I0772317

ARASELI'S WEB

MICHAEL SHAYNE

Araseli's Web

Michael Shayne

This is a work of fiction. Names, characters, places, and incidents
are either the product of the author's imagination or are used
fictionally, and any resemblance to persons, living or dead, business
establishments, events, or locales is strictly coincidental.

ISBN: 979-8-9891894-0-3

www.michaelshayne.net
michael_shayne@yahoo.com

CHAPTER 1

"Hey! Wake up!"

The man heard the words echoing as if underwater. Each syllable pounded inside his beaten brain like a sledgehammer.

When he felt the icy, salty brine of the Aegean Sea splash his face, he stirred, groaned, then opened his one unswollen eye to more darkness.

After spitting bloody mucus onto the fiberglass bow of the rising and falling dinghy, he managed to ask, "Where are we?"

Across the bow, the blurry figure said, "About a thousand feet above your grave. Give or take."

The voice was familiar, and it cemented the reality of his situation as it all came back to him. Where he was—and why.

Even in the darkness, he could see and feel the flex-cuffs binding his wrists. He couldn't see his feet, but knew they were cuffed too. He could make out a chain tied to a length of rope that snaked its way to where the figure sat balancing an anchor on the edge of the gunwale.

His situation was clear now. The end no longer a mystery. And he laughed through a bloody grin.

"What's the joke?" the figure asked.

The man spat blood again and said, "You were always so melodramatic. And so fucking predictable."

"Well, then, this won't come as a surprise either." The figure lifted his arm and let the anchor fall into the sea, taking the coil of rope with it.

CHAPTER 2

Moscow, Russia
Monday, March 11, 1996
25 Days Earlier
8:33 a.m.

Sleet pelted the faces of the four men following the narrow stone paths of the Novodevichy Cemetery on Moscow's south side, their gloved and frozen hands curled around the wooden handles of their tools. The area was crowded and too historic to allow heavy equipment, so the caretaker had demanded the dig be done by hand.

The only man without a tool was wearing slacks, a tie, leather gloves, a wool overcoat, and a ushanka fur hat and fought with a flapping map of the cemetery.

On the way to their destination, he paid little notice to the graves of Anton Chekhov and Nikita Khrushchev. March was too cold to loiter for long, even for seasoned Muscovite gravediggers.

The man in the suit stopped and pointed at a stone marking the plot. Hand-chiseled in large block letters was the name *BERGER*. And inches from there, embedded in the earth, lay three rectangular granite markers, one for each of the deceased: Karl, Sophya, and Liam. Their birth dates were missing, but the death dates were the same.

November 11, 1982.

Several minutes into their task, the men had picked their way six inches into the frozen ground when they heard, then saw, the screaming woman running toward them, her arms waiving wildly in the air. *"Остановка! Остановка!"* she cried. (Stop! Stop!)

The man in the suit ordered the diggers to halt while he met the crazy woman on the path. "Why do you stop us? We have permission from the highest—"

Bent over and out of breath, she struggled to speak. "You—won't—find—them."

CHAPTER 3

Russian Ministry of Defense
Khamovniki District, Moscow, Russia
Tuesday, March 12, 1996

General Grigori Urmanov, Russia's minister of defense, finished the call with his informant, then returned the phone's receiver to its cradle with a shaky, liver-spotted hand. After a long drag from his cigarette, he used it to light a new one while he leaned back in his chair and stared at the yellow-stained ceiling above his desk.

How long had the ceiling been like that? he wondered.

He had expected the call years ago. What he had done, what *they* had done, could never disappear into the dust of an evidence shelf. Not if Jurg Ivanovich, the head of the SVR (Russia's intelligence agency), had his way. And apparently, he had.

Checking his watch, Urmanov knew he had two, maybe three, minutes. His heart palpitated as he shuffled to the window, split the drapes, then opened the French doors leading to the narrow balcony. Leaning against the railing, he stared across the Moskva River one last time—a view he had come to cherish since taking over as Defense Minister.

Eleven floors below, three black SUVs belonging to the SVR skidded to a stop, blocking the Znamenka Ulitsa and the sidewalk as maybe ten agents poured out and disappeared into the building's ground floor, leaving one agent to take up a position on the sidewalk. With a submachine gun in his grip, the lone agent looked up, spotted Urmanov, and pointed.

The call Urmanov had received from his informant had been

timely. And accurate. The SVR had been to the cemetery. And they had dug.

Stepping back inside, Urmanov went to the wall behind his desk and opened the hinged portrait of Boris Yeltsin to reveal a wall safe.

After the third shaky battle with the dial, he removed the pre-stamped, pre-addressed envelope, closed the safe, then dropped the envelope down the mail chute.

As his office door rattled with angry fists, he strolled easily back to the window, waved at the SVR agent below…

… then threw himself over the railing.

CHAPTER 4

T hrough the plane's oval window, the slender man gazed down on the meandering dots of Irish serfs as the drooping sun warmed their pointless paths. *Why do they bother waking up?* he thought.

As the private jet owned by his Greek employer settled into its final approach, the man caught one last glimpse of the houses of Castlereagh and wondered if one of them might be *hers*. This bedroom suburb of Belfast might be mundane, but it was heaven compared with his war-torn birthplace of Tirana, Albania.

The man was only four when the communist-backed Democratic Front (successor of the National Liberation Front) murdered his father, a Russian Orthodox priest, for speaking out against them. Then, after the economy collapsed under the socialist's economic policies, his mother was forced into the streets to make a living. Riddled with shame, she had taken her own life, leaving the fate of her barely seven-year-old son to chance.

But not only had he survived, he had thrived. His talent for cruelty and stomach for the macabre served him well in the underbelly of socialism until he was old enough to start eliminating communists one by one. In Tirana, he became a folk hero to the oppressed, who helped hide him for years.

All that changed once the communists put a price on his head, and he was forced to escape to Greece, where he changed his name and put his talents to use working for Georgius Ruqur, the millionaire founder of the Hermes Corporation. Officially, he was hired as Georgius's personal aide. Privately, the rest of the staff knew him as the Fixer.

After landing in Belfast, the man instructed the raven-haired flight attendant—*was her name Angela?*—to arrange for rooms and wait for further orders. At the airport, he leased a Lexus SC 400 coupe and drove west into the Castlereagh suburbs.

He found *her* house on a street of similar brick structures with Georgian-style doors, dormered rooves, and sharp eaves, each separated by high fences, higher hedges, and rear alleyways. He parked the Lexus by the curb two doors from *her* house and watched the plebes live.

Late March was cool, but Ireland stayed surprisingly warm. Coming toward him, a mother, hand in hand with her child, kneeled to wipe his nose. A man passed by, walking his dog. The man shook his head. *I'd have to kill myself,* he thought as he turned his attention back to *her* house.

When they first met, *she* had been but a passing link in the chain of his quest. He thought about helping himself to her back then; only time and opportunity had not cooperated. But now, fate had proved powerful and had brought them back together in a more plausible scenario.

He'd get his second chance.

Satisfied he'd seen enough, he checked into the hotel suite, set his alarm for midnight, then reclined on the bed. But sleep never came. His thoughts of *her*, alone in the house, kept his mind racing with possibilities.

At midnight, he dressed in black jeans, sneakers, and a black shirt, then returned to Castlereagh, where he parked the Lexus a block away this time.

Ducking into an alley, he hugged the hedges until he reached *her* backyard. The gate was unlocked. Kneeling before a ground-level window, he unrolled the canvas pouch of picks, slipped a thin metal strip between the double-hung windows and its lock, then slid the bottom one up, bracing for an alarm.

Silence.

Pushing the pistol deeper into the waistband of his jeans, he retrieved the penlight from his pocket, then threaded his long limbs through the open window.

After his eyes adjusted, he found himself in a storage room. The dim beam from the penlight revealed boxes and furniture and lamps all draped by dusty sheets. In the corner, he saw another door and tried it. It opened into the garage, where he found another door that opened into the kitchen.

Once inside, he made his way to the living room at the front of the house and then the foyer, where a curved staircase wound upward to a dark second-floor landing that jutted left and right. A bedroom on each side—probably. One of them was *hers*.

And his heart raced again.

Satisfied *she* was still asleep, he returned to the living room and the tables and the curio and the mantle over a fireplace, each supporting items of joyous, pointless memories shaped like porcelain figurines.

Holding the penlight in his teeth, he examined the photos on the wall and the faces against backdrops of beaches and mountains and pubs and raised pints of beer. Some were of children. And a dog. *She* was in a few of the photos, but he recognized no one else, so he moved to the dining room, where he found a China cabinet and candlesticks and doilies on tables and more photographs, but still—not what he was looking for.

The China cabinet sat on a matching hutch with three drawers down the center. Squatting, he went through each one until promise revealed itself. Pouches and pouches of older photographs, no doubt developed at the local drugstore.

Taking them a pouch at a time, he flipped through each photo like a blackjack dealer until, halfway through the second pouch, he found the first black-and-white gold mine.

Then a second and a third. The fourth one was in color. Even better. He turned each photo over to examine the backs.

Perfect!

He clicked off the penlight and pocketed the four photos. Now that he had finished his entrée, it was time for dessert, and his gaze drifted to the ceiling and the bedroom beyond.

And the tingle returned.

She was in all four of the photos, only much younger. Still, she had grown up so very well. And having seen the younger her somehow amplified his hunger. His need. His addiction.

Stepping gingerly toward the stairs, he stopped when the floor beneath him squeaked.

Did she hear that? Does it even matter at this point?

But, as his hand touched the banister, a meandering beam from a passing car illuminated the front windows and sent ghosts across the walls. He found himself weighing the risk of losing the treasure he had found against his need for carnal release.

The dark angel on his shoulder urged him to climb the stairs, while the gray angel reminded him, *There's always the flight attendant. Angela, was it?*

The gray angel won—again.

After leaving the way he had come, he returned to the Lexus, where he was free to admire the photos beneath the dome light. Four thin squares of yellowing paper with fraying angulated edges. So benign on the surface, yet so powerful in *his* hands.

After putting the photos away, he checked his watch. His Russian contact had no doubt found the bodies by now and was one step closer to the point of no return. He couldn't help but take the photos out one more time for a satisfied glance.

Oh yes! They would burn for what they had done to him, he thought. *When the world was on fire, they would all burn.*

CHAPTER 5

Crossing over the rise, Liam Curran squatted behind a boulder on the hillside overlooking the war-ravaged landscape of Halabja, Iraq. Below, a crowd of at least a thousand moved toward a stage lined with banners and slogans memorializing the Halabja Massacre.

Eight years earlier, near the end of the Iran-Iraq War, Saddam Hussein had attacked the Kurds with mustard, sarin, and VX gases, killing more than five thousand civilians. Many of them children. Three weeks after the attack, his SEAL team, along with a squad of Green Berets out of Bragg, arrived to organize the now raging Peshmerga to bring down Saddam Hussein's Republican Guard.

But Liam certainly wasn't here for nostalgia.

Starting down the hill, dodging jagged tentacles of rebar protruding from car-size chunks of concrete, a cool, sand-filled gust pelted his cheeks, forcing Liam to rewrap his kaffiyeh.

Once he was on the street, he moved against the flow of the crowd to where the Peshmerga had blocked the streets with sandbags and rows of Isuzu pickups retrofitted with bed-mounted machine guns. Here, merchants lined the streets with carts and tents, waiting for the speeches to end and the people to return with their money. *Where liberty lives, capitalism blooms,* he thought.

As he approached the first soldier, he noticed the older Chinese type 56-II, 7.62x39 assault rifles, copies of the Russian AK-47, strapped to the man's shoulder. The soldier stiffened as Liam closed the distance but relaxed when Liam veered off the road and entered the Sheik Ismael Mosque.

Inside, Liam found himself in a stadium-size prayer hall with mosaic-filled walls bathed in candlelight. The musty aroma sent him back about six hundred years. In the far corner of the hall, a minbar rose above a domed arch, where a door had opened and quickly closed.

He was expected.

Making his way through the sea of prayer rugs, he pushed against the door, and it opened into a kitchen, where a Peshmerga officer in desert camo and a magenta beret waited next to a small table. Their eyes locked, but only momentarily. When the officer removed the beret and let her auburn hair flow down her shoulders in twists of gold, Liam felt the familiar attraction return.

Taking a cautious step toward him, her lips pressed into a thin line, then opened slightly as she was unable to hide her disbelief. Then, she glanced toward a dark corner of the candlelit kitchen, where an ancient man shrouded in robes and a chest-length gray beard had stepped forward, clearing his throat.

Liam recognized the man as the imam of the mosque from when he was last here as a SEAL. When she spoke in Sorani Kurdish, the imam nodded approvingly toward Liam, then exited calmly through the door.

"It's great to see you, Nadia," Liam said as his gaze drifted to the weapon strapped to her shoulder. Unlike the others, she carried the Colt M4 Carbine with a red-dot scope. American. The newest model.

Nadia al-Humana placed the M4 on the wobbly table and took a step toward the man she hadn't seen—and thought dead—for more than three years. Her eyes searched his, begging it to be true, right before she delivered an openhanded blow to his cheek.

Liam's kaffiyeh was all that prevented an imprint of her palm on his skin. He caught her second attempt in midswing and, then, her third. Now, with both of her wrists in his hands, he waited for her rage to cool before letting her go, and she collapsed into his arms.

"Oh, Trevor—I was told you were dead," she said, now in accented English.

When he heard the name *Trevor*, the rest of her words faded to mumbles. The name belonged to Commander Trevor Harmon, US Navy SEAL, an identity Liam had been forced to use for nearly twenty years. Still, coming from her lips, and given all they had been through, the name *Trevor* felt more real.

He pulled away and held her at arm's length, studying her in the dim candlelight and wondering how she would react when she learned the truth. The real truth.

"The bomb in my plane was planned," Liam said. "It was necessary to—"

His words were interrupted by her kiss, then reinforced by the pressing of her index finger to his lips. "You had a contract on your life for killing Al-Rasheed. I understand."

The killing of General Al-Rasheed was only the tip of the iceberg, Liam thought. In her eyes, he saw forgiveness, which only added to his guilt, fueled by the real reason he was here.

She kissed him again, long and hard. It felt familiar and natural. When he pulled away for air, Nadia reached into her pocket, took out a wallet-size photo, and held it between her fingers. It was the same photo he had carried for years but returned to her several months earlier as proof he was still alive.

If only he could say the same for the two others in the photo.

The picture was of Nadia; her sister, Aisha; and Aisha's four-year-old daughter, Lilliana—taken in a Baghdad marketplace. Nadia had first given it to him on their last night together in Romania before he left the SEALs to join the CIA. Two beautiful sisters holding the hand of a lovely, innocent child. Two lives cut short by Liam's own hand, marking the beginning of his recurring nightmare.

"Would you like the photo back?" she asked.

Liam lowered his gaze. "No. It's too…" He drew in a forced breath, then finished with: "You keep it."

She nodded, put the photo away, then took his hand and squeezed it. "I do not blame you for their deaths."

Liam said nothing. He didn't need her blame. He had more than enough already.

"I was thinking…" she said as she touched his cheek. "Tomorrow is your birthday."

"You remembered?"

She smiled. "Can we celebrate it together? Tonight?"

"I have to leave today."

Her eyes searched the floor. "You are still hunting the NEST, yes?"

Liam nodded. "There are only three left."

"I know. But Osprey is Munir Kateb. He is in Gaza guarded by the PLO. Eagle is a ghost, and we never knew Owl's identity."

Liam raised an eyebrow. "Sheik Tariq Al-Jabori knew. And he told me right before I sent him to meet his virgins."

Nadia gasped. "I heard that he— It was you?"

Liam nodded, then moved two rickety chairs to face each other and motioned for Nadia to sit across from him, knee to knee.

Nadia said, "We are still fighting with the KDP and the Turks. You have taken a great risk coming here."

Liam said, "When the US cut off your funding, I know the PUK turned to the World Hands Organization." It was a lie, but a white one. He only *suspected* they had turned to the WoHo. If he was wrong, Nadia would only deny it. But if he was right…

Her eyes widened and her lips parted as the natural reflex of denial met head-on with trust. But then, she sighed and said, "Why does this concern you?"

"The public face of the WoHo is a Brit named George Hanover, but the leader is Rufus Carmichael. He not only funds freedom fighters but also many terrorist groups. He was the money behind the NEST. His offices are in London, but I hear he's vanished. I need to find him."

"The sheik told you Rufus Carmichael is the Owl?"

"Yes."

Nadia shook her head as she fisted her eyes closed. "Then you ask too much. My people need his money for weapons."

Liam kept his gaze locked on Nadia. "I have intel proving Carmichael met with your leadership here, in Halabja."

She lowered her eyes.

"At least tell me what he looks like."

Nadia let out a breath, then said, "The atom bomb man."

"You mean Robert Oppenheimer?"

"Yes. Tall. Thin. Dark hair. Weak chin. He smokes a pipe and wears a fedora. I understand he prefers the company of men."

Liam let the image pinball through his mind, hoping to knock something familiar loose, but in the end, a past reference never developed. That was when Nadia picked up the M4 from the table and cradled it across her lap: a defensive move and a hint their meeting might be ending.

"I—I can't betray my people." Nadia pressed her lips together and lowered her eyes.

Liam said, "A minute ago, you blamed the NEST for the murder of your sister and Lilliana."

"No. I said that I do not blame *you*."

Liam shook his head. "Carmichael funded the NEST, making him directly responsible. I hope you can live with that, because I can't."

"Who can't? The dead Trevor Harmon?" Extending a finger, she poked his chest and asked, "And who are you now?"

"My real name is Liam Curran."

Nadia said nothing.

"Carmichael can lead me to Eagle, Nadia. This has to end."

"It did end! It is *you* who keeps it alive."

Removing his cell phone from a pocket, he dialed hers from memory. When she flinched at the buzzing in her pocket, she found it and eyed the number as Liam snapped his phone closed. Then, her eyes lifted to question him.

"You have my number when you are ready." But as he started to leave, he turned and said, "By the way, Turkey's seventh and eighth corps will be launching a major strike against your people."

"Where?" Nadia asked, her eyes wide with urgency.

This time, Liam said nothing.

"You are blackmailing me?"

"No. It's an offer."

"An impossible one. If I do not tell you, then my people die. If I do, we lose millions of dollars for weapons—and my people die."

"I'll help you find other sources." Reaching out, he stroked a strand of her hair, then kissed her nose. "You know how to reach me," he said, then pushed against the door, letting a line of brilliant sunlight part the dark room.

After a half an hour, he made it back to his Range Rover parked on the far side of the hill he had climbed down earlier. He started the engine and let it idle before easing it back onto the road. A few miles later, his cell phone buzzed in his pocket. When he saw who it was, he pulled the Range Rover to the side of the road and answered it.

"Are you testing the number?" he asked.

"Carmichael is no longer working out of Windsor. He relocated to a penthouse in Athens about eight months ago," Nadia said. "I hear he is running from something. That's all I know."

"Thank you," Liam said as he let the hiss build in his ear.

"Your turn," Nadia said.

"Eastern Turkey. Diyarbakir and Bingöl. The air attack is planned for early April."

"How do you know this?"

"Trust me."

Liam clicked off.

After pulling the Range Rover back onto the highway, he settled in for the long drive. In his mind, he repeated *Athens* over and over until the image of the city so familiar in his youth materialized. There could only be one reason why Rufus Carmichael, banker to terrorists, and killer of little four-year-old girls, would be running. He heard what happened to Sheik Al-Jabori. He knew it was now his turn. And, there was only one reason to choose Athens—Primo Ruqur.

Now, all Liam had to do was locate Carmichael (no doubt, he wasn't using his real name) in a city of a million people and force the man to give up the identity of Eagle. Then, like the other members of the NEST, Liam would kill him.

CHAPTER 6

Virginia Roosevelt-Woodburn, the executive director of the DC think tank known as the Billings Institute for the Conservation of Americanism—or simply BICA—left her town house for the three-block battle with the elements to her office on L Street. Tucking the wool scarf beneath the folds of her tweed overcoat, she shoved gloved hands deep into pockets and leaned into the icy breeze while eddies spun leftover snow mixed with litter around her fur-lined boots.

A block later, she ducked into her favorite café, ordered her usual, then carried the Danish and latte to the second floor. Saturdays were always crowded, but she found a table near the wall of windows overlooking Thomas Circle, completely unaware that she, too, was being watched.

She hadn't noticed the man when she'd left her town house, or even when he'd climbed the stairs carrying his espresso. But when she saw his skeletal reflection in the window, her neck jerked around in disbelief. Then, when he moved between her and the glass, her gasp escaped in a rush.

From the dossier BICA had on the man, his appearance was exactly as she recalled and unmistakable. A skeleton. He was tall and thin with sunken cheeks, wind-raked skin, and a shaved head hinting at a receding white hairline. He wore a gray wool peacoat over black slacks tailored so the cuffs broke halfway down the laces of Italian shoes. A platinum Rolex clung loosely to a bony wrist protruding from the cuff of his coat.

"May I sit, Miss Woodburn?" His cordial Eastern European accent was followed by a long palm extending toward the open seat.

"Franco Delgado," she said, scanning the café for more omens. "Or do you prefer Gjon Rockman? Which does your employer call you?"

"I *am* flattered the leader of BICA knows *me* so very well. May I call you Ginny?"

"No," Ginny said. When the man took the seat, she shivered. "What do you want, Mr. Delgado?"

"Only to procure your services."

"Did Primo Ruqur sent his errand boy this time?"

"I seek only what you would provide to any client. Your multi-billion-dollar endowment is maintained through the collection and sale of intelligence, and the gullibility of benefactors. I wish to join the club. To contribute."

"What are you asking?"

"Not what—who. Moscow. November 1982."

"Your English is failing you. That's a *when* and—"

When he saw the color drain from her face, his grin grew wider. Ginny said, "I'm afraid I'll need more."

Delgado lowered his considerable chin and said, "I would have been disappointed had you given in so easily."

The noise in the café grew as a tour group of junior high students, accompanied by a few adult chaperones, stormed up the stairs. Ginny said, "We should discuss this in my office."

"This will do. And, it is enough that you understand this: I know what you and your government did. In exchange for the information on the involved parties, I offer my silence."

Ginny drew in a breath. "Who are you looking for?"

"The two conspirators, of course." Delgado reached inside his overcoat and produced five folded sheets of paper, which he smoothed on the table.

One page was a 1982 *Pravda* article, and the other four were blown-up copies of photographs he had taken from the woman's house in Belfast.

Reaching out to touch each page, Ginny settled on the newspaper and the photos of two men and one woman staring back. The faces of the two men were circled.

"I don't read Russian, so—"

"You have people who do," Delgado said as he stood and buttoned his coat. Then, he handed her a business card. "I will be waiting for your call."

Ginny took the card and smiled at its simplicity. One single phone number. No name. No address. Perforated edges.

"My request will require some consideration, of course," Delgado said, interrupting her. "But you will come to the right decision. And when you do, you *will* tell me their whereabouts."

"Can you at least give me their names?"

"You already know their names."

She swallowed hard. "And if I refuse?"

"Then millions will die."

She glanced at the pages, then back to Delgado. "These photos mean nothing to me."

"But they mean everything to me. The color is gone from your cheeks, and terror has replaced the wonder in your eyes. All the proof I need that you know. And so will your enemies if I do not hear back from you."

"What enemies?"

"The Russians, of course. Millions of lives in exchange for two. It is a bargain." Delgado bowed slightly, then said, "Good day, Miss Woodburn." He then strolled easily away with his espresso and disappeared down the stairs.

Ginny turned to the window and searched the street below until Delgado came into view. He stopped at the crossing sign, a head taller than the crowd. When he turned and looked up at her, she shivered again. The walk sign changed, and he melted into the masses.

Picking up the pages in shaking hands, she tucked them away in her purse. At the same time, she found her two-way pager.

BICA had spent a great deal of time and money working with the pager's manufacturer to design a special version with a tiny GPS receiver giving each device an astounding price tag. Only certain individuals at BICA close to the executive director were issued the pagers Liam had comically dubbed as *Spytel*.

Using the tiny keypad, Ginny typed a message, praying for a quick reply.

It came seconds later: MONDAY. 1000 L

CHAPTER 7

Washington, DC
Monday, March 18, 1996

White House chief of staff, Patricia Woodburn—Woody to her friends—stood proudly in the blinding sunlight pouring down on the Rose Garden while the president announced her planned departure to the press. Then, he introduced her replacement, Lieutenant General Leon Carter.

It was the first time she had seen Carter in a suit without stars and medals, and the look seemed to make him fat and weak. Standing before them, the world press hung on the president's every word. The president took a moment to thank Woody for her service, and then lied about her wanting to spend more time with a family she didn't have before pouring on the accolades for Carter.

Staring into the eyes of the press, she wondered if anyone would ask why a lieutenant general would retire from the army and resign as director of the National Security Agency to become the chief of staff for a president under investigation by a special prosecutor: an investigation that had started after he'd vetoed an immigration bill the White House had helped to write.

The prosecutor hadn't leveled charges—yet—but if he ever discovered the blackmail and the bribe money from Mexico, the president and his family would burn. Woody's deal had been to keep that knowledge to herself and to resign before the next election cycle in exchange for the president vetoing his own immigration bill and moving away from his socialist agenda while in office. The carrot she would forever have on a stick.

After the press conference ended, and the president had retired to his private office for a closed-door meeting with his new COS, Woody retrieved her things from her office; met briefly with her deputy, Connie Perdew; then drove off the White House grounds. Four blocks later, she reached 1000 L, where she turned down the delivery ramp and stopped at the corrugated steel overhead door.

A guard appeared from a side door, checked her ID, then raised the overhead door to the private parking garage. Winding her way up seven floors, Woody guided her Chevy Suburban into what would be her new parking spot near the smoked-glass entrance with Thomas Jefferson's famous phrase etched at eye level:

The tree of liberty must be refreshed from time to time, with the blood of patriots and tyrants.

The organization housed inside had been founded as a conservative political party in the wake of the Progressive movement in the early twentieth century by Charles Edward Billings, an author and farmer. Immigrating as a boy from England in the late 1800s, he feared America's founding principles were being erased by Wilson Progressives, reviving the tyranny Americans had fled two hundred years earlier.

Over the next decades, the ranks of the organization grew to include the most brilliant minds from government, industry, academia, and the military, to eventually become one of the most revered foreign policy think tanks in the Western world. After the death of Billings in 1965, the organization officially changed its name to the Billings Institute for the Conservation of Americanism—or BICA.

At the entrance to the air lock, Woody swiped her card and entered her code. The doors parted and she stepped inside. After the air stopped swirling, the opposing doors opened, and she found herself in a bustling hallway of faces buried in reports.

Stepping across the hallway to the railing, she looked down onto the lobby of 1000 L seven floors below, where a coffee shop, chain restaurants, a credit union, and a health spa were already busy. Then, her gaze drifted upward to the stained-glass oculus of Howard Chandler Christy's "Scene at The Signing of the US Constitution."

Continuing down the hall, she entered the T-shaped executive suite. To the left was her new office, and to the right, the executive director's. And straight ahead was Curtis Steinberg's.

Amy, the administrative assistant, gave a cheerful smile and said, "Hello, Ms. Woodburn. She wasn't expecting you for another couple of hours."

"Is she available?"

"She's in a meeting."

"I'll take my stuff to my office and pop in on Curtis."

Curtis Steinberg not only ran BICA's digital operations at the Lake but was also the executive director's right-hand. Starting Monday, after Woody took the reins of the newly formed ICEBRG group, Curtis would report directly to her.

"He's on a call right now," Amy said. "I'll let him know—"

But Woody didn't wait for Amy to finish. Instead, she opened the door to the executive director's office, stepped inside, then closed it behind her, drawing a surprised look from the elegantly dressed woman in the sitting area.

"Well, good morning, Patricia," the woman said brightly with a Southern belle draw. After setting her cup on the table, she arose slowly from her chair, smoothed her dress, and said, "Aren't you the early bird?"

After Charles Billings died, he had left BICA in the hands of his deputy, who regrettably also died only five years later. The position of executive director was then passed to a woman who had been the first female fellow at BICA. Before that, she was the first female department head in the CIA's Directorate of Intelligence as well as the first female dean at an Ivy League university.

Virginia Roosevelt-Woodburn—or Ginny, as she preferred— stepped forward with a stately grace. Her traditional long dress yielded to her still shapely legs. Simple diamond stud earrings set off the single strand of pearls around her neck. Her conservative image betrayed only by a single gold ankle chain.

"Mother," Woody said, delivering a hug and peck on her mother's cheek. In the wall unit, the television was on the news but muted. "I take it you saw the press conference?"

"*We* did," Ginny said as a man cleared his throat and stood from the high-back Queen Anne chair in the sitting area. "I don't believe you've met Darren McFadden."

"No. I'm sorry," Woody said, greeting the distinguished older man with an outstretched hand. "Patricia Woodburn. Chief of staff for the next four days." But when their eyes met, a sense of déjà vu rushed over her.

"I understand you'll be leading our new ICEBRG initiative," McFadden said.

"*Our* initiative? Are you a member of BICA?" Woody asked.

Ginny chuckled. "Darren's been on BICA's board for, what, fifteen years now?"

"Sounds right." When he smiled, his dark-brown eyes set off the laugh lines that ended at the salt-and-pepper hairline near his temples. She guessed him to be in his early sixties with a chiseled, handsome face.

"I don't mean to stare, but have we met?" Woody asked.

"I'd remember if we had," he said, checking his watch, then turning to Ginny. "I should go and let you two talk." He delivered a hug to Ginny longer than Woody considered to be platonic, then left the office.

When she heard the door click, Woody turned to her mother and said, "I'm all ears."

Ginny motioned Woody toward the sofa, where she sat and listened as Ginny spent the next few minutes reliving her time at the café with Franco Delgado two days earlier.

"His name isn't ringing a bell," Woody said.

"He's an Albanian criminal born in Tirana during the takeover of the communist-backed Democratic Front. His father was a priest who was murdered by the communists, and his mother died a few years later, orphaning him. Later, he and his gang started killing off communists by the scores. The Russians put a price on his head, so he fled to Greece, changed his name to Gjon Rockman, and started working for Georgius Ruqur at the Hermes Corporation. After Georgius was murdered, he stayed on. Now, he's working for the son, Primo."

That name she knew well. Primo Ruqur was one of the world's wealthiest men, and he backed every socialist cause he could find. Woody stood and ventured to the snack cart. "So, who are the two men Delgado wants you to give up?" She chose a chicken-salad sandwich and a bottle of water, then returned to the sofa.

"Liam, for one," she said, then paused for several beats before adding, "and his father."

Woody paused in midbite. "I thought Liam's father is buried in Ireland. A fire or something?"

"It's a long story," Ginny said. "In the mid-seventies, Bryant Curran was recruited by the CIA away from the British SAS to spearhead a top-secret operation to infiltrate the Kremlin. It was called Operation: Jugular. He was given the identity of Karl Berger—an East German businessman—and gave up his own life and family to marry a widowed Russian woman who would eventually become Leonid Brezhnev's personal nurse. *She* was our ticket inside the Kremlin."

"That's dedication," Woody said. "What happened to Liam and his mother?"

"Gretchen, Liam's mother, eventually remarried. A Greek millionaire."

"Wait a minute. Are you saying Liam's mother married Georgius Ruqur?"

Ginny nodded.

"That means Liam Curran and Primo Ruqur are stepbrothers."

"Half-brothers, actually," Ginny corrected. "Gretchen was Primo's mother too. Different fathers, of course. Georgius's oldest child was a daughter by his first wife, whom he divorced to marry Gretchen. Primo was born a year later. Then after Gretchen drowned in '77, Georgius was about to remarry again but was killed only days before the wedding."

"Why am I just now hearing this? Liam isn't exactly our janitor. He's ICEBRG's top operator. The last time you kept me in the dark, I sent Paul to *kill* Liam. I'd like to avoid those misunderstandings going forward." After a beat, she added, "Funny, isn't it? Paul moved out, but I kept Liam. I hope it was a good trade."

Three years earlier, when Liam was still living under the alias of Trevor Harmon, two multimillion-dollar contracts had been placed on his life: one by Saddam Hussein for killing the head of his Republican Guard and another for the suspected murder of the director of the CIA, a contract Woody had placed herself.

"Let's get back to Delgado," Ginny said. "He must know we once had a spy inside the Kremlin. It's the only reason I can come up with for his interest in the Currans."

Since becoming the president's COS three years earlier, Woody had seen her share of spies escorted to prison or deported by the FBI and the CIA. It happened almost every day. In Russia, though it was less common for an American to be exposed, it happened. Swaps and extradition deals were cut at high levels. So, why did an Albanian man's threats to expose a fifteen-year-old spy ring warrant such concern?

Even in the best-case scenario, this Delgado person might be able to produce the *son* of a one-time spy, but not the father. At the same time, Delgado claimed to have information that could cost millions of lives if he were to spill it. And, whatever *that* was had Ginny scared.

"This makes zero sense," Woody said. "Giving him Liam is out of the question, and Bryant Curran is dead. And even if we could resurrect Bryant to trade him, Delgado could still give up whatever information he claims to have. That means he's either lying to the Russians about the Currans or—you're lying to me."

Ginny said nothing.

"Mother," Woody said easily, "what else is Delgado hanging over your head?"

Stiffening her posture, Ginny regained her poise, crossed her legs, and smoothed her dress. "Needless to say, Delgado and Liam have a contentious past, and Delgado has the resources of a billionaire. He needs to be stopped. Immediately."

"I agree. But I think I need to know more about Operation: Jugular before I send Liam out to kill a man."

"ICEBRG stands for *in case of emergency, break glass*," Ginny shot back. "I'm telling you that's exactly what this is. An emergency!"

Turning her back to Woody, Ginny crossed the room, opened the door to the outer office, and immediately called for Curtis before disappearing into the man's office, finishing with a slammed door.

Amy flinched, then looked up from her work, smiled sheepishly, then lowered her head again.

. . .

Ginny stood inside Curtis's office with her back against the door while her most trusted tech-guru watched her from behind his desk. When she heard Woody's office door close, she took out her pager and typed out a text message. When she finished, she let her finger hover over the Send button.

"Are you okay?" Curtis asked, standing from his chair and rounding the desk. "Is your pager acting up again?"

"No—it's fine," Ginny said. When she looked into Curtis's face and saw the man's smile melt away, she looked down at the pager in her palm...

And pressed Send.

CHAPTER 8

The Lake
Germantown, Virginia
Tuesday, March 19, 1996

After his flight from Qatar landed at Dulles, Liam retrieved his BMW 325iC convertible from the short-term lot and drove the sixty miles to Germantown, where he picked up a county road for five more miles before turning down an unmarked gravel drive normally flanked by cornstalks. But it was late March, and he could only smell freshly tilled soil and squinted at the brilliant sunlight reflected off the lake through the still bare trees.

The road narrowed to a single lane before he came upon a steel gate with a guard shack on its left. He flashed his ID to a man with the assault rifle, who waved him through, then he continued the last half mile to the Colonial-style plantation home owned by a BICA shell company. What appeared to be a well-kept historic home, the Lake—as it was called inside BICA—had been converted into the organization's technical heart.

As he parked, an attractive long-haired blonde in her late thirties stepped onto the wrap-around porch, leaned against a white column, and waved.

Bailey—a nickname Liam had given her in honor of the character on the sitcom *WKRP in Cincinnati*. In truth, Bailey was actually Luciana Renee Sabato, a Sicilian-born computer savant recruited by the National Security Agency who had lost her husband to cancer early in life and never remarried.

Right before leaving the NSA, Bailey had headed the organization's Technical Directorate—a team that acquired, operated, and maintained the vast communications, computer, and data storage systems. BICA had hired Bailey away from the NSA ten years earlier to build the team at the Lake from scratch, on a much smaller budget.

"I didn't know you were coming," Bailey said, her hand shielding her face from the rising sun.

"Me neither," Liam replied as he took the stairs two at a time.

"Happy belated birthday." Bailey hugged his waist and buried her head in his chest. "Why is it that every time I see you, I worry it will be the last."

"I'm not that old."

"That's not what I meant."

Liam pulled away, put an arm around her shoulder, then walked her toward the front door. "I need your help. It's an easy one."

"You always say that," she said as she opened the door, then held it for him.

The entire front of the house had been gutted to form one large room. On every wall, whiteboards had been mounted and were filled with colored dry-erase marker lines. In front of the whiteboards, workers sat at a dozen tables pecking away on PCs with giant monitors. It looked like a NASA command center—on a McDonald's budget.

Centered at the top of the whiteboard on the interior wall above a complex mesh of financial flowcharts were the words: *ARASELI'S WEB.*

Liam scanned the room for Araseli but didn't see the tiny Mexican woman. However, from behind one of the computers, another familiar face got up and walked over to meet them. When the woman stuck out her hand, Liam took it, tried to kiss it, then smiled when she yanked it back.

"Dr. Babbs. It's good to see you again," he said.

"You *know* I hate that shit," Babbs's cigarette rasp complained as she symbolically wiped the back of her hand on the thigh of her acid-washed jeans.

Like Bailey, Dr. Babbs was ex-NSA. But she was also ex-CIA and a genius in forensic accounting, banking, and digital commerce. The rumor was she had four PhDs. Liam was certain of at least two: One in applied economics from the Wharton School and one in accounting and MIS from the Ohio State University's Fisher College. The same school where he had recently completed his own PhD in economics.

Babbs said, "Please tell me my alma mater rejected your thesis like a dime novel." When Liam didn't respond, she let out a long sigh. "I guess you want me to call you Dr. Curran now?"

"You can still call me *asshole*."

"Count on it."

Their banter was legendary, but privately, Liam felt a sense of awe in her presence.

Babbs's gaze volleyed between Bailey and Liam. "What shit have you brought us this time?"

"Something right up Araseli's alley. Is she around?"

"I'll get her," Babbs huffed, then disappeared into the back offices. When she returned, a miniature, elderly Araseli was on her tail. When she saw Liam, she sped up and delivered a hug that hit him in the gut and took his breath.

"It is so very good to see you, Mr. Liam," Araseli said in her heavy Mexican accent.

Babbs may have come to BICA with Bailey, but Araseli had been Liam's contribution to the team after hijacking her from the Cartel Del Golfo in Mexico, where she ran their money-laundering operations.

The CDG had once enslaved Araseli's entire family until they had all escaped to the US. Everyone except Araseli. Eventually, the CDG hunted down and killed all but one of her relatives: her grandson, Stephan, who they forced to work as a coyote.

When the opportunity to grab Araseli *and* Stephan presented itself, Liam had taken it. New identities had been arranged, Stephan began attending college, and Araseli agreed to work for BICA.

Same slave. Different master.

After peeling himself from Araseli's hug, he pushed four folding chairs into a circle. They all sat, engaged in small talk, then every eye turned toward Liam.

"Rufus Carmichael," Liam said, his eyes gauging their reactions.

Babbs spoke first. "The Carmichael Group in London. Private investments and wealth managers for some of the richest people in the world. The man's a recluse. Invisible."

"He's more than that," Liam said, measuring his words carefully. He loved and respected all three of them, but only one *really* knew him. And even *Bailey's* knowledge of his past had its limits. He would keep the name *Owl* out of the conversation for now.

Liam said, "Carmichael runs the World Hands Organization."

"We know that," Babbs said. "WoHo operates as a charity. Billions flow in, and WoHo invests it in short-term financial vehicles and holds it until its highly questionable clients withdraw it. It uses tiny interest rates and huge deposits to fund its operations."

Liam stood and pointed toward the whiteboard with *ARASELI'S WEB* at the top. "I need a financial web built for WoHo and the Carmichael Group, just like the one she did for the CDG."

"Okay. But why the sudden urgency?" Bailey asked. "Those groups have been around for years."

Liam lowered his voice. "Rufus Carmichael recently vacated his Windsor estate and relocated to Athens. I need to know why."

"Maybe for the weather," Babbs quipped.

"No. I think he has a new client."

"Who?"

Liam shook his head. "You tell me."

Bailey turned to Araseli. "Can you get started tomorrow?"

"Already on it," Araseli said, poking her temple with a crooked finger, then tapping out a new cigarette from a pack.

"Thank you," Liam said.

Babbs and Araseli both stood. Araseli hugged Liam before following Babbs, no doubt heading for a smoke break. Liam and Bailey started for the front door.

On the porch, she stopped him before he reached the stairs. "I didn't want to bring this up in front of the others, but does this have anything to do with the NEST?"

Liam pursed his lips, then released a grin and said, "You tell me."

"I hope not." She kissed his cheek and delivered a quick hug, then stood on the porch until Liam had driven out of sight.

. . .

Liam waited a good ten miles before flipping open his cell phone and dialing. Araseli picked up right away.

"Are you alone?" Liam asked.

"Yes. I am in my bungalow," Araseli said.

"Good. Now let me tell you what I really need."

CHAPTER 9

Princeton, West Virginia
Tuesday, March 19, 1996

After hanging up with Araseli, Liam started his four-hour trek to Princeton, taking the back roads through Culpeper on his way to Charlottesville. There, he picked up I-64 west then I-81 south. With the Allegheny Mountains and the drooping sun on his right, he let the wind ty to beat the last four days out of his mind.

It failed.

He reached the outskirts of the tiny West Virginia town by 6:15 p.m. and his driveway fifteen minutes later. Using the remote, he raised the wrought-iron gate, drove over the cattle stop, then parked the BMW in the three-car garage.

After unpacking his bag, he went to the den and settled into his favorite lounger with a glass of Macallan's 18 and Stevie Ray on the speakers to enjoy the remaining few moments of spring break before returning to his students. But the promise of relaxation ended with his cell phone buzzing around in circles on the end table.

Liam recognized the country and area code as Belfast, so he answered the way he always did: in his native Irish.

"*Tráthnóna maith*, Brandon." (Good evening, Brandon.)

"Not here, it isn't," Brandon replied. "Brock Flannigan just came out of a three-month coma."

Brock Flannigan was not only a dear friend but also owned the law firm that managed the trust left to Liam by his mother. "Christ! What happened?"

"Some bugger shot him. When he came out of the coma, his

first words were to get in touch with James Jamison. He gave the nurse my phone number."

James Jamison was the alias Brannigan had set up for Liam in the trust. Only a handful of people knew this. Liam checked his watch, then said, "I'll grab the first available flight."

There was a long pause before Brandon spoke again. "Somethin' else you need to know. Stephanie's house was burgled a few nights ago."

"Is she okay?" Liam asked, launching forward in the chair.

"She's fine," Brandon assured him.

"What was taken?" Liam asked.

"Nothing. At least, not that we can tell. We'll talk more when you get here."

Liam clicked off the call, then dialed. Bill Shipman, one of his oldest and most trusted friends, and the man who leased Liam's farm, answered right away.

"Good. You got back in one piece," Shipman quipped.

"I survived," Liam said. "But I have to leave again. Can you keep an eye on the place another day or two?"

"It's what I do," Shipman said, his voice tentative. "Where are you headin'?"

"Belfast."

"To see *her*?"

"Not by choice."

"Bullshit! Can I ask what's going on?"

"I wish you wouldn't," Liam said. "Only because I don't know myself."

CHAPTER 10

Good evening, Miss Woodburn." The fifty-ish doorman in the blue blazer smiled from behind the desk as Ginny left the revolving door and stepped into the lobby. "The wind's picking up, I see."

Ginny plucked off her gloves and opened her coat. "How are you tonight, Bobby?"

"Pretty fair," he said, passing her a stack of mail. "Mostly ads today. Except for this telegram I signed for."

After a few pleasantries, she crossed the lobby to the elevator, inserted her key card, then pressed PH. The doors opened to a black-and-white mosaic-tiled sitting area with several gold-leafed, glass-topped tables. A teardrop chandelier centered the high ceiling over her front door.

Once inside, Ginny changed into sweats, then settled in front of the news with some chamomile tea. Tossing the ads aside, she opened the telegram first.

Inside, she found a single business card with only a phone number. The subliminal message was clear.

I know where you live and we need to talk.

Taking her cell phone from the table, Ginny entered the digits from the card but stopped before pressing Send; knowing that once she did, Franco Delgado would have *her* number too. She pressed Send anyway, and Delgado's Albanian accent answered.

"Have you forgotten our arrangement?" Delgado asked.

"We don't have an arrangement."

"It was—implied. Now, where are the men I asked for?"

"You gave me no names."

"Must we do this?"

Ginny sipped the tea. "If you've done your homework, you already know it would be impossible for me to deliver the men in the photos."

"Because they are dead?" Delgado said as he laughed a cackle befitting a Lugosi film. "We both know the truth, don't we?"

Fisting her eyes closed, Ginny absorbed the blow of his words. "Then you must be referring to two different men."

"I suspected you might require more incentive. Patience, please."

"Patience?" Ginny said. "I—"

But she was interrupted when her door bell chimed. After laying the phone down, she went to the peephole and found Bobby there. Before he could press the button again, she opened the door.

"Sorry to bother you," Bobby said. "But this came by courier a few minutes ago." He presented the bow-wrapped box, then delivered a wink.

"Thank you, Bobby," she said, closing the door between them.

With a fingernail, she tore into the wrapping, opened the box, and removed the VHS tape. She picked up the cell phone and said, "How very James Bond of you."

Delgado chuckled. "I will wait while you prepare the tape."

After sliding the tape into the VCR and pressing Play, the screen filled with what appeared to be security footage of a lobby lined with mailboxes—much like a Mail Boxes Etc. The camera was positioned high to catch the faces of people entering, and their profiles while they checked their boxes. The header in the upper right corner of the screen read: *Hilliard, OH. September 22, 1995. 08:10:02.*

Ginny put the phone back to her ear. "What am I looking for, Mr. Delgado?"

"Several months ago, my employer learned his half brother

might still be alive. He tasked me to find him. Without going into great detail, I was able to track him to a rented mailbox in Hilliard, Ohio. Imagine my surprise when I not only found my employer's very alive half brother on the video but also another familiar face. And not as dead as you pretend. Please fast-forward to ten fifteen."

Aiming the remote, Ginny pressed the FF button until the timer read *10:14:35*. She pressed Play and watched until the timer turned to *10:15:14* and a familiar face entered the store, kneeled to open one of the larger mailboxes, left a package, then locked it back. At *10:16:02*, he left.

Ginny's eyes closed. *How could you have been so careless?* she thought.

Delgado said, "I will take your silence as agreement. The older man who left the package is the same man in the photos I provided. And, oddly enough, he has the same face as the man in the *Pravda* article—Karl Berger. A man who supposedly lost his entire family in the fire. I wonder what the Russians might find in their graves?"

"Get to the point," Ginny demanded.

"The point," Delgado said, "will reveal itself. Now, please fast-forward to fifteen eighteen."

Jabbing at the remote until the timer read *15:17:56*, she watched for a minute more until Liam entered the store, opened the same mailbox, removed the package, then left.

Damn it! He knows, she thought.

Turning off the lights, Ginny stared out the window at the streets below. "If you have the video, then you already know the whereabouts of these men. You don't need me."

"Unfortunately, I only know where they both *were*—six months ago. But not where they *are*. The mailbox belongs to James Jamison, which we both know is false. As are the address and telephone number for Mr. Jamison. My offer remains on the table. The whereabouts of both men or I give the Russians their evidence."

Ginny said nothing as she stared out the window into the DC

night. She had lost her ability to speak as a plethora of scenarios spun out of control and in her head—nightmares of her own creation stored away as the risk of their reality waned from doubtful to probable.

"Your silence speaks volumes, Ms. Woodburn," Delgado said. "And you have not inquired as to what my evidence is, which proves its validity. I'll reach out to you one last time." Delgado paused for several beats, then said, "You can turn your lights on now."

A gasp escaped her lips as she snapped her cell phone closed and yanked the drapes together. Backing away from the window, she fell onto the sofa, where she buried her face in her hands. The fear of opening her eyes and finding another specter from the past standing in her living room was overwhelming.

Snatching her purse from the end table, she dug out her pager. Leaning back, she stared at the ceiling with the cell phone in her lap and the pager in her hands while her fingernails tapped its display.

After several minutes, she gave up on indecision then typed the message.

THEY KNOW YOU ARE ALIVE.

CHAPTER 11

Only a half mile north of the White House, in what was once the Mrs. George Pullman House but was now the residence of the Russian ambassador, two diplomats dined on smoked salmon, borsch, dumplings, caviar, and, of course, Nemiroff vodka chased with tomato juice. The white-gloved servers, mostly sons of high-ranking communist party officials, cleared the empty dishes and replaced them with saucers of fruit-topped custard-filled cakes.

Boris Travkin, the Russian ambassador to the United States, chose raspberry, while Jerry Manchin, the secretary of state, picked strawberry. After dessert, the conversation migrated to fishing and movie stars as they enjoyed Cuban cigars and fine sherry in the library.

Manchin propped his feet up and relaxed in the coolness of the deep cushions of the leather chair and waited for Travkin to drop the last shoe. The Russian ambassador didn't host a one-on-one dinner with the secretary of state only to break the seal on a new vodka bottle.

Travkin snapped his fingers and the servers left the room. A long exhale signaled the beginning of a night that Manchin would never forget.

"President Yeltsin asks that I extend his deepest gratitude for your country's neutrality in our Chechen difficulties," Travkin said. The rotund man wore his jet-black hair in a flattop that ended in a sharp widow's peak. His appreciable eyebrows gave him an Eddie Munster quality.

Manchin said nothing as his gaze wandered to the mahogany shelves filled with books and trinkets illuminated by a busy crystal chandelier—all potential hiding spots for cameras and microphones. He usually enjoyed Travkin's company and even liked the man personally, but the man's pinkie ring bearing the coat of arms of the Military Academy of the General Staff of the Armed Forces of Russia blared a constant reminder that Travkin was no run-of-the-mill diplomat. He was an adversary.

Travkin smiled at Manchin's skilled silence. "Our nations live in a time of extremists. In Chechnya and in Oklahoma City. Our condolences to the families, of course. We were saddened to hear of the deaths of so many children."

Manchin nodded, wondering where this was leading.

Travkin plopped onto the sofa. "Your president's visit to Moscow next month for the Nuclear Safety and Security Summit—as I see it—is a great beginning to a new friendship, yes?"

"Absolutely," Manchin said, putting the lighter to his cigar. "What's on your mind, Boris?"

The elder diplomat drummed thick fingers on the arm of his chair. "There is—one thing. We have learned of certain troubling activities threatening to undermine the summit. Of course, we are not naïve. Dark forces always exist, and it is up to men—like ourselves—to recognize them."

"Is there a plot to this story?"

Travkin picked up the lighter. "The story—as you say—played out long ago. The evidence proving this past transgression has only recently been revealed to us."

"Are you asking us to look into it?"

"*We*…are looking into it."

Shit! Manchin thought. By *we*, Travkin meant the GRU (Russian's military intelligence organization), the FSB (the new ruthless version of a Russian FBI), or the SVR (the KGB using different letters). And those groups were equally satisfied manufacturing evidence when none existed.

"Why are you telling me this?" Manchin asked.

Travkin leaned back, dipped the end of his cigar into his sherry, then sucked it dry. But his eyes never left Manchin, as if administering a telepathic polygraph.

Feeling the weight of the silence, Manchin brushed small bits of ash from his trousers, checked his watch without noticing the time, then announced, "It's getting late, Boris."

He stood and started for the giant oak doors, sensing Travkin wasn't far behind. On the other side of the doors, his DSS agents were waiting along with their Russian counterparts. When Manchin touched the handle, Travkin cleared his throat.

Manchin turned and their noses nearly bumped. "I'm tired of playing guessing games, Boris."

Travkin, his breath thick with cigar and sherry, whispered, "In the spirit of glasnost, I should mention that we have exhumed the graves of the three conspirators."

Manchin mused. "Where were these graves?"

"In a Moscow cemetery."

"Not to be insensitive, but why should I be concerned about the bodies of three Russian conspirators?"

"Because, dear friend, the graves were empty. And I never said they were *Russians*." Travkin placed a hand on Manchin's shoulder, then reached for the door handle. At the same time, he slipped something into the pocket of Manchin's blazer and patted it gently.

Manchin paused, his hand slapping the pocket. "What did you just give me, Boris?"

Travkin shrugged and backed up a step. "Thank you for coming, Mr. Secretary. Let me show you out."

CHAPTER 12

The White House
Wednesday, March 20, 1996
7:30 a.m.

Woody selected another trinket from her credenza, wrapped it in newspaper, then passed it to Connie, who placed it in the cardboard box with the others.

"This is too familiar," Connie said, referencing the day they had moved *into* the White House.

"Time flies," Woody offered as a thud from the hallway startled her.

Both women looked up to see an unfamiliar young man readjusting two file boxes he had dropped by the office door. He delivered a sheepish grin, then disappeared.

Connie stepped into the hallway, moved the stack of boxes to the side, then closed the door and locked it. "Looks like Carter isn't wasting any time moving in."

Woody smiled. "Were we any different?"

Connie clamped her hands onto her hips. "*We* had just elected a new president. And *we* were part of the transition team."

"Point taken," Woody said as her cell phone buzzed in circles on her desk.

Connie checked the display and said, "It's Manchin," then passed it to her boss.

Woody flipped open the phone. "Good morning, Jerry." She listened for a period, checked her watch, then said, "I'll be here. When do you—?" She stopped when the doorknob jiggled and then jumped when the pounding came.

Connie eyed Woody, shrugged, then opened the door. Jerry

Manchin stepped inside, slammed the door, then locked it.

"I'm available now," Woody joked as she closed her cell phone.

Manchin ignored her as he ran both hands through black hair that had grayed at his temples. His features appeared to sag, and his gold-flecked amber eyes were wide with urgency. He stepped to the window and parted the blinds to look—at nothing.

"Jerry?" Woody prodded. "Want some cold coffee?"

"Is it too early for bourbon?" he asked.

Woody reached into a box and unwrapped a half-empty bottle of Macallan 18. "Scotch okay? I have Styrofoam cups."

"I'll take it," Manchin said.

Woody poured two fingers into three cups, then passed one to Manchin and one to Connie.

Manchin wet his lips with the warm brown liquid. "Officially, for the next seventy-two hours anyway, you're still the chief of staff. I wanted to run this by you before I—" He stopped and took another sip.

"Run *what* by me?" Woody asked, sitting on the edge of the credenza.

Still staring out the window, Manchin said, "I had dinner with Ambassador Travkin last night. Actually, it was more like a catered ambush. He went down a rabbit hole about some new conspiracy they discovered from years ago that could disrupt the nuclear summit next month."

"What conspiracy?" Woody asked.

"He didn't say. But he *did* tell me the graves were empty."

"Zombies?" Connie quipped.

Machin grinned. "As I was leaving, he slipped this into my pocket." Manchin held out his palm and revealed a folded pink Post-it note.

Connie took the note and read the scribble, shrugged, then passed it to Woody. After squinting to make out the scribble, she sat down on the desk and hoped the others hadn't noticed her gasp.

On the note were scribbled two names:

Karl Berger

Bryant Curran

The same two names she and Ginny had discussed yesterday. Two names for the same dead spy. She had called it correctly; Delgado was already spilling his guts.

"Woody?" Manchin said. "Anything?"

"No," she lied, then passed the note back to Manchin. "Did Travkin say who these men were?"

"Were?" Manchin asked.

"I assume they are two of the missing bodies from the cemetery?" she said.

Manchin shook his head and sipped the Scotch. "He never said that. But he led me to believe Russian intelligence is already investigating."

"Did he ask for our help?"

"No."

Connie glanced at her boss. "Sounds like Travkin is baiting us."

Manchin held up the Post-it note. "I'm being played. No doubt about it."

You're not the only one, Woody thought as another possibility entered her mind. *What if the Russians and Delgado are working together? Travkin plants the info in Manchin's pocket—the official channel—while Delgado slips it to BICA through Ginny—the back door. Same evidence from two sources.*

When she came up from her thoughts and found Connie and Manchin staring at her, she realized she had another big problem. Manchin was right. She was still, officially, the chief of staff and already knew about the two names—and who they were. Or, more to the point, who *he* was. And given that Bryant Curran was dead and buried in Belfast, she wondered who the Russians thought they were digging up.

"The president needs to know," Woody said, then watched the tension leave his body.

Connie opened her planner. "The president has ten minutes in his schedule, and then Woody and I are with Carter for a few hours afterward." She closed the planner, then glanced at Manchin. "You'll need to brief Carter too."

Woody said, "This *has* to come from you, not me. If Carter discovers you came to me first—"

"This conversation never happened," Manchin said, studying his shoes in thought.

"Jerry?" Woody said, drawing his attention back to her. "His ten-minute window just opened."

CHAPTER 13

Liam's flight landed that evening a few minutes early.

After collecting his bag and passing through customs using the passport of Ronald Scott, he rented a Toyota Camry, then drove to the Hilton. He left the car at the curb, checked in, dumped his bag on the king-size bed, then immediately left for Castlereagh and the house with the red Fiat Barchetta parked in the drive next to the white Porsche Carrera.

After parking across the street, he used his burner phone to make a call, then waited three rings before the sweetest Irish voice he knew answered.

"Hello," Stephanie Maguire said, and in his mind's eye, he could see her pulling her strawberry hair away from her ear as her magnificent emerald eyes peered through the drapes, scanning the street.

"Hi, Stephanie. It's Liam," he said, raising a hand to wave as he crossed the street.

"I'm a seein' you," she said. "But I ain't believin' you actually came. How long has it been—six months? Been drinkin' on the flight, have you? And—"

"Can you let me in and complain later?" Liam asked. He closed the flip phone without waiting for a response, climbed the stairs to the porch, then tapped lightly on the door. When it opened, it wasn't Stephanie's face he saw but her brother Brandon's, and the two long-time friends embraced warmly.

Originally protestant planters from Enniskillen, their families (the Ó Corráins and the Maguidhirs) had been aligned since King James I established the Ulster Plantation in the early 1600s. Sometime over the next hundred years, both families had converted to Catholicism. The Ó Corráins (now Currans) created the next major riff when they left for America in 1966. Liam was only six, but it was assumed by many at the time, with Liam and Stephanie being only a year apart, they had been promised to each other.

A *broken* promise, Stephanie still reminded Liam from time to time.

Brandon and Stephanie had moved to Belfast, where they opened Maguire's Jewelers, and Stephanie took charge of the day-to-day routine, while Brandon used the business as a front to run operations for the Provisional Irish Republican Army (IRA) across the Ulster province.

The IRA was in a cease-fire with the British since August of 1994, but it ended two months earlier when it was demanded the IRA disarm. Privately, Brandon realized the IRA's power was waning and his Ulster team had refrained from carrying out any attacks.

Liam skillfully stayed away from conversations on the matter.

He took off his jacket as he followed Brandon to the living room, where he found Stephanie sitting in an armchair, pulling her hair into a ponytail and fuming. To most, it would seem innocent enough. But to Liam, she was sending a clear and defiant message: *My hair is going up, so stay the fuck away.*

"Don't you be a throwin' that rag over the back of my good chairs," Stephanie warned. "God knows what pestilence you brought with you."

"I missed you too," Liam said, drawing a grin from Brandon. He decided to keep the peace and hang the jacket over the closet door.

Stephanie crossed her arms. "So—someone had to shoot your

friend for ya to visit your people," she said, her finger drawn and shaking in his direction. Her chest heaved as she spoke, drawing his attention to the open V in her blouse and the ring dangling there on a chain. She touched it and said, "And don't you be askin' for this back."

"Have I ever?" Liam said. "My mother gave it to you."

"And just you be rememberin' that," Stephanie said. Her wagging finger stopped, and she tucked it away beneath her crossed arms.

Liam and Brandon exchanged knowing glances. "Tell me about the break-in," Liam said.

Brandon motioned for Liam to follow him into the garage, which was packed floor to ceiling with boxes and plastic shelving and jars of canned vegetables and—junk.

At the back of the storage room were three ground-level, double-hung windows. Brandon pointed to the crescent sash lock on the middle one. He said, "If we hadn't been in the back looking at the planters, we wouldn't have noticed the footprint or that the window was unlocked. Whoever broke in wasn't able to relock it after they left." He then pointed to the dirty footprints on the floor. "As best I can tell, they stayed downstairs."

"And nothing is missing?" Liam asked.

"Don't ya think we looked?" Stephanie's voice said from the doorway, and both men turned to look. "My purse was in the kitchen and so were the keys to my Porsche. Bastard ignored both."

And you were alone and asleep upstairs, Liam thought as he touched the window lock. *Someone breaks in, risks getting caught, but takes nothing?* "Maybe they *left* something," he said.

Brandon let his eyes search the dark storage area. "I'll have my people take a look."

Liam knew this meant an IRA security team would bring in equipment to do a sweep. He turned to Stephanie, who had moved a few steps closer. "Are you sure you've checked everything?"

"I am," Stephanie said, her eyes fiery again.

Liam looked at his watch. "Is it too late to go to the hospital?"

. . .

Thirty minutes after piling into Liam's rental, they were standing in front of the ICU desk at Royal Victoria Hospital and were being told Brock Flannigan had been moved to a private room.

When they arrived at his room, a nurse was removing a tray of food from the serving cart. Flannigan's bed was elevated but he was asleep. His head was wrapped with gauze and an IV leaked from his arm. Behind him, an EKG silently traced his condition.

"Hey, Brock," Liam said in a whisper.

With some effort, Flannigan's eyes fluttered open, focused, and he recognized two of his three visitors. His questioning gaze settled on Stephanie as crusted lips parted.

"This is my sister, Stephanie," Brandon said. "How are you feeling?"

"Like I've been shot." Flannigan's nod was weak and his voice was like sandpaper. Odd, because Flannigan had always reminded Liam of the country music singer Kenny Rogers. When he saw Liam glance at his head, Flannigan said, "Bad spot to shoot a lawyer."

Liam chuckled as he pressed against the bed's stainless-steel railing. "Heard you had a long nap."

"So they tell me," Flannigan said, running a tongue over cracked lips.

Liam found a container of ice chips and put a few on the man's lips. "You should be good and rested." He then gripped the man's hand and said, "I am so sorry, Brock."

"Not your fault."

Liam squeezed his hand tighter. "Can you tell me what happened?"

Flannigan closed his eyes to speak. "Bloke came in after we closed. I was working late. Started asking me about AquaMedTran and the trust your mother left. Then he asked about the sale of

AMT to Apollo Oceanic."

Liam closed his eyes. AMT was once a subsidiary of the Hermes Corporation Liam's mother was given to run—as a hobby—by her then husband, Gorgeous Ruqur. The gesture was more to keep her busy and out of his personal affairs. It was clear he never expected her to make a success of it. But she had, and the company was placed into trust that was left to Liam after her death. He had the trust sell it back to Apollo Oceanic—another subsidiary of the Hermes Corporation—at a sizeable premium.

Flannigan licked his lips. "The man knew the trust passed to you after your mother died. But since you were supposed to be dead too, he wanted to know who controlled the trust."

"What made him think I was dead?"

"Said he visited the cemetery in Enniskillen. Saw the markers." Flannigan's eyes closed for several beats. "He forced me to print out the information."

"It's okay. The trust is in the name of James Jamison."

"Yeah," Flannigan said. "That's when he shot me. I'm sorry, Liam."

"Don't be," Liam said. "Did you recognize the man?"

Flannigan shook his head. "He had a funny accent. Slavic, maybe."

"What did he look like?"

Flannigan considered the question. "Shaved bald. Tall and very skinny, like a skeleton."

Liam glanced at Brandon, who mouthed a name they both knew well. When he saw the IV tube move and felt Flannigan touch his hand, he leaned down to hear his words.

"This man is dangerous." Flannigan's eyes searched Liam's. "You have to—"

Liam patted Flannigan's hand. "Get some rest, okay? I'll handle it."

As they left the room, Stephanie gripped Liam's forearm and said, "You know who did this, don't you?"

After managing to unclench his jaw, Liam said, "Yeah—I do."

CHAPTER 14

The Lake
Same Day
3:00 p.m.

Woody flashed her new BICA ID to the guard and for the first time she was waved through without someone at the house vouching for her. As her lips lifted into a smile, it was less joy than pride. The members of ICEBRG were talented and brilliant. And better yet, she was now one of them.

Once inside the house, Woody found Dr. Babbs and Araseli at the whiteboard. After hearing her approach, they spun around, startled to see her.

"Good afternoon, ladies," Woody said. "I'm looking for Bailey."

"She's in the kitchen," Babbs said, a puzzled look on her face. "I didn't realize—"

"I know. Sorry about that," Woody said as she pressed the kitchen door open, leaving Babbs and Araseli to their work. In the kitchen, she found Bailey near the stove.

"Oh!" Bailey exclaimed when she saw her. "Ms. Woodburn? Hello."

"It's Woody, please. Ms. Woodburn is my mother. Sorry for not calling ahead, but I needed to get away from the White House and thought I would drop by and see..." She paused to measure her next words—Bailey seemed frightened enough. "I wanted to get acquainted with my new team."

Bailey only continued to stare while dunking the tea bag into the steaming cup.

"Looks like the web on the whiteboard is growing."

"It's part of the new project Liam gave us."

"Liam was here?" Woody asked, perhaps too quickly. Liam was supposed to be recovering from his trip to Mexico, where he nearly died bringing Araseli out. "I'm still playing catch-up. What did Liam ask you to work on?"

"Research on Rufus Carmichael and WoHo?" Bailey said with a question.

"WoHo? What is that?"

Bailey explained Liam's theory about the relationship between Rufus Carmichael and the World Hands Organization.

"I wasn't aware Liam had asked you to do that. Can you please keep me informed of your progress?"

"Uh—yes, ma'am," Bailey said with little commitment.

Smiling weakly, Woody leaned against the kitchen sink and asked, "I understand you and Liam are very close."

"He's like my brother," Bailey said, her smile brighter now. "We go back several years; even before he joined BICA, and—well, you know—you tried to have him killed."

There it is, Woody thought. *My first fire to put out.* She pressed a smile, then said, "You understand that what I did was based on a lie, right?" When she saw Bailey's face soften, she asked, "What do you know about Liam's family?"

"Only that he lost his parents when he was young." Bailey's eyes drifted to the ceiling and back. "He never really talks about them. Why?"

When Bailey stopped talking, Woody knew the look on her face. Like a coached witness in a trial, there was more behind her eyes, but it might be too early to press, so she eased into it with a political show of trust.

"Has Liam ever mentioned the name Karl Berger?"

Bailey shook her head as her eyes squinted a question.

Woody lowered her voice to a whisper and said, "This doesn't leave the room. Understand?"

Bailey nodded.

Woody let out a breath and said, "The Russian ambassador slipped a note to Jerry Manchin last night. The names Bryant Curran and Karl Berger were written on it."

Bailey's eyes darted away in thought. "Bryant Curran was Liam's father. Who is Karl Berger?"

"I need to know that too," Woody lied, not wanting to give up too much this early. "Can you discreetly search Russian communications to see if they might also be asking about those names?"

"You're asking me to *sniff* Russian chatter?"

"That's right," Woody said.

Just then, the kitchen door cracked open and a familiar face peeked through.

"Araseli? Come in. Please," Woody said.

Araseli slipped timidly into the kitchen with an unlit cigarette clinging to her lips.

Woody considered herself to be short at five five, but the top of the elderly Mexican woman's head met her nose. She recalled the first day meeting Araseli here at the Lake. She had joked that Liam could have smuggled her out of Mexico in a lunch box.

"Buenas tardes," Araseli said, each smoky syllable strained through a thick Mexican accent. She paused for several beats, her gaze shifting between the two women. "Is Mr. Liam here?"

"Not today," Woody said, then watched the woman deflate, produce a cigarette lighter from a pocket, then leave the kitchen for the patio—without another word.

Through the kitchen window, Woody watched the woman light up as she leaned on the birdbath. Woody turned back to Bailey and said, "She's very guarded."

"Very. But it's a good trade-off. When it comes to the dark world of money laundering, she even has Babbs beat. Which is why the CDG wants her dead. She trusts no one." Bailey sighed, then added, "But she loves Liam."

So do you, Woody thought, but said, "I'm going to get out of your hair. Please let me know if you hear those two names in the chatter."

"I will," Bailey promised, following Woody to the front porch.

As she drove away, Woody noticed Bailey in the rearview mirror, and that she stayed on the porch until she was gone.

On the drive back, using her government cell phone, she checked in with Connie.

"Carter's team is pissed you left," Connie said. "By the way, I met my replacement. Remember the *boy* who dropped off the boxes? Georgetown grad. Must be a relative of Carter's."

"Did Jerry update the president?"

"I think so. But he didn't brief me, so I guess we are officially out of the loop."

Woody hung up after promising to be more available to Carter's transition team tomorrow. It was getting late in the day and she needed to see Ginny.

Using her new BICA cell phone, she dialed her mother's apartment and her mobile, but both went voice mail. The same thing happened with her office phone. So, she tried Curtis, who picked up immediately.

"I was about to call you," Curtis said. "Ginny scheduled an emergency meeting for tomorrow."

"What time?"

"That depends. I'm still trying to find Liam. His BICA devices are off." After a long pause, Curtis asked, "Why were you at the Lake?"

Shaking her head, she scolded herself for ignoring the fact that Curtis was still in charge of the team at the Lake and she had little doubt Bailey had called Curtis. It pissed her off, at first, but then she began to appreciate the loyalty. She said, "See you tomorrow, Curtis."

After taking the exit to Alexandria, Woody stopped by her

favorite Chinese take-out place, ordered the pepper steak and an egg roll, drove to her condo, and ate the meal alone at the desk in Paul's one-time office.

On the television mounted high on the wall, Peter Jennings announced the guilty verdict of the Menendez brothers.

. . .

Behind the main house at the Lake, a set of four matching single-story bungalows had been constructed. Mostly used for visitors, Araseli had moved into the farthest bungalow from the main house eight months earlier, after Liam extracted her from Mexico.

Saying her brief good night to Babbs, she left the house through the kitchen and was in her bungalow in less than a minute. After washing her face and changing into jeans, she left the bungalow, started her new metallic-blue Acura RL, lit a cigarette, then left the Lake driving north on Route 15 into the town of Warrenton.

She parked at the side of a strip mall away from the road and walked to the front, where she entered the new internet café called Java Linx. She ordered a cup of coffee, purchased a password, then mulled over which of the sixteen computers to use.

After opting for one in the back, away from the windows, she entered the password, watched the timer start in the lower corner of the screen, then waited for Windows 95 to appear. She clicked on the Excite search engine, then navigated to her Hotmail account and logged in as *JustMe703*.

From: JustMe703
To: ReggyD5150
Date: Wednesday, March 20, 1996
Subject: Update

Patricia Woodburn was here today. She asked Bailey about Karl Berger and Bryant Curran.

Nothing more to report.

Gracias!

End of Message

CHAPTER 15

After leaving the hospital, Liam took Brandon and Stephanie home before returning to his hotel where he checked his email in the business center. His plan was to take a quick shower, attempt to move his return flight up to the morning, and then hit the sack. But Stephanie's call to his burner phone changed everything.

"Let's go to White's Tavern," Stephanie said.

For the first time since his arrival, her voice sounded cheerful. Liam sighed and said, "I'd love to, but I need to get—"

"I need to see you, without Brandon. It's the pub where our parents took us when we were children."

"I know it," Liam said. Part of him wanted to accept her invitation, but the other part wanted to get back to finding Carmichael and now—Franco Delgado. But then, an opportunity revealed itself. "Okay. Meet me there at ten o'clock."

"You're not picking me up?" she complained.

"Just meet me there."

After hanging up, Liam left the hotel immediately, and instead of driving to White's, he drove into Castlereagh and parked three houses away from Stephanie's. He cut his lights and waited for a half an hour until he saw her leave the house, lock her door, back the Porsche into the street, then speed away.

When her taillights had shrunk to red pinpoints, he waited another few seconds and was about to give up on his theory when another set of headlights came on three cars ahead and pulled away from the curb.

A Volkswagen Golf.

Leaving his lights off, Liam tailed the Golf to the intersection. It gave a right-hand signal and turned in the same direction as Stephanie. Once the Golf had made the turn, Liam hit the headlights and followed.

In Belfast, Stephanie circled the block until she found an open parking spot on North Street. When she stepped into the crosswalk, the Golf paused at the green light and waited for her. As she passed, the driver lowered the window and stuck his head out to watch her disappear down a narrow alley called Winecellar: the entrance to an enclosed shopping and dining area. The Golf then whipped around the block and parked in the first spot on the west side of the alley.

Liam followed and parked in the space on the east side.

When he saw the man slam the car door, Liam started toward the alley, approaching the man head-on, but slowed to let the man turn down Winecellar first.

A few steps ahead of him, the man stopped to glance into every café and bar until he reached White's Tavern. Here, the alley came to a T to form a dimly lit open-air plaza. The man peered through the tavern window, did a double-take, then took a seat at one of the small tables in the plaza, his gaze locked on the pub's entrance.

When the man had settled in, Liam hugged the buildings and worked his way behind him until he had reached a dark portico where he could pause to get a better look. The man was medium build with black hair over his ears touching his collar around a thin neck. The bulk of his jacket obviously wasn't hiding muscles.

Glancing around to make certain they were alone, Liam stepped from the shadows and asked calmly, "Waiting for someone?"

The man's head spun around so quickly, his neck popped, and

when his eyes found Liam, they bloomed from surprise to shock. Then, his hand dove into his jacket pocket.

Lunging forward, Liam gripped the man's hand while it was still in his pocket, absorbed an elbow blow to his shoulder, then delivered his own elbow to the man's jaw. The man's knees buckled and he started to fall, but Liam gripped him from behind and dragged him back into the dark portico. He checked the man's pockets and found a cell phone and a small-caliber pistol. No wallet.

Pinning the man against the door with a foot into his chest, Liam said, "Funny. A dog never knows what to do with the car once it's caught."

The man spat, then said, "Fuckin' jobby! I don't—"

Liam launched a fist across the man's jaw. "You were tailing the lady. Why?"

The man groaned.

Liam opened the man's cell phone and then scrolled until he found the list of incoming and outgoing calls. The last call made was to someone labeled *GM* and the number began with *011-30*.

"Who's GM?" Liam demanded.

The man's gaze dropped at the same time as he took a swing at Liam's crotch. Liam blocked it with a hand sweep, then, using the foot still against the man's chest, he drove the toe of his sneaker into the man's chin, sending a tooth across the pavers of the plaza.

The man still said nothing.

After driving another elbow into the man's cheek, Liam stepped back to deliver a kick to the man's head but stopped when the man spat out, "Gustov Mikos."

Liam searched his mind's Rolodex and came up empty.

"What did you take from her house?" he asked, but saw true surprise on the man's face. Liam slipped the barrel of the pistol beneath the man's chin. "Or maybe you *left* something?"

"I didn't burgle the totty's place, mate. I—I was paid to find *you*," the man stammered, his East London Cockney accent dripping now. "I was given your description and told to report back when you showed your ugly mug."

"Did Gustov Mikos give you my name?"

"Liam Ó Corráin, you fuckin' bugger!"

Surprised at hearing the old pronunciation of his surname, Liam centered the barrel of the pistol on the man's forehead. "Did Gustov Mikos also mention that I'm a psychopath and feed on the pain of others?"

He cocked the hammer.

"No. Please," the man begged. "I won't—won't do anything." He raised his hands in surrender and let a bloody grin spread. "Okay. I found you, right, mate? My job is done."

"No, it isn't. You were told to report back." Liam opened the cell phone, thumbed down the list, and highlighted the last call again. Liam pressed Send and put the phone on speaker as he winked at the man.

After three rings, a man's Albanian accent answered and asked, "Why are you calling me again?"

. . .

Liam's breath stopped involuntarily when his brain recognized the voice, sending him into the past; a blaze flushed through his body like a shot of grain alcohol. He took the phone off speaker.

"I found the idiot you hired. What do you want, Delgado? Or is it still Rockman? Or Gustov Mikos? I can't keep up anymore."

"Master Liam?" Delgado said, and he thought he could hear the man smiling. "It has been a very long while."

"October thirty-first, 1977. Ellinikon International Airport. Athens," Liam said.

"I was only following orders."

"I was seventeen when you dumped me at the terminal with nothing but a one-way ticket to Cyprus and a wish for luck. I understand you've been looking for me."

A cackle of laughter buzzed the speaker, and beneath his foot, the Brit stirred. Liam backed away and allowed the man to stand. He pressed the Mute button, locked eyes with the Brit, then shifted his gaze toward the dark alley. "Get the fuck out of here," Liam said through clenched teeth. "If I see you again, I'll end you! Is that clear?"

The man didn't wait. He took off down the alley, catching a shin on a bench and a hand on a metal garbage bin before disappearing. Liam went back to the phone, then pressed Mute as Stephanie poked her head from the tavern door. Her gaze darted left, then right, across the plaza.

Liam waved, smiled, raised a finger and the cell phone, then bore the brunt of a scolding glare as she ducked back inside. He returned to the call.

"Now, what do you want?"

"First, let me say how well you sound—for a dead man. Perhaps the caretaker of your family's plot in Enniskillen should change the dates on the headstones. I'm certain your mother's is correct, but you and your father have been playing—how is it—possum?"

Liam closed his eyes and thought of his mother's grave. Through gritted teeth, he said, "Castille. That's how you found me."

Manuel Castille was an immigration attorney (when he was still alive) and the managing partner of the Los Angeles–based law firm of Castille, Huerta & Sullivan. The *Sullivan* in the name was Lacey Sullivan, Liam's neighbor and one-time lover, who got caught on the wrong side of Castille's plot to affect the vote on an immigration bill and was murdered. It was her death that had drawn Liam out of hiding, to get involved with finding her killers—and exposing his identity.

Somehow, Lacey Sullivan's ties to Liam had reached Castille, who was being controlled by Primo Ruqur—Delgado's employer.

Delgado said, "My employer tasked me with finding his long-lost half brother—who he thought to be dead."

"Why would he care?" Liam said.

"That was not my concern, Master Liam."

"And if I'm not interested in attending a family reunion?"

"I have made the consequences of that decision quite clear."

"To whom?" Liam asked.

"To Miss Ginny, of course," Delgado said, then followed it with: "Tsch, tsch, tsch. Has the great Virginia Woodburn not briefed you on our conversation? Perhaps you should reevaluate your allegiances."

No, she hasn't told me, Liam thought, but said, "Why did you break into Stephanie's house. And why did you shoot Brock Flannigan?"

"Perhaps Virginia Woodburn has the answers you seek. Afterward, I am certain you will want to meet. Will you be arriving as Master Liam or Master Jamison?"

Fuck! Liam thought, fisting is eyes closed. Delgado wasn't bluffing. He needed to know how much the man knew, but something more pressing was driving him. And it had just opened the pub door.

"I'm leaving," Stephanie's voice called. She sent a glare his way before she huffed back inside.

"I'll get back to you," Liam said, ending the call. Then, after copying Delgado's phone number into his own contact list, he smashed the Brit's cell phone against the pavers.

"Bloody hell! Have you gone mad?" a man's voice said from behind Liam as he held the door open for his date, hurrying her inside the pub.

CHAPTER 16

Established in 1630 during the unrest of Charles I and the English Civil War (the same year the Maguidhirs and the Ó Corráin clans arrived from Scotland), White's Tavern billed itself as the oldest pub in Belfast. More than three hundred years later, the Maguires and the Currans were still frequenting the tavern during their weekly treks from Enniskillen to the big city.

The food, playing checkers, breathing the smoky ambience, his mother's laughter, and Stephanie Maguire were among the fondest memories Liam had from childhood. And they all came back when he stepped inside the crowded tavern.

Stopping by the bar and ignoring stares from the regulars, he ordered two drafts. He found Stephanie at a high table in the back corner.

"Sorry about that," Liam said, sliding a fresh pint in front of her.

"I doubt it." Pulling the foam from her beer, she added, "What was *her* name?"

Liam glanced over the menu. "Franco Delgado."

"She sounds—butchy."

Liam said, "Delgado is the man who broke into your apartment. And the same man who shot Brock Flannigan. He had you followed..." Liam stopped in thought, then added, "...to find me."

Her lips parted as her eyes darted toward the door.

"It's okay. I took care of it."

Stephanie crossed her arms, her face blazing with fury. "Who is Franco Delgado?"

"Residue from my past."

"Why did he break into my house and take nothing?"

Liam shrugged. "I think it was to get my attention—to draw me to Belfast."

Stephanie's gaze had drifted to her own reflection in the glass. "You're back with the CIA, *aren't you*? Have you not learned your lesson?"

"I'm not back with—" Liam said, then lowered his voice. "I'm working with an NGO. Delgado may be blackmailing my boss."

A boss who kept her conversation with Rockman from me, Liam thought.

Stephanie said, "They're all the same. Just different initials."

Liam shook his head. "No. It's different." But as he said the words, he wondered who he was trying to convince. "Rockman knows we are close; and he used that to find me."

"Are we?" she asked. "Close?"

"When you're not busting my balls," Liam said, his fingers massaging hers.

Stephanie smiled as she leaned back and touched the claddagh ring on the chain beneath her blouse. "I never take it off."

"I remember when my mother gave it to you."

"I loved Gretchen like my own mother," Stephanie said. "But she isn't why I wear it."

Taking in a breath, Liam leaned on his elbows. "You know I love you, but for Christ's sake, I left Ireland as a kid. My father was off doing God-knows-what, and I had to change my name twice and fake my death to stay alive."

"Are you trying to scare me away?"

"I don't have to try. My past is a fucking horror movie." When he saw his words had missed the mark, he added, "Since I left Ireland, we've seen each other, what, five times?"

"Eight," Stephanie corrected. "Three in the last year. You always say you've left, but then you always return. Ireland is *in* you." Using her nails, she stroked strawberry locks behind both ears.

Liam said, "I want you to stay with Brandon until I get this sorted out."

Her neck reddening, Stephanie crossed her arms and said, "I thought this isn't about me?"

"It's not. And I want to keep it that way."

She huffed a laugh. "You want me to stay with my brother, his wife, and two kids?"

"They might enjoy having their aunt around."

"They see me enough."

"Look—Rockman shot Brock Flannigan just to track me down."

"He didn't shoot *me*," she said.

"Please, stay with Brandon. A few days—tops. Okay?"

"I'll think about it." Her eyes dropped to the table as she asked, "What about tonight?"

Liam drew a breath. "If you want, I can—"

"You can be a sleepin' in the guest room, if you'll be behavin' yourself."

His heart skipped as his childhood friend morphed into the fiery woman he had never stopped thinking about. Their long-dormant friendship had always existed on the edge of volcanic intimacy. Their eyes met and threatened his self-control.

"I promise to be good."

She smiled. "Your promises don't mean much."

After leaving the pub, Stephanie followed Liam to his hotel and waited in the lobby while he retrieved his bag, leaving the key on the dresser rather than checking out. On his way back to the lobby, he turned on his PagSat for the first time and found it buzzing with missed texts. All from Curtis.

Liam called him back.

"Where are you?" Curtis asked.

"What's up, Curtis?" Liam ignored the question, knowing full well Curtis could track his location using the signal from his Spytel pager.

"Emergency meeting. Tomorrow. How soon can you be here?"

"How soon can the BICA jet be in Belfast?"

"I'll send it now. Why are you—?"

"Just send the plane."

Liam clicked off as he entered the hotel's lobby. Stephanie was waiting for him by the coffeepots.

"Bad news?" she asked, gripping his free arm.

"My departure was just moved up to the morning."

He followed her back to her place and settled into the guest room while she fussed over pillows and blankets. After a long hug and kisses on cheeks, Stephanie left the room, and Liam climbed beneath the covers, calculating the arrival time of the BICA jet.

I'll get maybe five hours of sleep, he thought.

But minutes later, when Stephanie opened the door and slipped out of her gown and into his bed, their friendship came to an end as Liam thought, *Okay. So, I'll sleep on the plane.*

In life, they had been each other's first—everything. First friends. First kiss. First heartbreak. They had been lovers before either of them knew what that meant, and tonight, for the first time in their lives, they would enjoy each other fully against all better judgment.

There was no *easing into it* or *testing of the waters*. They had spent years doing that and exploded onto each other as if emotionally starved. There was no grace period, no time for second thoughts. It would have been like turning the *Titanic* or throwing water on Hiroshima.

. . .

Liam awoke with a start.

Sitting up in the dark, unfamiliar surroundings, he wiped his hands over his sweaty face; the nightmare of Lilliana dying in front of him was fading. Then, when his PagSat buzzed from the nightstand, his heart raced again.

He checked the pager. It was Curtis, and the plane was two hours out.

It was time he wished he didn't have as he took stock of what had happened. He cursed his weakness as he rolled over to watch her sleep. She seemed at peace. Something he had never known except for watching others experience it. But then, they had gotten involved with him.

Stephanie stirred.

Her tan cheek dug into the pillow as her lips parted softly. He couldn't resist lightly kissing them. A smile curled the corner of her mouth, but her eyes never opened.

Maybe she was right. Maybe he had never left Ireland. He stroked her bare shoulder before pulling the sheet up. As her eyes opened, she rolled away, she spooned into him, and he draped his arm over her.

"How long do we have?" she asked.

"Maybe an hour."

She gripped his forearm and said, "You're sweating."

"I'm fine."

She closed her eyes again. "I know what you're a thinkin', but this was my decision. I only wish it happened sooner."

"I won't let you regret it."

She started to play with his hair. "I'll go to Brandon's tonight."

"Thank you," Liam said.

An hour later, they reluctantly tumbled out of bed, said their goodbyes, and an hour after that, Liam was returning the rental at Belfast International Airport. Walking through the terminal, he tried Woody's phone, knowing she was five hours behind.

She answered, groggy and pissed off.

He said, "Are you my new boss now or not?"

"I hope not. Curtis said you're in Belfast," Woody retorted.

"What's the big meeting about?"

"I'd tell you if I knew. What's your ETA?"

"I'm guessing wheels-down at eight your time."

"Come straight to BICA. We have a hell of a mess."

CHAPTER 17

Liam parked the rental on the seventh floor of the garage, passed through the air lock, and was met by Curtis on the other side. The man's face appeared melted from lack of sleep.

Without a word, he turned and led Liam across the hallway to the railing, where they both looked down at the seven-story drop to the lobby, where people were buying coffee, doing business with the credit union, or rushing to a yoga class.

"Why the fire drill?" Liam asked.

Curtis shook his head. "Ginny came in this morning with a man I've never met. They've been locked up tight in her office since." After a pause, he asked, "Why were you in Belfast?"

"Vacation," Liam said.

Curtis sighed, then led Liam to the suite of offices where the lone admin—Amy—looked up, smiled, then returned to her work. Curtis pointed in silence at Ginny's closed door before disappearing into his own office. Liam tapped a knuckle against Woody's door—waited—then opened it anyway.

He found her sitting cross-legged on the floor amid a sea of boxes. Surprised, Woody looked up, smacked her hands together, and said, "Pick a box—any box—and—"

Liam slammed the door. "Did Ginny tell you about Franco Delgado?"

She stopped unpacking. "Yes. I found out in our Monday meeting."

"Who was in the meeting?"

"Me, Ginny, and Darren McFadden."

"McFadden?" he repeated. "When were you going to tell me?"

"Maybe if you'd answer my calls…" Then, her eyes softened, and she asked, "Who told *you* Delgado contacted her?"

Liam chuckled. "Delgado did."

Woody looked up at him and said, "You're shitting me!"

"We had a nice chat—catching up on old times. Did Ginny tell you why Delgado was trying to lure me to Belfast?"

"Lure you? No, she—" But she was interrupted by a new voice coming from her now open office door.

"If you calm down, I'll tell you both," the voice said, and they both turned to find Ginny standing in the doorway like a gunfighter entering a saloon.

Her usual Southern belle ease had given way to a scolding glare as if she had caught her children playing with knives. When she stepped into the office, a stout man about her age followed her inside. He had graying-brown hair swept to the side over gray eyes with a Slavic slant set over jagged cheekbones. After casting a suspicious glance at the open blinds, he locked the door behind them.

Ginny tossed two envelopes onto the coffee table. One was large, manila, and closed. The other was legal, white, and open. "We have a lot to discuss," she said, then went to the entertainment console and slid a tape into the VCR. Picking up the remote, she paused the fuzz before it could play.

Ginny and the stranger each took a high-back chair on either end of the coffee table, while Liam and Woody took opposite ends of the sofa. After clearing her throat, Ginny turned to Liam and said, "It's over. We've been—compromised."

"What does that mean?" Woody asked.

Ginny's eyes shifted to Woody, then back to Liam. "Operation:

Jugular. You. Your father. The Kremlin. It's out there now." When she saw that Woody was about to speak, she raised her palm and added, "Let me bring you both up to speed."

"I've already lived this story," Liam said.

"Not all of it," Ginny said.

. . .

In the late 1960s, after seizing power from Nikita Khrushchev in Russia, Leonid Brezhnev developed his *doctrine* for dealing with the West, proclaiming that any opposition to socialism in the Eastern Bloc countries was a threat to Russia and the Soviet Union as a whole.

Not only did he create an overt policy against capitalism, he ordered his most trusted advisor, General Grigori Urmanov, to develop a plan for an all-out nuclear attack should NATO's posture become aggressive. It was called Operation: One Strike.

Urmanov, a proud communist and Brezhnev's closest friend, also believed in the future of Russia but never wanted to see it destroyed by a nuclear war—which is exactly what would happen if One Strike was ever put into motion. It was true that his country had nuclear weapons. But like their conventional forces, the numbers—the ones that actually functioned—were greatly exaggerated. And the ability of a missile to actually hit a target was a roll of the dice.

Still, like a good soldier, he developed the plan, presented it, then shelved it—never once implementing regular exercises to practice it. He hoped that by staying close to Brezhnev, he could keep watch and, if necessary, talk him out of ever going through with it. What he had misjudged at the time was the power of Brezhnev's cult of personality, and the inevitability of medical fate.

Brezhnev's first mini-stroke came in 1975. And when it leaked, the CIA and BICA were ordered, by the president, to come up with a plan to counter his lunacy, should it become necessary.

Addicted to smoking, sleeping pills, and tranquilizers, Brezhnev was a walking vascular time bomb. Each day brought more erratic behavior, and he grew dangerously unpredictable.

Then, in January of 1976, Brezhnev had a bigger stroke.

The world was led to believe he had recovered, but the CIA and BICA knew the truth: Brezhnev had lost his mind. He had grown paranoid. His agricultural reforms were failing, people were starving, and he believed the United States was behind the unrest in the Soviet bloc countries. Then, when he replaced his top generals with hard-liners who might actually go through with Operation: One Strike, the CIA's plan was put into motion.

"Operation: Jugular…" Ginny said as she took a sip of water, studied the faces in the room, then finished her story with, "…the assassination of Leonid Brezhnev."

Turning to Liam, Woody asked, "You knew about it?"

"Just the broad strokes. I know it destroyed my family."

Ginny said, "We needed to get close to Brezhnev. Which was damn near impossible until General Grigori Urmanov approached me at a defense conference in Paris.

"Grigori and I had known each other for many years. We had a mutual respect and perhaps a little trust. At the conference, he asked for a secret meeting, where he confirmed many things about Brezhnev the CIA and BICA already knew.

"What we *didn't* know was how terrified General Urmanov was that Russia, and his family, would not survive Operation: One Strike. He had already lost his wife to cancer, leaving behind a daughter and a son. After that conversation, we had our in. Now, BICA needed to find the right man.

"But the CIA already had the perfect man: on loan from the British SAS acting as a linguist who was already fluent in German and Russian. An Irishman named Bryant Curran." She turned to Woody and added, "Liam's father. After months of training, we moved Bryant; his wife, Gretchen; and Liam to West Berlin, where

Bryant posed as a special envoy to the ambassador. In reality, he was establishing a second identity: a German pharmaceutical sales rep named Karl Berger.”

Woody stirred when she heard the name, and filled her lungs with air, extending every ounce of restraint she had not to spill the intel from Manchin too soon. She let it out and leaned back on the sofa.

Ginny said, “Establishing the identity of Karl Berger in East Berlin was the easy part. Getting him inside the Kremlin was where General Urmanov came in.” She took another sip of water.

“Let me help you,” the strange man said, speaking for the first time. His accent confirmed he was Russian. “General Urmanov’s daughter, Sophya, was a trauma nurse in East Berlin. Arrangements were made for Bryant Curran and Sophya to meet socially, and they developed a friendly relationship. At the time, Sophya was married with a daughter, so General Urmanov arranged for her husband to be arrested and jailed in L’gov. Then, when he was murdered in prison, her affair with Bryant Curran—or Karl Berger—began. Once they were married, General Urmanov arranged for Sophya to become Brezhnev’s personal nurse. All three were moved to Moscow and given an apartment near Red Square.

“In February of ’82, Brezhnev ordered One Strike to be implemented. General Urmanov tried to convince Brezhnev otherwise, but his hard-line generals won out and deployments began. All the Soviet military needed was the final word from Brezhnev. Then, that November”—Ginny cleared her throat—“we got lucky. Brezhnev died before he could put One Strike in motion.”

“Thank God!” Woody said.

“Yes,” Ginny said. “But then, we had another problem. The Russians could never find out about Operation: Jugular, and we needed to get Bryan Curran and his new family out of Russia. At the time, only a handful of people knew about Operation: Jugular. General Urmanov, Bryant Curran, Sophya, the director of central intelligence, Walter Rehnquist, myself—"

"And me," the Russian added.

Liam turned to the Russian and asked, "Who the hell are you anyway?"

The man smiled as all eyes fell on him. He loosened his tie and leaned back in his chair. His response was cold as he pointed to the open white envelope on the table. "I received that letter two days ago from General Grigori Urmanov. It was sent the same day he committed suicide."

"Suicide?" Liam said as he looked at Ginny. "When?"

"Last Tuesday. Nine days ago."

Woody turned to the Russian. "Why would the Russian minister of defense send the letter to *you*?"

But it was Ginny who responded. "Because, until yesterday, Jaco was a special envoy working with Ambassador Boris Travkin."

"Jaco," Woody repeated. "Finally, we have a name. So, what happened yesterday?"

"I defected to the United States," Jaco said.

Ginny picked up the envelope and spun it to Liam. "You should read this to the team."

Liam removed the letter, unfolded it, saw it was handwritten—in Russian—never dated, and reeked of sour tobacco. "It's been a few years since I've read Cyrillic, so I might be a little—" But he stopped midsentence when he recognized the first simple word at the top of the letter. In Russian, it read as *Сын*. In English, it meant *son*.

Liam looked up, but Jaco answered his question before it was asked. "My name is Jaco Urmanov. And General Grigori Urmanov was my father."

CHAPTER 18

Liam said to Jaco, "If you're General Urmanov's son, then the woman my father is married to—"

"Yes. Sophya is my sister," Jaco interrupted.

Liam held Jaco's gaze for a beat longer, then returned to the letter and translated for the room.

"Son, if you received this letter, be assured my past has caught up with me and I have decided not to endure the pain. Do not grieve. Russia was saved, as were the lives of you and your sister. Please contact your cousin Miranda and inform her of what has happened. She has something for you. With most love to you and your sister, your father, Grigori."

Liam spun the letter onto the table with little interest. That was when he noticed that Woody was staring at him—transfixed—as if he owed more words. When she smiled and turned away, he knew something was up.

Looking at Jaco, Woody asked, "Have you contacted your cousin?"

"Yes," Jaco said as he turned to Ginny. "Meet Miranda."

Ginny leaked a grin. "It was my code name during Operation: Jugular. Jaco's defection had always been part of the plan, if it ever became necessary. And now—thanks to Delgado—it has." Then, she pointed to the manila folder on the table.

Woody snatched it up, reached inside, and removed the xerox copies of three black-and-white photos, one in color, and an article out of *Pravda* from November 11, 1982. Her eyes widened when she saw the three photos across the top of the newspaper. On the left was a woman she assumed to be Sophya. On the right was a teenage boy that was clearly Liam. And in the middle was the handsome face of a man who could only be Liam's father, Bryant Curran. Or Karl Berger, as the caption claimed. A circle had been drawn around the two men.

Woody sent another knowing glance at Liam and said, "Looks like you're dead—again."

"Actually, this article was the first time I died," Liam said as he took the stack from Woody's grip. "I remember this article. It's a tribute to Sophya—and an obituary for the rest of us." Rifling through the photos, he added, "And these are of me, my father, and my mother. The other people in the photos are the Maguires. The other two children are Stephanie and Brandon." Dropping the photos back on the table, he said, "Now we know what Rockman took from Stephanie's house."

"Yes," Ginny said. "Is that why you were in Belfast?"

"Partly. Brock Flannigan was shot back in September. When he came out of his coma, he asked for me. I went to the hospital, Ginny. He's in bad shape but was able to describe the shooter. It was Delgado."

"Who's Brock Flannigan?" Woody asked.

"The lawyer who manages Liam's trust," Ginny said as she closed her eyes and leaned back in the chair.

Woody asked. "Where did you get the photos?"

Ginny hesitated, then said, "Rockman gave them to me at the café."

Woody felt her face flush. "Meaning you had the photos when we met with McFadden but didn't show them to me. And now I know why."

Ginny said nothing.

"You knew I'd figure it out. Didn't you?" Woody said. "I think you'd better tell me the rest of story—now."

"I'm getting to that," Ginny said.

Woody snapped up the *Pravda* article from the table and pointed to the photo of the older man. "He's Karl Berger in the article, but he's really Bryant Curran, Liam's father."

Ginny said, "That's hardly a revelation."

"No. But this is. He's not dead! Because I met him three days ago in *your* office. Only, his name was Darren McFadden." Woody swung her gaze to Jaco and said, "I'll bet your sister isn't dead either." When she was met with curious silence, she added, "But we have a bigger problem because the Russian ambassador slipped a piece of paper to Jerry Manchin at dinner. It had the names *Karl Berger* and *Bryant Curran* written on it. Whatever information Rockman has, he's already releasing it."

"My God!" Jaco said, sending a worried gaze toward Ginny. "And they have the photos."

Ginny glanced at Liam; her eyes wrinkled in defeat. But she said nothing.

Picking up the photos, Woody said, "I don't get it. Why are those so valuable?"

"The copies aren't," Liam said. "But the originals have dates, places, and names on the back. The Russians know the face of Karl Berger in the obituary. And, thanks to my mother's writing on the back of the photos, they know the same face belongs to an Irishman named Bryant Curran." Liam then picked up the *Pravda* article and aimed it at Ginny and Jaco. "A spy in the Kremlin, married to Brezhnev's personal nurse." He spun the article back onto the table.

Woody said, "Okay...so, the conspirators Travkin was referring to are Bryant, Liam, and Sophya. But he also said the graves are empty. Maybe Travkin slipped the names to Manchin as a warning."

"Maybe," Ginny said with little conviction.

Liam glanced at Ginny, then at Jaco. After the volley repeated itself several times more, Ginny finally nodded and Liam released a long sigh. After fifteen long years, he could finally tell the story.

"Travkin must be lying," Liam said, "I know there were three cadavers buried in the plot. General Urmanov arranged for them—" But Liam stopped when he saw Jaco shaking his head. "What is it?"

Jaco said, "My father made sure the charred cadavers were cremated so they could never be tested. If the graves were exhumed, all they found were three urns."

Woody turned to Ginny. "If Brezhnev died on his own, why go to such great lengths to fake their deaths? Yuri Andropov would have his own people, his own nurse. Sophya would have been naturally replaced. She and Bryant could have taken their time leaving."

"Their escape wasn't about Brezhnev," Ginny said, then let out a long sigh. "In '82, the Soviets were in Afghanistan, and certain enterprising members of the CIA, and a few Russian generals, were exploiting a highly profitable business opportunity."

"Opium?" Woody said.

Ginny nodded. "And Walter Rehnquist, the CIA's chief of station in Moscow at the time, was running it. He offered to let Bryant in on the scheme, but when he refused, Rehnquist decided to set him and Sophya up."

Jaco said, "My father learned of the plan to frame Bryant Curran. And he knew that under no circumstances could Bryant ever be captured."

Ginny said, "Obviously, we couldn't use the CIA's original exit strategy, so we—me and General Urmanov—put plan B into motion. The fire and the cadavers. We used the British MI6 to smuggle them out of Russia."

"Meaning Sophya is still alive," Woody said. "Why was it necessary to fake your death? In November of '82, you were living in the States as Trevor Harmon."

"I was finishing up at MIT and getting ready to join the navy," Liam said absently.

Ginny said. "If the CIA thought Liam knew anything about the opium operation, Rehnquist would target him later—as long as he was alive. So, we arranged for Liam to visit his father in Moscow and perish in the fire too."

When Woody turned to him, Liam heard the unspoken question. Three years ago, DCI Rehnquist was murdered, and Liam had always been the prime suspect. It was the reason Woody had sent Paul Kelvington to kill Liam.

Liam said, "I know what you're thinking, but this is the first time I'm hearing that we were running from the CIA and not the Russians."

Woody involuntarily reached out and touched Liam's hand. "An empty grave in Moscow and in Ireland. You've been running your whole life, haven't you?"

Liam said nothing. Anything more than silence would reveal how right she was.

Woody turned to Ginny. "The photos are proof that Bryant Curran and Karl Berger are the same man, but they don't prove he's still alive. I mean, they still found three urns fill with ashes."

"You're right," Ginny said as she turned to the television, aimed the remote, and pressed Play. "I received this from Delgado two days ago."

Ginny started the video at the time Bryant Curran first left the package in the mailbox, then fast-forwarded to Liam retrieving it. After playing it four more times, Ginny ejected the tape and sat on the arm of the chair, enveloped in the room's silence.

Finally, Liam said, "The mailbox is leased under the name of James Jamison. It's how I receive mail from Brock Flannigan's law firm. My father and I also use it as a dead drop."

"And that's why Delgado shot Flannigan," Woody said. "To track you down?"

Liam nodded. "Delgado forced Flannigan to give him the information before he shot him. It's funny, though. When I spoke to Delgado, he admitted that he was searching for me, but he never once mentioned my father." Then he turned to Ginny and said,

"And he wondered why you never shared that you two had met."

"And now—I have," Ginny said coldly.

Woody said, "Delgado was threatening to release this evidence to the Russians if Ginny didn't give up you and your father. But the Russians already know about Karl Berger and Bryant Curran. The note to Manchin proves it. If Delgado's leverage is gone, why is he still playing us like it isn't?"

"Maybe he doesn't know yet," Liam said. "The KGB put a price on his head years ago. He could be bargaining to have the sanction lifted."

"It's more than that," Jaco chimed in. "Jurg Ivanovich has always believed the United States murdered Brezhnev, and he has been trying to prove it to the Kremlin for years. Delgado had been living—quite successfully—as Gjon Rockman for decades now. Why the sudden urgency to come out in the open and trade information for the removal of the contract?" He turned to Ginny and said, "We believe he's found a way to help Ivanovich prove Brezhnev was murdered."

"But why?" Woody asked.

"To start a war with the United States. To punish Russia for the murder of his parents."

"But the world already knows Brezhnev died of a heart attack," Woody said.

"Tell that to Ivanovich," Jaco explained. To Ginny he said, "We *must* keep the names Karl Berger and Bryant Curran out of the chatter at all costs. It can never be leaked that we know about the cremation of the cadavers. That alone would prove our involvement in Operation: Jugular."

Everyone in the room nodded in agreement except for Ginny— and she was pacing again, in deep thought. Finally, she stopped and looked directly at Liam. "When I first watched the tape, I was on the phone with Delgado. He argued that we both knew the truth, but he never once used the name Curran. Not even in the café. I think he wanted *me* to say the names," Ginny explained. "In fact, he *needs* me to say them—to prove that I know. He must have been recording our conversation."

Woody said, "When I look at the evidence, all I see is proof of a fourteen-year-old spy ring in the Kremlin. Russia's not going to start a war because of that."

Liam said, "And if I were Delgado, I'd be more worried the Russians might actually exhume Brezhnev's body for more testing. That would bring his and Ivanovich's plan to a screeching halt."

"There *is* another side to this," Ginny said. "Primo sent Delgado to Liam, right?"

"So now Primo's working with the Russians?" Liam asked. "Why?"

"How close are you to finding Eagle, Liam?" Ginny said.

Liam didn't answer. In truth, he lost his breath.

Ginny said, "This will come as a shock, but I've always suspected Primo Ruqur was involved with the NEST. Maybe this isn't about Russia at all, but the NEST trying to stop *you*."

"Are you suggesting Primo Ruqur is the Eagle?" Liam asked.

"The man is a socialist billionaire. He publicly admitted his Power of Progress organization is the revival of the Bilderbergs. He sits on the board of the World Economic Forum. And, if he believes you're getting close to finding him, who else has more motive?"

"And resources," Jaco added.

Liam turned and pointed at Ginny. "You'd better be damned serious about this. There's no half speed with me, and you know that. You have always tried to stop me from eliminating the NEST, and now—"

"I'm blessing it," Ginny finished for him. "Can you find him?"

Woody jumped in. "Primo is your half brother, for Christ's sake. How can you—?"

"If he's Eagle, I'll eat a sandwich on his corpse," Liam said.

Woody cringed, then glanced at Ginny. "Getting to Delgado is one thing, but Primo Ruqur is a billionaire who has bodyguards."

"Sheik Tariq Al-Jabori had guards too," Liam said as he put on his jacket and started toward the door.

"I want regular updates," Woody called out.

"I'll do my best." Liam closed the office door as he left the suite.

. . .

After Liam was gone, Woody looked up at Jaco and then Ginny, who were also staring at her. She said, "I hope you realize that sending Liam to hunt down Delgado *and* Primo is playing right into their plans."

"No, it isn't," Ginny said. "Liam means nothing. Delgado and Primo needs Bryant, not Liam."

"If they get to Liam, they could use him as leverage."

"A trade we'd never make," Ginny said. "Delgado's not stupid."

Jaco said, "Bryant isn't the only bargaining chip."

Woody nodded. "If I were the Russians, I'd want Sophya more than either Liam or Bryant."

"Yes," Jaco relented.

"Does Bryant know about the videotape yet?" Woody asked.

Ginny shook her head. "I tried to warn him that he's been exposed."

"And..."

"He's gone dark."

CHAPTER 19

Atli Hotel
Ankara, Turkey
Friday, March 22, 1996
1:15 p.m.

Delgado ordered the driver to pull the Cadillac to the curb in front of the hotel and wait. When the porter reached to open the door, Delgado waved him off. Several minutes later, a cab pulled up behind the Cadillac, and a medium-build man with a shaved head got out of the back, paid the cabby, then limped into the hotel.

Delgado placed a quick call from his cell phone and spoke only three words: "I am here." He then lowered his window and told the porter, "You may get my door now."

In the hotel's lobby, Delgado sent a quick glance toward the bald man before turning away. He was then met by a man in a suit and an earpiece who—after looking him up and down—escorted him into the elevator. As the compartment rose, the man searched him for weapons, then, touching his earpiece, said in Russian, "He is unarmed."

When the doors opened, he was escorted to the presidential suite, where another suit with an earpiece stood guard at the door. Delgado was let inside, where he was led to the bathroom.

"Get undressed," the suit said, tossing him a white robe with the hotel's logo.

"I thought I had a meeting," Delgado said.

"You still do."

Delgado left his clothes in a folded stack and slipped into the robe.

The suit returned a minute later and escorted him across the hall to the Turkish bath, where three lovely Turkish women proceeded to remove the robe and help him down the slope of the zero-entry jacuzzi, where Jurg Ivanovich was already seated. After serving a round of cigars and Cognac, the women were ordered to leave.

Delgado sat and let his body adjust to the warmth as his gaze settled on Ivanovich as he lit his cigar. "I trust your meeting with the Turks went well."

Ivanovich smoothed his black flattop and spoke around his cigar. "Not our concern, Mr. Delgado."

Glancing around the area, Delgado said, "You are a very cautious man, Jurg."

"You should be so cautious. The name Franco Delgado is still notorious in Russia. It was wise to not give your name to my men. A two-million-dollar bounty is hard to ignore."

"I hope the intelligence I am providing will get us past that."

Having lived with the price on his head for more than twenty years, removing it meant no nothing to Delgado at this point. But it was important Ivanovich believed it did.

Ivanovich tapped a log of ash onto a folded towel, his eyes dissecting Delgado as his grin faded to a scowl. "You are *not* keeping your end of the bargain."

"Why do you—?"

"There were no bodies. Only three urns filled with ashes! I cannot test ashes!"

"Ashes?" Delgado repeated. "How could that be?"

"We could ask General Urmanov, but we would need a séance to do it."

"He died?" Delgado asked, trying hard to keep his disappointment masked as shock. He had counted on the interrogation of Urmanov to help verify the intelligence he was providing.

"Suicide," Ivanovich said. "My team discovered documents proving the general had ordered the cremation of the bodies of the Berger family only days after their deaths. Someone tipped Urmanov off, and he leapt from his office balcony." Ivanovich pursed his lips, then said, "Our deal may have died with the general, Mr. Delgado."

"No. I have other means to prove the Bergers were not who they pretended to be."

"You mean that Karl Berger was an American CIA operative name Bryant Curran?" When he saw Delgado's eyes and mouth spread to O's, he added, "Our ambassador in America has suggested this fact." Then, Ivanovich threw his cigar at Delgado, missing his face by inches, and screamed, "You are making a fool of me in front of my superiors!"

Delgado's mind struggled with how the Russian ambassador to the United States could have come up with the tie between Karl Berger and Bryant Curran. Still, he had another ace to play but had been holding it for a better time. Apparently, that time was now.

Delgado said, "Granted—I was hoping that tests on the bodies would prove that cadavers had been buried in their place. Surely you can see this cover-up is more proof that the three conspirators are alive. Still, I have more convincing evidence."

Ivanovich had picked up the lighter but held it unlit near the tip of his Cuban. "What is this evidence?"

"Photographs proving Bryant Curran and Karl Berger are the same man."

"I already know this."

"And, I have both him—and his son—on videotape. Very much alive."

Sucking the flame from the lighter through the Cuban, Ivanovich asked, "And you have brought this tape with you?"

Delgado shook his head. "I will have it to you in twenty-four hours."

"You understand I am not interested in simply outing an American spy? I must prove the spy and his wife murdered

Leonid Brezhnev."

"I understand," Delgado said. "That is why I am also offering the conspirators themselves. Bryant Curran *and* Sophya Gubina."

"Both of them?" Ivanovich said. "That is impressive."

"And the interrogation of living conspirators would yield far better proof to President Yeltsin, would it not?"

Ivanovich nodded, in deep thought. If Delgado was telling the truth, he was so close to vindication, he could smell it now.

"You have earned a few more days," Mr. Delgado. "But no more."

Just then, a brown female face appeared at the door. Ivanovich waved the woman in, and she left two new glasses of Cognac on the edge of the pool. After delivering a fresh stack of towels from a rack, she left.

Delgado said, "There is one other thing. My sources believe the Americans have discovered what we are trying to do and have procured the services of a professional assassin."

"And you fear for your life, Mr. Delgado?"

"Not for mine."

Ivanovich cackled before gulping down the Cognac. "An American assassin? Sent to kill me?"

Delgado held back a smile as he thought about the bald man downstairs as he climbed out of the bath and back into the robe. "I will send you the videotape."

After being escorted by the suit back to the suite for his clothes, Delgado dressed and was escorted to the lobby. The bald man was gone. He then turned to the suit and said, "Come with me. I have something for you."

Outside, the porter opened the Cadillac's door, and Delgado climbed in the back seat. He found his briefcase, spun the lock on the dial, opened it, then passed a bulky sealed manila envelope through the window to the suit.

"Give this to Ivanovich," Delgado explained. "He will know what to do with it."

He raised the window and ordered the driver to take him to the airport.

Seven months earlier, when he discovered Bryant Curran was still alive, he thought his plan might be too complex to work. And, in reality, it was. But reality didn't interest Jurg Ivanovich. Blinded by his obsession with proving Brezhnev had been murdered by the Americans, Delgado predicted, quite accurately, Ivanovich would bite on anything.

Now, after delivering the photos and the tape to Ivanovich, Delgado knew that even *he* couldn't stop his own plan at his point. Ivanovich may think *their* plan was failing, but *Delgado's* plan was working perfectly. He only needed to wait for the rope he had fed the Americans to grow taut.

And when it did, he had a little something extra planned.

CHAPTER 20

At the counter, Araseli collected her blueberry bagel, cream cheese, coffee, and change from the young girl in the green Java Linx apron.

"You're becoming quite the regular, Ms. Estrada," the barista said. "I'm starting to know your orders."

"*Si. Gracias.* I mean, thank you," Araseli said, delivering a forced smile while keeping her eyes to the floor. In truth, being predictable made her nervous, but she didn't have much choice. Any communications leaving the Lake were monitored, and as long as she lived in one of the bungalows on the property, privacy was impossible. The internet café was her best option—for now.

After selecting the same computer in the back, she placed her bagel and coffee on the left so she could drive the mouse on the right. After logging into her Hotmail account, she found a new message in her inbox. As old habits die hard, she read from the first to the last message with the updated subject line:

From: ReggyD5150
To: JustMe703
Date: Wednesday, March 20, 1996
Subject: Suggestion

Suggest looking for ties to group called Power of Progress. Look for buys and shorts inside broker accounts.

Be safe.

End of Message

Araseli took out her pad, made a note to look into the Power of Progress, then started pecking out a new email.

From: JustMe703
To: ReggyD5150
Date: Wednesday, March 22, 1996
Subject: Suggestion

Have made some progress.

PoP and WoHo both have accounts is in Switzerland with subsidiary accounts in Hong Kong, Belize, New York, and London. Recently, they opened a Greek account at Athens Cooperative Bank owned by holding company called Hermes. History to 1983. Noticed large transfers to broker accounts started in 1991.

All accounts are inactive. Found buys in many defense stocks starting in 1991. Between the two accounts, about $20 million US purchased. If other accounts are similar, could be hundreds of millions. Confirmed by transfers from brokerage accounts to other accounts in 1993, total transfers were near one billion. Was able to gain access to bank in New York but no data yet.

End of Message

Araseli bit into her bagel. Looking away from the screen, she rubbed her eyes, then squinted at the glare from the morning sun off the chrome trim of the café's fixtures, where a line had now formed at the counter as the breakfast crowd arrived.

And that's when she saw the two familiar faces enter the café.

Araseli slid down in the seat until she could barely see over the partition and watched Dr. Babbs and Bailey get in line, their eyes fixed on the menu board. After several minutes, they collected their orders and searched the café for seats. With nothing available, they gave up and left, causing Araseli to breathe a sigh of relief and cross herself twice before hitting Send.

CHAPTER 21

CIA Director Paul James Sanchez chose to deliver the president's daily brief in person that morning. As were all PDBs, the information was highly classified. But this morning's would dovetail with the meeting of the National Security Council, meaning Richard Morrow, the national security advisor, would be there. And Sanchez was given a heads-up that *his* briefing would contain the name of someone Sanchez knew and cared for deeply.

He was glad today was Patricia Woodburn's last and there would be a cake shaped like the presidential seal in the conference room. It gave him the excuse he needed.

Sanchez was a true American success story. His entire family had immigrated from Cuba in the 1950s during the early phase of the revolution when Batista was still in charge and Castro was but a Marxist thug. A year later, Paul James Sanchez was born in Miami's Little Havana district.

After enlisting in the army as a private, PJ worked nights to finish college before being accepted into Officer Candidate School. He graduated as a second lieutenant, then worked his way to lieutenant colonel before being tapped to join the Defense Intelligence Agency at the Pentagon. There, he made full-bird colonel and attended war college, but was recruited away from the DIA to join the CIA by the previous DCI (the now deceased William Rehnquist).

Sanchez officially retired from the army to become the CIA's chief of station in Manila before being promoted to deputy director of intelligence and relocated to Langley. Then, after Rehnquist's death three years ago, he was named acting DCI until the senate could confirm him as permanent. Which they did.

After the doors to Oval Office were closed and locked, it appeared this morning's NSC meeting would consist of the president, his incoming chief of staff, Leon Carter; Secretary of State Manchin; the secretary of defense; the national security advisor; and the attorney general.

Sanchez opened the briefing with the possibility of peace talks between the Russians and the Chechen rebels, then led into the Middle East, where Hezbollah had launched a series of indiscriminate rocket attacks into Israel from Lebanon. This led to the group discussing possible counterattacks by the Israeli Defense Force (IDF) and the position the US should take.

After the PDB, Attorney General Rittenger commented the FBI was investigating new and credible leads on the identity of a person called the Unabomber.

The next item on the agenda had been added at the last minute at the insistence of the incoming COS, Leon Carter. It pertained to intercepted communications between two unknown individuals using an unsecured email account.

Retired Admiral Richard Morrow, the national security advisor, said, "Mr. President, after receiving the note Ambassador Travkin gave to Jerry Manchin, at the request of Mr. Carter, our ECHELON group began sniffing the airwaves for the names Karl Berger and Bryant Curran." (ECHELON was a supersecret network of global listening posts). "The only instances we've found so far is between two Hotmail accounts."

"Hotmail? What the hell is that?" the president asked.

Morrow explained the concept of the new web-based messaging service as he reluctantly passed a single page stamped *Top Secret* around the room.

From: JustMe703

From: JustMe703
To: ReggyD5150
Date: Wednesday, March 20, 1996
Subject: Update

Patricia Woodburn was here today. She asked Bailey about Karl Berger and Bryant Curran.

Nothing more to report.

Gracias!

End of Message

When the page made it back to Morrow, he returned it to his satchel.

The president spoke first. Turning to his national security advisor, he asked, "What does this mean, Richard?"

"It means that Patricia Woodburn was asking her new BICA team to look into the two names. That is less concerning than the fact she was overheard by someone whose screen name is *JustMe* and is informing someone called *ReggyD*."

"So, BICA has a mole?" the president asked, sending a glance toward his new chief of staff.

"Maybe," Morrow said.

Sanchez chimed in. "A Hotmail account can be opened by anyone. It could be the Russians baiting us into reacting."

"Russians who have found their way inside BICA," Carter said.

Sanchez said, "We need more information before making that claim, Leon." Then, he turned to the president. "Give us a few days."

After the briefing, the team retired to the Roosevelt Room, where

Woody and her team were waiting to mingle with Leon Carter's incoming team. The atmosphere was cordial but tense, so Woody decided to visit the punch bowl again. It was there that Sanchez touched her elbow and whispered, "Cabinet Room. Ten minutes."

Sanchez filled his cup, then pretended to take a cell phone call as he left the Roosevelt Room. Woody waited the full ten minutes before making a bathroom excuse.

The Cabinet Room was across the hall but visually out of range of the Roosevelt Room. Manchin was waiting and closed the door behind them. Sanchez was by the window looking out on the colonnade.

"I brought PJ up to speed," Manchin said. "I didn't think you'd mind."

She didn't. There were only three members of the president's cabinet she trusted without question, and two of them were standing in this room. When Sanchez held her gaze, Woody responded with, "What is it?"

"Because your security clearance is still active, I can tell you this…" He then let her in on the email discovered by the NSA and the fact that her name was prominent. "And before you start assuming Leon Carter is firing a political shot at BICA, this came to me from Morrow. The email is real, Woody. Care to explain it?"

"The email, I can't explain," she said truthfully. "But I *did* ask my team to look into the two names."

Manchin said, "We think you have a mole. Carter is hoping for the Russians."

Sanchez said, "You need to dig into this right away, Woody. But there's something else." Lowering his voice, he added, "Jurg Ivanovich has been in Ankara for the past two days meeting with Turkish military and intelligence groups. We have surveillance and wiretaps set up at the Atli Hotel, where Ivanovich always stays." He removed three photos from his pocket and passed them to her. "These were taken yesterday."

Woody examined the photos. One was grainy and showed a bald man leaving a taxi. The second was better and from the front as he entered the hotel. The third photo was clear and taken from the hotel's lobby. It showed a stocky man with a bald head and a pocked face sitting in the lobby and reading a magazine.

"Who is it?" she asked, passing the photos back to Sanchez.

"His name is Jasper Pinard. Canadian. He entered the hotel, stayed for an hour, then took a cab to the airport and boarded a one-way flight on Aeroflot to Moscow. Our people picked up his trail when he landed."

Woody nodded, but they were clearly waiting for her to say something. She came up with, "Your team identified him awfully fast."

Sanchez said, "Pinard was a member of Canadian Joint Task Force 2: a group of handpicked, best-of-the best, special forces fighters. He was a sniper in Yugoslavia and Bosnia who hunted down Serb snipers. Over thirty confirmed kills, with five of them over two kilometers. Decorations out the wazoo *before* he was wounded and discharged last year. He's been living on the streets of Quebec City. And, he's being treated for PTSD."

"An ex-Canadian sniper meeting with Jurg Ivanovich?" Woody mused. Then, her eyes flashed to PJ. "You believe Ivanovich is trying to hire an assassin?"

"Maybe. Pinard and Ivanovich didn't actually meet in Ankara, but he could have been slipped a note of some kind." He returned the photos his pocket, then said, "Pinard was wounded in Bosnia— ambushed by Serbian fighters as he was changing locations. A US Marine sniper unit was covering him. They took out one Serb, but they missed the second. And that Serb shot Pinard in the leg, giving him a permanent limp. He's been active in chat rooms blaming the US for his disability and making wild threats of revenge."

Woody said, "And now we have a sniper who hates America meeting with Ivanovich. You think POTUS is the target?"

"The Secret Service and the CIA *always* assume that. But let's not jump the gun," Sanchez said as he passed her another set of photos. "How about this man?"

Woody looked at the photos of the lanky, bald, skeletal man. She shook her head. "Who is he?"

"His name is Gjon Rockman, and he works for your old friend Primo Ruqur. He followed Pinard into the Atli Hotel."

Sanchez reached for the photos, but Woody snatched them back to take another look. *So, this is the infamous Franco Delgado,* she thought. And his appearance was exactly as she had imagined. When she looked up, she found the other two men staring at her.

"Do you recognize him?" Manchin asked.

"Only the name, not the face. How does Rockman fit in?"

"No idea," Sanchez said. "We have a thin file on him."

Woody listened to Sanchez regurgitate the same information on Rockman she already knew. When he finished, she said, "Have you considered that *maybe* the Russians are using Rockman as a conduit to plant false information?"

"It crossed my mind," Sanchez said. "The Secret Service already has a team in Moscow preparing for the nuclear summit, and we have serious concerns these two men were seen going into the same hotel as Ivanovich."

"And it's only a matter of time before someone starts questioning how *you* knew about the names Karl Berger and Bryant Curran," Machin said. "And that finger will point to both of us."

On her last day in the White House as a federal employee, sworn to protect and defend the Constitution of the United States, she had also taken the same oath at BICA—only, they went a step further and included the Declaration of Independence. Then, she thought about Liam hunting down Primo and Delgado. Was it time to play dumb, or spill the information she had?

Woody drew in a deep breath and said, "Gjon Rockman has been operating under the name—Gustov Mikos. He's also contacted BICA claiming to have proof that a one-time CIA contractor named Bryant Curran infiltrated the Kremlin in the seventies."

"Holy shit!" Manchin said. "Do you think it was Rockman who gave the names to Ambassador Travkin?"

"Maybe. The problem is this, releasing the information to the Russians kills his leverage with BICA, and there's no way Rockman would give up the name of a CIA contractor—"

Sanchez raised his palm and stopped her. When he spoke, his tone reeked of disappointment. "Before you continue to lie to me, Woody, you should know that Ginny and I have been friends and colleagues for many years. So, you're wasting your time playing footsie with me." After a few beats, he let out two words that chilled her to the bone. "I know the Gjon Rockman's real name is Franco Delgado. And I also know about Operation: Jugular."

anchez motioned toward the doors, and Machin crossed the room to lock both sets. Woody took the cue and sat in one of the twenty-four brown-leather chairs at the large conference table. When Manchin returned and took the seat across from her, Sanchez sat down next to Manchin, unwrapped a piece of hard candy from the bowl, then started talking.

"After I was confirmed as DCI—which your mother lobbied the Senate heavily for, by the way—she suggested I read the agency's brief on Operation: Jugular. I was fascinated to learn how successfully we had infiltrated the Kremlin—and how close we actually came to seeing it through. Today, in the Oval Office, when Morrow showed us the email with the names Karl Berger and Bryant Curran, my first thought was the Russians were trying to bait us. What I *didn't* know was that Delgado had also spoken to Ginny asking her to hand over two dead men. Quite the heavy-lift in my book."

They think Bryant and Liam are dead, Woody thought. At first, her thoughts went to the CIA's brief and story of the fire, but then something else came to mind. Maybe PJ was baiting her to see if she'd give up the truth willingly. She found herself torn between a trusted friend and telling PJ the truth about Liam—and perhaps inadvertently putting another price on Liam's head.

"It's impossible," Woody said calmly. When PJ didn't bark back, she felt a wave or relief.

Sanchez said, "In the early eighties, Jurg Ivanovich was a KGB agent who believed the United States had murdered Brezhnev. In fact, his obsession became a joke among his peers, and he had to be silenced by his own government. Delgado may be playing on Ivanovich's obsession to get the contract on his life lifted."

Woody gauged her next words carefully. "BICA believes it's more than that. When Delgado cornered Ginny, he said that millions would die if he released the information to the Russians. Exposing a spy from fifteen years ago would not trigger a calamitous response by President Yeltsin. Unless *he* was convinced that we killed Brezhnev."

Sanchez glanced at Machin, then back to Woody. "Trent Householder has his team watching Pinard now."

Woody said, "I also have a resource looking into it."

"This *resource*; are they capable of—more?" Sanchez asked cryptically.

Woody knew exactly what PJ was asking. "Perhaps. But why not use the CIA's Special Activities Division?"

"I'm not ruling out a SAD operation. I'm just gathering my options. And I also want to be assured that we're working together."

"We are," Woody said. "What about Leon Carter?"

"He stays in the dark—for now," Sanchez said. "But I will *not* withhold information if it jeopardizes the president's safety. Everyone in this room knows the president is an anti-American, IAF-trained Marxist and he needs to be impeached and tried for treason. But not assassinated."

You might change your mind if you knew the half of it, Woody thought as the president's two-hundred-million-dollar payday from Mexico popped into her head. "Agreed," she said half-heartedly.

Sanchez washed his palms over his face. "Look—I have no choice but to brief the Secret Service on what we know about Pinard. I'll ask they refrain from using real names in electronic communications. The rest, I'll keep to myself until we know more. That means it's imperative we coordinate our efforts so we don't run over each other. But it all might be a moot point given the email. Hotmail is an open platform, Woody. Anyone can use it and—anyone can hack it."

"Understood," Woody said.

Sanchez stood and said, "The guest of honor should probably get back to her own party."

After leaving the Cabinet Room, Woody returned to the Roosevelt Room. Leon Carter's eyes went right to her before wandering; no doubt trying to locate PJ and Manchin. Neither man had returned.

Woody posed for photos with her staff, the president, and Leon Carter before leaving the White House grounds.

Pulling out her cell phone, she started to call Curtis but then thought better of it. If she brought Curtis in on this, it would be like telling Ginny. And right now, Ginny didn't need to know what she was about to do. Then, she thought about calling Bailey to let her know about the mole inside her team. She nixed that idea too.

She had a better one.

After driving to her condo in Alexandria, she changed clothes, poured a glass of Chardonnay, then sat down at Paul's old desk to check her messages.

Paul's old desk, she thought.

Paul Kelvington, her ex-fiancé, was once a Secret Service agent who now owned a private security company, PeKay, Inc. But after the Mexican incident with Curran eight months earlier, their professional falling-out had ultimately led to a failed romance—all because neither of them could tell the other…everything.

And nothing had changed. Including the fact that she still loved him.

Still, that night, after setting her alarm for six a.m., she tossed and turned and wondered why the man she was about to drive five hours to see made her so damn uncomfortable.

CHAPTER 23

That morning, Alexi Orlov parked his faded-blue Volga GAZ-24 behind the warehouse two spaces away from the rusted and abused Buhanka van belonging to his helper. The thermometer in his kitchen window that morning had been at ten degrees Celsius, and the snow on the ground had turned to slush. As he started toward the loading dock door, he whistled a tune of spring, then stopped abruptly when he found the overhead door already open.

After climbing the concrete stairs to the dock, he stepped inside and found the six handcarts they had filled the evening before had been lined up, ready to load into the truck. His helper had been busy, and he heard the sounds of his farm calling him already.

"Malik!" Alexi called out to the warehouse. His echo replied, so he started toward the back, where plywood panels had been nailed into four walls and a drop ceiling to create an office. Through the murky window, he saw Malik rising from the floor, a rolled prayer rug under his arm.

"Good morning," Malik said with a bright smile. "My apologies, but it was time for Fajr." Performed before sunrise, Fajr is the first of Islam's five daily prayers.

"No apology necessary," Alexi said. "Come. Let us hurry so we can go about our day."

A half an hour later, they had the delivery truck loaded. Malik went to use the restroom, and when he returned, he started the process of securing the load and the truck's rear door while Alexi turned in circles. He knew it had been there a second ago.

"What is the matter?" Malik asked.

"I cannot find the pick sheet and invoice. Perhaps they are in the office."

Alexi headed back into the warehouse with Malik close behind, each of them checking the tops of boxes along the way. After making it to the office and searching the area and finding nothing, Malik slapped his own forehead with an open palm and said, "The restroom. I could have left it there."

Located across from the office, the restroom was unisex and doubled as a janitor's closet. They were the only employees working that morning, so Alexi didn't bother knocking. After pulling the light chain, Alexi scanned the area for the clipboard but saw nothing but scarred porcelain fixtures, a mop standing in a wringer bucket, a shelf full of chemicals, and a roll of plastic sheeting.

Then, he felt Malik's approach from the rear.

. . .

Slipping the curved jambiya knife from the scabbard tucked in his waist, in one fluid motion, Malik gripped Alexi's forehead from behind, yanked backward, slit the man's throat, then forced his head forward to let the man drown in his own blood.

After lowering Alexi to the floor, he watched the man twitch and burp red bubbles for better than a minute. Malik then cleaned the blade in the sink and, when he was finished, turned to admire how well his plan had worked.

Most times, they flailed their arms dramatically. But Alexi had gone down easy. And as he stared into his boss's dead eyes, a moment of sadness came over him. Murder was a sin in the Koran. But not in the fight against infidels. And with Alexi being a homosexual, Malik felt certain Allah would forgive him of this transgression.

After wrapping the corpse in the plastic sheeting and dragging it onto a handcart, he connected a long rubber hose to the utility faucet and sent the blood down the floor drain. He then pushed the cart through the warehouse and onto the dock, where he opened the truck, dragged the body into the back, fished the car keys from the corpse's pocket, then secured the truck's door. After walking through the warehouse one last time, he locked up.

In the parking lot, he opened the door to his boss's Volga and stuffed the keys over the visor. By this time tomorrow, half of Alexi's car would be on a chop-shop shelf and the other half would be crushed into a cube.

After returning to the delivery truck, he started it and pulled away from the dock.

On his way to the Yasenevo District of Moscow, he detoured into the countryside, where he parked on the shoulder, opened the truck's roll-up door, and kicked the corpse onto the gravel berm. Jumping off the bumper, he rolled the plastic-wrapped body down the embankment, then dragged it into the grave he had dug the night before.

From the bushes, Malik retrieved the shovel he had hidden, filled the grave with dirt, tamped it down, then covered it with brush. He then tossed the shovel behind the truck's seat before continuing to his only delivery that morning.

Once he reached Yasenevo, he drove to the headquarters compound of the SVR, where he stopped at the gate and waited for the guard.

"Open the back," the guard commanded.

It was the same routine.

Malik got out, did as he was told, and waited while the guard performed a once-over of the ten-wheeler's load. Satisfied, the guard lowered the roll-up door.

"Where is Alexi?" the guard asked as he initialed the page on his clipboard.

"He did not come to work this morning," Malik said as he signed the guard's paperwork. "The order is not large. I can handle it on my own."

CHAPTER 24

Princeton, West Virginia
Saturday, March 23, 1996

In his dream, Liam was back in Baghdad, lying on the mansion's icy marble bedroom floor while the general and his slave-wife, Aisha, lay sleeping. Looking beneath the bed, he could see Lilliana from her shins down—and her tiny feet sticking to the floor as she padded her way to where her mother slept. Only, in this version of the nightmare, her footfalls were deafening and grew louder as Lilliana moved closer to the bed until—

Liam shot up in bed, his face drenched with sweat.

Will this shit never stop?

Drifting through the open window, steel-on-steel pings pulsed through his head. Bill Shipman had started early.

After pulling on sweats and sneakers, he filled two large mugs with black coffee, doctored one with cream and sugar, then stepped shirtless into the chilly mountain air. Following the sounds to the pole barn, he found Shipman at the bench working a metal ring.

Shipman stopped when he saw Liam with a cup of steam heading in his direction. "Thank ya, brother. Good to see you up—halfway through the fucking day." The lanky, leathery skinned man met Liam in the middle of the high bay. This morning, his slight gimp—acquired after a fall into a pit of punji sticks in Vietnam—seemed more pronounced than normal.

Their friendship dated back to the mid-eighties when they served together in Central America during the Honduran-Nicaraguan-El Salvadorian conflict before it became known as the Iran-Contra Affair. *Back when we used to shoot communists instead of elect them,*

Shipman liked to say. At the time, Liam had been on loan from the SEALs, and Shipman was with the National Security Council (NSC). Both had been labeled *consultants* while helping to train the Contra's in the panhandle of Florida before turning them loose on the Soviet-backed Sandinistas in Nicaragua.

Retired since 1989, Shipman now leased half of Liam's six hundred acres for the bargain price of twelve dollars a year.

"Thanks for holding down the fort," Liam said, drawing in air smelling of grease mixed with hay from the empty stalls before dousing it with coffee.

Shipman chewed his cheek. "I was in the house this mornin'. Noticed your go-bag on the floor."

Liam took another sip.

Bill Shipman was the one person outside of the BICA who knew of Liam's past. Most of it, anyway. At this moment, Liam didn't want to add to that knowledge until he knew what was happening himself.

Shipman said, "Last time I saw your go-bag out, you ended up at Walter Reed."

Before Liam could respond, a woman appeared at the open garage door. Timid at first, she took in the huge bay. But when she saw the two men gawking, one of them bare-chested, she walked in as if she owned the place.

Rosalyn Sanchez had purchased the property next to Liam after his neighbor Lacey Sullivan was murdered the previous summer—part of the reason Liam had been in Walter Reed. After gutting the house, she moved in and started leasing her own open acreage to Shipman. It was a good way to keep the grass down and the place watched since she only used it as a getaway when she wasn't touring the planet as the mega pop star known to the world as simply—Sierra.

"Oh good. You're up," she said. Her sweet Latino accent echoed in the bay as she crossed to where Liam and Shipman were standing.

The sun had cast a slanted shadow, and Liam couldn't help but be disappointed when her smooth mocha skin was blanketed with shade. Still, her amazing curves could not be contained.

She hugged both men—Liam a little longer—then took Liam's cup and sipped. The sleeves of her oversized sweatshirt covered her hands and some of the cup's handle.

"What's wrong with *my* cup?" Shipman asked.

"No cream and no sugar," she explained. She took a second sip, then passed the cup back to Liam. "I saw you pull in last night and wanted to stop by to see you before I left on the next leg of my tour."

"Where to this time?" Liam asked.

"Madrid. Then Barcelona, Lisbon, Bordeaux. Working our way north, then east. We leave on Wednesday. Will you be around?"

"I'm not sure," Liam said, drawing a frown from Sierra. She knew nothing of his past earlier than the last eight months, but the horror they had shared centered around Lacey Sullivan's murder was enough to forge lifelong respect. Maybe even—trust.

Sierra said, "I had hoped we could spend some time together during your spring break, but you disappeared. Will you guys be around for a drink later?"

Shipman shot a glance at Liam. "Sorry, brother. Can't make it. Yooz two have fun."

"Actually, I—" But Liam stopped when his cell phone mercifully buzzed his pocket. He eyed the display, saw it was Woody, then stepped away.

"Hello, boss. Kind of an early Saturday for you, isn't it?"

"Don't be an ass. I'm about two miles out—I think. You need to guide me the rest of the way."

"You're in Princeton?"

"I'll explain when I get there."

Liam dictated some landmarks, then stepped outside and waited. Three minutes later, the black Chevy Suburban pulled up to the gate and honked.

"Who the hell—?" Shipman said as he and Sierra joined Liam at the open bay door. Liam pressed a button on the wall and the gate rose. Moments later, gravel crunched and pinged and the black Suburban stopped in the turnaround and Woody got out.

Liam waved her inside, and as she entered the high-bay, her gaze darted between him, Shipman, and Sierra.

"Aren't you Patricia Woodburn?" Sierra asked, holding out her hand. "With the White House, right?"

"I resigned," Woody said, shaking the woman's hand while sending Liam a hot glare before turning back to the singer. "And you're Sierra. What are you doing here? In Princeton?"

"She bought the place next door," Liam said. "It's kind of like her Camp David."

"Wasn't that Lacey Sullivan's place?" Woody asked.

Liam turned to Sierra and Shipman and said, "I'm sorry, but Ms. Woodburn and I have some business to discuss."

"Are we still on for later?" Sierra asked.

Liam turned to Woody, who was nodding her head. He said, "Tonight around seven? My bar. I'm buying."

Liam led Woody into the house, then to his basement recording studio, where the walls were lined with electric and acoustic guitars. A twenty-four-channel mixing board dominated the area next to a pane of glass separating the control room. After sitting down in front of the mixing board, he slid a guitar stool her way.

"I didn't know you were a musician," she said. "I'm impressed."

"Don't be," Liam said. "Now, why did you drive all the way from DC just to talk to little ole me?"

CHAPTER 25

After putting on a T-shirt, Liam spent the next minutes listening to Woody spill the details of her meeting with PJ Sanchez and Jerry Manchin. The email between JustMe and ReggyD took center stage. When she finished, he said, "You've got a mole at the Lake."

Woody nodded. "I didn't see the actual email, but from what PJ told me, it's not Bailey. But Babbs and Araseli were both there and—"

"No way," Liam said. "There are about two dozen techno-nerds working at the Lake. Babbs and Araseli would be at the bottom of my list. Have Bailey look into it."

"Not Curtis? He's their boss," Woody said but then paused. "Actually, I guess that's me now."

"You'll never convince Curtis of that. And if you bring him in, you'll be adding more names to the suspect list." He let it sink in, then said, "Let's talk about Jasper Pinard. I've heard of him, and some of his more exotic shots. The legend is always better than the truth, but PJ's right to be concerned. I wouldn't want Pinard shooting at *me*."

"Could Pinard pull it off during the nuclear summit in Moscow?"

"Anyone can be gotten to. The trick is getting away with it. The president's trips are planned well in advance to allow the Secret Service time to secure the locations, which also gives the bad guys time to plan."

"There's a reception at the Kremlin, but the actual summit is off-site."

"I was a SEAL—but not a sniper. I'm not the right person to ask."

The Secret Service's detailed planning was a process Woody knew all too well as chief of staff. Not to mention her ex-fiancé had once been a Secret Service agent on the presidential detail.

Woody paused a beat, then said, "Maybe sending you after Primo and Delgado is the wrong move."

"And you think sending me after Pinard is a better move?"

"Don't you?"

"Hey. Ginny gave me orders and I'm following them."

"Bologna! Your MO has always been to push back. Only, this time, you have a chance at Eagle. And not only a chance—you have permission. If Primo *is* Eagle, I don't need you going off half-cocked getting to a billionaire."

Liam studied her face. "You're imagining me kicking in a door and spraying a place with bullets, aren't you? Like Pacino in *Scarface*?"

Woody looked sideways at him. "Let me put it this way. If you and I were at SeaWorld, and I asked how many sharks were in the tank, I'm afraid you'd jump in to count."

Liam chuckled. "You're still new, so I'll forgive your lack of faith."

"Faith? I have three years of evidence."

Liam changed the subject. "I've been thinking about Delgado's motives."

"Any revelations?"

"Yeah. This isn't about *me*. Or my father. I think it's about getting to Sophya."

"After you left, Jaco, Ginny, and I came to the same conclusion."

"So now Ginny thinks Pinard is the better target?"

Woody shook her head. "I haven't brought it up yet. But he's central to whatever is going on, and the CIA and Secret Service already know where he is."

"Meaning—with that many eyes on him, you want him interrogated and not killed."

"We're *are* in the intelligence-gathering business, and Pinard is a major link in the chain."

"You mean, low-hanging fruit."

"Look—I'm not willing to send you into the lion's den yet, because that's—"

"Exactly why you were hired to take over ICEBRG," Liam interjected. "The doubts you're having is what the military calls *the burden of command*." He delivered a wink, then said, "Okay. I'll find Pinard first. Ginny's going to be pissed."

"Why? Are you going to tell her?"

Liam shook his head, then led Woody out of the studio to the den. Stepping behind the bar, he pointed to one of the stools, then waved a hand at the glass shelves lined with booze. "Pick your poison."

Woody's eyes scanned the three rows of bottles. "This is a test, isn't it? Like in *Indiana Jones and the Last Crusade*? If I don't choose correctly, I'll turn to dust?"

"An aficionado of fine films, I see," Liam quipped.

"Then I'll take a finger of the eighteen-year-old Macallan's," she said as she took in the enormity of the room and its vaulted-beam ceiling, the tapestries on the wall, and the hand-carved bar.

Liam said, "You have chosen—wisely."

"That was from the movie too," Woody said.

He reached into the freezer and came back with two ice balls. He dropped one into each tumbler before pouring two fingers of the Scotch. He touched her glass with his and sipped, then noticed her attention had gone back to the booze on the shelf. "Something else on your mind?"

Woody nodded. "My mother lied to me about the photos."

"I know."

"She had them the whole time we were meeting with McFadden. I mean—your father."

"To your mother—*not telling* isn't the same as *lying*. You'll get used to it."

Woody grinned. "Like the little project you gave Araseli?"

Liam's heart skipped a beat. "Just a little data mining."

"Bullshit! You're looking for Rufus Carmichael. The Owl," Woody said.

Liam didn't respond. Instead, he touched her glass and then watched her sip. Her eyes closed as her tongue swiped her lips, taking in what had been missed. It was a true sign she was enjoying it. Most women didn't like Scotch, and in a small way, he considered it proof that this master of the political universe wouldn't engage in something to fit in.

Three years earlier, she had tried to have him killed. But they had both been played by the same organizations: the CIA and the NEST. As Woody's understanding of the latter was purely academic, Liam felt a certain kinship with her that also brought with it the concern they both were being used again.

Liam said, "I've spent my whole life trusting almost no one, and now you know why."

Woody said, "In our meeting, did Ginny *not tell* anything else?"

"She should have told me about Delgado as soon as he contacted her. You should have too."

"You had gone dark, remember?"

He watched her eyes shift to the bronze coat of arms over the fireplace. When she returned, her eyes had narrowed. Not in suspicion but realization.

She said, "I didn't know about your relationship with Delgado at the time. I promise you it will never happen again."

Liam raised his glass. "Trust, but verify—right?"

Her smile was genuine as she sipped. "Can you get me Sierra's autograph?"

Liam lowered his glass. "Shit! And you were doing so well."

"What? You don't like her?"

"She's fine. It's that digital noise she calls music I hate." He made a face, then smoothed it with a sip.

Woody said, "That's a riot, because she obviously has a thing for you. And your bare chest."

"I hadn't noticed."

"You called me *Ms. Woodburn* in front of her."

"Out of respect."

She chuckled. "How can you be so good at—what it is you do—and still be so damn clueless?" Woody checked her watch, drained the Scotch, then got up from the stool. "Enjoy your date tonight. I need to get back to DC."

"It's not a date," Liam protested, but Woody had already pushed her barstool in.

Liam led her through the garage and back into the sunshine. Sierra was gone and Shipman had returned to his pounding. Woody climbed into the Suburban, and Liam closed the door, then leaned on the open window as she started it.

"What's the story with this Shipman guy?" she asked.

"That's for another time," Liam said. "Just know that I trust him with my life."

"Fine. Just be careful—and discreet. What will you do first?"

"I have to see an old friend."

"You mean your father, don't you? Ginny said he's gone dark."

"Depends on who's looking."

"You and your father look so much alike."

Liam shook his head. "You have no idea how lethal having that information is, do you?" When Woody didn't bat an eye, he asked, "What's *your* next move, boss?"

"To clear your path and then talk to Bailey. By the way, I promised PJ and Manchin that we'd work *with* them."

"You're so gullible," Liam said. "Did you tell them about me?"

"They still think you're dead. But I did tell them I had an asset working on the issue."

Liam let out a breath. "Did they ask if your *asset* would kill for them?"

"I made no commitments."

"So—yes."

She dropped the Suburban into Drive while holding the brake. "Your father, then Pinard. We'll figure the rest out later."

Liam snapped a half-assed salute as she pulled away. The gate raised automatically, and a minute later, she was gone. As he watched the Suburban disappear over the rise, he felt a hint of guilt rise in his throat.

They had agreed to be completely honest with each other, and he planned to keep his promise and go after Pinard. But if along the way he had the slightest opportunity at Owl or Eagle—all bets were off.

CHAPTER 26

Monday, March 25, 1996

Counting the stops for coffee refills, the drive to Columbus, Ohio, took under five hours, and Liam pulled into the parking lot of the Hilliard Bearing Corporation at eleven a.m., hoping to catch the owner.

"Is Darren McFadden in?" Liam asked the older woman at the reception desk.

She smiled brightly and said, "I'm sorry, but Mr. McFadden is traveling today."

No, he isn't, Liam thought as he stared up at the camera behind the reception desk and smiled. "Do you know when he'll be back?"

"I'm sure I don't. Was he expecting you? I could try to—?"

Without leaving his name, Liam thanked the woman and left the building.

When he was back on the I-270 bypass, he headed south, then took the second exit and followed Leap Road until it ended at an upper middle-class subdivision called Britton Farms. He drove to the farthest cul-de-sac, then pulled into the driveway of the two-story brick-and-stone home.

He rang the doorbell four times before the blinds on a window parted, then closed. The dead bolt clicked; the handle turned; and a tall, fit, and disappointed older man in jeans and an Ohio State University sweatshirt opened the door.

"'Bout time you figured it out." Bryant let Liam inside, then closed and locked the door.

Liam followed his father to the office immediately off the foyer. Liam removed his jacket and hung it on the back of the chair before he sat. Bryant closed the French doors.

The shelf over the credenza was filled with books, and the walls were stamped with photos of people Liam didn't know—and his father probably didn't either. Filling one corner of the office was the only familiar object: a bronze-trimmed globe twice the size of a beach ball.

"The last time I saw Pappy's globe, we were in West Berlin and Mom was still alive," Liam said. "What made you get it out of the attic?"

Bryant said nothing.

Liam let several silent beats pass before he asked, "How's business?"

"The world needs bearings," Bryant said as he sat behind the desk. "Tell me, boy, where you been hidin'?"

"I was in Halabja when you were meeting with Ginny and Woody. I guess you know about the photos. Delgado took them from Stephanie's house."

Bryant nodded. "The ones your mother left Stephanie in her old steamer chest."

Liam nodded. "And Delgado shot Brock Flannigan. Put him in a coma."

"Jesus jumpin' Christ!" Bryant said, raking fingers through graying black hair.

"Why'd you go dark after your meeting with Ginny?"

Opening a desk drawer, Bryant removed his own BICA-issued pager and held it up without turning it on. "Ginny sent a text last Tuesday. It said, *they know you are alive.*" He dropped the pager back into the drawer and asked, "Can you explain that?"

"Maybe. Delgado sent her a videotape."

"What fuckin' videotape?" Bryant asked.

Liam brought his father up to speed on his trip to Belfast; his conversation with Delgado; his meeting with Ginny, Woody, and Jaco; and the two names someone had given the Russian ambassador. With each passing sentence, Bryant grew more and more rigid and the tent he had made with his fingers jammed deeper into the flesh below his chin. Then, Liam told him about the tape.

Bryant closed his eyes and said, "Delgado must have found the records where your trust fund sold AquaMedTran back to Primo Ruqur. That's how Delgado found Flannigan. And Flannigan's records led him to James Jamison and the box here."

"That's right. He was looking for me but found both of us instead. There's something else." Liam pinched his fingers together and said, "I'm this close to finding Owl."

"Owl? Why you be a thinkin' that?" Bryant's brogue was slipping now.

"It's Rufus Carmichael, Dad. I got the info from Sheik Al-Jabori."

"Yeah. I read that he was tortured and then killed outside Toledo."

"Aggressively interrogated," Liam corrected. "Carmichael must have heard about it too, because he fled his Windsor estate. My source tells me he's in Athens."

"Your source? You mean your Kurd bitch in Halabja. Dip your wick again, did you?"

Liam shook his head, having heard this banter before. "Let's argue about Nadia some other time. We've got work to do."

"More than you may know," Bryant said in a defeated tone as he bent a slat in the blinds and scanned the street outside. "If the Russians already know about the Bergers and Currans, what leverage does Delgado have? Obviously, he's trying to offer us up in exchange for the price on his head."

"We think it's more than that," Liam said. "He may have convinced Jurg Ivanovich that you and Sophya actually murdered Leonid Brezhnev."

"Meaning Sophya is the big prize," Bryant added.

Their eyes locked for several beats, daring the other to speak.

Bryant jumped in first. "They'd need more testing on Brezhnev's body, but it would only prove the fat socialist bastard drank too much, had strokes, and died of a heart attack. And that would ruin Ivanovich's Christmas—again. You know, he has always obsessed over Brezhnev's death. He only backed off when he was ordered to."

"Ordered? By who?"

"Grigori Urmanov," Bryant said. "But Ivanovich has command of the SVR now, and he must have discovered that Urmanov was involved with the fire and the cover-up. That's why Urmanov jumped out the fuckin' window."

Liam nodded, satisfied that for the first time he and his father were on the same page. Still, there was one more thing he wanted to hear. "Ginny told me about the opium and the CIA framing you."

Bryant paused as he studied Liam's eyes. "How loyal is your new boss to the fuckin' CIA? And them to her?"

"She's loyal to BICA. And the CIA still doesn't know you and I are alive."

"How long will that last?" Bryant sprang from his chair and leveled a finger in Liam's face. "Don't be a fuckin' fool! Not again."

Liam leaned back, and at the same time, he smacked his father's hand away. "I'm only passing along intel, you old bastard! You decide how much weight to give it."

"You know how they operate, and we've both been screwed by 'em, and they'll screw us again. BICA too." Bryant stepped away and leaned on the globe, catching his breath. "One day, you'll learn they're all the same."

His father was right. He *did* know how the CIA operated and how they had betrayed them both. Liam—twice. But he couldn't let that affect the mission at hand. Realizing his father was going down the same rabbit hole he always did when the subject of the CIA came up, Liam tried to bring him back into the here and now.

"I promised Woody I'd get Pinard."

Bryant huffed a chuckle. "You're a lyin' to one of the best, boy. You'll be a goin' after Carmichael."

"He can wait because I haven't found him yet. I have someone looking, and besides, I gave my word—"

Liam stopped talking when the French doors parted and a tiny, worry-hardened face peered inside.

CHAPTER 27

Belfast, Northern Ireland
Monday, March 25, 1996
5:15 p.m.

With spring only days old, for whatever insane reason foreign to Stephanie Maguire, this was the season men liked to get engaged. Some brought their prospects with them to the store, while others preferred the surprise. And *surprise* meant a return to the store for a fitting and, many times, upping the carat.

The customer she finished ringing up—right at closing time— had decided to astonish his unsuspecting bride-to-be with a marquis-cut, two-carat shocker. Anything smaller, and Stephanie would have told the guy to come back tomorrow. The tiny bell mounted above the door jingled as the man left. She finished making her notes, then walked the main aisle between the display counters to lock the front door.

"I'm closing," she called out.

"I'll only be a moment more," came the reply from Brandon in the back.

"Whatever," she said under her breath. Realizing she was twisting the claddagh ring around the chain, she withdrew her hand and wiped at a smear on a glass case, dreading the end of the day.

Still living with her brother, his wife, and their two children, Stephanie was starting to go crazy. Liam had been gone for six days now without a single call. She had made up her mind that tonight would be her last night in her brother's house.

Danger be damned.

. . .

They had been watching the place since Thursday.

Brother and sister arrived together every morning at eight thirty and flipped the sign on the door to *OPEN* at nine. At noon, the brother crossed the street to the pub to get their lunch, returned twenty minutes later, then the sign would flip to *CLOSED* at five sharp.

Two hours earlier, the message came down from Mr. Mikos. The plan was a go.

The leader of the three, a chunky ex-con named Breckon, and the same man who had been tracking Liam Curran, ordered Con 2 to the alley to take care of the back of the store and the brother, while he and Con 3 parked the car in front. They popped the boot but left it down, then sat in the running car and watched the woman finish up inside.

When the last customer left, and the woman was still behind the counter, they pulled their balaclava masks down over their faces. When she stepped from behind the counter and started down the aisle toward the door, they left the car for the sidewalk. Only two people paid them any notice, but at this point, they were committed.

When the pretty redheaded woman reached to flip the sign and lock the door, Breckon and Con3 made their move.

. . .

As Stephanie reached to flip the sign, she noticed one of her newly manicured nails had a chip. She was cursing life as the front door burst open and the metal frame caught her in the shoulder, sending her flying across a display case and her elbow through the glass top. A jagged edge sliced her hand as an iron forearm gripped her throat from behind in a vise and began dragging her outside while Con 3 held the door.

Being dragged backward, Stephanie could see down the store's center aisle, over the cash register, and all the way to the open back door, where a third man in a mask was standing and drawing a pistol as Brandon burst into the hallway and started toward the front of the store, his own pistol cradled in two hands.

There was a flash from behind Brandon, and he fell face-first to the floor. The gunman then raced forward, leapt over Brandon's body, and met the others at the car.

"Brandon!" she screamed, but her words died in the thick palm over her mouth. Her kicks landed on air, and her flailing arms occasionally hit hair and cheek and shoulders as she was dragged toward the rear of a car and thrown into the open boot.

Two men stuffed her inside, then the third slammed the boot closed, putting her in complete darkness except for what leaked through the red taillights. She heard three doors slam before the car lunched forward, sending her rolling violently into the boot's latch.

After righting herself, she reached for her ribs and found a tear in the fabric of her blouse and a warm, wet, burning patch. Then, she felt for the cut on her hand.

Warm drips.

Panic raced through her as she blindly wrapped her hand in the tail of her blouse. Then anger set in as the vision of her brother falling to the floor replayed in her head, and she kicked at the door of boot.

Fumbling around in the dark with her good hand, she found the spare tire and, beneath it, the cold section of heavy steel she was hoping for. The car rose and fell, sending her face into the hatch and her back into the floor, so she rolled onto her good side and hugged the tire iron like a stuffed animal.

God help the first man who opened the boot.

CHAPTER 28

Hilliard, Ohio
Same Day

Not now, Sophya," Bryant said. "Liam and I are—"

"Yes, I heard. Moscow has found us," Sophya interrupted, her Russian accent still thick and as cold as Liam remembered.

Bryant stepped to the front of his desk and perched on the edge as his eyes met Sophya's. He started to reach out for her but let his hand fall and smack against his thigh.

Turning to Liam, she asked, "Where is my father?"

Liam said nothing at first, wondering how to tell Sophya that her father had committed suicide. All he could muster was: "Jaco received a letter from the general and—"

"Oh no!" she squeaked as she fell into a nearby chair. No more words. No screams of anguish. Only trembles of grief before her moist red eyes looked up into Liam's. "Where is Mika?"

"I don't know."

"You must find her and tell her about her grandfather."

He felt an impulse to reach out and touch Sophya's shoulder but held back. The two of them had never been close. In his mind, Sophya had always been the homewrecker who had stolen his father. And even though he knew now that wasn't true, the ditch between them had long been dug.

Liam turned to Bryant and said, "We have to stop to this."

"Do we now?" Bryant shot back. "Well, I'm doin' nutin' with you 'til you get that dead girl out of your head, boy! You're a walkin' time bomb; that's what you are."

Through gritted teeth, Liam said, "You ever kill a four-year-old and her mother, then watch them die over and over every night?"

"Does your Kurd bitch blame you for their deaths?"

"Her name is Nadia!"

"Does she?"

"No."

"And when you called in air strikes in Iraq, how many civilians died? How many were children?"

"I— It's not the same thing!" It was an argument he had had with himself countless times. But never with his father. Then, he felt a heavy hand grip his shoulder, and he looked into the icy eyes of the man he remembered from Enniskillen.

Bryant said, "Collateral damage is part of war, boy. And that's all they were. Your *feelings*"—Bryant made air quotes—"are what makes them different. As a soldier, your duty was to your team. But at the general's mansion, it was just you—up close and personal. You learned the difference between a soldier—and a killer. Left a bitter taste, did it? Well, spit it out!"

For the first time, Liam absorbed the advice from the one man he knew could truly understand. A man who had, in his own past, traipsed down the same bloody roads—as an SAS soldier and as a spy. But his thoughts were interrupted when his cell phone vibrated in his pocket.

Fishing the phone out, Liam eyed the display, then held it up so Bryant could see. He flipped the phone open and said, "Hello, Ginny."

Her tone was blunt and eager. "I have the team here with me. Are you in a good spot?"

Liam glanced at Bryant and Sophya, then said, "Yes. What's the problem?"

"Our friend called me again," Ginny said.

Our friend, she had said. Hiding something again.

"He asked why I haven't kept up my end of the deal. Then,

he gave me a phone number to call. It was Brandon Maguire's mobile and—"

Woody's voice interjected from the background. "Brandon's been shot. He's at Royal Victoria Hospital."

"And Stephanie?" Liam prodded.

Curtis chimed in. "The Belfast news is reporting that she was abducted from their jewelry store."

"Let me call you back."

After stabbing at the phone's key pad, Liam put it on speaker, and they all listened to the telltale clicks of an international call. After eight rings, they heard Stephanie's voice mail pick up.

Liam tried her home number. Ten rings. Same ending.

Liam ended the call and stared at the phone as if it had bit him. Then, his gaze met Bryant's. "Someone has Stephanie."

Bryant said, "Delgado has her. You're a knowin' this, yes? Bait for Curran fish."

Liam nodded. "I should have killed his stooge in Belfast when I had the chance." He dialed Ginny's number, pressed the SPKR button, then spun the phone on the desk.

"Liam?"

"It's me," Liam said. "Tell me someone traced the call from"—he paused, then finished with—"our friend."

Woody's voice came from the background. "It was from a cell tower near Red Square. It's the best we could do."

"Where's the MTS tower—physically?" Liam asked.

"I don't—"

"Then go get Curtis!" Liam fired back, raking frustrated fingers through his hair. As glances passed between the three of them, no one dared to speak. Then, over the phone, a door slammed and Curtis's voice came on the line.

"The tower is on the roof of the Hotel Baltschug Kempinski."

Across from our old apartment, Liam mouthed at Bryant, then said, "He's sending us a message and I hear it. Loud and clear."

After reaching out and pressing the Mute button, Bryant let out a breath. "What are you thinkin', boy?"

"Delgado lost his leverage when he spilled the names to the Russian ambassador. And you're right—Stephanie is his new pawn."

"And he's a knowin' you're impetuous. But this ain't about you and me anymore," Bryant said as he glanced at Sophya, then back to Liam. Then, he pressed the SPKR button on Liam's cell phone, and for the first time, he let his voice be heard, "Ginny. It's—me."

"My God!" Ginny's voice said. "Where have you been?"

Bryant ignored the question. "The man's playin' both sides."

"What do you mean?" Woody asked.

"Whatever he's a doin', *helpin'* the Russians or *punishin'* them, he's sellin' a lie."

"What makes you so sure?" Woody asked.

Bryant started to speak but then turned to Sophya and said, "Because there's no fuckin' way he could know the truth."

Ginny chimed in. "If their assassin takes a shot at POTUS in Moscow, it won't matter. Americans still remember JFK from '63. And if someone convinces the SVR that Brezhnev was murdered—it's war."

In the background, there was an echo of footsteps before Curtis said, "I just verified that a private jet owned by the Hermes Corporation left Belfast for Moscow earlier today. It landed about an hour before we got the call from—our friend."

Why would Delgado take Stephanie to Moscow? Liam asked himself. Then, it became clear. Looking into his father's eyes, he said, "I'm going to Moscow."

"Like hell!" Woody's voice fired back from the speaker.

Liam said, "You wanted me to go after"—Liam paused before mentioning the name—

"the shooter. If PJ's people are tracking him, he won't be hard to find."

There was a brief pause before Woody said, "Liam, you're

counting sharks."

Bryant's brow wrinkled into a question.

Liam, understanding her quip, asked, "How so?"

"The CIA's Moscow chief of station is—not a friend."

"Help him out," Ginny said.

Bryant hit Mute and said, "Trent Householder is the CoS in Moscow. I assume you remember him."

Liam did. When his alias—Trevor Harmon—was being hunted down three years earlier, Paul Kelvington hadn't been the only one Woody sicced on him. She had also used the CIA, and Householder had been the leader of the SAD team looking for him. And Householder had also been is SAD team leader the night he entered the general's mansion in Baghdad.

Bryant hit SPKR and said, "I'll go. The CoS doesn't know me."

Woody said, "I'll arrange the meeting."

"Ginny," Bryant said easily. "I'll be a goin' as WL. The same way I left."

"I understand," Ginny said.

Bryant searched Sophya's and Liam's eyes. It wasn't lost on any of them that the last time they were together like this was fourteen years ago at a kitchen table in a Red Square apartment preparing to run for their lives *from* Moscow using what he had always called *the Norse Channel*.

Woody's voice broke in. "I want you to stand down until he gets back and we know what we're dealing with. Meaning, you do not get on that plane."

"Understood," Liam said. He pressed End, then removed the battery from the phone and his pager.

"This will never end, will it?" Sophya said. "None of us will ever be safe. Not even Mika."

"We'll be a fixin' it," Bryant said, kissing her forehead. Then, he turned to Liam, his eyes blazing. "Idiot! You were 'bout to waltz into Moscow and offer your dick up to Trent Householder.

The worst of it is you have me agreein' with your fuckin' boss. You're a going nowhere."

"I didn't know Householder was the CoS," Liam said.

"Because you're impetuous," Bryant said, shaking his head.

Fuming, Liam went to the window and stared out at the cul-de-sac as the mail truck made its rounds to the boxes. Suburbia. The simpler life. He thought about his farm in Princeton before his thoughts went further back—to Enniskillen. How would things have turned out if his father had said *No!* to Operation: Jugular?

When he turned from the window and found Sophya and his father again, they were staring at each other. Surely Sophya was worried about Bryant going back into Moscow. Maybe she was worried that somehow Mika might be exposed too. Ivanovich would love to have the head of a traitor Vympel agent mounted on his wall.

After giving Sophya a quick hug, Liam went to the foyer and stopped short of opening the front door, letting his father catch up to him.

"We stay completely dark until I'm out of Moscow," Bryant said. "No pagers. No cell phones. Is that understood?"

Liam nodded. He started to leave, but his father gripped his elbow and stopped him.

"We'll meet back here when I'm finished. Agreed?"

"Agreed," Liam said. "But I could give a shit about Pinard. I need you to bring Stephanie back, Dad."

Bryant said nothing.

"Promise me you'll find her."

"I'll do my best."

After climbing into his BMW, Liam started it but remained parked in his father's driveway, staring at the three-car garage and the façade of a happy house. He wondered how much the neighbors knew about the Irishman and his Russian wife living next door. Nothing, most likely, which was turning out to be more than he knew himself.

Backing out, Liam aimed the BMW south toward Princeton and considered his next move, which turned out to be the easy part. Actually, finding the target of his next move might be trickier. Usually, he'd ask Curtis or Bailey to help him, but that was out of the question this time. And since BICA had supplied him with a superb computer system, it was time to see if this World Wide Web thing was worth all the hype.

. . .

After locking the front door, Bryant walked past Sophya to his office, found his cell phone in the desk drawer, then turned it on. After it found a tower, he pressed Redial and Ginny's voice answered immediately.

"Thank God!" she said. "We have a big problem."

"No shit," Bryant replied.

"He won't just sit around and wait. You know that. He'll go after..." Ginny stopped short of the name and said, "...and if he finds him, you know how it will end."

"I'm a knowin'," Bryant said. "But I've got a head start."

There was a long pause before Ginny said, "You know what's funny? After all we've been through, this is the first time I've ever been truly afraid. If *they* get their hands on either of you boys, then—"

Bryant glanced toward Sophya standing in the doorway, staring at her own entwined fingers. "It's not the boys you should worry about."

CHAPTER 29

Warrenton, Virginia
Monday, March 25, 1996
Noon

After collecting her chicken salad bagel and soda, Araseli strolled to the partitioned desks at the back of the Java Linx café, selected a computer in the corner, adjusted the mouse and pad, let the modem sync up, then logged into her Hotmail account.

From: JustMe703
To: ReggyD5150
Date: Monday, March 25, 1996
Subject: Progress!

In 1994, The Carmichael Group, PLC, opened several businesses using the same banks the WoHo organization uses in Hong Kong, Belize, New York, and London. Funds from the closed brokerage accounts were used as seed money. Private company financials not available and cannot access corporate computer systems— yet. Accessed London bank account of Richmond Automotive Distributors in England. Will try corporate systems today.

Brokerage accounts associated with WoHo show hundreds of stock shorts in 1993 during the thing about Iraqi nuclear weapons. It was in the newspapers.

Also, the London bank account of WoHo showed several EFTs,

totaling more than $50 million US from Power of Progress bank in Athens, Greece.

More later...

End of Message

. . .

In the parking lot, Babbs waited for Araseli to finish her session and leave Java Linx, which she did at exactly 12:35.

After entering the café, Babbs went straight to the corner machine Araseli had used, removed a floppy disk from her handbag, slid it into the drive, ran the executable file, then waited for the data to be transferred. She then removed the disk, exited the café, and drove back to the Lake.

Bailey was waiting for her on the front porch—and she walked past without a word.

After reaching her office and logging into her computer, Babbs inserted the disk into the drive and downloaded the simple TXT file to her desktop and opened it with Microsoft Word while Bailey leaned on the back of the chair, looking over her shoulder.

The TXT file had been generated by the keystroke logging software (KLS) program Babbs had installed on three of the computers at Java Linx the day before. The KLS program recorded every keystroke on that specific computer.

What Babbs saw at first was nothing more than letters and numbers and characters that occasionally came together to make recognizable words, phrases, and sentences. Because the file was downloaded immediately after Araseli had used the machine, the information she had typed was at the end of the file. Rather than decipher every word from the TXT file, Babbs was after something far more valuable.

To use the machines, a customer must first request a code from the barista at the Java Linx counter. The six-character code was tied not only to the user but also to the number of minutes they were logged in. Each user would get a different code, but Babbs knew it was always three letters followed by three numbers.

After searching the TXT file, Babbs found the one Araseli had entered, which gave her the starting point in the string. After that, the rest was easy, and she immediately brought up Internet Explorer 2 and navigated to Hotmail, where she entered Araseli's username, *JustMe703*, and her complicated password, *St1ep2ha3n*—though Babbs recognized the pattern as the name of her grandson with the numbers *one*, *two*, and *three* wedged in after every second letter.

Rather than stay in the Hotmail program, Babbs downloaded Araseli's emails to a file, then logged off so they could read them on the screen.

Babbs's brow wrinkled in confusion as she read the emails. Glancing at Bailey, still standing behind her, she said, "All the information is related to Liam's project. And she's giving the play-by-play to someone called ReggyD. The only information remotely interesting is where she mentions you, Woody, Karl Berger, and Bryant Curran. If memory serves, Bryant was the name of Liam's dead father." Spinning around in her chair, Babbs looked up at Bailey. "Did you see this coming? I mean, we put her on this project six days ago, and so far, she's reported no progress. Now, we know that's not true and she's been sending it to this—ReggyD. I thought Liam was like a son to Araseli, given all they went through in Mexico. Now she's spying on him? On us?"

"I can't explain it," Bailey said. "But we have access to her Webmail account now. We can stay on top of her activities." Then, her cell phone buzzed, and she held the display up so Babbs could see it. Taking two steps away, she answered it.

"Good afternoon, Ms. Woodburn," Bailey answered.

. . .

It was a subtle shot and Woody knew it. She decided to skip the pleasantries. "I'm going to speak in generalities."

After a short pause, Bailey said, "I understand."

"The property at the lake might have a mole problem." Woody let the silence play for a beat, then added, "A very large government agency has picked up on it—out of thin air. There was an email with two important names and—"

"We know," Bailey said. "And we're looking into it."

"Oh!" Woody said, legitimately surprised and unsure whether to be relieved or worried. "You said—*we*?"

"Yes. And *we* found the mole. *Comprendo?*"

Woody fisted her eyes closed. They had a problem alright. A *gigante* problem. She said, "Can you keep watching without the mole knowing?"

"Yes."

"Good. Let's see where it leads."

CHAPTER 30

I don't know what you see in this… man." Milo's effeminate British tones complained to Sierra as he fastened his seat belt on the final approach of the Bombardier Challenger 650 jet into Roanoke, Virginia. He tugged at a single earring before running a palm over his bleached-blond spiked locks.

Sierra smiled from the seat across the aisle and said, "It's not for you to understand, Milo."

Milo went back to his magazine.

After touching down, the jet taxied and parked outside a private hanger, where it was refueled. Sierra left the aircraft for the hangar floor to stretch her legs and wait. Less than ten minutes later, Liam emerged from a dark hallway and crossed the hangar floor with his duffle bag slung over one shoulder.

"Thanks for the lift," he said as he approached. His first instinct was to deliver a hug, but she beat him to the punch with a peck on his cheek.

"It's not a problem," Sierra said. "Especially after you ditched during your break." She smiled and added, "Milo will be happy to see you."

"I'll bet," Liam said.

Rather than letting the crew stow his duffle bag, he elected to carry it on and give it its own seat. At the top of the airstairs, he and Sierra were greeted by the friendly attendant. On his way down the aisle, he gave Milo's thigh a hearty slap, resulting in a sarcastic wince.

"Great to see you, Milo," Liam bantered.

"Mmmm," Milo hummed and delivered a toothless smile before going back to his *People* magazine.

Liam and Sierra took the seats over the wing, and twenty minutes later, they were airborne. Once the seat belt light extinguished, Sierra disengaged the lock on her seat and swiveled to face Liam. Her sneakers were off, and she let her stocking feet rest on his knees.

"So, you finally decided to take a vacation," Sierra said. "Without me."

"This one's been on the books for a while," Liam explained.

"I have a day or two to kill during the tour," she said a little too loudly, causing Milo to roll his meandering eyes.

"Touring Omaha Beach and the Ardennes might bore you."

"Try me."

Liam smiled. "I'm meeting some old military buddies for a European battleground tour. Patton's grave in Luxembourg. D-Day landing sites. Anzio. Verdun. The Somme. You probably wouldn't have a good time."

"How do you know?"

Liam chuckled. "I guess I don't. Still, this is a boys' trip."

"Is that your way of giving me a rain check?"

"Uh—sure," Liam said as Woody's words popped into his head. *How can you be so good at—what it is you do—and still be so damn clueless at times?*

After an hour, the attendant served their lunch, and that's when Milo decided to join them. Once he was out of snide remarks and engaged in real conversation, Liam discovered Milo was much older than he had originally thought and had once managed other big-name rock groups. By the time they reached Ponta Delgada for a refueling stop, Liam found the man downright interesting.

After they were back in the air, and Milo had returned to his seat, Sierra asked, "I'll be all over Europe the next few weeks. If you're close by, I'd love to have you backstage to see a show from start to triple encore. Your friends are welcome too."

Liam said nothing.

"This isn't really a boys' trip, is it?" she said.

"Sure, it is. We're heading up the coast of France until we get to Utah Beach, and from there—"

"Stop it, okay? Just stop it." Sierra lowered her voice and said, "I know what you are and what you do when you're not playing professor. I'm not your judge. So, if you're not going to tell me the truth, all I ask is that you *don't* tell me lies."

"You're right," Liam said. "From here on, I'll be as upfront as possible. Okay?"

Sierra nodded. "I guess it's a start."

. . .

It was dark when they touched down at Adolfo Suárez Madrid–Barajas Airport, where a limo was waiting and reporters were swarming. Liam made sure Sierra was off the plane and the reporters sufficiently distracted before he meandered down the airstairs, duffle on his should, in anonymity. Strolling easily across the tarmac, he left Sierra in Milo's capable care.

After finding the shuttle to the main terminal, he purchased a ticket for the last flight to Brussels. The flight landed at 1:15 a.m., and Liam breezed through customs using the passport and declarations for Rik Emmett. He rented a car and drove to the Hilton Brussels Grand Place.

As he entered the magnificent hotel, he was met by a large crowd milling around a marquee posted proudly in the lobby's center. Chuckling, Liam thought, *Maybe this internet thing had some value after all.*

After checking in and dropping his bags in his room, he returned to lobby to feign interest in the wall art and get a feel for his next challenge.

He made his way toward the conference wing, where he was

waved off by a frowning man in slacks and a bulging sport coat. The red lanyard around his neck supported a rectangular plastic sleeve with the word *SECURITY* in large black print centered against a white background. The right side of the backing had a single black stripe down one edge. At the top was the man's name and at the bottom were more letters: *SG-WEF-WG 1996-03-29*.

Liam smiled sheepishly at the man before making his way back to the lobby, where he found the bar and restaurant still open but closed to the general public. At the entry, another guard wearing the same red lanyard and same type of badge blocked the entrance between a set of horizontal brass railings.

The bar was filled with world-order types with drinks in their hands and perverted ideas dribbling from their lips. They poked and spoke and smoked and stroked each other until every faux-intelligence prick was at half-mast and had convinced each other of their brilliance.

All were wearing green lanyards.

The hotel was thick with security, but there were always weaknesses. And those gaps could be exploited if given enough time. Security was also about control and compartmentalization. Keeping everything layered and predictable. When deviations occurred, that's when uncertainty opened the doors for chaos. And that was going to be his greatest weapon.

Counting sharks in the water, Woody had said.

Finding his way to the hotel's business center, Liam checked his emails first, then opened up Microsoft Works. After printing his work, he went back to the lobby, where he snatched an empty red lanyard from the vacant check-in table and an abandoned program from another, then stopped next to the marquee once more and took in the poster-size photo of the man everyone was here to see.

How long had it been? Almost fifteen years.

Liam reached out and touched the marquee and blown-up familiar face. It read:

Community for Sustainable Globalization
A Strategic Partner to the World Economic Forum
Welcomes
Keynote Speaker: Primo Ruqur

CHAPTER 31

The Lake
Same Day

Araseli ordered her usual at the counter, except today she opted for a diet soda instead of a latte. After paying for her food and access code, she walked to the back of Java Linx to sit at the computer wedged in the corner. Once she had logged into her Hotmail account, she retrieved her notes from her purse and started typing.

From: JustMe703

To: ReggyD5150

Date: Wednesday, March 27, 1996

Subject: Progress!

Found subsidiary of the Carmichael Group called Pinpoint Holdings. September 1995, began regular monthly transfers to a property management company, Sun of Greece. Offices in Athens. Each transfer=10,000 pounds.

More later...

End of Message

After pressing Send, Araseli was about to log off when she noticed something odd.

In the upper left-hand corner of the Hotmail program, it always showed the current date and time. At present, it read, *Wednesday,*

March 27, 1996, 12:20:03, then *12:20:04*, then *12:20:05*. In the upper right-hand corner, the program displayed the last log-on date and time. It read, *Monday, March 25, 1996, 12:44:05*.

Thinking back to the last time she was on her Hotmail account, she realized it had indeed been two days earlier. But she had logged off a few minutes after noon, not sixteen minutes before one o'clock.

After closing out of the program, Araseli opened the Windows File Explorer, found the system programs, clicked the box that would unhide all the hidden files, then ran a search for suspicious EXE programs. After only a few seconds, she found what she was looking for.

Araseli cursed under her breath in Spanish as she logged back into her Hotmail account and sent her final, simple message.

From: JustMe703
To: ReggyD5150
Date: Wednesday, March 27, 1996
Subject: Hotmail!

End of Message

After logging off, she opened her cell phone and pressed the Speed Dial button. Her grandson answered on the second ring.

"Hello, Nanna," Stephan's voice said. "Please excuse the noise. I am on my way to class."

"I have not seen my grandson for so long. I would love to catch up with you," she said.

"I'd like that too. I can drive up this weekend."

"I thought we could meet in Harrisonburg this Saturday? They have a very nice arboretum at James Madison University."

"Well..." Stephan said, "...sure. We can meet. Are you up for the drive?"

"I'll be fine," Araseli said. Then, after a few more pleasantries—she ended the call.

CHAPTER 32

Helsinki, Finland
Thursday, March 28, 1996

After landing in Helsinki, Bryant instructed the BICA flight crew to get hotel rooms and enjoy the city for a day or two. Traveling under the name Wilbur Lee, he exited the hanger, boarded the shuttle for the airport parking lot, found the Volvo parked in slot seventeen, slid into the passenger seat, and introduced himself to MI6 field agent Mark Adams.

He sent a quick text to Ginny letting her know he had made contact, and by 2:12 a.m., he and Agent Adams had made it through the Vaalimaa checkpoint and crossed into Russia. By 4:20 a.m., they arrived on the outskirts of St. Petersburg, where Adams pulled behind a strip mall and parked. Across the way, headlights flashed, and he left Adams's car and approached the new one parked behind a dumpster. The car appeared to have a driver *and* a passenger, but when he opened the door, the passenger deflated into a briefcase.

In the mid-seventies, to fool KGB minders, the briefcase-passengers were developed from the concept of sex dolls. Only these dolls were very lifelike and inflated and deflated in a couple of seconds. It had been years since Bryant had seen this used and was surprised it still was.

After stowing the case behind the passenger seat, the agent introduced herself as Willow Truscott and ordered him to get in quickly. Four hours later, they were on the outskirts of Moscow. It was here that she asked Bryant to take the wheel while she tucked her long brown hair under a red page-boy wig.

Once they reached Moscow, Truscott pulled up to the front of the Hotel Baltschug Kempinski and waited while Bryant checked in at the desk using Wilbur Lee's documents. As the clerk typed the information from his fake passport, and he shrugged off the overhead cameras, he paused to take in the moment.

The last time he was here was November of 1982. He and Sophya lived across the street in an apartment building that had long since burned to the ground. Liam had arrived two days before so they could all die in the fire. The British MI6 agents had been parked almost in the same spot where Truscott was now. There was no hotel then, only another crumbling apartment building.

When the clerk passed him the room key, he smiled at her, avoided eye contact with the overhead cameras, then strolled easily toward the elevators. In the compartment, he wasn't fooled by the mirrored ceiling or the smoked-glass domes mounted in the hallway every twenty feet. In his room, microphones would be in the light fixtures and the telephone and the television. He also knew the passport of Wilbur Lee was in the FSB's and SVR's systems by now. It would take a little time before they got curious, and hopefully, he'd be long gone by then.

Back in the car, Truscott drove them across the Bolshoy Moskvoretsky Bridge over the Moskva River, then turned left toward the Presnensky District. That's when she noticed Bryant glance in the mirror—again.

Truscott smiled and said, "Your suspicions are warranted, Mr. Lee. Normally Agent Willow Truscott would have FSB minders following her everywhere." She tugged on her wig, then added, "That's why I'm Katie today. Katie works for the Department of Commerce at the embassy and stayed over last night so I could pull this off. I'm surprised you haven't asked about the inflatable dummy."

"I've seen it before," he said. "I guess the CIA sleeping with Hollywood was a foregone conclusion."

She took the turn onto Bolshoy Devyatinsky Lane before finishing with a hard right onto the US embassy compound. After flashing her ID and parking the pool car, Willow removed her wig and escorted Bryant to the CIA's offices, where they were greeted by Trent Householder, the Moscow chief of station.

Householder was a barrel-chested, graying man in his midforties who led them to a conference room at the interior of the building referred to as a sensitive compartmented information facility (SCIF) where they needn't worry about the FSB listening in.

But what about the CIA? Bryant thought.

After settling in and finally getting a good look at Householder, all Bryant could see was a man who had tried to kill his son three years earlier.

"Well—Mr. Lee," Householder started, his tone revealing he wasn't buying the alias. "I've been instructed by my boss, DCI Sanchez, to brief you in detail." But when he saw Lee's eyes darting to the walls and the column at the center of the room, he added, "If you're worried about the old listening devices found here in '85, they're gone. So, where would you like to start?"

Bryant thought, *If Householder has any inkling of who he was, it isn't showing.* He rubbed his eyes, then said, "Jasper Pinard."

Householder opened his satchel and removed a red folder marked *Top Secret* and slid it across the table to Bryant. "We started surveillance the second Pinard arrived from Ankara. Aeroflot. First class. I wonder how a homeless Canadian vet can afford that ticket."

Bryant slid the stack of photos from the folder and rifled through them. The one on top was the most detailed and showed a fortyish bald man wearing jeans, a sweater, and sneakers leaving a cab and entering a hotel. He appeared to be leaning to one side. "What's wrong with his leg?" Bryant asked.

Truscott chimed in. "Shot in Bosnia. His sniper team was changing positions and was being covered by a US Marine sniper team when they came under fire. The marines took out some bad guys but didn't get the one who got Pinard. He blames us for his limp."

"I see," Bryant said absently as he examined the remaining photos. They appeared to be in chronological order starting from when Pinard left Ankara to his arrival in Moscow. "Where is he now?"

"At the Kempinski. The same as you," Householder said. "He's scheduled to fly out tomorrow morning. Destination—Paris. After that, he has a flight to DC, then to Montreal."

Bryant held up a few photos showing Pinard in Red Square with a notebook in one hand and a camera in the other. "The bloke's been busy."

"Bloke?" Householder repeated with a chuckle. "The *bloke* has been stepping off distances between fixed landmarks and taking notes and photos. We followed him through Red Square, Tverskoy, St. Petersburg, and Yasenevo."

"Yasenevo? SVR headquarters?" Bryant looked up from the photos. "Any official events scheduled there?"

"No."

"Then why would Pinard waste his time?" Bryant asked.

"Hard to say. His room on the eighth floor of the Kempinski overlooks Red Square and the House of Unions, where the summit will take place, but neither are clear shots. And, there's no good egress. Plus, official arrivals at the Kremlin are in the courtyard, and it's surrounded on all sides. Dignitaries will be completely shielded."

"Unless the shot comes from *inside* the Kremlin," Bryant said.

"Suicide," Household said.

"Maybe that's why he's going to Paris—to prepare for the G7 summit at the end of June."

Householder shrugged, then leaned back in his chair, his fingers tented beneath his chin while his gaze fixed on Wilbur Lee. Studying him. Dissecting.

Bryant felt the stare and asked, "Something the matter?"

"Maybe," Householder said, his eyes narrowing. "I was in

Washington two days ago, face-to-face with Director Sanchez. He was more than happy to give me the who, what, when, and where. What PJ asked of us was to find out *how*—"

"And now, you want to know the *why*," Bryant finished. "The answer is: we don't know."

"What *do* you know, Mr. Lee?" Householder asked.

Bryant poured water from a pitcher into a spotted glass, then sipped. "I know a jet belonging to the Hermes Corporation arrived in Moscow from Belfast this past Monday."

"We know that too. Primo Ruqur comes to Moscow quite often." Then, Householder glanced at Truscott before he said, "But this time was different."

"How so?"

Truscott reached below the table, and her hand came back with another folder marked *Top Secret*. She removed three color photos and slid them to Mr. Lee, then said, "Those were taken at the Ankara airport and the Atli Hotel the same day Ivanovich was meeting with the Turks. The Hermes corporate jet landed in Ankara, but Primo Ruqur wasn't on it. But that man *was*."

Bryant rifled through the photos, taking in the familiar face in each. When he looked back at Truscott, it took great effort to keep from giving away his recognition of the man.

Truscott continued. "His name is Gjon Rockman. And he's Primo Ruqur's right-hand man. But now Langley is telling us his real name is Franco Delgado." She paused for a beat, then asked, "Did you notice the limo parked behind the cab Pinard got out of?"

Bryant did remember but had thought little about it at the time. He nodded.

Truscott said, "Delgado was in the limo and followed Pinard into the Atli Hotel."

"What are you saying? That Delgado and Pinard are working with Ivanovich?"

"Pinard's a Canadian sniper, Mr. Lee," Householder said.

Truscott let the comment go by. "We also know Delgado uses at least one more alias. Gustov Mikos. He's an Albanian and…"

Bryant let Truscott run through her spiel on Delgado. And she had gotten most of it right. What threw him was the name *Gustov Mikos*. That was a new one.

"You say they were both here in Moscow?" Bryant prodded.

Truscott nodded. "Pinard flew commercial from Ankara to Moscow, then checked into the Kempinski using his real name. Delgado *also* flew commercial from Ankara to Moscow but as Gustov Mikos. He checked into the Kempinski as Mikos too. The Hermes jet that took him to Ankara flew straight to Belfast— without him. It caught up with him in Moscow four days later."

Now we're getting somewhere, Bryant thought. If what Truscott said was true, the Hermes jet was in Belfast at the same time Stephanie Maguire was kidnapped. He asked, "When the Hermes jet landed in Moscow, who got off?"

"No one," Truscott said. "It refueled, then flew to Athens. It was on the ground in Moscow for a little over an hour."

Shit, Bryant thought, then asked, "Why would the jet need to refuel between Belfast and Athens? Are you sure no one got on?"

"Positive. Delgado never left the hotel the whole time he was there. He ate every meal in the hotel restaurant. But we believe he *did* meet with a man we've never seen before." This time Truscott passed him a larger stack of photos from the *Top Secret* folder. "He's in photos six and seven. The man with the backpack."

Bryant shuffled through the stack and found the two photos. The first showed the dark-haired man from the rear entering the Kempinski with the backpack in one hand. The next photo was of the same man from the front exiting the Kempinski. The backpack was slung over one shoulder.

Truscott continued. "We followed him into the hotel. We couldn't get any photos, but we know he didn't check in. He was handed an envelope at the front desk, then went straight to the sixth floor—the room adjoining Delgado's. He stayed ten minutes, maybe less, then went up two floors to Pinard's room. He stayed maybe another ten minutes, returned to the lobby, then left the hotel. He hailed a cab, and we followed him to an apartment building on the north side owned by the Tartar mosque."

Placing the two photos side by side on the table, Bryant said, "His backpack appears bulkier coming out than going in. Perhaps Mr. Delgado and Mr. Pinard would enjoy some company at dinner tonight."

Householder shook his head. "Pinard is scheduled to check out tomorrow, and Delgado left yesterday morning. The Hermes jet flew from Athens to Moscow, picked him up, took him back to Athens, and we followed him to the Ruqur Mansion in Kalopigado, Greece, where he took a helicopter to a yacht docked in the cove."

"*Gretchen's Emerald,*" Bryant said under his breath, struggling to even mumble the name of his dead wife and the only love of his life.

"That's right," Truscott said, sending a quick glance to Householder.

Bryant grinned. "It's world-renowned. I have a thing for boats."

After a beat, Truscott said, "Mr. Lee—who were expecting to get off the jet in Moscow?"

Bryant said, "Delgado may have hired men to kidnap a woman there. I thought maybe they brought her to Moscow."

Truscott shook her head. "We don't know if she got on the jet in Belfast, but she didn't get off in Moscow. That much we know for certain. But she could have gotten off in Athens without us knowing. We didn't have anyone watching at that time."

Householder sat up in his chair. "What's *her* name?"

"Stephanie Maguire," Bryant said as he watched the wheels in Householder's head turn.

"Maguire?" Householder repeated. "Any relation to the IRA's Brandon Maguire?"

Bryant only nodded. "His sister."

"How do they fit into this?" Truscott asked.

"That's what I'm trying to find out," Bryant said. "And so far, I'm batting a zero."

Householder eyed him for several seconds before slamming his portfolio closed. The meeting was over.

Bryant thanked Householder for all he and his team had done and asked that he please stay on top of the whereabouts of Delgado in Athens. Householder promised to collect every piece of intelligence he could but would only communicate through Langley. What that meant was that Bryant would only receive updates from BICA, after the intel was days old.

Back in her car, Truscott pulled on the wig before leaving the embassy compound.

Bryant closed his eyes and leaned back. "What room is Pinard in?"

"Eight twenty-two. Facing Red Square." Truscott read his thoughts, then added, "C'mon—the Secret Service away team is here in Moscow preparing for the summit. Half of them are at the Kempinski, same as you. They know Pinard's name and they'll never let him out of their sight."

She was right. Pinard had weak motive and had lost the element of surprise. But, if Jurg Ivanovich was paying his bills, Pinard certainly had the means. And with the SVR helping him, maybe Pinard didn't need surprise.

Bryant wanted to look into Pinard a little more, but his opportunity was gone. The Secret Service was no doubt all over Pinard. And that meant they'd be all over him if he tried to make contact.

Bryant closed his eyes in thought. He was missing something. And nothing was making sense as the circular reasoning spun out of control in his head. He was exhausted and needed to regroup.

"What time is your MI6 expecting us to return to St. Petersburg tomorrow?" Truscott asked as the tires hit the curb ahead of the turnaround in front of the Kempinski.

Bryant opened his eyes, shook off the fog, and said, "We need to leave Moscow by seven?"

"Seven, it is."

Bryant thanked her, climbed out of the car, then kept his head down until he reached his room, where he picked up the phone and ordered a sandwich. He showered while he waited for his food then set his alarm for six a.m.

Room service arrived twenty minutes later, and halfway through his sandwich, he checked his pager.

Nothing. And that was good. Maybe Liam would do the right thing—for a change.

Still, he knew Liam was dying to know what he had found out in Moscow. And not knowing would drive his son to be predictably unpredictable. So, Bryant typed a quick message into his pager: MOSCOW A BUST. SM NOT HERE. FD LEFT YESTERDAY. JP LEAVING TOMORROW. PARIS. RETURNING ON

But then he stopped typing and gave it a few beats of consideration. He pressed the delete key and got rid of RETURNING ON, before pressing Send.

CHAPTER 33

BICA Headquarters
Washington, DC
Friday, March 29, 1996
5:25 p.m.

Ginny spun the lock on the filing cabinet safe, gave a drawer a reassuring tug, found her purse, and made it into the hallway as her cell phone rang—again.

Drawing a frustrated breath, she stepped to the railing overlooking the lobby below, checked the display, and was relieved to see the call wasn't from a colleague at the Defense Policy Board Advisory Committee.

The number on the phone's display was Bailey's, which she happily answered. A sentiment that would soon change.

"Virginia Woodburn."

"It's Bailey, Ms. Woodburn. I'm sorry to bother you so late on a Friday, but I wanted to make you aware of a breach in security protocol."

"What kind of breach?"

"Araseli has been sending sensitive emails about Liam's project to an outside third party."

"A third party? What project?"

"Liam requested we construct a financial web for Rufus Carmichael and the World Hands Organization, like we did for the CDG cartel."

"Why wasn't I informed?" Ginny asked. Her ears had heard the words *Rufus Carmichael* and *World Hands Organization*, but all she could think of was Owl, the NEST, Liam's obsession, and her world spinning out of control. "How could she contact anyone on the outside using our system?"

"She can't. She's been accessing a Hotmail account at an internet café in Warrenton."

Ginny left the railing, crossed the hallway, and stepped into a dark office, where she sat in a visitor's chair. Bent over, with one palm pressing against the side of her head and the other pressing the cell phone to an ear, she said, "Tell me everything she's sent so far."

"You want me to read you the emails?"

"Word for word."

"But there are two names that—"

"Hum them, for Christ's sake!"

Ginny listened to silence until Bailey returned to the phone. Papers rattled on the other end before she began her dictation. It was during the first few words of the first email that Bailey hummed two of the names rather than reading them out loud.

"Bailey," Ginny said with a forced calm. "Are the initials of those two names KB and BC?"

"Yes."

"And my daughter asked you to look into them?"

"Yes."

"I see," Ginny said, her head pounding now. "Do you have any idea who ReggyD is?"

"No," Bailey answered. Then after several beats, she asked, "Have you by chance heard of Richmond Automotive Distributors? They're out of England."

Ginny swallowed hard. It was the first time she had tasted terror, and it was stuck in her throat. Pressing the phone harder against her ear, she lied, "No. How long has Araseli been working on this project?"

"Since last Tuesday. The nineteenth."

Ten days, Ginny thought. *Before the meeting in her office.* Ginny drew in a long breath to calm her racing heart. It didn't help.

"Are you still there?" Bailey asked.

"Yes. What's your assessment of the damage?"

"Based on what we've seen, it's all old banking info. Araseli's been looking into WoHo investment accounts that have been inactive for years. She's pulled some old statements, tied some EFTs together, linked a few banks, but that's about it. Nothing that could harm BICA."

"Which banks?" Ginny asked.

"Let's see," Bailey said, followed by more paper rustling. "WoHo has accounts in Switzerland, Hong Kong, Belize, New York, London, and Greece. Statements go back as far as '91. Looks like she's trying to establish a client list and money trail. The only oddity is—again—this Richmond Automotive Distributors."

"Listen to me very carefully," Ginny said. "I need you to shut her down. Capture everything she's done. She's gone far enough."

"Far enough?" Bailey said. "What's that mean?"

"Suspend—her—access! Is that *clear*?"

"If we shut her down, she'll know. She might even run."

"Where would she go with the CDG looking for her?" Ginny said. "But go ahead and tag her car, just to be sure. I want to know her every move."

"Why do you want—?"

Ginny didn't let Bailey finish. Instead, she snapped her cell phone closed, cutting off any new argument.

After passing through the air lock, Ginny stepped into the parking garage and then onto the private elevator. She inserted her key, the doors closed, and once she was outside on the street, she allowed herself a moment to lean against a concrete planter and stop her shaking hands by jamming them deep inside the pockets of her overcoat.

She scolded herself for having misjudged Araseli. And, for what she had to do next. Before she stepped to the curb, Ginny had already made up her mind.

Beneath the flashing *DON'T WALK* sign, Ginny took out her pager and typed a message she prayed she would never have to send. EXECUTE ENDANGERED SPECIES—IMMEDIATELY!

CHAPTER 34

Athens, Greece
Friday, March 29, 1996
11:30 p.m.

Sitting in bed with his back against the headboard, Rufus Carmichael set the laptop aside, careful not to wake George, who was sound asleep next to him. Easing out of the satin sheets, he stepped onto the balcony and closed the twin glass doors behind him.

Twenty stories below, the headlights of Athens were thinning as the city shut down. In the distance, the brilliantly lit Acropolis offered some sense of promise. If that was life or death, he wasn't sure. Then, as the reality of the torture and murder of Sheik Tariq Al-Jabori this past fall returned, every dark window in the city became a possible hiding place for the murderer.

And there was no doubt in his mind that he would be next.

Going back inside, he sat on the edge of the bed and calmed himself with thoughts of one day returning home to his estate in Windsor. It had been in the family for ten generations. But there was no tradition requiring him to die there.

Only days after the sheik's murder, he had leased the penthouse, leaving George behind to run the estate. *Has it been eight months already?* Since then, he and George had been together twice. Once in Paris and once in Barcelona. Then, certain that George's life was in danger too, he brought him to Athens until the man killing off the members of the NEST was stopped.

He was about to nudge George awake when his cell phone lit up and buzzed its way across the cover of his original 1901 *Complete*

Works of John Keats, volume 2. When George stirred, Carmichael cupped the phone in his hands and stepped into the hall, closing the bedroom door behind him.

When he saw the number on the phone's display, a sense of dread fell over him, but he swallowed it back as he flipped open the phone.

"Tell me you've found him," Carmichael said. His normally gentle and precise Oxford diction had been replaced with contempt. Over the years, it had been refined to intimidate. But that wouldn't work with the man on the other end of the phone known only as...

Eagle.

"Not yet," Eagle said. "But I know *who* it is. It's Trevor Harmon."

"That's not possible. Harmon is dead."

Eagle said, "Apparently not. Our immediate concern is that he never finds *you*."

"No one knows I'm here. And I never leave. It is like a prison."

"Is that a fact? I hear you are doing business with the Peshmerga now."

Carmichael closed his eyes. "In Halabja, yes. Not here. How could you possibly—?"

"Harmon paid a visit to his Kurd woman in Halabja two weeks ago. She is a commander with the KDP."

His panic doubled as his lips trembled his next words. "If you want me to move again, I won't do it! If you know who this man is, why can't you just kill him? We never should have formed the NEST. We need to—"

"*You* need to calm down," Eagle broke in.

"Calm down? Do you think the sheik was calm when he was being tortured—like the others?"

"If we're smart—and calm—we'll get through this. I have a source close to him helping me track him. I need you to keep low a while longer. Do you think you can do that?"

"I've *been* doing it!" Carmichael exclaimed in a hushed whisper.

"Is George there with you?" Eagle interrupted.

Carmichael involuntarily touched the bedroom door, then pulled his hand away. "No. Do you think I'm stupid?"

"Sometimes—yes. When did you last meet with Primo?"

Letting out a long sigh, he said, "Last evening. Before he left for Brussels. Why?"

"Again. You *claim* you never go out."

"My penthouse has a helipad. I live in squalor for no man."

"Very admirable," Eagle said. "Get some sleep. I'll know more tomorrow."

The phone went dead.

Carmichael stared at the device as if it would wake up at any second. It didn't, but judging by the thumping and grinding noises coming from the room down the hall, someone else *was* awake.

After dropping the phone into the breast pocket of his pajamas, Carmichael padded down the hallway until he reached the door of the interior room. The thumb-turn on the dead bolt was still pointing to twelve o'clock.

A good sign.

Another thud came from inside the room. When he peered through the peephole, he saw only darkness.

A bad sign.

"Everything okay?" Carmichael asked as he pressed his ear to the door.

"Fuck you!" the woman's voice responded.

He eyed the thumb-turn again, reached to touch it, then thought better. "One more day. Maybe two." Then, after a beat of thought, he added, "Are you in need of any—feminine products?"

"No! And fuck you, again!"

CHAPTER 35

CIA Headquarters
Langley, Virginia
Saturday, March 30, 1996
8:22 a.m.

After checking in at the gatehouse using her new civilian contractor's badge, Woody parked in the visitor's spot and battled the stiff breeze all the way inside, where her flats echoed in the empty lobby as she crossed the seal of the Central Intelligence Agency.

Avoiding the reception desk, she went straight to security. After passing through the metal detector and collecting her things on the other side, she smiled at the guard, then looked up to find PJ Sanchez waiting by the elevators.

"Good morning," Woody called out as she approached her friend.

"Long night," Sanchez responded. "I received a diplomatic pouch at home—late."

Normally, Sanchez would be in a three-piece suit but had implemented a casual policy for the weekends. For him, that meant slacks, a sport coat, and a missing-in-action tie. The elevator doors parted and they stepped inside.

"How does it feel to be a civilian again?" Sanchez asked as he swiped his card and pressed the top button.

"I was only at the White House for thirty-nine months. I never drank the water."

"That's okay. *It* drinks *you*."

The doors opened to the seventh floor. Woody stayed on Sanchez's shoulder as they walked toward his office, and he asked,

"Is Mr. Lee the resource you mentioned when we were in the Roosevelt Room?"

"One of them."

"He's kinda—seasoned—isn't he?" Sanchez held the office door open for her, then closed it behind them. After fixing them both teas, he joined her in the sitting area, then spent the next several minutes bringing her up to speed on his Moscow team's meeting with Wilbur Lee. After letting it sink in for a beat, he added, "Bottom line is, we have a new actor in the play. Moscow calls him—Backpack Man." Then, he chuckled.

"What's so funny?" Woody asked.

"I'm imagining a yellow ball-eating ghosts on a computer screen. Anyway, with Delgado, Pinard, and Ivanovich at the same hotel in Ankara—at the same time—we have proof they are working together. Add in the Backpack Man and…" he said, combing his fingers through his hair, "…we have no fucking idea what they're up to." Leaning back in his chair and tenting fingers beneath pursed lips, he studied her then asked, "Who the hell is Stephanie Maguire?"

Woody had expected this might come up but hoped it wouldn't. She was prepared but hated that she couldn't be completely transparent with Sanchez. It was like his almost complete knowledge of Operation: Jugular. He knew everything—everything except that the Currans had all survived. He'd shit if he knew his Moscow team had met with one of them. It was the same, except…

Sanchez would not have asked about Stephanie Maguire if he didn't know some of the answers already. How much he knew, she wasn't sure. But she had known him long enough to recognize this was a test. And it was critical she pass, or risk losing Sanchez as an ally.

Time to tread very carefully, she thought.

"Stephanie Maguire was abducted in Belfast from a jewelry store she co-owns with her brother," Woody explained. "Her brother,

Brandon Maguire, was shot and is in the hospital. And we know he is linked to the IRA."

"I see. And how did BICA happen to learn of this kidnapping?"

"From Delgado," Woody said. "He called Ginny and took responsibility."

Sanchez gave a satisfied nod, then said, "Brandon Maguire is the *head* of the IRA's Northern Command in Belfast. And if Delgado took credit for the kidnapping, it makes what I'm about to tell you even more sensitive. I'm struggling with how much I can say because the murders of my predecessor and national security advisor, Cruxfield, are still under investigation."

Woody nodded calmly, but in the back of her mind—the past screamed.

National Security Advisor Donald Cruxfield and CIA Director Walter Rehnquist had been secretly working with the NEST three years earlier to assassinate an Iraqi general and to plant false information on his computer. Information that had sent the stock markets into a fury and world powers into mobilizing their forces. And in response, the CIA's operative—Lone Wolf—was supposed to die before leaving the general's compound.

But he hadn't. And in response, Cruxfield and Rehnquist had sent a team from the CIA's Special Activities Division to hunt down and kill Lone Wolf. A team Householder had led.

Only Lone Wolf, or Trevor Harmon, had survived. Rehnquist and Cruxfield—had not. And that made Trevor Harmon the number-one suspect in the murders of a national security advisor and a director of the CIA. Thus was born the ruse that Trevor Harmon had died in a fiery crash over the English Channel on his way to turn himself in. That was supposed to squelch the murder investigation.

Apparently, it hadn't.

Clearing her throat, Woody said, "You think there's a tie between the IRA and Ivanovich?"

Sanchez said, "Two years ago, Sinn Fein and the IRA agreed

to a cease-fire with the British government. And it held until the Canary Wharf bombing two months ago. Publicly, Sinn Fein condemned the bombing, but we know they were involved. And our sources inside the IRA have indicated some descension inside. Brandon Maguire condemned the bombing—to his superiors. There was even talk of replacing him. But that plan was nixed. Maguire has strong relationships with certain Estonian groups. Weapons and explosives.

"The SVR could give two shits about the IRA as long as they give the Brits grief," Sanchez continued. "But what they don't like is the money the IRA gives to the Estonians. The Estonians also work with Islamic militants from Chechnya, and that deeply concerns the SVR."

"Are you suggesting the SVR kidnapped Stephanie? To send a message to the IRA?"

"Just—thinking out loud. But if Stephanie Maguire got on that jet in Belfast, she didn't get off in Moscow. Maybe Athens. Your man—Mr. Lee—seemed very disappointed to hear this. Care to tell me why?"

"BICA sent him to find Delgado. I guess he's following every lead." *Not a total lie,* she thought.

"Why would Mr. Lee believe Delgado was involved in the abduction?"

Woody shook her head. "Mr. Lee has gone dark. I can't answer that until he returns from the field. What's your theory about Backpack Man?"

"He may have facilitated some kind of transaction between Delgado and Pinard at the Kempinski." Sanchez tented his fingers beneath his chin for several beats before adding, "Pinard's in a hotel in Paris right now."

Woody wanted to let out a long sigh of relief that she would no longer need to send Liam to Moscow after Pinard. Instead, she deflected by asking, "Are you working with the RG?" The RG was the Direction Centrale des Renseignements Généraux, the intelligence arm for the French police.

"Hell no! Pinard hasn't broken any laws, and all we have are a few anti-American posts to message boards. If the RG were to pick him up, Pinard would know he was being watched, and right now, we know where he is. We want to keep it that way."

"Any talk of canceling the summit?"

"Not publicly. But the Secret Service is pushing for it." He paused briefly, then said, "Is Mr. Lee your only resource?"

"Active—yes. I have another I can activate, if necessary," Woody said, then thought, *The other dead Curran.*

Sanchez nodded as he checked his watch. "I'm afraid I have another meeting. Can you let me know when you hear from Mr. Lee?"

"As soon as," Woody promised.

Sanchez escorted her to the lobby, where they shook hands before she stepped back into the biting Langley wind.

Once she was on the Beltway heading toward Alexandria, she found her cell phone and saw she had multiple missed calls from Ginny. When she called her back, Ginny picked up immediately, her voice—frantic.

Woody expected to hear that something had gone wrong with Bryant, but what she actually heard, according to Ginny, seemed far worse.

"Araseli has vanished," Ginny said. "She left early this morning, and the tracker on her car went dead soon afterward. Bailey and Babbs are trying to find her right now."

"Why was Araseli being tracked to begin with?" Woody asked reflexively.

Her question was met with dead air that lasted for several seconds, a habit her mother was prone to when calculating a response. When Woody was still with the White House, this caution was understood. But now that she was the director of operations for BICA, and it was unacceptable.

So—she hung up.

It took a few seconds for the phone to ring again.

Woody flipped it open and launched in immediately. "I've had it with this half-truth shit! Go dead air on me again, and I'll resign for the second time this week."

Ginny said, "Araseli has been communicating with someone outside of BICA using a Hotmail account, so I had her access suspended and asked Bailey to start tracking her movements. Last night, Araseli retired to her bungalow, and this morning, she was gone. She was working on a project for one of your employees and—"

Woody interrupted her. "She was constructing a financial web for *him*."

"You knew?" Ginny asked, clearly shocked.

"I did." *And the girls were supposed to keep watching Araseli—not turn her in,* Woody thought.

"And you knew about the emails?"

Woody started to answer, then paused when she heard the plural—*emails*. "I knew about one email," she said. "The one that mentions me and the two names we don't mention. There was nothing about"—she paused—"the project. I doubt she's gone far. Not with a price on her head."

"Really?" Ginny retorted. "Because your employee is gone too."

"I gotta go," Woody said. Snapping the phone closed, she dropped it back in the cup holder before pounding the steering wheel. Liam had lied to her. Had he agreed to stay behind so he could help Araseli escape?

Breaking out her pager, she typed a quick text to Liam, second-guessed herself a few times, then pressed Send.

Dropping the Suburban into Drive, she left the parking lot and merged onto I-495 south. When she reached the I-66 exit, she found herself with a decision to make. West toward home…

or east toward a confrontation. After a beat of debate, she hit the turn signal and took the ramp.

Opening her cell phone, she called Bailey, who answered on the first ring.

"Good morning, boss," Bailey said cheerfully.

"I'm on my way to the Lake. Meet me there in thirty minutes. Babbs too. And I don't care if it's Saturday."

"We're already here," Bailey said.

CHAPTER 36

Brussels, Belgium
Saturday, March 30, 1996
3:00 p.m.

An hour before he was scheduled to deliver the closing remarks to the Community for Sustainable Globalization, and flanked by two dapperly dressed guards, Primo Ruqur left his second home in the Saint-Gilles section of Brussels for the short limo ride into the heart of Brussels.

After making the turn onto the Rue d'Assaut, crowds of protesters flanked the streets, waving signs and spewing chants laced with the words: *Nazi, fascist, socialist, communist,* and *Bilderberg.* Constrained only by single runs of nylon rope strung between police barricades, they took every opportunity to breech the line and pound on the limo.

In response, Primo gave only cursory notice, electing instead to enjoy his cocktail and review his notes. The protesters were correct, of course. Not that it mattered. It was the destiny of every person on earth to eventually be controlled by the World Economic Forum, and there was nothing they, nor their governments, could do about it—except get on board the coming corporate republic.

Once they had passed the Rue de Loxum, the route opened up, and in less than a minute, the limo was through the security checkpoint and its destination—the Hilton Brussels Grand Place.

When the limo squealed to a stop at the rear entrance, a guard stepped from the curb and opened the limo's rear door, releasing the two guards inside, who then ushered Primo into the hotel to a separate hall set up as a safe room.

While the two guards inspected the impressive spread of food and drinks, Primo wiped his forehead, then ran both hands through curly receding black locks.

There was a knock at the door, and it was answered by a guard. After closing the door, the guard turned and held up two fingers. Primo nodded, straightened his suit, felt for his notes, then stepped to the door. When it was his time, the doors were opened, and he was rushed across the hall to the back entrance of the grand auditorium. Once inside the dark backstage area, a man in a suit passed him a cool bottle of flavored water and a fresh handkerchief.

After the two-hundred-plus guests had resettled into their seats, and the doors were secured, the founder of the World Economic Forum took the stage and was soon bathed in applause. He thanked the room for their dedication to a better world and for making the conference a great success. Then, in German-accented English, he introduced their closing speaker.

"Our speaker is not only a distinguished member of our board, but he comes to us from a remarkable pedigree. His grandfather Linus Ruqur founded the Hermes Corporation with only a single fishing troller and two trucks. Ten years later, he had six container ships, three trucking companies, and had founded his first bank.

"The son, Georgius Ruqur, and the *father* of our speaker, expanded the Hermes Corporation into a banking and shipping conglomerate. And now, two decades after the tragic murder of Georgius, our young speaker has taken the Hermes Corporation to even higher plateaus in not only banking and shipping but in energy and media, holding each to the highest standards in social and environmental benevolence.

"Our speaker is also the founder of the Power of Progress, an organization dedicated to battling climate change and promoting peace and harmony across the globe and one of the first to embrace the corporate concept of environment and social governance. The WEF has partnered with the PoP in many successful endeavors.

"Our speaker is ranked by *Forbes* in the top two hundred wealthiest men in the world. Please join me in welcoming Primo Ruqur."

Stepping from the shadows, Primo embraced the WEF founder while the room boomed with applause. They hugged and waved and smiled at the crowd of government leaders, corporate magnates, oligarchs, and academic idealists. After thanking the crowd and settling them down, Primo cleared his throat, took a large gulp from the bottle, then set it down on the podium. He smiled into the bright lights and, in Greek-accented English, thanked the VIPs before beginning his remarks.

"I stand before you as a child of good fortune. A benefactor of what is possible when that means meets vision and opportunity? Hope and change."

As applause erupted, Primo raised his hands. When he noticed the tingling in both arms, he quickly gripped the sides of the podium.

"It is the privileged who must drive vision and opportunity to a critical mass, if you will. A nuclear explosion of oneness."

At first, he thought his fibrillating heart was only his nerves. But he had faced audiences much larger and more distinguished than this. So, why was he now sweating?

"Communal peace cannot be built on the crumbling foundations of individual sovereignty, self-interest, capitalism, or the myths of religion and natural rights. Through the smoky glass of time, efforts to propagate this message have been nearly impossible. But now, for the first time since the fabled Tower of Babel, all ears can hear and all eyes can see. Now, we have the internet."

Digging into his pocket, he withdrew a handkerchief, wiped his face, glanced at the lights above the podium with contempt, pocketed the handkerchief, finished off the bottle, then continued.

"The ability to communicate to the masses could not have come at a more opportune moment in mankind's history as we face the common enemies of global climate change and the dissolution of civil rights.

"Throughout history, the opportunities that arise from a common struggle have always been settled by those best positioned to lead the people to victory—and justice. We must embrace the opportunity this crisis provides—not for the good of nations but for the survival of the world."

The tremor in his left hand started first before radiating into his right by way of his shoulders.

"And we accomplish this—not through obsolete nations—but through public-private partnerships, social entrepreneurship, global citizenship, and ultimately through a central corporate republic. Through education and the media, we can bring people to a common mindset of dedicating each life—at birth—to the service of the many. From each, according to their gifts—to each, according to their needs. But only when leaders have turned away from unsustainable constitutions can they embrace their seats at the world table and bring about peace.

"Our efforts at the WEF and the Power of Progress have been to remove the cultural viruses that attack the human mind. We seek complete egalitarianism built around the leadership of a new set of founding fathers, based here, in Europe—the cradle of the world and the only hope for the future.

"Since the founding of the WEF in 1971, we have grown exponentially and we now partner with industries that will eventually control the income of no less than ninety percent of all peoples worldwide. Do you still believe elected politicians control the fates of peoples, or their economic selfishness? I can say definitively, that now...they do not!"

Applause erupted, but it sounded distant. Then, near the back of the room, a familiar face stepped from the shadows. He knew the face. He knew the man. And he knew him well.

From the back of the stage, his bodyguard stepped forward and touched Primo's elbow. "Is everything alright?"

"I-I'm not sure," Primo said as his eyes settled on the face at the back of the room. "Do you see the man standing to the right of the rear door?"

"Yessir."

"Without causing a commotion, escort him to the safe room. And check him for weapons."

"Yessir." The guard hesitated, then asked, "Sir—you are pouring sweat. Are you sure—?"

"Just do it!" Primo commanded with a forced calm.

The guard stepped away and disappeared backstage. As Primo settled his hands on the podium, he saw his bodyguard reappear at the back of the room and whisper in the man's ear. Together, they quietly left the auditorium.

After finishing his speech, Primo thanked the audience. Then, without pausing for the traditional photographs with VIPs, he reached for his bodyguard. Weak-kneed, nauseated, and leaning on the man's shoulder, he demanded to be taken back to the safe room.

CHAPTER 37

Standing before a giant bowl of melting ice filled with floating containers of yogurt, Liam held his hands shoulder high as the two guards finished patting down the suit he'd purchased the day before.

The guard who had led him from the auditorium snatched the badge from the lanyard around his neck, removed the laser-printed credentials from the plastic sleeve, then examined them with feigned expertise.

"Where did you get this?" the guard asked in Greek as he waved the fake in the air.

"Microsoft and HP," Liam said, then watched as the guard tore the square to shreds.

The second guard removed Liam's suit jacket and tossed it over the back of a chair as the doors burst open and a visibly perspiring Primo Ruqur was ushered inside between two more guards.

It was the first time in twenty years that Liam had seen his half brother in person. The last time was in 1977, the evening before Rockman had dropped him at the airport.

Of course, Liam had seen photos of Primo over the years in *Time, Forbes,* and *USA Today.* They made him out to be larger than life. But in person, Liam found him short, and his hairline had receded dramatically for a man in his late twenties. But that hadn't stopped him from growing it long in the back. And, unlike in the puff-piece photos, Primo's natural olive complexion was now pallid, waxy, and dripping with sweat.

Wiping his forehead with one hand, and gripping his chest with the other, the billionaire staggered closer while a guard squeezed Liam's elbow tighter. After returning the handkerchief to his breast pocket, Primo stopped short of where Liam stood, one fist in a tight ball.

"You were the one who handed me the bottle backstage," Primo said.

"I remember you love grape," Liam said, then braced for the coming punch. But what he received instead was an even bigger blow.

Primo hugged him.

In his native Greek, Primo spoke into Liam's shoulder: "Brother. It is good to see you after all these years."

Liam absorbed the hug, then let his free hand pat his half-brother's back. The fabric of his suit jacket was soaked.

"Yeah—sure," Liam said. He delivered one more backslap before the man pulled away.

Primo smiled, but it quickly melted to a frown. "Why would you poison your own brother?"

"I have the antidote," Liam said.

"Where is it?" the guard demanded before delivering a punch to Liam's gut.

Liam doubled over, his hands on his knees. After catching his breath, he waved his arms toward the fifty or so iced beverages. "It's in one of these bottles. I think I remember which one."

"Get it! Now!"

Before the guard could deliver a second punch, Primo spoke. "Stop it! And leave us."

"Sir?" the guard protested.

Pointing toward the door, Primo said, "All of you. Leave us."

The guard hesitated another beat before nodding to the others. A moment later, the door closed and they were alone.

After removing his suit coat, Primo found a metal folding chair and plopped down. "When I asked Gjon to find you, this is not the reunion I had imagined."

"His name is Franco Delgado. You have to know that," Liam said.

Primo smiled. "I've only known him as Gjon. His past is his own."

Liam studied Primo's face and the sweat running down his cheeks. "I'm not here because you sent *Gjon* to find me. I'm here because he kidnapped a friend of mine. I'm here to get her back."

Primo dabbed at his forehead with the handkerchief. "Kidnapping? If Gjon has done this thing, it was not on my orders."

"Let's say I believe you. I'm here. What do you want?" Liam asked.

"Only to see my brother again." Primo opened his dress shirt to the second button. "I hoped we could spend some time on *Gretchen's Emerald*, like when we were children."

"Our mother died on that yacht."

"She fell into the sea." Primo swallowed hard as his thumb and forefinger pinched his own left wrist as his face turned ashen.

Liam said, "Before you catch enough breath for another lie, I already know you are the man called—Eagle. And you're going to tell me what you and the Russians are up to, or I'm going watch you piss and shit yourself as you die." Liam checked his watch. "In less than hour, I expect."

"Brother, I swear I do not know what is happening here." Primo melted further into the chair. "You have poisoned me, accused me of working with the Russians and kidnapping a woman. And now I am supposed to be—an eagle? Perhaps *you* need the antidote."

Liam gripped Primo by the lapels and pulled him forward in the chair. "Where is Stephanie Maguire? And while we're at it, where's Rufus Carmichael?"

Pinching his brother's cheeks with one hand, Liam could feel the fire of his own rage burning a hole through Primo's face. But in the man's eyes, he saw something more. But not fear. And not deceit.

"Carmichael?" Primo said. "Now, I understand about the Eagle. The man who once led the NEST. Yes, I heard Carmichael may have been associated with them. But I have hired his company to manage the financial affairs of my Power of Progress organization. I was never associated with the NEST, and I am *not* this Eagle person."

Liam shoved Primo back against the chair. "Each heartbeat could be your last—brother!"

With great effort, Primo lifted his pitiful eyes to find Liam's. "I can see the pain on your face. But I cannot give what I do not have. I only wished to reunite with my last sibling."

"What do you mean, *last sibling*? Where's Leena?"

Four years older than Liam, Leena was Georgius Ruqur's daughter from his first marriage, making her Primo's half sister and Liam's stepsister.

"It was an overdose. Five years ago," Primo said, then smiled weakly.

"I hadn't heard," Liam said, genuinely sad to hear his free-spirited stepsister was gone.

"She was in Samoa with her fiftieth boyfriend. They wanted to be the first to celebrate the new year. She took something called *ice*."

"Crystal meth," Liam said. "I'm sorry to hear this."

Primo nodded, then opened his shirt another button, revealing a carpet of moist black hair. Then, he crossed his legs. Liam knew the man must be close to pissing himself.

"Where's Delgado?"

"Still searching for you, I suppose."

Liam shook his head and passed Primo a wad of napkins. "And Carmichael?"

"He has rented the penthouse in a building Gjon's company owns in Athens. I do not know the address."

"C'mon. I'm sure you meet with him regularly."

"My helicopter picks him up, and we meet at my home or on *Gretchen's Emerald*. He refuses to go out in public."

"And why is that?"

"He believes someone is trying to kill him." Pausing for a beat, Primo leaked a smile. "Might that be you, brother?"

Liam said nothing.

As he stared down at Primo, Liam considered how easy it would be to end him and his progressive goals. Maybe he wasn't Eagle, but his death could be as rewarding.

Primo said, "I know you do not believe me, but I am equally as curious to know what Gjon has been doing. If you give me the antidote, I promise I will help you."

"Delgado doesn't know I'm here, and I want it to stay that way," Liam said.

"Then, it will remain our secret. I promise you."

"Yeah, right." Liam chuckled. But then, it could speed things along if—

Helping Primo from the chair, Liam led him to a large tub filled with melting ice and bottled drinks. After selecting a random bottle of water, he wiped it on a cloth napkin, cracked the seal, then handed it to Primo.

"Drink it," Liam said. "Then take a good, long piss. Then, drink another one. The more you piss, the better."

"I don't—"

"There's no antidote for caffeine tablets," Liam said.

Primo's frown spread to a grin. Then, he drank the water greedily.

"I want to make something clear," Liam said. "You're a progressive globalist. An enemy of Americanism."

"I see," Primo said. "Then the rumor was true. You *are* working for BICA." After a long pull of water, he added, "Is that what my Irish brother has been doing with his life? Killing for the Americans?"

"I am an *American*," Liam fired back.

Primo chugged water, then shook his head. "Such a shame that we would find ourselves on opposite sides of a future neither of us could possibly stop."

"Forgive me if I don't follow you off the cliff of Mount Bilderberg. Right now, all I care about is finding Stephanie Maguire, Delgado, and Rufus Carmichael. In that order."

Reaching into Primo's suit coat, Liam found his money clip and a gold business card holder. After taking one of the cards, he said, "Now I know how to reach you." He started to walk away but couldn't resist one last shot. "By the way, your security sucks."

Liam crossed the room and pushed opened the door to the atrium, surprising the three guards and a crowd of onlookers. The one who had punched him in the gut tried to block him, but Liam planted a flat palm into his chest, sending him to the carpet on his ass. Another guard went to draw his gun but stopped when Primo called out, "No! Let him go!"

Liam directed a grin toward the guard on the floor, then wedged his way through the crowd as he headed back to the lobby and then—his room.

. . .

After ditching the suit for jeans and a sweatshirt, Liam returned to the lobby and exited the hotel to an adjacent park, where he found a bench beneath a monstrous oak. Nearby, children chased a puppy through the grass; their squeals echoed in his mind, sending him back to a simpler time. A time when he and Stephanie had been the same. Innocent. Unworldly. And, in Enniskillen.

In his mind, Stephanie hadn't changed. She may have grown to be beautiful, intelligent, and street-smart—a woman who had witnessed firsthand the scars The Troubles had left on Belfast, but that was in a different world. In her world, that was the exception.

In Liam's—it was the rule.

His world was dark and home only to people who operated there. Shadows offered both safety and opportunity. Emotions were obstacles and lives were currency. And Stephanie had unwittingly become a pot of gold at the end of a black rainbow. A pot he was going to find, no matter who got hurt. He would not let her become another Lilliana.

His sanity couldn't survive it.

Snapping out of his melancholy, Liam powered on his pager for the first time since leaving the states knowing he was giving away his location. It buzzed with new messages.

The first was from his father.

MOSCOW A BUST. SM NOT HERE. FD LEFT YESTERDAY. JP LEAVING TOMORROW. PARIS.

"Damn it!" he whispered in frustration. No Delgado. No Pinard. And no Stephanie. They were spinning their wheels, and he wondered if it could get any worse. Then, he looked down at the second message. It was from Woody, and he realized that it *could* get worse. Much worse.

WHERE HAVE YOU TAKEN ARASELI?

Taking out his burner phone, he dialed Araseli's number. It went straight to a digitized voice mail.

Liam slapped the phone closed.

How much deeper can this pile get?

CHAPTER 38

Woody found Bailey and Babbs in the kitchen staring at each other over empty mugs. A stack of papers lay between them next to the flying-saucer-shaped conference phone. On top of the papers lay two sections of a disk that resembled a broken hockey puck.

After taking the empty chair, she let the silence thicken before asking, "When we last spoke, why didn't you tell me there were more emails?"

Bailey's brow wrinkled as she exchanged glances with Babbs, then said, "We were speaking in code. Moles. Humming names. Remember?"

Woody thought back to the conversation from two days earlier and realized that Bailey was right. "Where do you think Liam took Araseli?"

Bailey cocked her head to the side. "Liam? I never said—"

"How else could she have disappeared so easily?"

"I don't think you give her enough credit," Babbs added as her gaze settled on the broken disc.

Picking it up, Woody asked, "What is this?"

"It was…" Babbs said, "a GPS tracker. We found it in the parking lot of the Fair Oaks Mall about an hour ago."

Woody studied the two women for a beat, taking in the faces of defeat. "What about the emails? Any ideas about ReggyD?"

Bailey let out a long sigh. "Nothing yet." Then she spun sideways in her chair and looked at Woody. "Other than the names *Karl Berger* and *Bryant Curran*, we couldn't find anything of great importance in her emails. And Richmond Automotive Distributors was the only entity still in business."

"Who are they?" Woody asked.

"A wholesale auto parts company outside London. It's a legit company. Been around for about forty years."

Woody's pager vibrated in her pocket. After glancing at the display, she eyed the conference phone at the center of the table. "What's the number for this—thing?"

Bailey rattled it off, and Woody typed the message and hit Send. Thirty seconds later, the lights on the conference phone flashed, and Woody reached across the table and pressed the green button.

There was a hiss of white noise. When it faded, she answered with, "Where the fuck are you?"

. . .

"I love you too," Liam returned. He pressed the burner phone to his ear as he left the hotel through the rear entrance and stood upwind of the dumpsters.

It was Bailey who spoke first and said, "Araseli's gone, Liam."

"And Woody thinks I have her."

"*I* don't," Bailey said as she glared at Woody.

"I'm in Brussels, Woody," Liam said. "And no—I didn't bring her with me. So, tell me this: Why would she run?"

Baily said, "We discovered she was sharing information on your project with a third party using a Hotmail account. When Ginny had us pull her BICA credentials, she disappeared."

Liam swallowed back the anger rising in his throat and said, "Why didn't you just watch her? Throw a net over who she was emailing?"

"That's exactly what we *were* doing," Babbs chimed in.

Liam said, "Her cell phone is going straight to voice mail."

"She left it in her bungalow," Bailey replied.

"Where are you looking for her?"

"*We* aren't," Woody said.

But I'll bet Curtis is, Liam thought, then said, "Do you have the emails handy?"

"Right in front of me," Bailey said.

"Read them to me."

"All of them?"

"Yep."

"Not again," Bailey said as she picked up the pages.

"What you mean, not again?" Liam asked.

"Ginny had me do the same thing. I'll hum the names, just like I did with her."

"Fuck that," Liam said. "Just read the damn things."

Liam heard pages rustling before Babbs's voice croaked, "I'll do it. Her emails were being sent to ReggyD five-one-five-zero. The first one is dated Wednesday, March twentieth."

Babbs read through all but one email, then stopped and said, "The last one is odd. It's dated Tuesday, March twenty-six, and sent only minutes after the one before it. It has no message. Only has a subject line. It says *Hotmail.*"

"Babbs," Liam said calmly. "When was the first money transfer between Pinpoint Holdings and Sun of Greece made?"

Pages rustled. "Back in September."

In his mind, Liam did the quick math. The drachma was about one three-hundredth of a dollar—and the dollar was also close to the euro and the pound. If Pinpoint Holdings was paying ten thousand a month in drachma, it wouldn't buy a month in a tent. But if they were paying in pounds, it could get them a palace. It could get *Carmichael* a palace in Athens. And, it made sense that he Carmichael would use a shell company to make the payments.

In the background, he heard a cell phone ring followed by the scooting of chair legs. He let it go as he chuckled in silence at Araseli's brilliance. And as smart as Curtis was, he'd never find her.

But Liam could. Only, finding Araseli was a lower priority than finding Stephanie Maguire. And if she had been on the Hermes jet in Belfast, but didn't get off in Moscow, the odds were better than even that he'd find Stephanie in Athens.

Liam said, "I need a list of properties owned or managed by Sun of Greece in Athens. I know it's a pain, but could you send the info over the PagSat?"

"I can send it from the computer. No problem," Bailey broke in.

"Good. Now—can I get a ride to Athens?" he asked as Woody's voice returned.

"From fucking Brussels?" she barked. "You're supposed to be at home. What's in Brussels?"

"The EU. Do I get a ride or not?"

After several beats, Woody said, "I'll send the jet. But forty-eight hours is all you get. No more. After that, you're coming home to regroup. We've got this all wrong and you know it."

She was right. He *did* know it. Delgado didn't *want* them—he was *playing* them. But he had brought Stephanie into the game, and that changed everything. Liam no longer cared about what Delgado was trying to do. All that mattered now was finding Stephanie before planting Delgado and Carmichael in the ground.

"Is he still on the line?" Babb's asked, her raspy voice distant in his ear. Then, it was loud and clear. "You won't believe this, but Sun of Greece is owned by Gjon Rockman. I'm still trying to find a list of properties."

"Perfect!" Liam said. "I'm getting close."

Woody chimed in. "Be careful. ReggyD is still out there. Maybe looking for you."

"ReggyD is the least of my worries, but thanks for caring," Liam said, then closed the phone.

On his pager, he thumbed a text to his father while he walked back toward the hotel's rear entrance.

WHAT'S YOUR ETA?

Then, he pressed Send.

After pocketing the pager, he checked his watch. Helsinki was close, and his father certainly had the crew ready by now. Realizing he didn't have much downtime, the old SEAL in him knew exactly what to do. Time to bank up some calories. He could sleep on the flight.

After wolfing down a steak, sides, and a beer in the mostly empty hotel restaurant (now the saviors of the world had gone), Liam felt the pager vibrate. He checked it while walking back to his room. This time, it was Curtis.

Curtis: `TICKET WAITING FOR RIK EMMETT`

Liam typed back: `WERE'S THE JET?`

Curtis: `UNAVAILABLE`

. . .

After the meeting, Woody left the house and leaned against her Suburban beneath the shade of the willow and thought about the last two couple of weeks. Delgado and his blackmail. The lies her mother had told, and not told. The disappearance of Araseli. McFadden and Karl Berger and Bryant Curran and Liam Curran—all still alive.

Opening her phone, she dialed Curtis's number and he answered immediately. After bringing him up to speed on all that had happened, the explained what she needed from him. He argued—at first—then reluctantly agreed.

After hanging up, she chewed on the phone's plastic antenna for a beat, then dialed one more number.

PJ Sanchez answered on the second ring.

And after a few pleasantries, Woody said, "I wasn't completely open with you this morning."

"About what?" he asked.

"Not on the phone. Tonight. Your place. Is it okay if I invite myself?"

CHAPTER 39

Harrisonburg, Virginia
Saturday, March 30, 1996
11:45 a.m.

Araseli had left the Lake right after seven that morning. She headed east on I-66 toward DC before taking the Fairfax exit, where she stopped at the Fair Oaks Mall. There, she had removed the GPS tracking device she knew Babbs had placed in the trunk before smashing it on the pavement. She then left the two sections of the device on the lamppost's concrete foundation before driving to the opposite side of the mall.

The main part of the mall opened earlier than its stores. After spending less than ten minutes inside, she had returned to her car and doubled back on I-66 heading west. Two hours later, while Woody was inviting herself to meet PJ, Araseli drove onto the campus of James Madison University.

The day was unseasonably warm for late March, and the students were out in force, hiking and biking and walking and nuzzling. Araseli found her way to the Edith J. Carrier Arboretum, where she parked near the entrance to the first walking path.

Ten minutes later, Stephan arrived and parked next to her.

He opened her door and helped her out of the car. Gripping his elbow, she let him escort her into the Andrew Wood Memorial Garden to a stone bench dedicated by a local family, where they sat in silence until a group of giggling students had passed.

"Nanna?" Stephan prodded. "What's happening?"

"*En español, por favor,*" she said. (In Spanish, please.) After lighting up a cigarette, she dug into her purse and removed a brass key embedded in a cylindrical piece of plastic with the number *20* printed on it. "Keep this someplace safe."

"Safe? From who?"

Araseli smiled. "Only give this to Mr. Liam. Understand?"

Stephan pocketed the key, then washed his hands over his face. "You're running, aren't you? Where will you go, Nanna? The CDG is still looking for us both."

"I worry more about BICA than the CDG," Araseli said. When she saw the concern in his eyes, she patted his leg and added, "Do not worry. I will send for you later."

After a few more minutes of small talk, Stephan helped his grandmother to her car and watched her drive away.

CHAPTER 40

Athens, Greece
Saturday, March 30, 1996
11:15 p.m.

There were no windows in the room.

Had her captors not allowed her to keep her watch, she would have no idea how long she had been here—almost six days now—or if it were night or day. It was close to midnight.

After being shoved into the trunk of the car, she had been taken to a private hangar at the airport. When the car's boot opened, she had plunged the tire iron into the first human she saw and buried the end of it high into one man's shoulder. The man had screamed and fallen to the pavement while the other two wrenched the iron from her hand.

In the end, her kicking and screaming and punching had resulted in little more than cuts and bruises on her own calves and forearms and a bruise on her cheek after one man had slapped her before binding her hands, throwing a bag over her head, and carrying her into a waiting plane.

After several hours in the dark tied to a leather seat, with only one trip to the bathroom, the plane landed. They were on the ground for less than an hour before they took off again, landing a few hours later. And from what she could surmise, they had taxied to a private hangar, where she was dragged from the plane into a car and then to a helicopter. That flight had been surprisingly short, and after landing, she was led down a flight of metal stairs.

Once inside and away from the whooping blades, the bag and cuffs were removed, and she was shoved into this windowless room with a double bed, one chair, one lamp, and a half bath all behind a knob-less metal door with a keyed dead bolt. There was a peephole, but it didn't seem to work.

Since then, her only human contact had been with one of two men who would deliver her meals along with fresh towels and clean panties a size too large. On the second day, they brought two gray sweatshirts and a toothbrush, which they left with her food tray. Then yesterday, they brought two plain white T-shirts.

Each time a knock came, she was ordered to step into the half bath and close the door. Only then would the steel door open and one of two men would deliver the items. One time, she had left the bathroom door cracked to see. All she caught was the back of one man as he was leaving.

He was quite tall with salt-and-pepper hair neatly squared off at a shaved neck. He wore tailored slacks and a dress shirt with the sleeves rolled up a lap. And his gait was odd—for a man. His arms didn't dangle at his side as he walked but remained wrapped in a perpetual hug.

The second man she never saw in person. But she had heard him through the steel door, especially after one of her many door-smacking tantrums that lured them both to check on her with minor attempts at comforting words.

Most times, it pissed her off even more. And what was even worse? The men were English.

It was getting late, and her yawn told her it was time to wash her face and take a whole-body sponge bath. The sink was shallow, making it difficult to wash her long hair, but she managed it once since arriving. What she wouldn't give for a shower and her own clothes.

After pinching her hair dry in the softest towel she had ever used, she heard the distant ringing of a phone. Pressing a moist ear against the door, she absorbed the vibrations of the muffled one-sided conversation. Then, it stopped.

If the phone was hung up, she couldn't tell. But it must have been because she could hear the two Englishmen speaking to each other. Then, she heard footsteps approaching from one direction before trailing off as they passed. It turned quiet after that except when the stereo came on and music hummed in the background. It sounded like "Let Her Cry" by Hootie & the Blowfish.

Returning to the end of the bed, she was pinching her hair in the towel when she heard the opening and closing of the door at the end of the hallway. Then, there was a thud followed by more footsteps going the other way, and she ran back to the door and pressed her ear flat against it again.

Hootie was over and "Long, Long Way from Home" by Foreigner had taken over. But the footsteps had stopped. Then, very clearly, she heard the Englishman who always brought her food, scream four words:

"Bloody hell! It's you!"

Then, as she adjusted her ear against the door to capture more, she heard the worst sound yet—a loud, spitting crack—followed by a whomp, as if someone had dropped wet laundry. Then came two more spitting cracks, and this time, she recognized it for what it was. A gunshot through a silencer.

She knew the sound well, having practiced many times with her brother at the range. She recalled being surprised at how loud a supposedly silenced shot actually was, and that's exactly what this had sounded like.

Gasping, she hit the light switch, plunging the room into total darkness except for the sliver below the door. Backing away from the door, she tripped on the serving tray and her half-eaten chicken before stepping on an upended fork and an empty water bottle.

Kneeling down, she felt around and picked up the steak knife, fell onto the bed, then rolled off the far side until she was between the bed and the wall. The handle of the nightstand drawer dug into her shoulder. Her breath was quick and loud, and the only sound she could discern was her own heartbeat in her ear and the final hum of Foreigner in the distance.

Then, beneath the door, there was a break in the light. Patterns of gray mixed with the blacks and whites against the hardwood flooring. Then, there was a faint clicking sound.

The dead bolt was turning.

Then, the door cracked open, letting an L-shaped blade of light inside.

Turning away and shielding one eye, she watched the door open completely. Light spilled around the dark silhouette holding a silenced pistol at its side, and taking up the entire opening. Oddly enough, the silhouette was very tall but appeared to be wearing—was that a dress?

The figure took a step inside, and she raised the steak knife until it was in front of her face, the light spilling around the figure reflected off of the blade. When the figure raised the pistol in Stephanie's direction, she pressed harder against the nightstand.

With adrenaline pulsing through her body, causing uncontrollable tremors, she held the trembling steak knife near her nose and watched as the figure made one last adjustment before lowering the pistol at her face.

Then, in a surprise move, the figure sprinted toward her, stopped at the end of the bed, raised the pistol again, and for the first time, she noticed the figure hadn't been wearing a dress at all but a bathrobe.

And, after the figure spoke, Stephanie realized the voice belonged to a man, and not one of the two Englishmen.

The man cursed as if he'd picked up the wrong brand of bacon at the supermarket.

"Son of a bitch!" he said. Then, with a shaking hand, the man raised the pistol again...

And fired.

CHAPTER 41

Athens, Greece
Sunday, March 31, 1996
12:34 a.m.

Having fallen asleep before the jet's wheels left the ground in Brussels, Liam was still trying to shake off the fog in his head, but Curtis's text kept popping in there. Why was the BICA jet unavailable, and why wasn't his father answering his texts? Something must have gone wrong.

After retrieving his duffle bag from the overhead compartment, Liam filed along with the rest of the passengers to the jetway, navigated through customs as Rik Emmett, then stepped outside into the crisp, salty night air.

The line at the taxi stand was four deep, making him the fifth. While he waited, he turned on the pager, then held his breath. When the tiny LCD letters in the word *SYNCED* appeared, and the pager didn't vibrate, he let the breath out.

It had been several years since he had last been to Athens, the city he had called home as a teen. And even with all the turmoil in his past, it felt oddly comfortable.

The cab stand operator waved the next taxi forward. The driver got out, helped the attractive middle-aged woman in front of Liam with her bag, then held the door open and asked where she was going.

She gave him the name of a hotel, and as she extended a leg into the taxi, Liam took notice of a smooth, shapely thigh spreading the slit in a snug skirt before the cabbie closed the door. Then, the woman rolled down the window and showed him a nervous smile.

"Taxis are expensive," she said in Greek as her eyes locked onto his. "Are you going into the city? We can share."

Liam was about to decline but then realized what she was actually asking and decided to accept.

The cabby, seemingly annoyed, took Liam's duffle bag and tossed it into the trunk before opening the rear driver's-side door. Liam slid in beside the woman.

After climbing behind the wheel, the cabby eyed the rearview mirror and asked in Greek, "Where are you going?"

"Take her first," Liam replied.

She smiled at his response.

Liam had recognized the hotel she mentioned, and that it was on the north side of the Acropolis. He recalled it not being the best part of Athens. He also recognized that when she had spoken to him in Greek, her accent was not native.

Once they left the airport property and were on Attiki Odos, the main road into the city, she said, "Thank you for sharing. My name is Ivona."

"Constantine," Liam lied, staying in Greek. The passing street-lights lit up her lovely, tired eyes, and he saw real gratitude. "Your accent—it isn't Greek."

"Neither is yours," she quickly returned, then added, "I am from Constanta. You've probably never—"

"Romania," Liam said quickly, drawing a bright smile from the woman.

"You know my city?"

"I vacationed there once," he replied as his mind drifted back to mid-May of 1991 and the week he had spent at the Black Sea resort with Nadia. The first two days, they never left the room.

"It is the oldest city in Romania," Ivona said with some pride.

Liam said, "If you don't mind me saying, your choice of hotels—"

"My company made the reservation. It's okay. I've stayed there before." She shot him a smile, then turned back to the window.

After a few miles, the Mesogeion turned onto the Vasilissis Sofias. As they passed the Benaki Museum, the driver took the exit and stopped in front of the woman's hotel. Dropping the taxi into Park, he retrieved Ivona's bags before opening her door and helping her out.

After the driver slammed the door closed and collected his fare, she tapped on the glass with a fingernail.

Liam lowered the window.

"Thank you again," she said. "I know it was out of your way. I am still on Lisbon time, if you would like to have a drink."

"Unfortunately, I am on Hong Kong time," Liam returned. "But thanks for the invitation." Liam raised the window, then said to the cabbie, "The Athens Gate Hotel."

Turning on the dome light, Liam checked the pager again. Before he left Brussels, the ever-efficient Dr. Babbs had texted him the address of a luxury apartment building owned by the Sun of Greece management company. It was the only one they owned in Athens that might command a monthly rent of £10,000. When he found the cabbie's eyes in the mirror, he also found a wide grin.

"What is it?" Liam asked.

"You turned down a night with a very beautiful woman. Are you deranged?"

Liam ignored the quip and said, "Take me to this address." He read it from the pager, then turned off the dome light.

"I know this building. You must be very wealthy. Still, you travel with a duffle bag?"

Liam ignored the cabbie.

After turning onto the Leoforos Vasilissis Amalias, and only moments after passing Hadrian's Arch, a sea of flashing blue and red lights splashed the sides of every building on the west side of the highway. Liam opened his mouth to speak, but the cabbie spoke first.

"That is Makri. And the lights are near your building. Perhaps we should—"

"No. See if we can get through," Liam said.

After taking the exit, the cabbie did his best to navigate to the address but was met with orange-and-white barricades at every intersection. Liam instructed the cabbie to stop and pop the trunk. "I'll walk from here," he said, climbing out of the cab.

After shouldering his duffle and slamming the trunk closed, he paid the fare, tipped the cabbie generously, then slapped the hood, sending the taxi away. He then strolled casually to the first intersection and stopped at the flashing sawhorse barricade.

There were no cops at this point, so he went around the barricade and walked easily down Makri until he reached the next intersection and the first batch of curious onlookers.

And, the first cop.

The officer's back was to him, and the words *Elliniki Astynomia* (Hellenic Police) had been embroidered across the back of his uniform. The muzzle of an assault rifle poked out from the left side of his body.

From this vantage point, Liam could make out the numbers on the fronts of the buildings. His eyes followed each in sequence until he found the correct one, and it had barricades and yellow tape blocking its entrance.

Not good.

Easing his way nearer to the cop, Liam asked, "What happened?"

"Stay back," the cop responded without conviction.

Liam felt a tap on his shoulder and turned to find a younger man of college age, whispering, "It was a murder."

"How do you know?" Liam whispered back.

"We live in the building. I phoned my mother, and she says it was one of the Englishmen in the penthouse."

"Have you met them?" Liam asked.

"Only one of them. Mr. Johnson. He drives a great Mercedes. I've only seen the other man, Mr. Sebastian, from a distance. It's like, he never leaves, and I think..." The boy hesitated, and Liam felt the boy's gaze searching for something. Then, the boy said, "…I think they were lovers."

"Which one was murdered?"

The boy shrugged. "My mother did not say."

Taking a step back, Liam looked around for a way to get closer.

Melting into the shadows, he turned down a side street. A half block later, an alley ran between the adjacent buildings, so he took it, zigzagging around bums and dumpsters until he was back on Makri but one block closer to the building.

The police presence was thicker.

Looking up the face of the building, Liam recalled the boy hadn't mentioned a woman. And he hadn't mentioned Rufus Carmichael either. Had he gotten it all wrong and neither of them were here? And what if Delgado had taken Stephanie to Primo's villa on the coast? Or maybe even the yacht? Did that mean Primo had lied to him in Brussels and had been part of the plan all along?

Still, there was the question of the two men. Mr. Sebastian and his maybe-lover, Mr. Johnson, living in the penthouse. Two Englishmen, the boy had said. Liam shook his head. One of them had to be Rufus Carmichael. And that brought about a selfish inconvenience.

A living-and-breathing Rufus Carmichael could be interrogated. And he was Liam's best chance at finding Eagle. A dead Carmichael meant he had been cheated—again.

Now, it was imperative he get inside.

In front of the building, the police began pushing the crowd aside and removing barricades to let a forensics van through. It was followed by the coroner's van. Tilting his head back to take in the roof and the police helicopter that was now hovering to land, a possibility started to take shape.

CHAPTER 42

Narva River, Three Miles North of Lake Peipus, Russia
Sunday, March 31, 1996
1:05 a.m.

In his newly purchased 1991 Autokam Ranger, Malik Anzorov held the map beneath the dome light in one hand and the steering wheel in the other as he navigated the pitted, narrow, unlit gravel road north until it crossed the low bridge traversing the Vtroya River. The bridge couldn't have been more than ten meters long, meaning the width of the so-called river had to be less. To the west, it emptied into the much larger Narva River that divided Russia from Estonia.

Pulling to the side of the road, he studied the map. He needed to stay on 41K-164 for another four kilometers before taking a left onto another road that paralleled the Narva River on the Russian side. Ten minutes later, he arrived at the T, then turned south.

It was still too dark to enjoy the landscape, but he knew the border with Estonia ran down the middle of the Narva, and immediately ahead, on the Estonian side of the river, would be the ruins of Vasknarva Castle and the first twinkling of a streetlight. When he saw it through the still bare trees, he pulled the Ranger to the side of the road and killed the engine.

After jamming his pistol deeper in the waistband of his trousers, he took the backpack from the passenger seat, retrieved the flashlight from the glove box, locked the Ranger, then started his trek through the forest along the narrow footpath until he arrived on the east bank of the Narva. He could hear the gentle flow as it made its way to the Gulf of Finland and then, fifty kilometers to the north, the Baltic Sea.

Raising the flashlight and aiming it at the ruins across the river, he pulsed the beam three times. Then twice more. Then once. Then—he waited.

A few seconds later, a flurry of pulses responded from the distant bank before he heard the purr of a trolling motor.

It took a few minutes before he could make out the dark shape of a bass boat easing its way through the black water and the outline of the two men aboard. One was carrying a large sack, and both men were clearly holding pistols. As instructed, Malik flashed his light once more to give away his exact location, and the boat ran ashore a few meters from where he stood.

The man operating the trolling motor leapt to the bank and held the boat while the second man with the sack stepped off ,and they both paused, eyeing Malik through the darkness. Their pistols in silhouette by their thighs.

"Do you have the money?" one man asked in broken Russian, his accent clearly Estonian.

Malik held up the backpack. "I need to inspect the merchandise first."

He watched as the Estonian reached inside the sack and came back with what looked like a handful of string. After setting the sack down, the Estonian walked the short distance to Malik and passed him the length of wire.

Squatting down, Malik turned on the flashlight, careful to keep the beam in control while he inspected the wire and the blasting cap on one end. Satisfied it was legitimate, he turned off the light and stood to face the Estonian. He asked, "And the Tovex?"

The Estonian turned toward his partner, who retrieved a larger bag from the boat and carried it to where they stood, placing it gingerly at Malik's feet.

Malik knelt down once more and unzipped the bag to reveal a half dozen tubes of a gelled explosive resembling orange bratwurst.

At the bottom of the bag, he also found three pages of instructions. He smiled as he stood and faced the two men and asked, "Where's the rest of it?"

"In the boat. One hundred and eighty kilos."

"And the detonators and det cord?"

The Estonian nodded to the man who had brought the Tovex sample, and he retrieved another bag from the boat.

Malik knelt down, zipped open the bag, then counted each detonator. They were all there. This time, when he stood, he lifted the backpack and presented it to the Estonian.

"Fifty thousand, as agreed." He shouldered the bag filled with the detonators while the Estonians knelt down to count the rolls of fifty-dollar bills—only a small subset of what Gustov Mikos had given to him in Moscow. Some of the money he had used to purchase the Autokam Ranger and the fertilizer. But most had been deposited in a bank for his family now living in the United States.

When they finished counting the money, the Estonians picked up the backpack and started toward the boat. It took three men four trips to carry everything to Malik's Ranger.

Malik slammed the rear door closed, checked the latch, then turned to the Estonian. "Are you sure this will work?"

The Estonian who had carried the detonators turned around and replied, "It worked in London for the IRA."

Malik waited until the men had disappeared into the forest and he heard the motor on the boat start before beginning his ten-hour drive back to Moscow.

Unlike the trip to the river when he struggled to stay awake, he now tingled with anticipation of the many godless Russian lives he would take in revenge for what they had done to his beloved Chechnya and Islam.

But more than the deaths of hundreds of Russians, there was one in particular he couldn't wait to vaporize.

CHAPTER 43

Athens, Greece
Sunday, March 31, 1996
1:38 a.m.

Rummaging through his duffle bag, Liam found the business card he had taken from Primo in Brussels. Flipping open the burner phone, he punched in the number on the card. On the fourth ring, a voice answered in Greek.

"*Chaírete?*" Primo said through a yawn.

"*Geia sou aderfé,*" Liam replied. "Hello, brother. I trust you are feeling better."

A chuckle erupted on the other end. "I cannot stop peeing. But my heart rate is back to normal."

"There was a murder in Athens this evening. In the building Gjon owns."

"I am in Cologny and have not heard." After several beats of silence, Primo said, "Please tell me you have not killed Mr. Carmichael."

"No. But someone might have. I need to get inside—tonight. The cops have the building sealed off, but there is a helipad. And *you* told me that your helicopter picks Carmichael up from time to time."

There was no answer at first, and Liam wondered if he had lost the connection. But then Primo said, "There is a better way. Ask for Captain Dominic Vasco. Tell him Lieutenant General Lampros has sent you. You may show my business card, if you like."

"Why should they let me in?"

"You are a consultant, of course. Working for me."

"Won't they check with General Lampros?"

"Of course. I will make the call. Will you be arriving as Rik Emmet? As you did in Brussels?"

Liam froze for a beat as the fact settled into his head. Of course, Primo had checked up on him at the hotel. He almost made the man piss himself to death. "Rik Emmet is acceptable," Liam finally said, then clicked off the call.

Shouldering the duffle, Liam turned back to the barricade, where two cops were standing inside the crime-scene tape. Both were facing the crowd and both had Heckler & Koch MP5 machine guns slung beneath their shoulders. Liam pinched a run of the yellow tape to duck under but then stopped as something else came to him.

Maybe Primo was setting him up.

In Brussels, he had gotten the better of Primo. But now, perhaps Primo was returning the favor and leading him straight into the hands of a police force clearly under his influence. And presenting himself as Rik Emmet, then getting caught in the lie, would only make things worse. Especially if it happened at a murder scene.

Overhead, a police helicopter hovered near the edge of the roof. Craning his neck to look up the face of the building, Stephanie popped back into his head. Alive or dead, she could be up there.

Ducking under the crime-scene tape, Liam walked toward the nearest cop.

"*Na stamatísei!*" the cop demanded as he brought the MP5 to ready.

"I need to speak with Captain Vasco," Liam said in English.

The officer, puzzled by the request, switched to English as well and demanded, "Back behind the line."

"Lieutenant General Lampros sent me. My name is Rik Emmet."

The cop's eyes grew wide and his posture stiffened. He keyed the mic on his lapel and spoke, listened, then spoke again.

The moment of truth, Liam thought.

Then, the cop's eyes shifted to Liam before motioning him

forward. Pointing toward the white forensics van parked on the sidewalk, the cop said, "Ask for Sergeant Boosalis."

Liam thanked him then started toward the commotion. When he reached the van, he found the rear doors open and a man in a white jumpsuit, gloves, and booties fumbling through some compartments. "Are you Rik Emmet?" the man asked before turning to face him.

"Yes," Liam said, opting not to shake the man's gloved hand. "Are you Boosalis?"

"*Sergeant* Boosalis." After eyeing Liam for a moment, he reached inside the van and came back with a sealed plastic bag. Handing it to Liam, he said, "Put it on."

After slipping into his own paper-thin white jumpsuit, booties, and gloves, Liam followed Boosalis through the revolving door and into the building.

They crossed the lobby to the twin brass elevators but then took a hard right down a hallway that led to the parking garage. Boosalis stopped short of the glass door, took another left, and punched the Up arrow by a different elevator. Reading Liam's mind, he said, "It is the private elevator to the penthouse."

Liam nodded, then eyed the ceiling-mounted camera pointing at the door to the parking garage. Another one like it had been mounted in the lobby above the brass elevators aimed at the front entrance.

The elevator door opened and they stepped inside. Boosalis inserted a fire key into the slot, then pressed the Up arrow. Moments later, the doors opened to the twentieth floor.

Liam followed Boosalis into a hallway decorated with tapestries and portraits and landscapes and shiny light fixtures with dripping crystals. Gawdy, even for a penthouse.

To the left, the hallway ended at a propped-open door and a set of metal stairs leading up. *The helipad,* Liam thought as two men in windbreakers descended from the roof.

"This way," Boosalis said, motioning for Liam to follow him to the right.

The hallway led them past a second, grander staircase leading up and down—then a kitchen, a dining room, an office, a storage room, and at the end, it opened up into a den complete with a well-stocked bar and a wall of windows overlooking the city. A swarm of white jumpsuits buzzed in every direction.

On the far side of the room near a U-shaped white sofa, a pajama-clad body lay face down in a crumpled pose. Around the head, a lake of black had formed and a creek ran beneath the sofa.

"Captain?" Boosalis called out to the white jumpsuit kneeling by the body.

The man looked back at them—clearly annoyed. As he stood, his lips pressed into a thin line and his head shook. "Mr. Emmet, is it?"

Boosalis turned to Liam and said, "You are *his* responsibility now." Then, he hurried away.

Liam turned back to the tall jumpsuit. The man had removed his gloves and was running fingers through thick salt-and-pepper hair. Liam figured him to be about his own age, mid to late thirties. When he smiled, his teeth were slightly crooked but bleached white.

"I am Captain Vasco. You have very powerful friends, Mr. Emmet."

Holding up Primo's business card, he said, "I was sent to be of some assistance."

Vasco gave the card a cursory glance, then asked, "Assistance? To me or to Mr. Ruqur?"

"That depends on the victim."

Vasco motioned for Liam to follow him to the corpse. "The deceased is Winston Sebastian. An Englishman leasing the penthouse."

Kneeling down, Liam's attention went to the two tiny entrance wounds in the back of the corpse's head. The collar of the man's paisley-patterned silk pajamas was soaked in blood.

"Have you contacted Sun of Greece?" Liam asked.

When he heard the name of the property management company, Vasco's eyes went wide. "We have. I assumed that is how you came to be here."

Liam didn't answer. Instead, he craned his neck over the corpse to get a look at the face, but it was too close to the back of the sofa and turned downward. A pair of wire-rimmed glasses lay half under the sofa and twisted like a lemon slice in a spilled bloody cocktail.

Liam turned to Vasco. "Is he the only victim?"

"So far."

"What's that supposed to mean?"

"Another man, Mr. George Johnson, was living with Mr. Sebastian. And they had a guest. Both are missing."

Liam asked, "Have you seen security video?"

Vasco nodded.

"Can I have a look?"

Vasco shook his head.

"Can you at least give me a summary?"

After delivering a disapproving glare, Vasco stepped away from the corpse. When they were well out of earshot of the other jumpsuits, he said, "At eleven thirteen this evening, Mr. Johnson entered the garage using his card. After parking, he used the private elevator to access the penthouse. Several minutes later, one of the tenants complained to the desk clerk about a car alarm. The clerk called upstairs, and a few minutes later, Mr. Johnson came back down and walked into the garage. The alarm stopped and he then went back inside. That's when the tenant who lives below the penthouse heard popping sounds and a thud. He called the front desk to report the noise. The clerk ignored the tenant. Ten minutes after that, Mr. Johnson came back downstairs, entered the parking garage, then drove away in his Mercedes."

Liam said, "And you believe Mr. Johnson murdered Mr. Sebastian?"

Vasco nodded. "Witnesses tell us that Mr. Johnson and the deceased were—intimate. There may have been an argument before Mr. Johnson used the excuse of silencing his car alarm to retrieve a pistol and conceal it inside a box he was carrying. He returned to murder Mr. Sebastian before leaving the building."

"Why would he need an excuse? Why not go to the garage and conceal the pistol in his pocket?"

Vasco didn't respond.

Liam let out a long sigh. "What about the guest?"

Vasco stepped away, and Liam followed him down the hallway to the open door that Liam had originally thought was a storage room.

With a gloved fist, Liam rapped on the open door. It may have looked like wood, but it was obviously steel-cored. Inside, he found an unmade bed, dime-store furniture, a working lamp on a nightstand, a serving tray on the floor, an empty plate nearby, food scraps, and utensils scattered around the room. Off to one side, a door opened into a half bath.

Liam took a few steps forward but stopped when a lab tech popped up from behind the bed. "The bathroom has not been processed," she scolded.

"Sorry," Liam said as he stepped sideways and peered through the door into the half bath. Something was definitely off.

The toilet was new, but its water source was fed by a flexible hose from beneath the pedestal-style sink. On the linoleum, a square stain surrounded the toilet, and another one was beneath the sink. Over the toilet, a rectangular opening covered by a stainless-steel hinged door had been tack-welded shut.

Turning back to Vasco, he said, "This used to be a laundry room."

"Yes. But here is the strange part," Vasco replied before stepping away.

Liam followed Vasco back to the steel door, where the man pointed to the dead bolt and the peephole and said, "They were installed backward."

"So, the guest was a prisoner." Liam stepped over to the bed, where the tech was stuffing a pillow into a plastic evidence bag. "Would you mind?" Liam asked.

"Mind what?" the tech asked.

Liam bent over and sniffed the pillowcase. As the hint of sweet perfume engulfed his olfactory receptors, he had no doubt it was the same brand Stephanie had been wearing their last night together in Belfast.

"Did you find any long red hairs?" Liam asked.

The tech replied, "Yes. How did—?"

"Any clothing?"

"T-shirts and panties."

"Blood?"

This time, Vasco nodded toward the numbered tag on the wall. The tag's arrow pointed to a small bullet hole in the plaster. When Vasco turned off the light, the tech took the hint and sprayed the area with a liquid from a plastic bottle. The area around the hole glowed with tiny blue spots that quickly faded to black.

Vasco turned the lights back on.

The tech said, "The bullet is still in the wall."

Liam laced his fingers behind his head, then closed his eyes. Stephanie had definitely been here. And she had been alive—at the time.

After turning back to Vasco, Liam said, "When did the prisoner arrive?"

"A mystery," Vasco said. "My tech has reviewed the security videos. Neither man ever used the front elevator, and no one except Mr. Johnson has used the private elevator. Mr. Sebastian only traveled using Mr. Ruqur's helicopter. There are no cameras above the first floor." Vasco paused for several beats, but when Liam didn't take the bait, he added, "Perhaps the helicopter brought the prisoner."

"Was there a maid service?"

"No."

"With the laundry room converted to a bedroom and bath, where did they—?"

"Laundry service," Vasco said. "Pickups and deliveries are in the lobby."

Liam nodded. "I want to see the security video."

With the faintest of head shakes, Vasco said, "Mr. Ruqur is an important man in this country and has the ear of Lieutenant General Lampos. But this is *my* case. I agreed to allow you inside, as I was told you could help. But so far, you have not. Why should I—?"

His words were interrupted by the squeak and rattle of wheel bearings in the hallway and two orderlies in white coveralls pushing a gurney with a body bag.

"Stop!" Liam called as he stepped to the doorway. The orderlies complied, and Liam reached across the bag and pinched the zipper. He looked back at Vasco and said, "It's your case."

Vasco nodded, and Liam unzipped the bag, peeling away the sides to expose the face of the corpse for the first time.

His slightly gelled black hair had been professionally cut, but was thinning and receding well above the wrinkles in his forehead. A gaunt face with caterpillar eyebrows topped sunken sockets over prominent cheekbones set over a too-narrow chin and a broad mouth. Tiny ears sprouted from the sides of his head. The lapels of his silk pajamas were open to reveal a small bullet hole where his thin neck met his collarbone, like a tracheotomy done by an amateur.

This was the first shot, Liam thought. *And the two in the back of the head were for good measure.*

Liam thought he had seen the face before, but he *knew* Nadia had. In the Halabja mosque, she had described the man perfectly. In his mind, Liam placed a fedora on the corpse's head and a pipe in his mouth.

Robert Oppenheimer, Liam thought. "Fuck," he let slip out as a feeling of defeat swept over him.

"Well, Mr. Emmet?" Vasco prodded as a new white jumpsuit ascended the stairs.

"Captain Vasco. We found the Mercedes near the airport. And, we found Mr. Johnson," the man said.

"Good," Vasco said, clapping his hands. "Take him to the station for questioning."

"He's dead. Shot himself while sitting behind the wheel."

"What caliber?" Liam asked, drawing the man's stunned attention.

"Small. Looks to be a twenty-two."

All eyes drifted back to the body on the gurney and the tiny bullet hole in the man's throat.

Vasco said, "A murder-suicide? Crime of passion?"

"Ten-to-one, you're wrong," Liam said.

Glaring and fuming now, Vasco pointed a finger at Liam's chest. "And you can prove this?"

"Yes. If I can review the security tapes?"

Stepping back and looking down his nose, Vasco gave it great thought. "How can you be so sure?"

"Because, the man on the gurney isn't Winston Sebastian," Liam said. "His name is Rufus Carmichael."

CHAPTER 44

Athens, Greece
Sunday, March 31, 1996
2:05 a.m.

Vasco ordered his detective to check on the name *Rufus Carmichael* while he and Liam waited for the orderlies to maneuver the gurney down the stairs to the first floor of the penthouse. When they reached the hallway and the main elevator bank, Vasco pressed the Down arrow multiple times, then stepped back and stared impatiently at the numbers over the doors. When the doors opened, they let the orderlies and the gurney carrying Carmichael in first.

Back in the main lobby, Vasco led Liam through an unmarked door that opened into a small office stuffed behind the main elevator bank. They both managed to squeeze inside.

While Liam tore off his jumpsuit, Vasco sat at the desk, retrieved the top CD from a dozen others next to an empty evidence bag, then fed the disk into the computer's drive. On the shelf mounted over the desk, three nineteen-inch monitors flickered to life.

Vasco asked, "Where would you like to start, Mr. Emmet?"

"When the tenant reported the car alarm to the desk clerk," Liam said as he studied the view on the third monitor. It came from a camera he hadn't seen yet that was mounted at the street entrance to the parking garage.

"Here we go again," Vasco said under his breath as he drove the mouse and fast-forwarded the images on the three screens. Then, he pressed Play.

Monitor one belonged to the camera mounted over the elevator doors in the main lobby, and they watched in silence as the top of an irate tenant's head appeared at the front desk, wagging a finger at the clerk. When the clerk picked up the house phone and dialed, the tenant turned back to the main elevators and disappeared from view.

Vasco said, "The clerk is calling the penthouse to report Mr. Johnson's car alarm."

On monitor one, the clerk went back to his book.

Shifting to monitor two, the camera facing the glass door leading to the garage, the faint flashing from Johnson's car headlights could be seen. But then, there was a subtle change in the brightness caused by light from inside the private elevator spilling out as the door opened. As the camera faced the door to the garage and not the elevator, Liam couldn't see inside the elevator. But, using the reflection in the glass door, he could, and he watched the distorted face of a man leave the elevator and extend a hand to hit the Door Release button.

"That is Mr. Johnson," Vasco said.

The view of Johnson on the monitor was high and from behind, and he was wearing a bathrobe. He pushed the door open, entered the parking garage, then disappeared up the ramp. A minute later, the flashing stopped.

Then—nothing.

For five minutes, they stared at the video of the door leading to the parking garage until Johnson returned, this time carrying a cardboard box hoisted on his left shoulder. He swiped his card at the door, adjusted the box, entered the building, then stepped behind the wall to the private elevator and out of view of the camera.

All Liam could see was the reflection of Johnson's backside in the glass door. That's when Liam noticed something and said, "Pause it."

Vasco did, then asked, "What is it?"

"Look at the bottom of his robe."

Vasco said, "Loafers and dress slacks."

"That's right. Now, go back to when he first came off the elevator."

Vasco reversed the video and paused it on the image of the back of Johnson's head as he pressed the Door Release button to enter the garage.

"Now, look at the bottom of the robe," Liam said.

"I can't see his shoes," Vasco said.

"That's right. Because the robe is too long. And who wears a robe over slacks and dress shoes? Now, look at the top of his head." Liam found a Sharpie in a cup and placed a tiny black mark on the monitor where the top of Johnson's head met the doorframe. "Go back to when Johnson was coming in with the box."

Vasco did, then chuckled. "Mr. Johnson grew a few centimeters in the garage."

"Except it isn't Johnson," Liam said. "Okay. Let it play forward."

After the person in the bathrobe disappeared in the elevator, for the next several minutes, they watched absolutely nothing happen except when the desk clerk flipped the pages of his novel. Then, at 11:21 p.m., the clerk set his novel down and picked up the house phone, spoke for a few seconds, hung up, then went back to his novel.

Vasco said, "That call was from the tenant who reported the popping and thud sounds. The clerk said he hadn't heard anything so didn't bother to call us. The tenant told us he waited a half hour before calling us himself."

They watched the clerk read until 11:32 when the bathrobe reappeared on monitor two, still carrying the box. Only, this time, it was on his right shoulder and still blocking the view of his face. He left the building, walked up the ramp, and then disappeared. At 11:35, headlights appeared coming down the ramp and panned toward the exit.

Liam and Vasco shifted their attention to monitor three. But the camera was mounted to view the faces of drivers entering the garage, not leaving. All Liam and Vasco could make out was the rear of the Mercedes and the license plate as it made the turn onto Makri.

"Did you at least run the plate?"

"Yes. It is Mr. Johnson's Mercedes," Vasco said. "And no one else left the building with him unless they were inside the cardboard box. But it was too small for a human unless—"

"I got it," Liam interrupted, then added, "The killer didn't have time to cut up a body and clean up the mess." But then, he thought about Carmichael's body on the gurney and said, "Fast-forward to when the first person came off of the lobby elevators."

Vasco pressed Play and they watched monitor one at four-times speed. No one entered or left the building until the first two cops arrived and spoke to the desk clerk. Then they all disappeared into the main elevators. Minutes later, people started filing out of the building en masse as more blue lights arrived and secured the building.

Stepping off the main elevator, the first person had been an older man in pajamas. He was followed by a gaggle of others in various levels of disruption. Many of them wore caps and hats and robes and coats, but all Liam could see was the tops and backs of their heads.

"Shit!" Liam said as his fist hit the desk.

Vasco studied Liam for a moment. "You realize that if this woman *did* leave during the evacuation, she becomes a suspect."

Vasco is right, Liam thought, then said, "I think Box Man triggered the car alarm to bait Johnson into coming down to disarm it. Box Man knocked Johnson out, took his robe, tied him up, and left him in the trunk of the Mercedes."

"Where did he get the box?"

"Johnson's car. The dumpster. Who knows? He used the box to conceal his face when he entered the building. He murdered Carmichael, returned to the car, then left with Johnson still in the trunk. After finding a remote place to park, he staged Johnson's suicide."

"Staged?" Vasco repeated. "What about the woman?"

Deflating, Liam said, "I can't explain her yet."

"This woman, she was your lover?" Vasco asked.

"She is a dear friend."

"*Is* a dear friend?" Vasco said. "I admire your optimism."

Liam closed his eyes and thought about his personal cell phone he left behind. *If Stephanie's alive, and she tried to call me… Fuck!*

Vasco shut down the computer.

Liam rubbed his eyes, picked up his duffle bag, then followed Vasco back into the lobby. When Liam saw the empty front desk, something else came to mind.

"Any chance you know the last time a helicopter landed on the roof of the penthouse?"

Opening his notepad, Vasco thumbed through the pages, then stopped halfway in. "The clerk said it was late Monday evening—six days ago."

The same day Stephanie was taken from Belfast, Liam thought. So, if she was brought by helicopter on Monday, she could have left anytime between then and tonight. Maybe the blood on the wall wasn't hers, and maybe—

What in the fuck is going on?

"Something the matter?" Vasco asked. Before Liam could respond, the detective from the penthouse entered the lobby, saw them, and made his way to where they stood, an open notepad in his grasp.

"I checked the name, Rufus Carmichael," the detective said. "He is the founder and principle of the Carmichael Group in London. He has an estate in Windsor. No photos exist that I can find. And, his dead gay lover—is George *Hanover*, not Johnson. He lives with Carmichael at his estate."

Liam and Vasco exchanged glances as the detective's forehead wrinkled, and he said, "If Carmichael was renting this penthouse under an alias, he must have been hiding from someone." He then scampered off toward the main elevators.

Yeah. He was hiding from me, Liam thought. Carmichael had heard what happened to Sheik Tariq Al-Jabori and knew he was next. And now, Liam had been cheated out of his chance to interrogate Carmichael—to find the identity and whereabouts of Eagle. Someone had beaten him to the punch. Had his visit with Primo in Brussels triggered the murder of Carmichael?

Maybe Primo sent an assassin to take out Carmichael before Liam could beat the identity and whereabouts of Eagle out of him? If that were the case, then maybe Primo *was* Eagle. And if his father also suspected Primo was Eagle, there was a good chance Liam would catch up with them both in Kalopigado—after Primo returned from his trip. Maybe he'd find Stephanie there as well.

But it wasn't to be.

When his pager buzzed, Liam gave it a cursory glance and immediately regretted it. Fisting his eyes closed, he let out a long breath in an effort to ward off the inevitable pounding in his head.

"Everything okay, Mr. Emmet?" Vasco asked.

"Yeah. I need to check into my hotel and get some sleep."

"I can have one of my men give you a lift."

"That's okay. It's only a few blocks from here." He reached out and touched Vasco's shoulder. "I appreciate everything you've done for me tonight. You didn't have to let me in."

"On the contrary. Your boss is a very powerful man. But I am glad to have met you. Admittedly, you have helped us immensely."

Liam shook the man's hand, shouldered his duffle, then left the building.

The chill of late April hit him as he ducked beneath the yellow tape and started toward the Athens Gate Hotel. On the way, he stopped at the corner where the taxi had first dropped him, retrieved the pager, then stared at the text in disbelief. The letters hadn't changed. And no matter how hard he wished them to, they wouldn't.

It was 3:02 a.m. when he entered the lobby of the hotel. Instead of checking in, he had the concierge call a taxi to take him back to the airport. He waited until he was in the taxi before taking out the pager and—in disbelief—read the message again.

ARASELI'S DEAD! JET WAITING. RETURN IMME-
DIATELY!!

Kalopigado would have to wait.

CHAPTER 45

Liam had wanted to use the eleven-hour flight back to DC to catch up on sleep. Instead, the thoughts of Araseli's death and leaving Athens without Stephanie or his father denied him of slumber. Plus, there was the selfish thought any operator worth his salt would be having.

If Araseli is dead, what good am I in DC?

Still, he felt he owed it to Araseli to return after all they had been through. Plus, if the CDG had found Araseli, Stephan might be next.

He had tried to reach Woody on the jet's airphone system several times, but it was still using terrestrial sites to communicate and was at the mercy of the civilian systems. The technology at the Lake may have been ahead of its time, but the jet-to-ground cell service over the Atlantic was stuck in the eighties. Meaning it was dead air.

Once the plane was inside the BICA hangar at Washington National, Liam grabbed his duffle bag and hovered behind the flight attendant while she lowered the airstairs. Over her shoulder, he saw Woody waiting for him on the concrete wearing a blue suit and low heels.

After descending the airstairs, he crossed the hangar and stopped short of her, letting their gazes lock. No words. Her face showed embarrassment, while her eyes beamed disappointment.

His burned with fire.

"Where did you find her?" Liam asked as he slung his duffle over one shoulder and started walking toward the exit.

"*I* didn't," Woody said, jogging to catch up to him. "The CDG sent a VHS tape."

"To BICA headquarters?"

"In my name."

He started to ask how the CDG could possibly know to send it to her when he remembered Mexico and how she had given up her name to Juan Garcia Lopez, the leader of the CDG, in order to trade guns for Liam's life. Truthfully, he had been unconscious the whole time, but his best friend, Rick Michaels, took every opportunity to remind him that it had been Woody's now ex-fiancé, Paul Kelvington, who had actually saved his life.

"Regretting your trade with the CDG?" Liam asked.

"Jury's still out."

Liam pushed through the glass doors and stepped into the parking lot, where he let Woody slip by. She pressed her key fob, lights flashed, and they jogged to her Suburban. Liam tossed his duffle into the back, then climbed in the passenger seat. A few minutes later they were on the George Washington heading north in stop-and-go traffic.

Woody said, "I'm sorry that—"

"I was this fucking close!" Liam interrupted her as he pressed his thumb and forefinger together in the air. "I could smell her perfume on the pillow."

"Her perfume?" Woody said, her eyes squinting as she studied him.

"Yeah. Next to a wall splattered with blood and a bullet hole."

"You okay?"

"Why wouldn't I be?" he spat back.

But Woody knew him better than that. She could feel the rage radiating from him. Right now, she could only hope it wasn't aimed at her. "Can you fill me in on Brussels *and* Athens?"

Liam did. And by the time they crossed the Potomac into DC, they were caught up and he could tell that Woody was holding something in.

She said, "I know you're pissed about Carmichael, but still, that's one less bird, right? We'll figure out who did it and why, but right now—"

"So, it's *we*, is it?" Liam said, his gaze fixed on the Washington Monument. Then, he pounded his fist on the dash. "Carmichael was my ticket to finding Eagle." He shook his head in disgust.

"You were ordered not to go anywhere."

"Whatever. Where are *we* going?"

"BICA first. Then Ginny wants you on a plane back to Princeton."

"Home? There's no way in hell! My father and Stephanie are still in Greece and—"

"I only said that Ginny *wants* you on a plane," Woody interrupted him. "A lot has happened, and I need to catch you up. Your father met with the CIA in Moscow." She could feel his glare burning the side of her face, so she added, "Bryant is still dark, so PJ filled me in on the meeting."

"Then you can be pretty sure it's a lie."

Woody spent the remainder of the drive bringing Liam up to speed on Delgado, Pinard, and the Backpack Man. By the time they reached the seventh floor of the BICA garage, she had finished.

She chirped the lock on the Suburban as they walked toward the entrance. After swiping her access card, she held the door for him, and they stood in the air lock together, her nose to his chest. Waiting for the all-clear beep felt like forever.

"I need to say something," Woody said as they stepped clear of the air lock and started toward the offices. "No matter what you see or hear in this meeting, I promise you, there's more to the story. We have a meeting at the Lake afterward."

Liam turned to go but stopped when he felt Woody's hand grip his bicep.

"Promise me you'll stay calm in this meeting," she said.

"I'll stay calm."

"Good. Because Ginny doesn't know about our second meeting."

"Why not?"

Woody walked away without answering. When she reached the executive suite, she touched the door handle and looked back at him. "Remember. Stay calm."

CHAPTER 46

Curtis was the first to greet them in the suite and followed them into Woody's newly furnished office, where he closed the door behind them.

"Ginny's on her way," Curtis said, choosing a spot at the end of the new sofa. "And she's—not herself." After sending a knowing glance toward Woody, he added, "None of us are, I guess."

Before Liam could ask for clarification, the door opened and Ginny stomped in—almost unrecognizable.

Blue jeans and a blouse had taken the place of her usual long dresses, and she had let her brown hair rest on her shoulders, making her appear younger, at first glance. But when he saw her face and sleep-deprived eyes, she looked ten years older.

Without a word of welcome, she fell into an armchair and locked gazes with Liam.

"Did *you* do it?" she asked.

"Do what?"

"Kill Carmichael."

Liam shook his head.

"Then who?"

He shook his head again. "But it was definitely a pro."

"How do you know?"

"I saw the corpse...and the security tapes."

"How did you—?"

"The man *you* were certain was Eagle used his pull to get me inside Carmichael's penthouse." Liam then ran through the details he had given Woody.

"So—Primo *helped* you?"

"It fits," Woody interjected. "Primo legitimately sent Delgado to find Liam. But, when Delgado discovered Bryant Curran was still alive, he decided to take advantage of the situation and—do whatever it is he's doing."

"So, we're worse off now than when we started," Ginny said. "A Canadian assassin is still on the loose, and Delgado's trying to use him to start a world war. Now we have a dead British financier, Stephanie Maguire has been kidnapped—or worse—and this Backpack Man joins the cast."

Woody said, "Pinard isn't exactly *on the loose.* We at least know where he is."

"Don't forget Araseli," Liam said.

"Unrelated," Ginny replied as she settled into a chair and looked away.

Leaning over, Curtis touched Ginny's forearm, and the two started a whispered conversation. Then, he went to the entertainment center, picked up the remote, and pressed Play.

At first, everyone watched snow fill the screen. Then, it flickered to an image of two men in balaclavas against a cinder-block backdrop. Between them, and kneeling, was a short old woman.

It was, without a doubt, Araseli.

Each man had a grip on a frail shoulder. They could have been mistaken for an Islamic hit squad until the shorter man began his rant—in Spanish.

He blamed BICA for the deaths of CDG comrades, for stealing their weapons (purchased from a Nicaraguan dealer), and then using those weapons in Bosnia. And though BICA could certainly take peripheral credit for killing CDG thugs, it was the FBI and the Mexican military who had confiscated the weapons after

Woody's trade.

As the shorter man spoke, the taller man reached behind his back and removed a large, curved knife. Liam recognized it as a Spanish Moorish dagger, and the man placed the blade beneath Araseli's chin.

Then, the shorter man looked directly into the camera and said, "*Esto es tu culpa*, Liam Curran," before turning to the larger man and nodding.

At that point, Curtis stopped the video.

Liam closed his eyes as his fists clenched into stones. He knew the video had been made for two reasons: to prove to the CDG leadership the assassins had accomplished their mission, and to send a symbolic middle finger—to him.

Juan Garcia Lopez had gotten his revenge after all.

Liam got up and walked to the screen. He touched the frozen image of Araseli's wrinkled and terrified face. "*Es mi culpa*, Araseli," he said. "*Lo siento mucho.*"

"What did you say?" Ginny asked.

But it was Woody who answered. "It wasn't your fault, Liam."

"That's right," Ginny agreed. "Araseli knew she had a price on her head, and she chose to run. It's time to move on."

"*Move on?*" Liam spewed as he spun around to face Ginny. "She was working on *my* project when she was murdered by the CDG. I'm not *moving on.*"

"Okay. Let's talk about *your* project!" Ginny fired back. "Araseli was researching Rufus Carmichael—for you. Then sharing it with someone called ReggyD. Maybe that's why Araseli and Carmichael were murdered. Have you thought about that?"

"Not once," he said through gritted teeth. Lifting his eyes and latching onto Ginny's, Liam poked his own chest and said: "*I'm* ReggyD!"

"You?" Woody said, leaning forward in the chair.

"Of course." Curtis chuckled as he snapped his fingers. "ReggyD.

Reginald Dwight. Elton John's real name."

"Then what's *five-one-five-zero*?" Woody asked.

"*5150*," Curtis said. "Van Halen's first album with Sammy Hagar. Why didn't anyone let me see the emails? I could have saved us—?"

"I'll tell you why, Curtis," Liam broke in. "Lack of trust and this compartmentalization bullshit. The same mindset that nearly got me killed three years ago…" Then, he wheeled around and pointed a finger at Ginny. "And I won't fall for it again. Want to know why I didn't use the BICA systems to communicate with Araseli? Because I don't trust *you*!"

"You've lost your mind," Ginny said. "I'm shutting you down."

"Like you shut Araseli down?" Liam said, his finger pointing at Ginny like a gun.

The room fell into a queasy silence as Liam let his gaze drift to Curtis, who was studying the floor. Then, Liam's eyes met Woody's—and hers motioned toward the door.

Woody gathered her things from the table, then turned to Ginny and said, "I'll see that he gets on a plane."

Siding up to Liam as she passed, she touched his elbow and led him out of the office, through the suite, then into the hallway.

Keeping a step ahead as they walked, she looked over her shoulder and said, "Nice work. You promised you'd stay calm."

"That *was* calm," he said.

Neither spoke until they were in Woody's Suburban and pulling out of the parking garage onto L Street.

"So, tell me, what's at the Lake?" Liam asked.

"The truth, I think," Woody said. When the sign for I-66 to Arlington appeared, she put on her turn signal.

"Why did you pull me out of Athens? Araseli is dead. My being here is a waste of time."

"Weren't we just in the same meeting?"

Liam thought about it, then said, "I give up. What did I miss?"

Woody shook her head. "Maybe you *do* need some time off. What was the first thing Ginny asked you?" She merged into traffic, then set the cruise control.

"She asked if I killed Carmichael," Liam said. "I knew her ass would be chapped about it."

"Mm-hmm," Woody said, her eyes staying fixed on the road. "And how did Ginny know Carmichael was dead?"

Liam studied his boss's profile for a beat. "From you, I thought."

"Really. Because I didn't know until *you* told *me* on the ride from the airport."

"Son of a bitch!" Liam said, smacking his own thigh. "When I told her I was at the crime scene, she must have pissed her pants?"

Woody nodded. "Still think being here is a waste of time?"

"Okay. If you didn't tell her, how did she know?"

"I have a hunch, but there's so much going on."

"Like what?"

"I'd rather you hear it from someone who doesn't have the last name—Woodburn."

CHAPTER 47

The Lake
Same Day
11:24 a.m.

Woody parked the Suburban next to a black Lincoln Town Car. As they walked by, Liam immediately noticed the plain white government-issued plate and stopped in midstride.

"What am I walking into, Woody?" he asked as his gaze drifted to the two men in boxy suits on the front porch now taking a cautious step forward.

"You're not walking into anything," she said. "But it's time you stopped running."

As they approached the porch, the boxy suit twins met them at the top of the stairs. Liam recognized them as PAs (protective agents) for whoever was inside.

"Miss Woodburn," the suit on the right said. "It's good to see you again."

"You too, Andre. I'll vouch for this man," Woody said as her thumb shot toward Liam.

"Can I see some ID anyway?" the suit asked.

"No, you can't," Liam said curtly.

Woody held the door open as Liam passed.

Inside, the normally bustling *war room* (as Liam liked to call it) was empty. But when Woody pushed open the door leading to the kitchen, Liam heard mumbles. When he entered, the mumbling stopped—and the Hispanic man in the first chair stood up.

"You must be Liam Curran," the man said, extending his hand.

"My name is Paul James—"

"I know who you are, Director," Liam said, stunned the director of the CIA had called him by his real name. He didn't need three guesses to figure out how the man knew. So, he shot a murderous glare toward Woody.

Sanchez let his unshaken hand drop. "It's okay. If I were you, I wouldn't shake my hand either."

Liam said nothing.

"Still…" Sanchez continued, "I, for one, am glad you are still alive."

Woody said, "I told PJ everything. It needed to happen."

Sanchez offered his hand again.

"Sure, it did," Liam huffed as he finally gripped Sanchez's hand, making certain the DCI could feel the loathing in his grip. What Liam felt were crumbs from the remains of a pizza on the table—no doubt baked by Bailey, who despised the chains.

After holding Sanchez's gaze for a moment longer, Liam circled the table to the empty chair. Babbs still hadn't acknowledged him but kept her eyes glued to what was left of the pizza. Bailey, on the other hand, leapt from her chair to hug him, and Liam could feel her gentle sobs against his chest.

"Araseli," Bailey managed to get out.

"I know," Liam replied, his tone low and breathy in her ear. "I saw the tape." He helped Bailey back to her chair before taking the empty one at the head of the table.

Woody had taken the opposite end, next to Sanchez.

Bailey cleared her throat. "Roanoke cops found her car on a side road off of I-81. Her body was behind the wheel, but her head—"

"They found it in the trunk," Babbs finished coldly, her eyes still on the pizza.

Liam seethed with rage, but when Babbs finally looked at him, he saw an equal amount of contempt.

"Curtis told me about ReggyD," Babbs said. In her hands, she waved a single sheet of paper.

So that's why you're so pissed off.

"What is that?" Liam asked.

"Araseli's last email, we think. We read it you over the phone. Remember?"

She spread the page on the table for Liam to see.

From: JustMe703
To: ReggyD5150
Date: Wednesday, March 27, 1996
Subject: Hotmail!

End of Message

Babbs said, "At first, I thought it was sent in error because it has no content. Then, it dawned on me. This might have been a code."

"And you'd be right," Liam said. "Araseli knew she had been compromised."

"Compromised," Babbs repeated. Then, she looked at him with disappointment and asked, "Why would you do this to us?"

Liam started to answer, but Woody spoke first. "Show him the other email."

Babbs slid another page his way, and Liam recognized it as having been sent from an America Online account. Then, when he realized what he was reading, he felt his blood pressure soar.

From: <HIDDEN>
To: chopperlover186@aol.com
Date: Wednesday, March 29, 1996
Subject: Lost Vehicle Found

Near Warrenton, VA. Metallic Blue Acura RL. BBR-598

Danada

Slamming the email down in front of Babbs, he asked, "Who the hell is *chopperlover one-eight-six*?"

"Carlos Fuentez," Woody said.

Then Sanchez chimed in. "Fuentez is the number-two man in the CDG. He's high on our watch list."

"He just went to the *top* of mine," Liam said. "And whoever sent the damn email, their Spanish sucks. Who was it?"

"We're looking into it," Bailey said.

"If you need help—" Sanchez started but was interrupted by Woody.

"Not necessary," she said. "This isn't really why *you're* here, PJ."

Sanchez took the cue. Reaching into a folder marked *Top Secret,* he retrieved a photo of a dark-skinned man with fuzzy black hair worn in a flattop. After spinning it to the center of the table, he said, "This person is who my Moscow team *was* calling Backpack Man. We now know his real name. Malik Anzorov." Sanchez then dealt each person a one-page copy of Anzorov's dossier.

Liam studied it, shifting between the dossier and the photograph. Nothing was registering.

Sanchez continued. "Anzorov snuck into Moscow from Chechnya two years ago after escaping the Battle of Grozny. The Russians had seized the city and indiscriminately attacked civilians, schools, libraries, and mosques; many Chechen Muslims were murdered by the Russian socialists. His mother and father included."

"Just like Franco Delgado's family in Albania," Woody added.

Liam said. "He's had two years to plan something. What is it?"

Sanchez leaned forward, his elbows on the table. "He's been working in a warehouse for a food distributor. One of their customers is the cafeteria at SVR's headquarters. About ten days ago, Anzorov's boss, a man named Alexi Orlov, vanished. So, in true Russian style, Anzorov's employer made *him* the boss. They hired a new helper, but our sources say Anzorov worked the last weekend delivery to the SVR on his own. He had been living in a one-room apartment in a complex owned by the Tartar mosque, but—and here's the suspicious part—lately he's been squatting at his late boss's farm."

"You think he offed his own boss to take his house?" Liam asked.

Sanchez said, "You read the dossier. Anzorov was an explosives expert with the Chechen resistance in '94."

"Someone is going to come looking for Orlov sooner or later."

Sanchez shook his head, "*Later* is more likely. Alexi Orlov had no family in the area. No girlfriends. He kept to himself. If anyone comes looking, it might be a while."

"Have you been through the place?" Liam asked.

"Not yet. And so far, the only combustible substance we can see is an aboveground tank filled with diesel. Every farm has one."

"Do the Russians know about Anzorov?" Babbs asked.

"If they do, they haven't been watching him," Sanchez said.

Woody said, "Anzorov has motive to murder Russians, but not Americans. Pinard is just the opposite. Delgado hates both. And all of them were at the Kempinski Hotel at the same time."

Liam said, "It's clear that Delgado's playing in the space between these two killers and the SVR. He has a sniper, a bomber, and an obsessed Jurg Ivanovich. What's the end game?"

Sanchez said, "Last night, Russian Ambassador Travkin informed Secretary of State Manchin they were considering canceling the Nuclear Security Summit because the FSB believes Pinard poses a threat to President Yeltsin."

"They know his name?" Woody said.

Sanchez nodded.

"So, which is it?" Liam asked. "Is Pinard planning to shoot *our* president or *theirs*? If the summit is canceled, both sides miss an opportunity."

Woody said. "It's a senseless circle. Obviously, the Russians are linking Pinard to us, but we have every reason to link Pinard to them."

Liam heard her, but his mind had long drifted back in time to when his mother was alive and married to Georgius Ruqur, and the two of them were living in the Ruqur mansion in Kalopigado. Liam had been a teenager but old enough to understand Delgado's hatred for the Russians. The man had demonstrated it from time to time in raging fits that resulted in shattered items around the Ruqur home.

Liam got up from his chair and turned toward Sanchez. "Where's Pinard now?"

"Back in Quebec City. We have people on him."

"Good," Liam said. "He'll be easy to find." He gave Bailey a kiss on the cheek and Babbs a touch to her shoulder as he passed. He then rounded the table and his gaze locked onto Sanchez as the man stood.

Woody's pager vibrated across the table. She picked it up and read the message as she followed Liam and Sanchez outside, where the PA team followed them to the Town Car.

Sanchez pulled Liam and Woody aside. "If you contact Pinard, you'll expose our hand. If he's really planning to shoot the president, we can't take the chance of losing him."

Liam said, "It won't matter because he'll be dead in less than forty-eight hours. And I need him alive."

"You think Delgado's going to kill him?" Woody asked.

"Nope. But I think Delgado has *hired* someone to do it."

"Why would he do that?"

"Because he knows what I know. Pinard's the pivot man—the weak link. Think Ruby and Oswald."

"But he hasn't killed anyone yet."

"He doesn't have to," Liam said, then turned to Sanchez and asked, "How do I find Pinard?"

Sanchez appeared to give it some thought, then asked, "What's your number? I'll give you a call when—?"

"Not a chance," Liam said. "Work through Woody. She'll get me the message."

Sanchez chuckled. "You used to be one of us, Mr. Curran. And I'm not my predecessor."

"I know that. Because Director Rehnquist is dead."

Leaving Sanchez shaking his head, Liam climbed into the passenger seat of the Suburban. Woody got in seconds later, her fingers working the PagSat's keyboard.

Liam said, "If Sanchez was your non-Woodburn source, he never mentioned Carmichael's murder. Or Ginny."

"PJ isn't who I had in mind," she said, dropping the pager into her blazer pocket and firing up the SUV. "The jet's fueled and a new crew is ready to go at National. We have reservations at the Marriott in Quebec City. But first, we need to stop by my place."

"What's at your place?"

"My suitcase."

Liam chuckled. "Ginny's going to be pissed."

"Why? I promised to put you on a plane, and that's what I'm going to do."

CHAPTER 48

Same Day

After leaving the Lake, they drove to Woody's condo in Alexandria, where she changed into jeans and a sweat-shirt. While she packed a bag, Liam took a shower. Ten minutes later, he emerged from the steaming bathroom pinching a towel around his waist.

Looking up from her suitcase, Woody couldn't help but stare at Liam's damp and bare V-shaped torso, hard stomach, and the massive calves that protruded from the bottom of her yellow bath towel. She always wondered what was beneath the loose clothing he favored.

Now—she knew.

Liam said, "My clothes are starting to get a little gamey. Any chance that Paul—"

"I'll check," Woody said, almost jogging out of her bedroom and into the one across the hall.

Paul had moved out after the Mexico incident eight months earlier. Like Liam, Paul was a big man. But Paul was more mass than muscle and his weight more evenly distributed. Liam's was sculpted with a specific design in mind.

Woody found a couple pair of baggy jeans and a few sweatshirts Paul had left behind, then placed them on the bed like an offering. "These might fit," she said before leaving the bedroom in a rush.

Dry and wearing a navy-blue sweatshirt, Liam found her ten minutes later in the kitchen. The jeans he had chosen—were his own. When he saw the question on her face, he said, "Paul's were too tight in the thighs and big in the waist."

They left the condo and drove to Washington National, where Woody parked the Suburban two spaces from the one that she had vacated only hours earlier. Inside BICA's hangar, Liam was surprised to find Curtis at the base of the airstairs, a file folder in his grip.

"I shouldn't be giving you this," Curtis said, passing the folder to Woody. He appeared sick—as if he'd eaten bad sushi.

"What *is* it?" Liam asked.

"We'll talk on the plane," Woody said, then turned back to Curtis. "It was the right thing to do."

Curtis shot Liam a nervous glance. "We'll see, won't we?" he said before walking away.

After stowing their luggage and buckling in, Woody ordered two Scotches from the attendant—one that Liam didn't recognize.

"Is she new?" Liam asked.

"I don't know. Curtis handles personnel for the jet?" Woody said absently as she studied the folder's contents. "Why? Want her number?"

Liam said nothing.

Once his lips were sufficiently coated with the Scotch and they were airborne, Liam spun his seat around to face Woody, and for the first time, he saw her as something other than his boss—and the woman who tried to have him killed three years earlier.

She was leaning back with her footie-covered feet on the rest and crossed at the ankles. Her toes were fidgeting, and the *T* and *R* in *STANFORD* across the front of her sweatshirt popped out atop the hint of breasts. When her fingernail hooked a loose strand of brown hair with blonde highlights behind one ear, he noticed the golden loop dangling against the soft outline of her jaw. Her lips parted as she took in a dreamy sigh.

Holy crap! She's a girl, he thought.

"Something the matter?" she asked, glancing up from her reading.

"I guess Curtis is your *non-Woodburn* source?" Liam asked.

"That's funny because he and your mother are welded at the hip like Siamese twins."

Woody smiled as she pulled two laser-printed emails from the folder and handed them to Liam. He read while she explained.

"The first email is Ginny replying to Jaime de Ojeda y Eiseley, Spain's outgoing ambassador to the United States. He had thanked her for convincing the Smithsonian to return to Spain a spear from Francisco Vázquez de Coronado's expedition. The second is one she sent to Carlos Salinas de Gortari two years ago at the end of his term as president of Mexico. He thanked her for all of her support in the past. Tell me what you see."

The emails were in English with some Spanish sprinkled in. But one phrase more than any other, Ginny seemed to favor. The Spanish phrase for *you're welcome*.

De nada.

Only Ginny had misspelled the phrase the same way every time.

Danada.

Liam remembered it was the same misspelling in the email sent to chopperlover186. When he finished reading, he looked up at Woody, his face bright crimson. Before he could speak, Woody broke in.

"Remember in my office when you blamed yourself for Araseli's death and mumbled something in Spanish? Ginny had no clue what you said." She studied Liam's face for a beat, then spoke the obvious. "It was Ginny who gave up Araseli to the CDG."

"And that's why Curtis gave up Ginny—to me," Liam said.

Closing his eyes, Liam buried his face in his palms. He had been right not to trust Ginny. But what had Araseli discovered to warrant this kind of betrayal? Her emails had contained nothing but old financial transactions—information that had helped Babbs locate Carmichael's property in Athens but nothing more than that.

"There's something else," Woody said, removing another page from the folder and passing it to Liam.

"What am I looking at?" Liam asked, studying the single page.

"Curtis printed out the PagSat messages Ginny sent to your father. Look at the last one."

Liam read it out loud. "Execute endangered species immediately?"

"She sent it last Friday evening—*after* Bailey told her about Araseli's emails. Carmichael was murdered the next night. She questioned you in the meeting not knowing you had been at the murder scene." She paused for a beat, then asked, "Guess which endangered species she's referring to."

"The spotted-fucking-owl," Liam replied. "Your mother and my father knew where Carmichael was the whole time. But it was something Araseli discovered that prompted them to kill Carmichael. If it was in the emails, I must have missed it."

Woody said, "I just thought of something. If Stephanie was in the penthouse when your father—" She paused to let the weight of her lead-in take hold, then continued with: "Is he capable of such a thing?"

The air in his gut was prepared to bark out *Fuck no!* but Liam choked it back. Whatever Araseli had found, it was enough for Ginny to send his father to murder Carmichael and George Johnson. But was it important enough for his father to kill Stephanie to cover it up?

Liam lowered his head and said, "I don't get it. Ginny has always hated the idea of me going after the nest. But she's never actually tried to stop me. What was so damn important in those emails? In her office, she all but begged me to kill Eagle."

"Who she said was Primo," Woody said. "Maybe, in her mind, making you believe Primo was Eagle—and letting you take him out—would stop you from hunting Eagle."

"Again—Ginny has never tried to stop me from taking down the NEST. Why this time?"

"Oh shit!" Woody said. "Your father."

"What about him?"

"Ginny sent you both to Eagle. To him, that's still Primo. Maybe he's—"

Liam pulled out his pager and eyed the device anxiously. Before he could hold down the On button, Woody reached over and covered the device with her hand.

"Don't," she said. "Curtis isn't the only one who can see every text."

Lowering the pager, Liam clicked off the overhead light and stared out the window into the darkness below. This had all started with Delgado hunting him and his father. So, how had it become an issue about the NEST?

"Pinard's the key," Woody said. "Let's focus on that—for now."

Liam allowed his attention to drift back to the window and the familiar coastline of Lake Saint Louis. "We're over Montreal."

"Mmm," Woody responded as she closed her eyes and reclined her seat. "I couldn't help but notice a few scars when we were in my condo."

"I had my appendix out when I was twelve."

Woody chuckled. "There was a long one on your back, above your waist on the right side."

"That was Nicaragua," Liam said.

Woody glanced at him. "I've seen your service record. Or should I say, Trevor Harmon's service record. I don't recall any orders for Nicaragua."

"They were stapled to the orders sending me to Syria."

"Syria? There wasn't—" She stopped when it occurred to her that she had once been the White House chief of staff and knew better than anyone that special people were sent on special assignments without the shackles of paper trails. "Point taken," Woody said. "So, tell me about the scar."

"It's classified," Liam said with a grin. "Besides, Shipman tells that story better than I do."

CHAPTER 49

Jurg Ivanovich arrived early that morning. Even so, he found SVR headquarters already buzzing with activity. On his way to the lobby elevators, workers eyed him with reverence—and fear. But no one spoke. That was the rule. His rule. He didn't have time for small talk. Ever.

After taking over the SVR three years earlier—and the traitor, General Grigori Urmanov, was made minister of defense—Ivanovich had assembled his most trusted men to lead a secret operation to reopen the investigation into the death of Leonid Brezhnev. And for more than two of those years, it had gone nowhere. That was until an unlikely source contacted him personally.

That source had turned out to be Franco Delgado. The Albania the KGB—and now the SVR—had wanted dead for decades. And the deal? Lift the contract on his life, and he would deliver proof the Americans had murdered Leonid Brezhnev.

Ivanovich had agreed.

Once Delgado's information started to flow, the case started to come together. General Urmanov and his daughter, Sophya, were proven to be traitors. Sophya's husband, Karl Berger, and his son, Liam Berger, were exposed as the American spies Bryant and Liam Curran. And none of them had died in that fire.

The now dead Urmanov had been behind the planting of Bryant Curran inside the Kremlin by arranging to have his own son-in-law arrested, prosecuted, and murdered in prison—all to pave the way for his daughter to marry Bryant Curran, aka Karl Berger, before becoming Brezhnev's personal nurse. And there was only one reason for Urmanov's actions, and that was to put in motion a plan to murder Secretary General Brezhnev.

Ivanovich had long suspected General Urmanov had been behind the cover-up of the Currans' escape from Moscow. Why else would they be the only three people to perish in the fire that destroyed an entire building? Then, when Delgado delivered the photos proving Karl Berger was actually Bryant Curran, and the video proving they were all still alive, Ivanovich had all the evidence—and ammo—he needed.

It didn't take long for his team to uncover documents proving that General Urmanov had ordered three cadavers for military testing purposes two weeks before the fire—and more documents proving Urmanov had ordered the cremation of the cadavers before they were autopsied. I was enough evidence to have him arrested.

And apparently enough to coax General Urmanov to leap to his death.

Not only was it more proof of his guilt, but in Ivanovich's mind, it was more proof of a conspiracy. But even that hadn't been enough.

Yesterday, Ivanovich had presented his findings to President Yeltsin and his closest aid, Valentin Lukashenko, in a private meeting. Finally, after being laughed at and chastised by every official in Gorbachev's administration, Ivanovich had left the meeting with a win and a loss. President Yeltsin believed there was a conspiracy, but not a murder.

Lukashenko had made it clear: previous testing on Brezhnev's body had been done, and the official cause of death was a heart attack, multiple strokes, and poor life habits. And, if there were spies in the Kremlin in 1982—so what? Russia had spies in the White House, State Department, and even the IRS.

Ivanovich left the Kremlin dejected.

After months of real progress, his three-year effort to prove the Americans had assassinated Leonid Brezhnev was in danger of going nowhere—again.

On the way to his first meeting of the day, Ivanovich stopped by his office to retrieve a fax he was expecting from Delgado. The laser-printed pages were lying in the tray beneath a plain cover sheet. There was no name on the fax. No official logo. Only two names scribbled across the second page:

Rufus Carmichael

Liam Curran

After filling his drip coffee maker with water to heat for his tea, he settled in behind his desk to review the fax.

Beneath the first page were several grainy snips taken from multiple security cameras. Each photo contained only one face belonging to one man, and most were far too grainy to make a clear identification.

The face was much older than it had been in the *Pravda* obituary from November 12, 1982, but there was no doubt it was also the face from the video Delgado had given to him in Ankara.

Liam Curran.

However, the relevance of the name *Rufus Carmichael* was still a mystery, but at this point, the more evidence, the better.

Ivanovich slid the two clearest photos into his portfolio and sent the blurry ones through the shredder. After pouring hot water from the coffee maker into a mug and dropping in a tea bag, he left his office and started down the long hallway.

Rounding the corner, he paused in midstep when he saw Felix Trubnikov leaning against the closed door to the conference room, the knob in his grip behind his back.

Trubnikov, the first deputy of the SVR's Directorate K (Russia's external counterintelligence group), had been leading the top-secret task force.

"Are we still meeting?" Ivanovich asked, disappointed.

"Yes, Comrade Director. But I wanted to let you know I have asked Victor Fradkov to join us." Fradkov was the first deputy in charge of the SVR's Directorate X, the scientific and technical support arm of the SVR.

"Now I *am* intrigued," Ivanovich said.

Trubnikov opened the door, letting Ivanovich enter first, then closed the door behind them. At the far end of the twenty-seat conference table, a ceiling-mounted projector broadcast the SVR logo against a blank white screen extending from the ceiling.

"Good morning, Comrade Director," Fradkov said, rising from his chair.

"Sit," Ivanovich said as he tossed his portfolio onto the table.

Fradkov returned to his chair, and Trubnikov stood in the front of the room immediately out of the projector's light. Picking up the laser pointer, he tested it by making red circles on the screen.

"One of our latest weapons?" Ivanovich asked through a scowl as he dunked the tea bag.

Trubnikov smiled at his director's rare moment of levity. "There is good news. We have identified the assassin. His name is Jasper Pinard, a decorated sniper in Canada's special forces." The screen changed to a collage of photos of a man in various locations around Moscow. "After scouting out shooting positions, he flew to Paris, then to Washington, where he stayed for one night in a Hampton Inn near Langley before returning to Quebec City," Trubnikov added.

"Near CIA headquarters," Ivanovich said under his breath.

"Yes," Trubnikov said. "His handlers most likely met him at the hotel."

Ivanovich asked, "And you are certain he plans to kill President Yeltsin here, in Moscow?"

"Not anymore, Comrade Director."

Ivanovich drew in a long, angry breath. "What does that mean, Felix?"

Trubnikov said, "The assassination attempt will be in Moscow. But we no longer believe the target is President Yeltsin."

"Then who?"

Turning on the laser pointer, Trubnikov circled two photos on the screen where Pinard was standing in front of SVR headquarters. "It is you, Comrade Director."

CHAPTER 50

SVR Headquarters
Moscow, Russia
Monday, April 1, 1996

"You have my attention," Ivanovich said.

Trubnikov nodded at Fradkov, who changed the photo on the screen. Using the laser pointer, Trubnikov drew a red circle around Pinard's face. Only, this time, the backdrop in the photo was the Atli Hotel in Ankara.

Trubnikov said, "This photo of Pinard was taken in Ankara while you were in the hotel. He arrived at one sixteen in the afternoon, sat in the lobby for an hour, then took a taxi to the airport. He landed in Moscow, then checked into the Kempinski Hotel for three days while he scouted shooting positions."

Fradkov chimed in. "Also, Directorate X has been monitoring American communications channels for signs they might know we are close to uncovering their treachery. It has been unusually quiet, but finally, they made a mistake." He pressed a key on the laptop and an email appeared on the screen.

Trubnikov began circling the names in the first line.

From: JustMe703

To: ReggyD5150

Date: Wednesday, March 20, 1996

Subject: Update

Patricia Woodburn was here today. She asked Bailey about Karl Berger and Bryant Curran.

Nothing more to report.

Gracias!

End of Message

When he saw Ivanovich's eyes grow wide, Fradkov added, "The daughter of the head of BICA is asking about Karl Berger and Liam Curran? They know we are close."

Ivanovich asked, "Who sent this email?"

"The embedded IP address is from a router near Washington. We cannot pinpoint the sending computer. But after hacking the two accounts, we know ReggyD logged in from the Hilton in Belfast, Northern Ireland."

The screen changed and another face appeared. The photo was from a camera mounted in the ceiling of a hotel's lobby.

"Liam Curran," Ivanovich said. "The son of Bryant."

"Yes," Trubnikov said. "But he registered as Ronald Scott and left the hotel the same night. We also know he flew from Heathrow to Belfast as Ronald Scott, but there is no record of him ever leaving Belfast."

Fradkov said, "We found five emails between ReggyD and JustMe, but the names Karl Berger and Bryant Curran appear in only one. The others concern the financial activities of a man named Rufus Carmichael, a British financier known to fund terrorist organizations."

Ivanovich thought about the photos faxed to him earlier and the two names scribbled on the cover page. He couldn't help but leak a grin. His two most trusted advisors had blindly validated another piece of intelligence from his confidential source.

Trubnikov said, "Four days ago, the BICA jet flew from Washington to Columbus, Ohio, then to Helsinki. After landing, the passenger crossed into Russia at Vaalimaa and was dropped at the Kempinski Hotel. He checked in before being driven to the American embassy."

"Driven by whom?" Ivanovich asked. "Known American agents are constantly watched."

"With the American Secret Service in Moscow preparing for the summit, our resources are stretched thin. We do not know who the driver was, Comrade Director."

Fradkov cycled to the next image of two men leaning against a car at a security checkpoint. He said, "This photo was taken at the Vaalimaa border crossing two hours after the BICA jet landed in Helsinki."

The driver, Ivanovich didn't recognize. But the passenger, he did.

"Bryant Curran," Ivanovich said.

Fradkov grinned. "At the border and the Kempinski, he used the passport of Wilbur Lee."

Trubnikov nodded to Fradkov, and two more photos appeared side by side on the screen. The photo on the left was clearly Jasper Pinard in profile, registering at a hotel reception desk. The photo on the right was from the same camera, only the man in the photo was standing directly below it. All they could see was the top of his bald head.

"Who is *this* man?" Ivanovich asked, struggling to make out the face.

Trubnikov said, "He registered as Gustov Mikos and took a room on the sixth floor. Pinard registered using his real name, and his room was on the eighth floor, facing Red Square."

He nodded, and Fradkov changed the slide.

The next screen was tiled with photos of a short black-haired man in a light jacket hoisting a loose-fitting backpack. There were photos of him entering the Kempinski, standing at the reception desk, riding the elevators, exiting the elevators, stopping at two rooms, then leaving the hotel.

Trubnikov pointed the laser as he spoke. "The man did not check in. But a desk clerk passed him an envelope. Afterward, he entered a room on the sixth floor—the same room adjoining Gustov Mikos's. He stayed for only a few minutes before taking the elevator to Pinard's room. Again, he stayed only a few minutes before leaving the hotel."

After aiming the laser pointer at the photo of the man exiting the hotel, Trubnikov circled the backpack and said, "Notice it is much fatter. He must have been given something."

Ivanovich leaned back and laced his fingers on top of his head. "Did Bryant Curran also meet with these men?"

Trubnikov cleared his throat. "Gustov Mikos left Moscow the day *before* Bryant Curran arrived. If he and Pinard met, they did it without being caught on camera."

Ivanovich studied the screen and the photos of the man with the backpack. Turning to Trubnikov, he said, "If you have photos of *this* man with the backpack inside the hotel, why do you not have more of Gustov Mikos?"

Trubnikov swallowed hard as he nodded at Fradkov. Fradkov touched a key, and a new collage of photos from inside the hotel appeared. Only, this time, it was the lanky man with the bald head wearing a trench coat.

Ivanovich recognized the face immediately, and it caused the vein in his temple to pulse.

Trubnikov said, "This is the man who registered as Gustov Mikos, but we know it is not his real name. Certainly, Comrade Director, you recognize the man whose life you yourself put a contract on."

"Franco Delgado," Ivanovich said.

Trubnikov nodded, and Fradkov changed the slide. The photo on the screen was from the hotel in Ankara again. This time, it was Delgado's face on the screen.

Drawing in a breath, Ivanovich lifted his chin and stared down his nose at his advisors. The FSB had full access to the Atli Hotel's cameras. It was why FSB executives used the hotel.

Now, it appeared the FSB's excellent resources had worked against him.

"What are you suggesting?" Ivanovich asked.

Trubnikov said, "Comrade Director, you met with this man at your hotel. You shared a Turkish bath with him. We know Delgado is your informant."

"He is," Ivanovich relented. "And the intelligence he has provided has been impeccable, has it not?"

"Without question. But what are his motives? He has lived with a price on his head for more than two decades, and suddenly he is your best friend?"

"Watch your tone!" Ivanovich barked. "Do not forget yourself. This man is not my friend. He is only a valuable asset—at this particular time."

"And what is his price for providing this intelligence, Comrade Director?" Fradkov asked.

"The contract to be lifted," Ivanovich said. "It is a small price to pay."

"Are you certain his life is all he is trading?"

"What do you mean?" Ivanovich asked.

Fradkov said, "When Delgado flew to Ankara, it was on a jet owned by the billionaire Primo Ruqur. But when he flew to Moscow, it was on Aeroflot as Gustov Mikos. The private jet that brought him to Ankara flew to Belfast without him. Four days later, the same jet left Belfast and refueled in Moscow without a single passenger getting on or off. Two days later, it returned to Moscow, picked up Delgado, then flew back to Athens. Were you not aware of Delgado's association with Primo Ruqur?"

Ivanovich shook his head at the vital fact Delgado had failed to mention.

Fradkov continued. "Two days ago, ReggyD accessed his Hotmail account from the business center at the Hilton Brussels Grand Place, where Primo Ruqur was delivering a speech." He then cycled to the next screen and a clear photo of Liam Curran in the lobby.

Trubnikov aimed the laser pointer and said, "He checked in as Rik Emmett." Drawing in a deep breath, he added, "Liam Curran and Primo Ruqur are half brothers, Comrade Director. Same mother, different fathers. I think we now know who ReggyD is."

The room fell into a dead silence as his two advisors allowed the information to sink in. After nearly a minute, Trubnikov added, "Yesterday, in Athens, Rufus Carmichael was murdered. The same man mentioned in the emails."

Ivanovich dug into his folder and spread out the two photos he'd received that morning. Both Trubnikov and Fradkov bent over the table to look, taking in every detail of the face in the photos and the names *Rufus Carmichael* and *Liam Curran* written on the first page. One photo showed the entrance to an apartment complex and its address written in mirror image on the plate glass window.

Ivanovich said, "Delgado sent these to me this morning."

Trubnikov and Fradkov examined the photos, then Fradkov stepped away, opened his cell phone, and made a call. Two minutes later, he closed the phone and said, "The address is an apartment building in Athens. Rufus Carmichael was indeed murdered there. But not by Liam Curran." Turning the two photos around, he pointed to the faint time stamps in the corners. "These photos are from early Sunday morning. Carmichael was killed before midnight on Saturday while Liam Curran was still on a plane."

"Then who did this thing?" Ivanovich asked.

Trubnikov shook his head. "Comrade Director, Bryant Curran was here in Moscow using a false name. He was seen going into the embassy. His son was in the same hotel in Brussels as Primo Ruqur."

Fradkov added, "There is the email with the names Karl Berger and Bryant Curran. Add to it Pinard at your hotel in Ankara and in Moscow and at SVR headquarters and Langley—these are not coincidences. And the fax you received is—"

"Is *what*?" Ivanovich barked.

"How was Delgado able to obtain these photos of Liam Curran so quickly? He must have known where the man would be."

"Are you suggesting they are working together?"

"No, it's… If the Americans have discovered how close we are to proving the assassination of Brezhnev, there is ample motive for them to want to kill you. And there is one more thing to consider. The day after General Urmanov committed suicide, his son, Jaco, defected to the United States. If you will recall, one of our best Vympel agents, Mika Gubina, General Urmanov's own grandchild and the daughter of Sophya, Bryant Curran's wife, also defected to the United States six years ago."

Ivanovich studied the concerned faces of his advisors. It was obvious they believed Delgado and this Canadian assassin were working with the Americans. But he wasn't so sure.

When Delgado first contacted him eight months earlier, Ivanovich had also been wary of the man's motives. But his own team had validated every piece of Delgado's intelligence many times over. Why would Delgado provide him with verifiable evidence *against* BICA and the Currans if he was working *with* them?

Ivanovich closed his binder and picked up his empty cup and said, "President Yeltsin was very interested in our findings but is still not convinced Brezhnev was murdered. To prove it, we must go to the source."

"Sophya Berger?" Trubnikov asked.

"Yes. But let's start by finding the assassin."

"Why not Delgado?" Fradkov asked.

"Let me worry about him," Ivanovich said as he stood from his chair.

"You should not leave without protection, Comrade Director," Trubnikov said. "Let me assign more men to—"

"My current detail is fine," Ivanovich said.

After leaving the conference room, Ivanovich returned to his office, where he locked the door before anyone could distract him from what he needed to do. Sliding open the top drawer of his desk, he retrieved the tiny slip of paper he had taped beneath the edge and dialed the phone number scribbled there.

Franco Delgado answered on the fifth ring.

CHAPTER 51

Athens, Greece
Same Day
8:30 a.m.

After faxing the photos of Liam Curran to Ivanovich earlier that morning, Delgado returned to the apartment building, where he stood before the private elevator, his extended finger hesitating to press Up.

Waiting for him in the penthouse were certainly more questions—questions from a man who worked for an agency Primo Ruqur had great influence over. It wasn't that he was afraid, but only that his patience wasn't up to the challenge.

He pressed Up anyway.

When the elevator doors opened, he stepped into the hallway and was met with voices echoing from the distant end. One voice belonged to the woman who owned the cleaning service, and the other belonged to Captain Dominic Vasco.

The forensic team was gone.

It was Vasco who had given him the photos from the security cameras. And on the surface, the face of a Curran appearing on any camera in Europe played perfectly into his plans. In fact, it was critical to his ruse.

What troubled Delgado had less to do with Liam Curran getting closer and more about how had the younger Curran had managed to gain access to the murder scene. That answer had come from Vasco when he'd revealed the man in the photo was someone named *Rik Emmett*, and it had been Primo Ruqur who'd pulled the strings to get him inside, meaning only one thing—Primo Ruqur was now helping Liam Curran.

Delgado decided to put the Liam-Primo sideshow in the back of his mind. There was also the disappearance of Stephanie Maguire to consider. But though her mysterious exit was somewhat troubling, her kidnapping had served its purpose. She had drawn at least one of the Currans to Europe.

Perhaps the Irish beauty had sweet-talked her way out of the room, something Delgado thought impossible with two gay men. If that were the case, they both got what they deserved. Hell, they only needed to play along for another day or two until Primo left for Turkey and she could be moved to the villa.

On his way toward the voices, he stopped at the door to the converted room, and a somber thought came to him as his gaze settled on the bullet hole in the wall. *Maybe the Irish beauty didn't survive.* Which begged two questions: If she had been killed, then where was her body. And who was the killer in the bathrobe?

Continuing down the hallway to the living room, he smiled at the cleaning lady as she passed, then he sided up next to Vasco, who was hovering over the outline of where the corpse had been.

"How well did you know your tenant, Mr. Rockman?" Vasco asked without acknowledging his return.

"Mr. Carmichael and my employer were business partners. That's all I know."

Reaching inside his suit coat, Vasco removed a folded set of stapled papers. "I have a copy of the lease—and the strange requests in the addendum."

"Carmichael was very eccentric."

"No argument from me," Vasco said. "This penthouse has four bedrooms—three were not being used—yet the laundry room was converted into a fifth bedroom with no windows, and a steel door with a dead bolt and peephole installed backward."

"Mr. Carmichael's eccentricities are not my concern," Delgado said.

"Perhaps. But if Mr. Carmichael was the one who requested the room, it was not in the addendum."

"The work was requested by Mr. Carmichael after the lease was signed." It was a lie, of course. But dead men couldn't testify, Delgado knew. He then turned back to the outline on the floor and asked, "Can my cleaning contractor begin?"

"I think so," Vasco said. But as Delgado turned away, he said, "I wonder why Mr. Carmichael's name appears nowhere on the lease. Pinpoint Holdings is paying the rent, and Winston Sebastian is listed as the tenant?"

Delgado grinned. "Wealthy people use shell companies and aliases for privacy concerns. Just ask my employer."

"I see," Vasco said. "Thank you for your time, Mr. Delgado. I will leave you to clean up your property."

Delgado watched Vasco until the man had reached the end of the hallway and disappeared down the main stairs. When his cell phone buzzed and he saw the number, he bolted to the end of the hallway, through the door, and up the metal stairs until he was standing in the center of the helipad. Only then did he flip open the phone.

"I was expecting your call much sooner," Delgado said as he caught his breath.

"I had a meeting," Ivanovich said. "I have good news. President Yeltsin is convinced the Americans were behind the conspiracy."

"Then we were successful," Delgado said. He closed his eyes as he pressed the phone closer to his ear, waiting for the other shoe to drop.

"As agreed, I have removed the contract on your life. And once again, your sources have proven to be accurate. The Americans hired an assassin to kill me. We have learned the contract is with a Canadian."

Delgado's smile widened against all efforts to control it. Not only had the Russians removed the contract on his life but they had discovered Pinard, another event critical to his plan.

"How can I help?" Delgado asked, suppressing a chuckle.

Ivanovich said, "We have certainly proven a conspiracy, but President Yeltsin requires absolute proof of a murder. Given that your sources are impeccable, I wish to bring you deeper into the fold of my team so we may see this through to our mutual gain. I would like to discuss this matter further, but not over the telephone."

Delgado's radar immediately went off, but at the same time, he was relieved. Ivanovich had grown suspicious and wanted him in Moscow. A move Delgado had long anticipated—and needed—for the fulfillment of his plans for Ivanovich, the SVR, and for Russia.

"I accept your invitation," Delgado said.

"Excellent! Is tomorrow too soon?"

"Certainly, appointments can be changed. Let me get back to you."

Delgado clicked off the call.

It felt foreign, this emotional reaction to the ebbs and flows of life. But, this time, as he stood at the center of the helipad, he couldn't help but let his euphoria run free. His cheeks burned with unfamiliar joy as he looked up into the morning sky and, for the first time in many years, allowed himself to enjoy the warmth of a coming spring.

For decades, he had suffered hatred for the Russian communists without recourse for relief. But when his search for Liam Curran had miraculously resulted in the discovery of Bryant Curran, it almost made him believe in the god his father had died for. He had manipulated the obsessed and naïve Ivanovich into believing his own fantasy; the Americans had assassinated Leonid Brezhnev. And now the Americans were convinced the Russians were plotting the assassination of their own president.

War was almost certain, and vengeance for the death of his family at the hands of the communists in Albania was in reach.

And if the discovery of mutual assassination plans wasn't enough to start a fight, Delgado still had one more catalyst up his sleeve.

He relished the knowledge that, after tomorrow, scores of books would be written about the event, and every author would get it wrong. But in the end, it wouldn't matter. Tensions between the world's two superpowers would escalate beyond return.

After opening his cell phone, he pressed the speed dial and waited. Three rings later, a Slavic accent greeted him in Russian. "Good morning, Mr. Mikos."

Delgado begrudgingly switched to Russian. "Good morning, Mr. Anzorov. Our operation has been moved to tomorrow. Will this be a problem?"

Anzorov replied, "Not at all. What time should I be there?"

"The same time you normally make your deliveries. We do not want to arouse suspicion—now that we are so close."

"The device will be there at nine forty-five."

"Thank you."

After clicking off, Delgado dialed a second number. He had one more loose end to tie up before his trip to Russia. His call was answered by an English accent.

"Yessir," the man's voice said.

"Are you in Quebec?" Delgado asked.

"I am."

"Good. It's time," Delgado said. "Kill him now and call me when it is finished. Once I have proof, I'll move the rest of your money."

He clicked off the call, then meandered to the edge of the helipad to take in the whole of Athens.

So many millions of people. All so willing to believe their own fantasies at the slightest endorsement by another. No wonder Primo Ruqur was a billionaire.

Delgado recalled a saying Georgius Ruqur had been so fond of repeating. *It is easier to move a million people than to move but one.* Perhaps because they fed off of the lies of those they congregated with. What did psychologists call it? Mass hysteria? That which was desired to be believed would be. If a million could be so easily moved, nations would be even easier.

Delgado made one last call. This time to his pilot. They were returning to Moscow.

CHAPTER 52

Outside Moscow, Russia
Monday, April 1, 1996
1:18 p.m.

After ending the call with Gustov Mikos, Anzorov faked the flu and left his job at the warehouse. Back at the farm owned by his late boss, the infidel Alexi Orlov, he finished the afternoon's Dhuhr prayer in the kitchen, then went to the barn to begin his final preparations.

Half of the fertilizer and all the diesel fuel had already been on the property when he killed Alexi Orlov. The rest he had ordered the day he'd moved onto the farm with part of the one million dollars Mikos had fronted him.

In the back corner of the barn, Anzorov mixed the diesel fuel, powdered aluminum, and the ammonium nitrate fertilizer to create the ANFO, a high-powered explosive. In the end, he had used all the fertilizer and most of the diesel to fill fourteen 208-liter steel drums with the explosive packed around every sausage of Tovex from the Estonias. One more than was used in Oklahoma City. All that was left to do now was to load the drums, shape the explosion with the hay bales, and wire the control box he'd bought from the Canadian.

The refrigerated truck came equipped with a hydraulic lift on the tailgate, which made for easy loading, and the truck's storage area was spacious, giving him the necessary room to not only arrange the barrels but to place the water-soaked hay bales to direct the explosion. With the explosives ready, it was time for the delicate part.

Using the instructions the Canadian had given him, Anzorov constructed the wooden box to house the control unit and the fresh car battery. When he finished, he thought the contraption looked like a high-tech shoe-shine box.

Mounted on the top of the unit were four sets of twelve position bus bars to land the detonator wires and a set of aluminum brackets to mount the cell phone. Through the top of the control unit poked a single insulated wire with a TRS audio plug.

Also at the top of the unit, aligned in three rows, were three LEDs, three toggle switches, and three labels. Finally, set off by itself at the upper-right-hand side, a large red-and-yellow switch had been installed.

After drilling a hole between the cab and cargo area of the truck and carefully measuring and stripping the end of the detonator wires, Anzorov fed the wires through and secured the ends to the bus bars on the control unit. He then positioned the control unit in the passenger seat while he sat on the driver's side with the instructions in his lap and read.

The first toggle switch on the control unit was labeled *Voltage*. Flipping it up, the LED above the switch glowed green, while the other two LEDs glowed red. According to the instructions, this indicated the device had come up to the correct voltage to deliver the necessary current to set off the blasting caps.

He toggled the switch off.

The burner phone had come with the device, and Anzorov secured it between the aluminum brackets, then plugged the TRS end of the wire into the audio jack. He toggled the Voltage switch again, and the three LEDs on the control unit went to green-red-red. Then, he toggled the switch labeled *Phone*, and the LEDs went to green-green-red. This meant the voltage was up and the phone was recognized. The third switch in the row was labeled *Arm*. When he flipped it up, there was a three-second delay before all three LEDs went green.

According to the instructions, when he called the burner phone and the connection was made, all three lights would start to flash.

Anzorov flipped off the three switches in reverse order and powered off the phone.

If everything went as planned, tomorrow morning at exactly 9:45 a.m., he would park the truck in front of SVR headquarters, walk three blocks to his getaway car, and wait for Ivanovich's limousine to arrive. He would then enter the six-digit code on the phone's key pad, receive a tone, press and hold the Pound and Star buttons simultaneously, then witness years of Russian treachery go up in a massive fireball. If everything *didn't* go as planned…there was always the fourth switch.

. . .

Immediately inside the tree line at the edge of the farm, Agent Alfonse Millwood and Agent Kevin Stricker of the CIA's Moscow station were watching the barn. When Millwood saw Malik Anzorov open the barn's doors and drive the truck inside, he nudged Stricker awake.

"He's moving," Millwood said.

Stricker rubbed his eyes to clear them before looking through the binoculars. When Anzorov closed the barn doors, Stricker leaned back against his tree, lowered his binoculars, then said, "Do *you* want to call Truscott or should I?"

"And tell her what? The guy moved the truck into the barn? Let's keep watching. He came home early for a reason."

Three hours later, Anzorov had yet to emerge from the barn. And Millwood sent Stricker back to the car in search of dinner. The relief team wouldn't arrive until eight p.m., and if this current level of excitement remained constant, they'd have a long night ahead of them.

CHAPTER 53

Quebec City, Canada
Monday, April 1, 1996
8:12 a.m.

When his watch alarm went off, Liam slowly opened his eyes.

Last night, he and Woody had arrived at the hotel late with the only plus being he hadn't had time to fall deep enough into sleep for Lilliana to invade his dreams. For the last three years, the specter of the little girl had her own alarm clock—and it went off routinely three hours into his slumber.

After starting the coffee maker with a complimentary pouch of Maxwell House, he opened the drapes and stepped onto the balcony. A cold breeze off the St. Lawrence Seaway found its way up his borrowed shorts. *That's better*, he thought, then leaned against the stone-capped railing and took in the view.

Opened in 1893 and situated on the highest knoll in Quebec City, the historic Château Frontenac hotel watched over the ships sailing up the seaway toward Lake Ontario. Across the river and through the mist lay the city of Levis. And beyond that—Maine. The view was amazing, but Liam had no doubt the plush hotel suite had been chosen as enticement—or, a bribe—to keep him from killing Ginny later.

Once again, Ginny had lied to them all. In war, shit happened sometimes. But while hostile fire was part of war and friendly fire was unavoidable, what Ginny had done to Araseli was neither. It was murder. Even worse, it was betrayal. And betrayal had a price that must be paid.

How Woody would handle it going forward was something Liam was dying to find out.

Through the open French doors, the coffee maker gurgled.

He went back inside, showered, slipped back into his jeans and the navy-blue sweatshirt Woody had given him, picked up the mug of coffee, then went downstairs in search of the business center. He found it around the corner from the elevators.

Through the glass, he saw that a single guest was already sitting behind a computer screen. After swiping his card and walking inside, Liam chose the adjacent machine to prevent the woman, and anyone passing by, from viewing his screen.

After logging into the Hotmail account of ReggyD5150, and finding he had received no new emails—not even an ad—he logged off and stared at his reflection in the monitor and wondered for the first time if Stephan knew his grandmother was dead.

Surely, Stephan had tried to call her a few times by now. At least Araseli had left her cell phone at the Lake, preventing the CDG from gaining access to her contacts and call history. If they ever found Stephan—they'd kill him too.

After exiting the Hotmail account, he found the aquatic center down the hall. When he found the pool empty, he swiped his room card and stepped inside.

The water in the Olympic-size pool was like glass, and Liam took his coffee to the far end and stood by the hot tub inside the bay window overlooking the St. Lawrence. After digging his cell phone from his jeans pocket, he held it to the glass, checked the bars, then made the call. It took several rings before a groggy male voice answered.

"*Hola.* Who the hell is this?"

"It's Liam, Stephan. Sorry to wake you." He paused in thought as candor—his greatest skill, according to Woody—threatened to take over as he imagined the unsuspecting college student sitting up in bed unaware his class schedule was about to be interrupted by very bad news. And what could he say to start the conversation? *How's Calculus class? Do you like your professors? Getting laid?* Mercifully, the decision was made for him.

"I can't reach Nanna," Stephan said. "Have you talked to her?"

"No, I haven't," Liam said. "Look, Stephan—I have— Your grandmother has been—" Then he stopped himself and changed words. "She's dead."

There was no response.

"I don't have a lot of details yet," Liam lied but swallowed it back with some coffee. He paused for a beat, then said, "But I think—"

"BICA has killed her!" Stephan blurted out.

"*BICA?*" Liam exclaimed. "Why would you say that?"

"Nanna told me they would."

"When did she—?"

"Two days ago. Saturday. At James Madison University. The same day she gave me the key."

"A key to what?"

"She would not tell me. Only that I was to give it to you."

What Liam needed for Stephan to do right now wouldn't happen if the man knew the whole truth. So, he said, "Stephan, your grandmother was murdered by the CDG, and it must have been right after you met with her. I need you to get to the Lake and wait for me. You'll be safe there."

Maybe, he thought.

"I guess maybe tonight I can come," Stephan said.

"No. You need to leave now," Liam said. "And don't stop on the way. Not even to piss."

"Okay," Stephan said. "When will—?"

"Just go! I'll be a couple of days behind you. When you get there, ask for Bailey. Tell her you spoke to me, but don't tell anyone about the key."

Liam clicked off the call, then left the aquatic center for the elevators, where he jabbed at the buttons until a set of doors finally opened, and he leapt on ahead of an elderly couple getting off. The man muttered something rude in French as the doors closed.

Liam didn't know what Araseli had found that was important enough for Ginny to have her murdered, but the answer might be in Stephan's hands. And though what he had just asked of Stephan might expose him to the CDG, if he could make the journey to the Lake—without getting killed—he'd be far better off than sitting in a Virginia Tech dorm room only thirty minutes from where his grandmother's body and head had been found.

When the elevator doors parted, Liam flipped open his phone again and dialed.

"Good morning," Woody answered.

"What time are we meeting PJ's guys?" Liam said as he jogged down the hallway. He reached his room and swiped his card, slamming the door once he was inside.

"In an hour. Why? What's going on?"

"Where's Pinard now?"

"On the east side somewhere. The CIA team has him under surveillance. Has something happened?"

"I'll be in the lobby in thirty minutes. Be ready."

CHAPTER 54

Kalopigado, Greece
Monday, April 1, 1996
3:18 p.m.

Bryant parked the rented Ford Explorer close to the edge of the bluff on the north side of the cove. After opening the rear hatch and sitting cross-legged in the cargo area, he removed the binoculars from the case, then focused the lenses until he could clearly see Primo Ruqur's mansion atop the cliffs on the south side of the cove.

For the first time in days, he turned on his cell phone and pager and waited for the inevitable call.

It was cramped in the cargo area, but the shade relieved the glare from his binoculars. It also had the benefit of shielding his actions from the curious driving by—much like a sniper would keep the barrel of a rifle from protruding through the window.

After biting into the wrapped sandwich he'd purchased at a café, he chased it with bottled water and watched the mansion's guards meander around the grounds for close to an hour before the whooping sound of a helicopter beat against the silence. It landed on a section of the cliff jutting out from the mansion where a helipad had been constructed.

Finally, he thought as he watched the chopper settle. A beat later, two men jogged from the mansion beneath the turning blades with their heads low and their hands firmly planted on caps. They boarded the chopper, slid the side door closed ,and were soon airborne and heading toward the yacht anchored in the bay a half mile off the inlet's coast. After landing on the pad at the rear of the yacht, the same two men left the chopper and disappeared inside *Gretchen's Emerald*.

Not Primo Ruqur and not Delgado.

Where are you guys? Bryant thought.

A moment later, one of the yacht's side hatches at the waterline opened to reveal the tender boat storage of the lower deck: a garage-like area where smaller utility boats were stowed. Off to the side, a crewman operated a set of buttons at the end of a cable.

Inside, a landing craft was hoisted forward, then lowered into the sea. Once the two-man crew boarded, its engine came to life and it chugged across the cove toward the shore, where a large white van was parked.

Ignoring the dock, the landing craft opted for the beach, where its bow-ramp was lowered and the crew was able to step directly onto the sand like a two-man marine unit.

Turning his attention back to his sandwich and the mansion, Bryant finished his last bite at the same time as a cream-colored Bentley Azure convertible pulled up to the gate. The driver's window lowered, and a long, thin arm delivered a knowing wave to the guard, who immediately let it pass.

"One down," Bryant whispered as he focused to get a clearer view of Delgado's face disappearing behind the tinted glass of the rising window. A twelve-foot-high stone wall surrounded the cliff-top mansion, but from this high vantage point, Bryant could see Delgado pull into the center spot of the five-car garage.

As the door was going down, Bryant's burner phone buzzed in his pocket. *That didn't take long,* he thought as he eyed the display, swallowed the bite of sandwich, then answered the call.

"Yeah," he said curtly, pressing the phone to one ear while holding the binoculars up with the other hand.

"Where are you?" Ginny's anxious voice asked.

"You know damn well where I am. News flash. Delgado just pulled in."

"I have some disturbing news. Liam and Primo met in Brussels. Primo survived," Ginny said. "And—he helped Liam get inside the penthouse."

Closing his eyes, Bryant let a long breath out and adjusted the binoculars to watch two guards cut a path outside the perimeter wall, confirming the shifts were staggered in regular intervals. Habits and schedules were the worst enemy of security.

Ginny added, "You know what this means? Liam no longer suspects that Primo is Eagle."

"I get it," Bryant said as he shifted the binoculars toward the yacht. "What about the old woman?"

"Araseli is out of the picture. She did gain access to the bank account of Richmond Automotive Distributors, but that's as far she got."

"Are you sure?" Bryant asked as he stared through the binoculars.

"Yes. But there *is* one other thing."

"I'm listening." On the beach below, the two men had returned to the landing craft with a cart and what appeared to be an engine manifold.

That'll take some time.

"The Russians are threatening to cancel the nuclear summit, citing security concerns. What we are hearing from our back channels is they have uncovered a plot to assassinate a high-ranking official in their government. They think it's us."

Bryant lowered the binoculars and stretched out his legs. "That's rich. They're the ones working with Pinard to assassinate our president and are trying to put it back on us. It's another red herring."

"Perhaps. But they're standing by their ruse. The Russians had canceled a military exercise ahead of the summit. It's back on now. NATO is responding in kind."

"Where's Liam?" Bryant asked.

"In Quebec City with Patricia."

"Pinard is from Quebec City," Bryant said. "Why would he take Patricia on an op?"

"I can't answer that."

"Just keep him away from Kalopigado. Is that understood?"

"I'll do my best, but as long as Stephanie is still missing—well, you know your son."

He did, and Ginny was right. Nothing would stand in Liam's way until he found his oldest friend—which wasn't going to happen anytime soon.

Raising the binoculars and finding the beach again, he saw the two men had finished loading the manifold and were now carrying cardboard boxes toward the landing craft.

"I'm going dark again," Bryant said. "See you when it's over." He clicked off the call.

Drawing in a frustrated breath, Bryant watched the landing craft battle the chop as it made its way back to the yacht. Once its cargo was unloaded and the craft was hoisted inside the tender storage area, he swung the binoculars back to the mansion, where the middle garage door was swinging up and the Bentley was backing out.

Where are you going now, Delgado? Can't drive to the yacht.

After the Bentley had cleared the gate and had taken a left down the hill, Bryant stowed the binoculars, closed the Explorer's rear hatch, and sat behind the wheel, contemplating his next move.

Delgado leaving didn't change anything. He had wanted Delgado and Primo to be in the same place at the same time so he could get them both. But Primo was the real prize, and taking out Delgado first might alert Primo. Better to have Delgado go underground than a pissed-off billionaire with unlimited resources.

CHAPTER 55

Quebec City, Canada
Same Day
9:20 a.m.

He waited in front of the hotel until Woody pulled up. As he slid into the passenger seat of the leased Taurus, Liam dropped a plain white paper bag onto the console.

"What's in the bag?" Woody asked as she pushed the gearshift into Drive.

"Donuts I lifted from the breakfast bar."

"A rich guy like you steals donuts?"

"I slept about two hours, took a dump, drank a shitty cup of coffee, and now I'm wearing about fifty dollars, including my sneakers. Does that scream rich to you?"

"Paul's sweatshirt was forty dollars by itself."

"I stole it. Doesn't count."

Liam gripped the dash as Woody took a hard right out of the hotel, then navigated the swirling streets down the hill, past the Citadelle de Québec, before catching the A-440 north.

"Can I ask where we are going?"

"Rue des Sables," she replied. "Pinard lives in a high-rise overlooking the confluence of the St. Charles and St. Lawrence."

"I thought the guy was homeless and living out of a box."

"He *was*," Woody said. "I spoke with Agent Dabler this morning. He told me Pinard moved into a new place right before he took off to Ankara. Cash deposit and—"

From the console, Woody's cell phone chimed. She flipped it open with her lips, then pressed it to her ear. After several seconds of nodding and uh-huh-ing, she said, "We'll meet you there." After flipping the phone closed, she pulled back into traffic, signaled, then swung a U-turn through the median. "That was Dabler. Pinard just got a call from a guy who said that he had the rest of his money and wanted to meet in Levis."

"Levis is on the other side of the St. Lawrence," Liam said. "Did Dabler give you a name?"

"Only that Pinard called the man *Breckon*? He said the guy sounded like a character from *Oliver Twist*."

Liam chuckled. "That's Cockney, from the East End of London. Breckon is a Welsh surname and—" But then his grin faded and his heart began to race as reality sunk in. "We need to move! How far back are the CIA boys?"

"I don't know. A couple of minutes. Why?" Woody asked as she took the exit to cross the Pont de Quebec.

"Because neither of us has a gun."

"So?"

"This isn't a payoff. It's a hit." His eyes drifted to the rearview mirror and the top of his duffle bag poking above the seat. "Damn! We should have gone to my place first."

"What makes you so sure it's a hit?"

"Trust me. I met Breckon in Belfast."

. . .

After crossing the St. Lawrence to the Rue Jogue, Woody followed it about ten miles to the farming town of Levis, where she pulled into to a McDonald's cohabitating with a gas station and parked at the pump. That's when her phone rang again.

"Woodburn," she answered, then listened. "What's he driving?"
Pause.
"Okay. And what are you guys in?"
Pause.
"Got it," she said, then clicked off. "The CIA boys are in a

charcoal Camry. Pinard is driving a beat-up green Astro van."

"Should be easy enough to spot," Liam said.

"Except they aren't coming here," Woody said, squealing the tires as she pulled away from the pumps and onto the street, turning back in the direction they had come. "Dabler said the van turned north instead of crossing the bridge and now they're on Route 138 heading toward Beaupre."

"I know it," Liam said. "That puts us about thirty minutes behind *them*."

They crossed the St. Lawrence River again.

Woody ran two lights getting to Route 138, the main highway through Quebec City that followed the river on the northwest side. Fifteen minutes later, they passed the first sign for the Sainte-Anne-de-Beaupré basilica. By the time they saw the magnificent tourist draw on the left, Woody's phone rang again. This time, Liam answered it.

"It's Curran. Give me a sitrep." He waved for Woody to pull into the basilica's parking lot.

Dabler said, "Pinard made it to Beaupre, but he turned around and is heading back toward Quebec City. How far did you get?"

"The basilica. You guys need to back off. They must be on their cell phones and Breckon is sending Pinard in circles, checking for a tail. That means Breckon is following him. Hopefully he hasn't made you guys. When Pinard passes the basilica, we'll pick him up and you can hang back."

"Roger that," Dabler said, and the line went quiet for several beats, then, "Okay, he's coming up on you now. Old green Chevy van."

Liam turned his attention back to Route 138 and caught the Astro van speeding by. He pointed, but Woody was already pulling out. By the time she got up to speed, the van was ten cars ahead.

"We have him," Liam said into the phone. Jabbing his finger at the windshield, he said to Woody, "See if you can get a couple of cars closer."

Woody did, then settled back into the flow of traffic. Pinard switched lanes a few times, but she didn't bite on it. "He's definitely paranoid," she said.

They followed Pinard back to Quebec City, where he turned north onto Route 73 toward Tewkesbury, where he doubled back again, only, this time, he swung north onto Rue Jacques-Cartiers, following the river of the same name. As they passed by a rafting company on the opposite bank, Liam checked his mirror and noticed a blue Bronco had caught up to them, and was trying to pass.

"Let him by," Liam said.

He felt Woody ease up on the gas and then caught a glimpse of the driver's silhouette in the mirror. Definitely a man and definitely uncertain about passing. Then, the car's left blinker flashed, and Liam caught a glimpse of the driver in profile as the Bronco blew by.

The man was on the phone, probably with Pinard, and he immediately recognized the man's face from outside White's Tavern in Belfast, the night he had kicked his ass. It was also the last night he and Stephanie had spent together. He should have killed the bastard then and saved them all a lot of time and trouble.

Liam went back to the cell phone. "You still there?"

Dabler replied, "Still with you."

"Good. Breckon is in the blue Bronco."

"And he just passed Pinard's van," Woody said, pointing through the windshield.

Liam nodded, then went back to the phone. "The Bronco's leading the van. He's probably looking for a place to pull off."

"Okay. When they do, we can drive by and—"

"No time for that," Liam said. "Breckon's going to kill Pinard, and we need them both alive. Stay behind us and follow my lead. You're armed, right?"

"Sidearms. But in case you got turned around, this is Canada, not the US. We don't have the authority to just nab two Canadian citizens."

"I have news for *you*," Liam fired back. "One, you don't have the authority to do it in the States either, but you do anyway. Second, Breckon isn't Canadian. You take him and let me deal with Pinard."

Ahead, the van's right blinker came on.

Liam said, "They're turning. When they pull off, slow down to a crawl, then ride the shoulder."

Woody tapped the brakes, then eased the Taurus to the right, dropping two wheels off the pavement. Ahead, the Bronco and Astro van pulled into a wide spot and disappeared, blocked by a thin row of trees.

"What are we doing?"

"Giving them a little space," Liam said.

The wide spot was a half-assed rest stop with a couple of rotted picnic tables on the edge of a forest. As they approached the wide spot and the Bronco and Astro van came into view through a cloud of settling dust, he found both had pulled up to two cut logs seven spots apart.

"Stop here," Liam said. "And when I tell you to, I want you to drive into the back of the van."

"You want me to *what*? This is a rental."

"Just give it a real good jolt," he said as the CIA boys stopped behind them.

In the clearing, Breckon got out of the Bronco and started toward the van.

Checking his mirror, Liam saw the agent in the passenger seat of the Camry, shrugging. Turning back to the wide spot, the van's back-up lights flashed, then extinguished along with the brake lights. Pinard stayed in the van.

Turning to Woody, Liam said to her and the phone, "Now!"

There was a moment of hesitation before Woody drew in a

breath, and then the sedan lunged forward. The last two wheels left the pavement with a bounce as the bumper bit into the gravel.

Liam knew Pinard, who was still in the van, would have no idea what was happening. But Breckon would. He was half way to the van when he whipped around to face them, an O of surprise on his lips. Liam could make out a heavy bulge in the thigh pocket of the man's camouflage shorts.

As Breckon reversed course and sprinted back toward the Bronco, his hand fumbled in the pocket as Woody's arms stiffened against the wheel and her face turned away from the windshield. It was then that he realized she was going way too fast.

Rather than bracing, Liam threw himself between Woody and the steering wheel, gripping the door handle for a breath before the sedan slammed into the back of the van, sending it forward over the cut log and into a tree. The impact drove Woody's face into Liam's side, and he lost his wind at the same time that the airbags deployed, scorching him through the sweatshirt as the car filled with smoke.

After crawling back into his seat, he slammed the gearshift into Park. To their left, he heard the Camry skid to a stop in the gravel. It was followed by muffled excited voices.

The impact with Pinard's van had shoved the right fender of the Taurus into the passenger door, and Liam had to press it open with his feet. Leaping over the hood of the Taurus, he pressed himself against the driver's side of the van and waited. When the van's driver door burst open and a pair of sneakers swung out, Liam gripped both of them and yanked so hard that Pinard landed in the gravel on his ass, causing the pistol he was holding to bounce toward the front bumper.

Ignoring Pinard, Liam stepped around the open door toward the pistol. Pinard had the same idea and tried scrambling beneath the door. Crawling through the dust and gravel, his arms stretched desperately toward the pistol that Liam now had beneath his sneaker. The other foot came down hard on Pinard's outstretched hand.

Pinard snatched his hand back in pain as Liam knelt down, picked up the dime-store revolver, then pocketed it. Woody had eased around the van and was eyeing Liam while he dragged Pinard by the collar toward the front of the van and away from the prying eyes of passing drivers.

Kneeling down, he put a knee between Pinard's shoulder blades and started patting him down. Then, he looked up at Woody, who was approaching slowly.

"You okay?"

She nodded.

"Car still running?"

She looked, then nodded again.

"Good. Park it so it doesn't look like we were in an accident." She started to walk away, but he stopped her. "Do you see the CIA boys anywhere?"

Her neck craned toward the Bronco, and she nodded. "Yes. They have Breckon."

Woody was able to pull the sedan away from the van and park near the tree line. Surprisingly, the damage wasn't as bad as she had thought. The bumper and the right fender had seen better days, though.

Checking beneath the car, she found nothing leaking, so she started back to the front of the van, where Liam had Pinard sitting against a tree. Moments later, the two CIA boys arrived, each with a hand on one of Breckon's shoulders.

The blond agent with the crew cut said, "I'm Dabler, by the way. This is Agent Yancy." He tossed Liam a set of flex-cuffs.

"I'm Curran and this is Woody. Sorry we had to be introduced this way, but I'm all about a good meet-cute." Liam yanked Pinard's hands behind his back, then zipped on the cuffs. "We can't do this here. Let's get them deeper into the woods."

Dabler instructed Yancy to move the Camry and the Bronco to less conspicuous spots, then shoved Breckon forward and deeper into the forest. Liam and Woody followed close behind with Pinard in tow. Once they were deep enough, and they couldn't see the highway, they sat the two men down, back to back, against a tree.

Liam made a show of pulling the revolver from his pocket as he looked directly into Breckon's now terrified face. The man shook his head, closed his eyes, and lowered his chin.

"You remember me, don't you?" Liam said as he squatted, his knee pressing into Breckon's ankle, causing the man to wince. "Remember what you promised me in Belfast?"

Breckon said nothing.

"You lied, didn't you?"

Breckon nodded weakly right before Liam slammed an open palm into the man's forehead, sending it back against the tree. Liam looked up as Yancy returned. "Got anymore flex-cuffs? And a knife?"

CHAPTER 56

Yancy went back to the Camry and returned a minute later with more flex-cuffs and a folding Buck knife. Liam instructed both agents to watch Pinard and Breckon while he cut the flex-cuffs from their wrists and installed new ones; only, this time, he cuffed Pinard's left wrist with Breckon's right, and Breckon's left to Pinards right so they were hugging the tree—back to back. He passed the revolver to Woody, then went to the other side of the tree and squatted down Indian style on Breckon's outstretched shins.

"Bloody hell, man!" Breckon cursed. "Gonna give me another kickin', are you?"

Laughing, Liam turned and looked up at Dabler and Yancy and said, "You were right. *Oliver Twist*." But then he turned back to Breckon and used his full motion to drive an elbow into Breckon's jaw. A bone popped and, behind him, one of the agents grunted.

"Liam!" Woody said, taking a step toward him. "What—?"

Liam stopped her with a raised finger, his eyes never leaving Breckon, who was now working his jaw left and right and groaning. Then, he leaned forward and delivered a slap to the right ear of Pinard on the other side of the tree. The man screamed.

"You paying attention back there?" Liam said. Turning his focus back to Breckon, he waited for the man's eyes to clear. "What happened to Stephanie Maguire?"

"Who?" Pinard asked from the other side of the tree.

"I wasn't talking to you," Liam said as he plucked at the growing knot near Breckon's ear. The man winced, and when Liam dug his thumb into the man's shoulder joint, he howled.

"Wow!" Liam said. "I know it hurts, but you're bucking for an Oscar." Reaching out, he gripped Breckon's shirt, ripped it open, and found a large section of gauze held by several strips of white surgical tape. When Liam dug his thumb directly into the wound, a tear streaked down the man's cheek.

"This isn't going to be your day," Liam said. "One more time. And honestly—for the last time—where is Stephanie Maguire?"

"We flew her to Athens," Breckon choked out.

"By way of Moscow?" Liam added.

"It's what we were told to do."

"By whom? Delgado?"

"Who the fuck is Delgado?" Breckon asked.

"My bad," Liam said. "I mean, Gustov Mikos. But for our purposes, let's just call him Delgado. You listening back there?" Liam called out.

Woody glanced down at Pinard and then nodded.

"How much did Breckon owe you, Pinard?" Liam called out. His question was met with silence.

Liam pressed Breckon's head against the tree. Then, reaching down, he felt for a set of ten fingers where Breckon's and Pinard's hands were cuffed together. After gripping one finger, he bent it back until he heard a pop. It was Breckon who screamed.

"Ooooh. Did you hear that crunch?" Liam asked. "I have nineteen more to go." He nodded at Woody again.

"How much, Mr. Pinard?" she asked.

"A quarter of a million," Pinard said.

"Wow!" Liam exclaimed, then focused on Breckon, who was now sobbing openly. "How much was the down payment?"

"Fifty," Pinard yelled back.

Liam pursed his lips as the first crack in the story emerged. "I see. So, Breckon here was meeting you to deliver the last two hundred grand?"

"Yeah."

"But you haven't killed anyone yet."

"I wasn't hired to kill anyone," Pinard said.

"Shut up, you fuckin' arse!" Breckon said.

"Fuck you!" Pinard fired back. "I was hired to *plan* two shots in Moscow. One near the Kremlin and one near SVR headquarters. Then I was instructed to fly to Paris for a day and Washington for a day. That's all. It would cost a hell of a lot more than two hundred thousand dollars for me to kill the American president."

Woody said, "I don't get it. You were ordered to plan it, but not to execute? Why? Is there another shooter?"

"I don't know and didn't ask," Pinard said. "I needed the money, so I did it. Seemed like an easy way to earn a quarter mil."

Liam reached around the tree and flicked Pinard's ear. "You need to come clean. Breckon wasn't sent to pay you. He was sent to kill you."

"That's a fuckin' whopper," Breckon said.

"Really?" Liam said. As he stood up, Breckon retracted his legs to his chest. Stepping around to the other side of the tree, Liam's eyes met Pinard's. Liam then waved for Dabler to join them. When Dabler arrived and looked down at Pinard, Liam asked, "How much money did you find in the Bronco?"

"Two hundred euros and twenty dollars Canadian," Dabler said. "And change."

Liam knelt down and pinched Pinard's cheeks. "Maybe Breckon has two hundred grand stuffed in the pockets of his shorts. What do you think? C'mon, Jasper. You were a member of Task Force 2. Stupid wasn't one of their prerequisites."

Pinard studied Liam's face until their eyes finally locked. "Where did you serve?"

"He was a SEAL," Woody responded.

The crusted blood at the corner of Pinard's lip cracked when he grinned and corrected her. "*Is* a SEAL." He turned back to Liam. "I was in Bosnia."

"I know. I also know how you got your limp. A Serb got you with an AK round when you were changing positions. A marine sniper unit was covering your move, but you still got bit. You should also know the same marine snipers picked off six Serb fighters that day." When he saw doubt on Pinard's face, he added, "I hear you weren't discharged because of your limp. They wanted to make you an instructor. So, what happened?"

Jasper swallowed hard. "The gunshots. I couldn't take them. I could hear them in my sleep and woke up screaming every night. You have no idea what that's like."

"Actually, I do," Liam said. "Only, I don't hear gunshots."

Pinard continued. "They put me on prazosin, but it made me puke, and lithium made my…" He paused then shot an embarrassed glance at Woody. "It stopped working. So, I accepted a discharge and a monthly stipend."

"Why would this Delgado guy do this?" Agent Yancy asked.

"Revenge," Liam said. "But Pinard is only a small part of a bigger plan. We just don't know what that is."

Pinard scratched an itch on his left cheek, then said, "I'll tell you everything. Nobody uses me and gets—"

He stopped in midsentence and brought his palm up to his face. His eyes locked onto his hand and his fingers as if he'd never seen them before. Liam saw it too, and that meant only one thing: Pinard's left hand was no longer cuffed to Breckon's right.

From behind the tree, there was a scuffle, and Agent Yancy went down into the leaves. Rolling clear, he came up on his feet as his hands felt around his belt buckle. Something was missing, and that's when the shot rang out and tree bark exploded over Yancy's left shoulder, sending him diving.

Breckon had Yancy's gun.

Liam's first thought went to Pinard's revolver, but Woody had tucked it into her front pocket and the bulge was still there. Regardless, he shoved her away before wheeling around the tree where Pinard's right hand was still cuffed to Breckon's left and was being yanked upward.

Dabler was sprinting away, his pistol drawn as he put a tree between him and Breckon.

With the pistol he had swiped from Yancy in his free right hand, Breckon had some choices. He could send another shot at the tree Yancy was hiding behind or swing the pistol to the left and try to pick off the armed Dabler. Better yet, he could swing farther to the left, around the tree, and take out Pinard or the two Americans.

Using the tree as cover, Liam rounded it on the right as Breckon was getting to his feet, yanking Pinard's arm up in the process. Breckon was panning his gun hand toward Dabler. Woody had recovered from Liam's shove and had also gone right, her hand digging in her front pocket for the revolver.

Rounding the tree on Breckon's blind side, Liam sprang forward and gripped the wrist of Breckon's gun hand. Letting his momentum and gravity do the rest, Liam kept a tight grip on Breckon's wrist with two hands as he spun completely around in the air, twisting Breckon's arm like a wet towel. He felt the man's arm and shoulder splinter like a piece of firewood. The semiautomatic pistol fired once, and the bullet caught a nearby tree.

Liam hit the ground with Breckon's limp wrist still in his grasp. But with Breckon's left wrist tied to Pinard's right, his motion stopped abruptly as Pinard was yanked hard against the tree.

Breckon screamed in agony as his now useless hand dropped the pistol, and Dabler sprinted to snatch it up.

After regaining his footing, Liam stepped toward Breckon just as Woody leveled the revolver on him. Liam sent a knee into Breckon's gut while Pinard tried hopelessly to scramble away.

Gripping Breckon by both cheeks, he screamed, *"Who killed Stephanie Maguire?"*

"I—I don't know! Ahhhggg!" Breckon yelled as Pinard tugged against his good hand.

"Was it Carmichael?"

"I don't know," Breckon insisted. "We took a helicopter to the top of a fuckin' building. We locked her in a room and left the key with a couple of homos living there." Then his eyes drifted to the bandages on his shoulder. "She stabbed me with a fuckin' tire iron."

Liam let a grin spread across his face. "Good for her."

"She was alive when we left Athens and—"

Liam didn't wait for him to finish his sentence.

Shifting his weight, he spun around with Breckon's neck in the crook of his arm. At first, it appeared as if he would try to flip Breckon over his shoulder—an impossibility with Pinard still cuffed to his arm. But then Liam dropped to one knee and twisted hard, there was a muffled snap, and when Breckon went limp, Liam let him drop to the ground.

"Oh fuck!" Pinard exclaimed, turning away.

"What did you do?" Dabler asked as he knelt down and put two fingers to Breckon's neck.

Behind the tree, Woody vomited.

Liam brushed leaves from his clothes. "We have some cleanup to do before we get Pinard back to the States."

"He's a Canadian citizen, for shit's sake. You can't just—"

"I'll go," Pinard said, interrupting Dabler.

"See? He's being a good sport," Liam said.

"What about the dead Brit?" Dabler asked, his chest heaving with anger.

Liam ignored him as he knelt by Woody. "Are you okay?"

"I'm fine," she said, wiping her lips with her sleeve. Then, she smiled. "I didn't get to thank you for what you did in the car and—"

"You're the boss. Employee evals are coming up." Liam winked, then went to the dead Breckon and gripped him beneath the armpits and lifted. His eyes then shifted to Dabler. "You going to help or what?"

Dabler tucked the pistol away and helped hoist the dead man across Liam's shoulders before following him deeper into the woods, where they crossed a dry creek bed at the base of some low cliffs, where Liam let the body fall. When Liam looked up the face of the cliff, Dabler only shook his head and walked away.

When they reached the clearing, Woody was already behind the wheel of the Taurus with the cuffed Pinard in the back. Yancy was closing Woody's door, and Dabler was heading toward their Camry, when Liam put his arm around Yancy's shoulder.

"Hey! Dabler," he called out.

Dabler stopped, spun around, then came back; his eyes burned with fire.

Liam said, "The Bronco will stay here. The driver is probably rock climbing or something." He paused for a smart-ass remark from Dabler, but when one didn't come, he said, "Yancy, you're driving Pinard's van to the Maine border, where you'll leave it by the side of the road near a farm on the Canadian side. Take the keys with you when Dabler picks you up. We'll catch you back at Langley—or wherever."

After reaching the Taurus, Liam yanked Pinard from the back and told him to take the front passenger seat. He then ordered him to hold the door closed while Woody drove. Liam took the back seat but kept his right hand on Pinard's shoulder.

They rode in silence for several miles until Woody broke it. "You didn't have to kill him."

"Kill who?" Liam said coldly.

Woody shook her head, glanced at Pinard, then caught Liam's eyes in the mirror. "How are we going to explain Breckon?"

"We're not," Liam said as he squeezed Pinard's shoulder. "Right?"

"Don't worry," Pinard said. "It won't come from me." His gaze turned toward the shattered passenger window and he added, "But there's something I need to tell you both. Something bigger than a fake assassination."

"Such as…" Liam prodded.

Pinard smiled. "When we are on the plane, I will tell you."

CHAPTER 57

Vnukovo International Airport
Moscow, Russia
Tuesday, April 2, 1996
8:35 a.m.

The Cessna Citation touched down, then taxied toward a hanger controlled by the SVR.

Delgado had chartered the jet certain that Primo—if the man was working *with* Liam Curran—was now monitoring the whereabouts of the Hermes corporate jets. And he was so close to success now, he couldn't take the risk of having his plan upended by his billionaire boss.

Through the oval window, he could see the limo inside the hangar, and the two men in boxy suits waiting for him. Given the uncertain tone of their last conversation, Delgado knew Ivanovich had something more planned than to bring him into the folds of the SVR. Something had happened.

But, in about an hour, none of it would matter.

By the time Delgado descended the airstairs to touch the concrete, the ground crew was already transferring his bags to the limo. As he crossed the apron, one of the suits opened the limo's rear door, and Jurg Ivanovich's face peered out.

Ivanovich was sitting in the rear-facing seat, and he greeted Primo with a smile and a sweep of his hand, offering him a clear path inside. When he was inside, and had settled across from Ivanovich, the man picked up the bottle of Louis XIII Cognac from the bar. Ivanovich poured them both two fingers, neat, passed one glass to Delgado, then offered up a toast.

A guard slammed the rear door.

"To the coming end of a fourteen-year quest, Mr. Delgado," Ivanovich said. "Soon—with your help—there will be justice for Leonid Brezhnev."

And revenge for me, Delgado thought as he sipped the expensive brandy. He said, "I delight in your—vindication."

"Of course," Ivanovich said as he studied Delgado over the rim of his glass.

"Something on your mind, Jurg?" Delgado asked as his eyes drifted to his watch. Anzorov was no doubt on his way to SVR headquarters by now.

Ivanovich sipped again, then said, "The Canadian assassin—Jasper Pinard. We have photographs of him at the Atli Hotel in Ankara. The same day I was there. He then flew to Moscow and stayed at the Kempinski."

Delgado said nothing.

"Bryant Curran was staying at the Kempinski at the same time. Only, he registered as Wilbur Lee. So, we know Pinard is working with the Americans."

"You seem surprised," Delgado said.

"Not at all," Ivanovich said. "But I am surprised that you were also at the Atli Hotel, and the Kempinski, those same days. Only you registered under the name Gustov Mikos. My people tell me this is not a coincidence."

"Do you believe I am working with the Americans?" The confusion on Delgado's face was genuine, but when Ivanovich pulled the pistol from behind his back, all doubt was removed.

. . .

Outside Moscow, Russia
8:40 a.m.

Agents Millwood and Stricker had relieved their counterparts forty minutes prior and were settling into another boring day of watching nothing happen at the farm when Anzorov opened the barn doors and eased the refrigerated truck into the clearing. After closing the barn doors, he climbed in and drove the truck toward the main gate.

"He's moving," Millwood said, peering through the binoculars.

"Running a little earlier than usual," Stricker added, firing up the Ford Taurus as Millwood stowed the binoculars and buckled in.

Following the dirt road for a quarter of a mile, Stricker paused long enough to watch Anzorov and the truck go by on the main road before pulling out to follow.

After a couple of miles, the truck veered to the right on the M2 heading north, and Millwood commented, "Looks like he's skipping the warehouse this morning and heading into Moscow. Give Truscott a call and let her know."

. . .

Quebec City, Canada
1:45 a.m.

Gazing through the window, Liam watched the runway lights fade to black as the BICA jet climbed, then banked south. Sitting across the aisle from him, and diagonal from Woody, Pinard was staring at his own reflection in the glass.

The attendant lowered the cabin lights, delivered three hot towels, refilled Liam's empty glass with fresh ice and Scotch, then returned to her station near the front. She was cute, Liam thought. And reminded him of someone from his past he had tried desperately to forget. When he turned toward Woody, he caught her grinning as she wiped her face and hands, then tossed the towel onto a vacant seat.

"What?" Liam asked.

Woody held up her empty glass and said, "You're so clueless."

Swiveling his chair toward Pinard, Liam cleared his throat to get the man's attention, then said, "Okay. We're on the plane, Jasper. What's the big secret you couldn't tell us on the ground?"

Pinard spun to face him. "The fifty grand I was given wasn't a down payment for planning an assassination. It was full payment for delivering a detonator box."

"There's a bomb?" Woody blurted out. "Where?"

Pinard's gaze shifted between the two Americans before he said, "Somewhere in Moscow. A big one, I think."

"How big?" Woody asked.

"Hard to say. The specs called for four sets of twelve-position bus bars. That's forty-eight possible blasting caps."

"That's why Anzorov went to your room at the Kempinski: to pick up the device and pay you so Delgado could keep his exposure to a minimum," Liam said.

"I've never met with this Delgado person. Everything was done through Breckon. But when Anzorov paid me, it was in rolls of new fifty-dollar bills."

When Woody turned to Liam, he said, "Call PJ. Now!"

"And do what? Talk to him in Navajo? You know these airphones aren't secure."

"We're way past that now, don't you think?"

She studied his eyes for a beat, then, reaching for the console beneath the window, she pulled out the handset and started dialing.

Liam turned back to Pinard. "Tell me about the detonator box."

"It's sweet," Pinard said, his chest inflating. "All you need is a cell phone with an audio output jack and you can detonate it from anywhere."

"So—what? You call it and it blows up?" Liam asked.

"Give me a little credit. It can be remotely detonated, but it must be armed locally. Once the call connects, there's a six-digit code to enter. Then, you have to press the Star and Pound buttons at the same time, and—it's foolproof."

"If you're relying on the Russian cell phone system, you're up against a whole other set of oh-shits."

Pinard grinned. "That's why I installed a martyr switch."

Liam washed his hands over his face. "Shit! Who else has the phone number and the code?"

"Anzorov, the man you call Delgado"—Pinard paused when Woody turned his way—"and me."

"Dammit!"Woody said as she stabbed at the buttons on the phone.

"What now?" Liam asked.

"I had PJ long enough to tell him about the bomb, but then the call dropped. I warned Ginny about these phones and—" Woody stopped in midsentence as her lips melted to a frown. "I'll keep trying."

Pinard said, "What was it you were saying about the Moscow cell system?"

. . .

Moscow, Russia
8:46 a.m.

Bouncing in the seat, Anzorov divided his attention between the road and strapping the detonator box in the passenger seat. He still had two kilometers to go before reaching the first outer belt around Moscow, and traffic was starting to get heavy. SVR headquarters was another thirty kilometers.

He should be a few minutes early, just as he had planned.

Being late or on time for his normal delivery would mean he'd be ushered into the rear of the building, immediately putting the bomb into a less-than-perfect position to take down the building. Plus, the guards would search the vehicle first. Arriving early was much better. It meant the SVR guard would make him wait in front of the building until the kitchen was ready to receive him. The bomb would be in the perfect position.

Structurally, the front of the headquarters building was optimal for the blast to take out the main vertical support columns. Personnel-wise, the explosion was timed for when most of the SVR's workforce would already be inside. Politically, he'd wait to set off the device as Ivanovich's limo arrived. By then, he'd be two blocks from SVR headquarters, on the second floor of a parking garage, sitting in a car he had parked there two days earlier. From there, he would call the device, enter the code, then watch Ivanovich and hundreds of SVR scum—vaporize.

Anzorov reached over, powered up the burner phone mounted to the control unit, and flipped the first toggle switch up. The LED above it turned green.

And he smiled.

. . .

Over Lake Ontario, Canada
1:55 a.m.

"It's PJ," Woody said, pointing at the handset. "Where are they now?" she asked, listened, then relayed, "PJ's men are between the south outer belts of Moscow. Anzorov is in front of them."

Liam turned to Pinard. "Where do you *think* they're heading?"

Pinard shrugged. "It could be anywhere."

Woody cupped the phone and said, "News flash. PJ's team assigned to Ivanovich spotted Delgado getting into Ivanovich's limo at Vnukovo International."

Liam stood while combing fingers through his hair. What did all this mean? *A Chechen bomber on his way to Moscow and Delgado in a limo with Ivanovich.* He glanced toward Pinard, then thought, *And I have the sniper with me?* Then, it all became clear.

Turning to Woody, he said, "Delgado's been playing us, alright. But not how we thought."

"Hang on," Woody said, cupping the phone as she turned to Liam. "What are you talking about?"

"Delgado never intended to turn me and my father over to the Russians, just like Pinard was never supposed to shoot anyone. He only wanted us to be seen. *By both sides!*"

"But why?" Woody asked.

"To create two false narratives. Both Russia and the US believe the other is setting up a political assassination, when Delgado's real plan is to explode a bomb and make it look like the US actually went through with it."

"Who's the target?" Woody asked.

"If you wanted to stop the Russians from finding out if Brezhnev was actually murdered, who would you take out?"

"Ivanovich," Woody said. "But Delgado's with him in the limo. He's not going to blow himself up. Are you saying someone's been playing Delgado too?"

It was a good question. But not one that needed to be answered at this second. He said, "If the bomb's as big as Pinard suggests, the truck is probably filled with ANFO. No better place to hide that kind of stuff than a farm in Russia. I'm thinking Oklahoma City."

"Don't," Pinard said. "The basic ingredients for ANFO, ammonium nitrate and diesel, are easy to come by, but it can't be set off with blasting caps alone. It needs a booster. The Oklahoma City bomb was thirteen barrels of ANFO. But they used nitromethane instead of diesel and Tovex as a booster. The nitromethane would be impossible to get, but the Tovex—it's possible. Think Canary Wharf instead of Oklahoma City."

"Okay—so now I'm thinking Estonians," Liam said. "How many possible blasting caps did you say?"

Pinard's eyes grew wide. "Forty-eight."

"We have to stop that truck," Liam said. "The Russians will have no choice but to believe the United States used a Chechen separatist to kill Ivanovich, possibly taking hundreds of Russians with him." Then he turned and stared at Pinard. "And *we* used a Canadian bomb expert to deliver the detonator device."

Woody un-cupped the phone. "PJ? We need your agents to—"
She stopped and her face went white. "PJ? Are you—? Dammit!
I lost him again."

. . .

Vnukovo International Airport, Moscow, Russia
9:06 a.m.
"You're being paranoid, Jurg." Delgado squirmed in his seat,
and at the same time, he gripped the cell phone in his pocket. "The
Kempinski is the most popular hotel in Moscow. Where else would
Pinard and Bryan Curran meet? And what would have happened
if I registered as Franco Delgado in Moscow? Your people would
have arrested me. I always stay in the Kempinski as Gustov Mikos."

Lowering the glass divider between them and the driver, Ivanovich said, "You can go now." The car eased forward, and Ivanovich
raised the divider.

"Then perhaps you can explain the man who visited the
adjoining room to yours before visiting Pinard's room. Is that,
too, a coincidence?"

Delgado brought his hand to his lap and opened the flip phone
nonchalantly as if checking for text messages. What his eyes
focused on was the two Speed Dial buttons and the time on the
display. Given the traffic, they should arrive at the SVR complex
as Anzorov was parking the truck.

The Chechen would have enough time to arm the device, but
not enough time to get away before Delgado could call and tie
up the line. Anzorov would not be able to dial in himself, giving
Delgado enough time to detonate the bomb while he and Ivanovich
were still shielded by the other buildings.

The world would soon believe the Americans had leveled the
main SVR headquarters building and had timed the explosion
to coincide with the arrival of Jurg Ivanovich. It would be a near
miss. But because Delgado was in the limo with Ivanovich, any

suspicions of his involvement would vanish along with the truck bomb and Anzorov.

"Tell me this," Delgado said. "Did Bryant Curran also meet with the CIA?"

Ivanovich pursed his lips.

"Then it proves the CIA is leading this conspiracy. Not me."

"We'll see. My staff will have more questions for you at headquarters."

Delgado said, "You are making a big mistake."

. . .

After the third try without any luck, Woody put the phone to her cheek and gazed at Liam and Pinard, her head shaking. "What can we do?"

Liam turned to Pinard. "Can you access the detonator box with your phone?"

"As long as the signal holds."

"Can you disarm it from here?"

"No."

"What if we tie up the line?" Liam asked.

Pinard considered it, then said, "The martyr switch overrides everything. And, someone near the device could simply drop the call and—"

"Hold on," Woody said as the phone chimed. She eyed the display, then sent a questioning glance to the others. "Hello?" She listened briefly and then her face lit up. "It's an Agent Millwood. He says they're following Anzorov."

"Have them stop the truck," Liam said.

Woody started to speak into the phone, but Pinard stopped her.

"Remember Anzorov is not only a Chechen separatist, he's

also a militant Muslim. A militant Muslim with a truck bomb."

Liam said, "Ask them where they are."

Woody did and relayed back, "They're between the A-108 and the A-107 outer belts. There should be a good cell signal there."

As long as ours holds up, Liam thought, then said, "Have them stop the truck. I don't care how they do it. We're going to try to tie up the device."

. . .

Anzorov saw the Ford Tempo in the mirror. It had sped up and pulled in behind him.

He thought nothing of it at first. And then when it passed him, he thought even less. The passenger, a Caucasian man of about thirty in a gray suit, only raised a finger to wave as they went by. But then, when the Tempo signaled and pulled in front of him and began to slow down, he noticed the diplomatic tag.

Something had gone wrong.

Reaching for the detonator box, Anzorov flipped up the second toggle switch, causing the second LED to glow green. Then, he reached inside the glove box for the pistol. After cranking the window down to get a clear shot…the Tempo slammed on its brakes.

Anzorov stood on the truck's brakes, smoking all ten tires as his arm stretched out to prevent the detonator from sliding off the seat. The weight of the truck was one thing, but the extra tonnage from the drums of ANFO and the saturated hay bales was another. There was nothing he could do to prevent the truck from slamming into the back of the Tempo. Somewhere behind him, cars screeched and metal crunched and Anzorov's forehead hit the steering wheel.

Shaking it off, he fished for his personal cell phone on the floorboard and stuffed it into his shirt pocket. He found the pistol and gripped it in his left hand as he stuck it out the window and fired, shattering the rear window of the Tempo as it limped forward.

Flinging the door open and standing on the running board, he used the open door as a shield and fired two more rounds at the Tempo. Traffic on both sides of the highway came to a crashing stop.

Ahead, he could see the interchange for A-107, the thirty-kilometer mark from his target. But now, he'd lost his window to arrive early. Immediately beyond the interchange was the first set of skyscrapers. At this point, a dead Russian was a dead Russian.

. . .

Over Buffalo, New York
2:29 a.m.

"Millwood says they stopped the truck, but I heard a gunshot!" Woody said.

She listened again.

"He says Anzorov is shooting at them."

Liam bolted toward the front of the plane, past the nervous attendant, who was strapped into the jump seat, then opened the door to the cockpit. Both the pilot and co-pilot spun around, wide-eyed with surprise.

"I need you to circle a city. And stay low—in cell tower range."

"The closest is Buffalo," the pilot said. "I'll have to clear it with—"

"No, you won't. Just do it."

"I'll try," the pilot said.

Liam flipped open his cell phone and watched the bars on the screen. There were two.

"Want me to land?" the pilot called back over his shoulder.

"If you can."

Leaving the cockpit door open, Liam sprinted into the cabin and stopped short of where Pinard was sitting. The man was already scrolling through his phone's contact list. He stopped on the one he had named *La Malbaie*, then said, "Ready?"

"Dial it!" Liam demanded.

"I don't have a signal! I'm on a Canadian—"

Liam opened his own phone. "Then read me the fucking numbers!"

. . .

Two Kilometers from SVR Headquarters
Moscow, Russia
9:42 a.m.

Ivanovich had relaxed his posture and now had the pistol resting in his lap beneath tapping fingers. Still, the two men hadn't spoken since turning onto the A-130 heading north.

Delgado could have cared less.

Their driver had taken the exit for the Moscow inner belt, and that was a good marker for Delgado to connect to the detonator box.

He felt the limo veer to the right and saw signs for Ulitsa Pavla Fitina. Delgado knew he was less than a kilometer away from the SVR complex.

"I need to check this text," he said, then flipped open the phone and pressed Speed Dial #1. When he saw the display change and the call timer start, he knew he had connected.

He pressed Speed Dial #2, sending the six-digit code. Then, he waited until the limo had taken the last turn toward SVR headquarters before holding down the Star and the Pound buttons.

. . .

Over Buffalo, New York
2:43 a.m.

"Fuck! It's busy," Liam said.

He pressed End, then hit Redial.

Busy.

"Someone's already dialed in." He turned to Woody. "Tell Millwood to get as far away from that truck as they can. Now."

Woody relayed the message, then looked back at Liam. "He says their car is wrecked but he'll try. I still hear gunshots. And car horns. And a siren."

. . .

Moscow, Russia
9:44 a.m.

Anzorov fired another round at the Tempo as one of the men dove into the front of the car from the passenger side and lay across the seat.

What could he possibly be doing?

Then, when the car started limping forward, he knew exactly what he had done. The man had put the vehicle into neutral, and the other man was pulling it forward.

Perfect, he thought. Now, he could drive around the car and detonate the device as soon as he crossed into the Moscow Oblast. It wasn't SVR headquarters, but he'd still kill a lot of Russians.

Anzorov climbed back into the cab, tried the ignition, but the truck wouldn't turn over.

He tried again.

And again.

Finally, it started. But the motor sounded sick, and the sweet smell of white smoke poured from the hood.

On both sides of the highway, cars were stopped in a heaping jam. People were outside, straining to see what was happening. And ahead, the two men tugging on the Tempo had made it only twenty meters. Time to make the most of his situation.

Leaping back inside the cab, Anzorov eyed the detonator box. He had already thrown the first two toggle switches up, and they had both turned green. The last toggle switch, the one that would arm the box, he hadn't yet thrown. But that hadn't stopped the two green LEDs from flashing. That could only mean one thing.

Someone had dialed into the box and was connected.

It had to be Gustov Mikos. He must be trying to detonate the device himself.

"The hell with you!" Anzorov screamed as he reached across the seat and disconnected the call before starting the sequence again. This time, he flipped up all three toggle switches, flipped open his cell phone, then pressed the preprogrammed Speed Dial button. When he saw that all three LEDs were flashing green, he knew he was connected—and armed.

After dropping the gearshift into Drive, he felt the truck lurch before slowly starting forward. The front left fender was cutting into the tire as the sounds of a medieval sword fight scratched from beneath the hood. The truck might make the interchange and overtake the Tempo at the same time.

Pressing the second Speed Dial button, he sent the six-digit code to the device.

Across the highway, hundreds of drivers were straggling toward the action, curious to see. Killing them wasn't as good as killing Russian SVR, but they would have to do.

Anzorov stomped on the accelerator until the truck caught up with the Tempo, clipped its rear bumper, and sent the smaller vehicle spinning away, throwing the two infidels onto the shoulder.

The interchange was only seconds away now.

Gripping the cell phone and feeling for the key pad, Anzorov turned toward the open window and screamed at the agents and the onlookers on the other side of the highway. He screamed at the Tempo in the mirror as one of the infidels raised up to shoot.

"I win!" Anzorov screamed, then fired a random shot out the window toward the crowd. Then, realizing the truck had limped into the shadow of the overpass, he dropped the pistol and gripped the cell phone in both hands—one thumb on the

Star and the other thumb on the Pound.

Then, as the truck's transmission gave up, he rolled out of the cab to the concrete, came up to his knees, and screamed "Allahu Akbar!" as he pressed the Pound and Star buttons.

. . .

Delgado pressed and held the Star and Pound buttons, then flinched, anticipating the explosion that should follow. He couldn't help it. He was about to level the main SVR building and still be close enough to rock the limo's world with a blast bigger than the one in America's Oklahoma City.

But there was nothing.

He tried the two buttons again.

Nothing.

The limo took the turn and started down the street in front of the main building of the SVR complex. It was still there. When he looked down at his phone, he saw the connection had been broken. And when he looked up, there was no delivery truck.

That little bastard! Delgado thought.

"Something the matter, Mr. Delgado?" Ivanovich asked.

. . .

"I got it!" Pinard said, shaking his cell phone.

"Great! Now what?" Woody asked.

Liam turned to her. "What's going on in Moscow?"

She went back to the phone. "Millwood. What's happening?"

She listened, then said, "Anzorov smashed through their car. The truck is smoking, but it's still moving toward the interchange. He's waving his gun out the window and screaming nonsense and—wait." Woody paused to listen, then said, "Millwood says they're about a quarter of a klick from the A-107 ramp."

Liam turned back to Pinard. "Enter the code."

Pinard pressed the six digits.

Woody looked up at Liam and asked, "What are you doing?"

"I know that interchange. On the north side, there's a large number of skyscrapers. I think he's trying to get there."

"Yeah. And?" Woody asked.

Liam turned to Pinard. "Give me the phone."

Pinard did.

Liam let his fingers hover over the Star and Pound buttons as the flight attendant jogged down the aisle and gripped a seatback as the plane started to bank.

"We can't get clearance and were ordered to stop circling," she announced.

"I'll lose the signal," Liam said.

Woody closed her eyes, nodded, then pressed the phone against her ear.

Liam drew in a breath—then pressed the Pound and Star buttons.

Two seconds later, Woody dropped the plane's phone, and it fell to the floor, bobbing by its curly cord. Her hands went to her mouth before she buried her face in them and whispered, "Oh God!"

CHAPTER 58

Over Buffalo, New York
Tuesday, April 2, 1996
2:55 a.m.

No one spoke. Only the hum of the jet's engines offered any reassurance that another reality existed.

Pinard's gaze had returned to the window and his own reflection. Woody had retrieved the phone but had yet to speak. Liam had flipped Pinard's cell phone closed and was sitting on the edge of the vacant seat, across from Woody.

The flight attendant took a step back and studied her three passengers curiously. "Did I do something wrong?" she asked, breaking the silence but not the pressure. Her words drew the attention of the others, and she retreated another step.

"You didn't do anything," Liam said softly and forced a smile. "Can you give us a minute?"

"Sure," she said before sauntering up the aisle and into the cockpit, where she slammed the door closed.

"Woody," Liam said to the back of her head. Her face was still buried in her palms, and a section of phone cord had caught around a pinkie. "Patricia," he said again, and this time, she turned enough to let one eye appear.

"What?" She sniffed.

"Call PJ."

After an imperceptible nod, she dialed, listened, then shook her head.

"Keep trying," Liam said.

After several minutes, she finally pressed the phone to her ear, but Liam held out his hand as he shifted to the seat facing her. She hesitated before passing the phone to him, stretching the cord to its limit. Liam could already hear a tinny male voice in the speaker.

"PJ. It's Liam Curran." He swallowed back some uncertainty, then added, "We lost the connection with Millwood."

Sanchez said, "That's because the truck exploded on the M2. It's already on CNN."

"Millwood and Stricker?"

"Householder can't reach them and—" Sanchez paused for several beats, then said, "CNN is showing a smoldering crater in the middle of the M-2 northbound."

"North or south of the interchange?"

"South—it appears. Why?"

Liam pinched his eyes shut and said, "We think the truck was heading to SVR headquarters. Your agents may have stopped a war."

"You mean, *postponed* one," Sanchez said. "You know how this is going to play out. Just yesterday, Chechen Prime Minister Zavgaev praised Yeltsin's peace plan for the two countries. Now, because of the evidence Delgado has manufactured, we'll be accused of using a pissed-off Chechen in a failed attempt to assassinate Ivanovich."

"You're probably right," Liam relented.

"My other agents followed the limo as long as they could, but it turned into the SVR complex. Delgado was still with Ivanovich."

In the background, Liam heard a phone ringing and the squeak of a desk chair before the phone was put on mute. Sanchez came back seconds later and said, "The president is requesting a meeting with entire National Security Council."

"Don't give Delgado what he wants," Liam said. But then, he glanced across the aisle at the window-gazing Canadian. "Have you spoken with your agents in Quebec City yet?"

"No. Why?"

"Delgado sent a man named Breckon to kill Pinard. Breckon was not successful," Liam said, then gave Sanchez the rundown on Quebec.

"So, you were right," Sanchez said. "I guess none of that matters now. Delgado can say anything he wants at this point."

"Maybe. But we know something he doesn't. His man is dead, and Pinard is still alive—and we have him."

"He's on the plane?"

"Yup."

"Of his own volition?"

"Yup again," Liam said. "Pinard is the key to undoing what Delgado has done. He's the common thread between us and the Russians. You need to get a meeting with Ivanovich."

"Are you suggesting the director of the CIA call the director of the SVR—a man who believes we are trying to kill him—and ask for a meeting? Even in friendlier times, that would be a diplomatic chore. Those meetings are highly secretive and well-orchestrated. Time. Place. Security."

"Ever try to schedule one to stop a war?"

"Not yet," Sanchez admitted. "I gotta go to the White House. See you when you land."

Liam dropped the call and returned the phone to Woody. She placed it back in its cradle, then eyed him curiously. "Now what?"

Liam said, "Tell the pilot to take us to Bart's. Have Bailey call ahead to wake him up, then meet us there. We'll need a ride from his place to the Lake."

"What's at the Lake?"

"Not what—who!"

CHAPTER 59

Warrenton, VA
Tuesday, April 2, 1996
5:15 a.m.

Bart—as Liam had called him—was Bartholomew Blackwell, a retired software magnate who owned a large plantation-style home surrounded by a hundred acres north of Warrenton, Virginia, with a mile of paved runway. Better yet, farmer Bart was once Brigadier General Blackwell, United States Army Special Forces—retired.

Perched on a golf cart near the fuel pump, the old general's shirt was open, revealing a bare chest, a leathery tan, and puffs of white hair. Below the waist, he wore cutoff sweatpants and sandals. Frosty breath mixed with the smoke from his cigarillo leaked from his nose and mouth in equal measure as he watched the BICA jet taxi to the front of the open-air hangar attached to his garage.

As the airstairs extended, Liam appeared and stood at the top. Beyond the cyclone fence, a Ford Bronco flashed its headlights, and he raised a reassuring palm toward Bailey. Then, when he found Bart on the golf cart, he flashed a middle finger.

Bart returned the gesture.

Woody and Pinard followed Liam down the airstairs. At the bottom, they went right toward the Bronco while Liam approached the golf cart. The scowl on Bart's face melted around the cigarillo.

"Eat something sour, General?" Liam asked as he delivered a walking salute.

"Had a couple of SEALs for breakfast." He then eyed the jet. "You know, my boys jump while the plane's still in the air."

"SEALs do too. We use parachutes, though."

Bart chuckled. "Bunch of pussies."

The two men had a good chuckle before exchanging a back-slapping embrace.

His history with General Blackwell went back ten years to Eglin Air Force Base in Florida when Bart was in command of the army's 7th Special Forces Group in support of operations in Central America. It was Bart who had introduced Liam to Bill Shipman. And, Shipman who introduced Liam to Honduras and the Contras.

When Woody approached with Pinard in tow, Liam started to introduce her, but Bart interrupted him and extended a hand.

"Thought you retired?" Bart said.

"Resigned," Woody said, shaking the older man's rough hand. "You must be Bart."

"No one else wants to be," he quipped.

"Ms. Woodburn's my new boss," Liam added.

Bart let his eyes scan her from head to sneaker and back before settling his gaze on Pinard. "What are you, her stunt double?"

"This is Jasper," Liam explained. "He'll be staying at the Lake for a few days."

"Mm-hmm. Nice to meet you—Jasper." Bart stuck out his hand, and Jasper shook it, receiving a viselike grip as the general examined the Canadian's two taped fingers and the thin marks around his wrists left by the flex-cuffs.

When Bart let go of Pinard's hand and eyed Liam, Woody said, "Bailey's waiting. Be quick."

Liam nodded and watched as Woody and Pinard met with the flight crew before starting toward Bailey's Bronco. Bart had been watching her too.

"She's got fire. And an ass. Are you sure she's only your boss?"

"Positive," Liam said.

"Then you're dumber than I remember." Bart studied Liam for a beat, then said, "Heard on the Chicken Noodle Network someone's been doin' some blastin' in Moscow. Any of that your fault?"

"Maybe," Liam said as he glanced around. Lowering his voice, he asked, "Do you remember the old Mexican woman Michaels brought through here last fall?"

"Sure do. Why?"

"The CDG caught up with her in Roanoke and—"

"Saw something in the paper about that," Bart interrupted. "That was the same woman?"

Lian nodded. "Any chance you've seen some suspicious Mexicans hanging around?"

"Can't say that I have," Bart said as he studied Liam. "Are they on your to-do list now?"

Liam only nodded and Bart didn't press.

"I keep a tank full of Jet A on hand for you guys. Your nickel, of course."

"Got enough for two?" Liam asked. When he saw the question on Bart's forehead appear, he said, "Do you think you could reach out to Michaels and have him meet me here?"

"Probably," Bart said.

"Today?"

"A taller order, but I'll check. Don't know if I like having *two* fuckin' SEALs here." Bart's gaze then focused over Liam's shoulder. "Here comes trouble."

Liam turned and found Woody jogging his way, her finger wagging him forward. Bart slapped Liam's shoulder before pulling away in the golf cart. Liam met Woody a half dozen steps later.

"I called a cab for the flight crew," Woody said before looking left, then right. "Curtis picked up your father's PagSat and phone. He was in Kalopigado right before he went dark again."

Liam said, "I can't be here. I need to stop reach him before he does something that can't be undone."

Woody shook her head. "We have other things to do. PJ called.

He made contact with Ivanovich."

"That's great," Liam said with little conviction. "I have a big surprise for you at the Lake."

"Bigger than a meeting with Jurg Ivanovich?"

"Possibly."

CHAPTER 60

The Lake
6:20 a.m.

s soon as they arrived at the Lake, Woody assigned a guard to mind Pinard while Liam went to the bungalow Bailey had assigned to their guest. When he opened the door, Liam found him sitting on the edge of a freshly made bed with an open can of Sprite.

When Liam closed the door and Stephan looked up, he saw something he had witnessed many times before in the eyes of interrogated Iraqi and Taliban prisoners—total defeat.

Over the years, the CDG had murdered Stephan's father, his mother, and now his grandmother. What little fight and understanding of the world the one-time coyote had was gone.

Liam said, "Juan Lopez sent Carlos Fuentez to kill Araseli. And I'm going to burn them both."

"Remember when you first brought us here?" Stephan asked, his voice breaking. "You promised we'd be safe. That we would have better lives. The CDG could never find us."

They didn't find you, Liam thought. *You were betrayed.* Then he said, "Now's not the time. C'mon. Let's go inside and get started."

He led Stephan from the bungalow into the main house to the room of whiteboards filled with colored lines and boxes titled *ARASELI'S WEB*.

After everyone assembled, Woody cut the chitchat short. She introduced Pinard, then quickly bid him farewell, sending him and his guard away to one of the bungalows. Now, it was only the five of them. Liam, Bailey, Babbs, Woody, and Stephan, all sitting in folding chairs around a whitewashed wooden table, staring at each other.

Babbs still hadn't acknowledged Liam.

Looking at Stephan, Liam asked, "Where is it?"

While the others shifted in uncertainty, Stephan dug into his jeans pocket, then slammed his palm on the table. "Nanna said to only give this to Liam. It was her last wish." After several beats, he raised his palm and Liam picked up the tiny key.

Holding it up to the light, Liam examined it. It was brass and about an inch long. One end was embedded in a cylindrical piece of plastic with the number *20* embossed in black on the edge.

"You've got to be kidding," Babbs said as she dug into her own pocket, produced a ring of keys, then held up one nearly identical. "It's to my locker at the bowling alley. There must be a million of these around DC."

"Did Araseli say anything else?" Bailey asked Stephan.

He shook his head.

Woody turned to Stephan and asked, "When did Araseli give you the key?"

Stephan checked the ceiling in thought, then said, "Last Saturday. We met in the arboretum at James Madison University."

"What time?"

"About three o'clock."

Woody said, "I think I know where the locker is."

Bailey said, "You're thinking about the GPS tracker Araseli smashed and left at the Fair Oaks Mall."

Woody nodded.

Liam said, "I'll be damned! By smashing the tracker, she established her own dead drop."

"There are lockers in the hallway behind the Toys "R" Us next to the restrooms," Bailey said. "Jesus! I've been by there twice this week."

Woody stood up and gripped Liam by the hand, pulling him up with her. "C'mon. We're going shopping."

. . .

The Fair Oaks Mall sat on the western border of the city of Reston, Virginia, making it a thirty-mile drive from the Lake but a forty-five-minute drive this time of the morning. When they arrived, Liam made a comment about the bare parking area and the age of the shoppers.

Woody chuckled and said, "You don't get out much, do you? The stores don't open until ten o'clock, but the mall doors open early so the elderly *mall walkers* can get their exercise."

After parking near the JCPenney, Woody led Liam to a side door that opened up to a narrow service hallway that exited across from the Toys "R" Us. After dodging a few walkers, they managed to cross to the opposite service hallway marked by three overhead signs: *RESTROOMS. LOCKERS. EXIT.*

On the left side of the service hallway, a six-by-ten array of lockers had been mounted along the wall. They found Locker #20 at the end of the second row down, close to the women's restroom. It was one of only two lockers in the array with a missing key.

Woody was two steps ahead of Liam and had the key in her hand ready to insert it when she stopped.

"Something wrong?" Liam asked.

Woody glanced at him and said, "You're sure she liked you?"

Liam chuckled. "Just open the damn thing."

Woody inserted the key, turned it, then pulled the door open. Reaching inside the space, her hand came back with a legal-size manila envelope. She let the spring close the door as she ripped open the envelope and took out a three-and-a-half-inch blue floppy disk with *Sony* etched on the shutter. The label was blank.

Liam chuckled and shook his head. "C'mon. It's time for Babbs to earn her money."

CHAPTER 61

The Lake
8:40 a.m.

Bailey was waiting for them on the porch.

"Any luck?" she called out.

Woody chirped the lock on the Suburban, then held up the disk as she and Liam approached the stairs.

"Let's see what treasure Araseli left for us," Woody said.

"You mean, what she left for Liam," Bailey corrected.

Woody stopped on the porch and caught Bailey's gaze. There was no doubt where her allegiance lay, and she wondered if Bailey's devotion to Liam was truly sibling-like, or was there something more?

"Sure," Woody said as she passed the disk to Bailey.

They followed Bailey inside and up the stairs to where the bedrooms of the old plantation house had been converted into offices. They found Babbs in the one at the end of the hallway behind a computer screen. Stephan was seated in a corner chair and stood when he saw them.

Babbs said, "I guess you found something."

"We'll see," Bailey said, then passed the disk to Babbs.

Babbs went to work. First, she ran a program that checked for hidden executable files—viruses—before opening up the file directory. Then, after a chuckle, she pointed at the screen. "It's just one big unprotected Visio file." A few clicks later, she had the massive flowchart open on the big screen above her credenza.

"Holy hell!" Babbs said. "When did Araseli have time to do all this? It looks like she recreated the whole damn web. But this looks bigger than the one on the wall downstairs." She enlarged an area of the web on the monitor, then said, "This section is information from your project. I recognize the bank names. This box labeled *RAD* is probably Richmond Automotive Distributors. But there's more info here than what was in her emails to you—ReggyD."

Liam let the quip go by and took in the screen and the massive web while Babbs and Bailey followed colored lines to colored boxes to bullet points. In true form, Araseli had outdone herself.

"What was Nanna doing?" Stephan asked, staring in wonder at the web on the screen.

"Helping me locate a man and—" He caught himself in midsentence to glance at Stephan, then to Woody, then said, "But someone found him first."

"So, she died for nothing?" Stephan asked.

"I don't think so," Babbs said, pointing at the screen. "There's a ton of new financial activity linked to RAD not in the emails. This is very curious. The middle box is clearly a bank in New York, and the line to the right ties to Richmond Automotive. But the line to the left goes to an empty box that's referred to in a footnote."

Grabbing her mouse, Babbs highlighted the area and magnified the initials *HBC*. She said, "Money was transferred between their two bank accounts at the same New York bank. Who the hell is HBC? And why would Araseli keep this out of the emails?"

"Because she found out she was being watched," Woody said through gritted teeth.

When he heard the initials, Liam's heart had leapt into his throat. Surely, what he was thinking couldn't be true. "Tell me about the transactions."

Checking the web again, Babbs said, "As best I can tell, starting in early '93, HBC received regular transfers from Richmond Automotive Distributors. It started out at a million per month but increased over time. She even posted the invoice numbers issued by HBC to RAD, matching the payments. And then there's this." Babbs traced the screen to another footnote. "I don't believe it."

"What?" Woody asked.

"Richmond Automotive is owned by a subsidiary of the Carmichael Group. And the RAD account in the New York bank was closed after the last transfer to HBC was made."

"When was that?" Liam asked.

"This past September," Babbs said.

"Right after you took out Sheik Tariq Al-Jabori," Woody said as she ran her finger along the footnotes until she found the first payment between RAD and HBC.

February 1, 1993. One million dollars. Invoice *01251993-48756*.

Then, her head spun to Liam so fast a muscle popped. "Do you have any idea what this is?"

Liam took a step back. He felt as if he'd been gut-kicked.

How could I have been so stupid for so long?

After years of navigating a foggy road through the shambles of the life he had been dealt, it was if a breeze had blown away the mist, and the path behind him was clear, while the path forward was now filled with barbed wire and IEDs.

And it led straight to hell.

Looking up at Stephan, Liam said, "Don't go back to Virginia Tech. Have Babbs get you a new name and go somewhere else. The CDG is still looking for you."

"I don't understand," Stephan said.

"Just listen!" Liam said. "Araseli and I setup a numbered account in a Belize bank. You are the sole beneficiary. It's a little over three million dollars. I'll get you the information later."

"Liam? What's happening?" Bailey asked, her eyes pleading with his.

"You're giving me a ride back to Bart's." He drew in a breath, then looked back at Woody. He noticed a subtle shake of her head delivering a clear request. He heard it. Processed it. Then walked out of Babb's office.

Liam was almost to Bailey's Bronco when he heard the porch door slam behind him.

"Wait!" Woody called from the stairs. She caught up to him beneath the willow and let her hand reach out and touch his palm. "Where are you going?"

"I have some non-BICA business to attend to."

"I don't under—"

"Let me make it clearer. Fuck off!"

"You fuck off! We have a meeting setup with Ivanovich and—"

Liam jabbed a finger in her face "*You* and PJ are on your own! I'm out. Your mother started this shit, and now you can fix it. Welcome aboard."

"Dammit!" Woody belted out as she hammered his shoulder with her fist. "I don't deserve this. We're a team here, Liam."

"A *team*?" he pressed through gritted teeth. "We can't turn our backs on each other without getting butt-fucked. And your mother is queen of the dildo brigade. She's racking up more bodies than my team did in Iraq. The difference is this—in Iraq, I killed the enemy. She's feeding off her own."

"I don't— I'm not letting you go after my mother."

He let a grin spread across his face. "Keep on thinking you have a choice."

They glared at each other until Liam broke off and climbed into the rear seat, slamming the door. Woody slid into the passenger seat, and they breathed in each other's anger.

"And you're not using the BICA jet."

Liam said nothing.

"This isn't going to fix what Ginny did. She'll still be here when we get back. The Russians believe the bomb was ours and—"

"Well—I did set it off," Liam interrupted. "You and PJ can wriggle on the hook of that fact. Hey! Here's an idea. Why don't you get Ginny to help you?"

Instead of responding, Woody drew in a long breath. His words had hurt her deeply, but she knew him well enough now to know she wasn't his target; his aim was simply bad.

Bailey finally arrived, climbed inside, glanced at Liam's face in the mirror, started the Bronco, threw it into reverse, then hammered the accelerator. After Liam's and Woody's heads settled back against their headrests, the cabin fell into a forced silence.

After several beats, Woody said, "We've come a long way together—even before we were friends. I got fucked back then the same as you. We can deal with Ginny after we meet with Ivanovich. Isn't that clearly more important?"

"I'm out, Woody!" Liam said.

"Out of what?"

"BICA. ICEBRG. Whatever the shit this is."

"You're fucking impossible!" she barked.

They rode in silence while Bailey broke a half dozen traffic laws on the way to Bart's. When they pulled into Bart's driveway, Liam jumped out of the Bronco, and so did Woody. She caught him by the arm before he could walk away.

Woody said, "I think you're right. Maybe it's probably best that you not come to Moscow."

"Moscow?" Liam said, shaking his head. "PJ agreed to meet in the bear's cave?"

"You don't get a say in the matter," Woody said, refusing to look at him now.

The garage door started up. Bart ducked under and stepped onto the driveway—waiting for them.

Woody said, "Soooo, you're just going to hang out with Bart?"

"Not your concern."

Behind them, the door slammed as Bailey climbed out of the Bronco.

"You can't win this fight!" Woody said.

"I agree. I lost a long time ago. I just didn't know it until today."

Liam turned away from Woody, retrieved his duffle from the trunk, then started toward the open garage, but Bailey stopped him at the front of the Bronco. Tears streaked her cheeks.

Wrapping her up in a hug, he whispered into the top of her head, "Stop it. This isn't about you."

"I know," she said, pulling away from him and wiping her face with her sleeve.

"Then why are you crying?"

"Because—" Reaching out, she sandwiched his cheeks with her palms and whispered, "HBC. I figured it out." After reading the disappointment on his face, she said, "I won't tell her, if that's what you want."

"Thank you," Liam replied.

"You don't have to do this."

"Yeah, I do," Liam said. "My whole life, nothing has ever been up to me. But this is my choice."

He kissed her on the cheek, then turned and walked to where Bart was tapping his watch and shaking his head.

"Woman problems?" Bart asked.

"Sort of," Liam replied. "Did you reach Michaels?"

"He's about an hour out. I was hopin' that maybe you cooled off and changed your mind about going after the CDG."

"As usual, you're half right," Liam said.

CHAPTER 62

Moscow, Russia
Wednesday, April 3, 1996
8:16 p.m.

They had taken the CIA's Gulfstream C-20 to Moscow. The delegation—consisting of PJ Sanchez, two protective agents, Woody, and Pinard—deplaned inside the hangar and ducked into the waiting black Mercedes sedan. PJ had requested the car through Householder, who had assigned Willow Truscott to play guide, and they arrived at the Radisson overlooking the Moskva River and the Russian Federation Government House (aka Russia's White House) ten minutes later.

After freshening up and crossing the hall to PJ's suite, Woody stopped outside his room before knocking and powered up her pager for the first time that day. No messages. She closed her eyes, then simply pocketed the device before delivering a knock. The chances that Liam had changed his mind were nil. Still, the seed had been firmly planted.

She was let inside by one of the two PAs. In the living room, PJ handed her a bourbon with ice, and she joined Pinard and Truscott in the sitting area. The deaths of agents Millwood and Stricker came up once, but Truscott put an end to the subject by raising a hand to stop the conversation before using it to swipe a tear.

Thank God, Woody thought. She was almost forced to break out her prefabricated denial of any knowledge as to how the bomb actually went off.

Once Sanchez had dismissed the two PAs from the room, she wetted her lips and said, "I have something I want to run by you."

Sanchez leaned back on the sofa and propped his feet up on the table. "Does it differ from what we discussed on the plane?"

"It augments it," Woody said. "Ivanovich will no doubt blindside you by having Delgado there."

Turning to Pinard, Sanchez said, "And I'll be blindsiding them by having him." Then, he turned back to Woody. "They're not expecting you."

"I'm counting on it. Because Delgado isn't either. And he's aware I know him as Gjon Rockman. This should be good."

Reaching into her purse, Woody removed a burner phone and held it up.

"What's that?" Sanchez asked.

"Breckon's old phone. My team at the Lake unlocked it."

Sanchez grinned, then said, "Of course. Tragic climbing accident. How does the phone help us?"

"In two ways. Delgado doesn't know Pinard's still alive, and he doesn't know Breckon's dead."

"And that's good because…?"

Woody said, "If we can get Delgado away from Ivanovich, I have something in mind."

She spent the next several minutes explaining her idea. After a few adjustments by Sanchez and agreement by Pinard and Truscott, the plan was set.

"We all need to get some sleep," Sanchez said as he stood. "Our meeting is at ten o'clock tomorrow morning." Then, he turned to Truscott and asked, "How far is it to the home of this—criminal?"

"Oligarch," Truscott said with a chuckle. "Andrei Listin is a very pleasant and likeable man. Just don't tell him more than he needs to know. I'm sure he'll be in the meeting too. It's his fee for the use of his home. Knowledge is power. I'll meet you at the side exit at nine o'clock sharp. Remember to dress down."

"See you then," Sanchez said, then showed Truscott out while the PAs escorted Pinard to the suite next door. After they were alone, he turned to Woody. "I like your idea, but I hope we don't need it. But if we do, let's hope the Russians fall for it."

"Falling for it isn't the issue," Woody said. "I'm afraid that Ivanovich's obsession will prevent him from even giving a damn."

CHAPTER 63

Hay-Adams Hotel
Washington, DC
Wednesday, April 3, 1996
1:26 p.m.

Named for John Hay (the personal secretary to Lincoln and a one-time secretary of state), and Henry Adams (a descendant of John Adams), the Hay-Adams hotel was constructed in 1927, near the White House, on the site where the homes of the two famous men once stood. It opened for business in 1928 and is thought to be the most historically exquisite in downtown DC.

Occupying the uppermost floors of the hotel was the Top of the Hay conference center. Today, the entire floor had been reserved for select members of the CIA's Directorate of Intelligence. And that afternoon, Virginia Roosevelt-Woodburn had delivered the keynote speech during the luncheon. Her topic: "Radical Islam and the New Weapon of Mass Destruction—The Internet."

Having managed her way through the presentation over the clinking of glasses, scraping of forks, and complaints the servers weren't more available, Ginny took a few questions before the doors were unlocked, the servers were allowed back, and she rejoined her table to finish what was left of her cold lunch. That's when Curtis appeared—and the ashen tint of his face spoke volumes.

Leaning over her shoulder, he whispered in her ear, "We have a problem."

"Excuse me, please," Ginny said to the table. "There's a matter that needs my attention."

"Nothing too serious, I hope," Secretary of State Manchin said as he courteously rose with her.

"Probably not."

After following Curtis out of the banquet hall, Ginny stopped next to an ancient phone booth. Decorative but still functional.

Curtis turned on his heels, looked both ways. then said, "Woody's pager was turned on. She's in Moscow."

"Moscow?" Ginny blurted out, then lowered her voice to a whisper. "But the jet's still—" Ginny glanced down the hallway at the room full of dignitaries. Jerome Manchin passed by the open door, glanced at her, waved, then continued on. Turning back to Curtis, she said, "PJ canceled at the last minute."

"You think he and Woody are together?"

"That has to be it. But why would she keep from me?" Then, something worse came to mind. "What about Liam?"

"He's gone dark," Curtis said. "What do you want me to do with this?"

"I'm not sure," Ginny said, delivering a faux smile to a passerby. "I need to give this some thought. I'll call you."

She left Curtis standing alone as she started back to the conference.

If Woody had slipped away to Moscow with PJ, that meant she had been purposely left out of the loop. That fact alone was bad enough, but now Liam had gone dark. Was he with her in Moscow, or worse yet…

Araseli had been close to discovering information she had no business knowing. Information that, if placed in the wrong hands—Liam Curran's hands, to be exact—could cost someone their life: a death she had already swapped with Araseli's.

As she watched the banquet room doors close, she decided not to return to the conference yet. Ginny needed to know Liam's whereabouts in the worst way, but since that wasn't possible, her only other option was to send out a warning.

Stepping beside the fake Ficus tree, she found her pager and typed a message, praying it would be received in time.

CHAPTER 64

Over Piana, Greece
Wednesday, April 3, 1996
10:05 p.m.

Rick Michaels stuck to the flight plan until he and his passenger were about a hundred kilometers from Ellinikon International. Only then did he deviate to circle an area above the Arcadia region of Greece, and begin his lies to the control tower.

Bottom line—he was going to land. Taking off again before the authorities arrived was still a crapshoot.

After his second trip around the dark patch of ground, runway lights flashed, then stayed on. Ignoring the hails from the tower at Ellinikon, he landed the small jet on the private airfield. As soon as he made the end of the runway, the lights extinguished and Michaels began a hasty taxi toward the Quonset hut on the far side of the strip.

Liam had been in the co-pilot's seat, but as soon as the wheels smoked pavement, he left the cockpit for the cabin to grab his go-bag. He had missed having it in Brussels and Quebec, and it felt like an old canvas friend was tagging along.

Michaels stopped the plane with a jerk in front of the Quonset hut and then lowered the airstairs without shutting down the engines.

"Be careful, amigo," Michaels yelled over the engine whine as they stood at the top of the airstairs.

"I owe you big," Liam replied.

"About that—" Michaels said, gripping Liam by the forearm. "I'm turning in my papers. I'm leaving the SEALs."

"Why in the hell would you do that? We were in BUDs together. You only need eight more years to retire." Then, after a sigh of understanding, he said, "Or did Ginny's offer cover that cost to get you to come to ICEBRG?"

"Bingo! But it wasn't Ginny who made the offer."

Fuckin' Woody, Liam thought. "Why are you just now telling me?" Michaels only grinned.

"Do me a favor, Rick. Give it some more thought." Liam slapped his friend's shoulder and stepped down. "Devil you know and the one you don't, right?"

At the bottom of the airstairs, an elderly white-haired man in jeans and a button-up work shirt was waiting with twin yellow-coned flashlights blazing. As Liam approached, the man yelled to him over the engines in Greek: "Are you Ronald Scott?"

"You must be Marco," Liam yelled back in Greek.

It was Bart who had arranged the meeting with Marco. The two had served together when Marco was a soldier in the Greek army and Bart was on loan from the Pentagon as an advisor during Operation: Niki, the Greek airlift during the Turkish invasion of Cyprus in 1974.

Taking a step forward, Liam embraced the man as a brother-in-arms, and they exchanged pecks on the cheeks.

"Bart spoke highly of you," Marco said. "That is why I must shoot you now—yes?" He let out a belly laugh, but his smile faded quickly. "You must hurry. The police will be looking for your plane."

Liam delivered a salute to Michaels, who was already retracting the airstairs. Marco disappeared inside the Quonset hut, and moments later the runway lights returned. In less than two minutes, Michaels had the private jet airborne. Seconds after his wheels left the pavement, the runway lights extinguished.

"Follow me," Marco said and led Liam around the corner to where two cars were parked. One was a black Jeep Wrangler. "Bart said you needed a vehicle. I hope this will be okay. It is my wife's."

"It's perfect," Liam said. "And I promise to return it." Reaching into his pocket, Liam peeled off five one-hundred-dollar bills. "For your troubles. If something happens, I promise to buy you a new one."

"Thank you," Marco said. "Now, you best be on your way. I do not know where you are going, but I wish you luck."

. . .

The drive across Greece to Kalopigado took a little less than three hours. After taking the exit, Liam navigated along the Leof Glinis until it came to a T at the Aigaiou coastal road that followed the shore of the Aegean Sea.

Turning north, the Aigaiou wound its way through fishing villages where mansions atop low cliffs contrasted with the shanties near the edge of the sea. With each passing mile, the scenery grew more familiar as Liam returned to a time when he and his mother and Primo and Leann were still living in the massive Ruqur villa.

Twin peninsulas jutted into the Aegean, forming a rocky horseshoe and creating a shallow cove that made up the bay. It was here the Ruqur villa presided over the village from atop the steep bluffs of the southern peninsula. Georgius Ruqur had built a high perimeter wall. But not high enough to obstruct his view of the village from the second story of the home.

After passing the entrance to the villa, Liam slammed on the brakes, got out, then leaned on the Jeep's cloth top, forcing himself to take in the massive house that had once been his home.

A few good memories lingered, but most were only disguised hauntings. At the time, Liam had been old enough to understand his mother's marriage to Georgius Ruqur was only for convenience. Perhaps even as a punishment to his father for leaving them.

Still, it didn't take long for Georgius Ruqur's well-known infidelities to resurface, but Liam's mother seemed to take the many trysts in stride. In fact, she seemed happiest when Georgius was away on business—alone or not. In many ways, Georgius's philandering had kept his mother sane.

Liam climbed back in the Jeep and followed the Aigaiou until he reached the access to the beach and the tiny wharf and docks and the restaurant his faux-family frequented when his faux-father wasn't screwing someone else. On the far side of the cove, the elevation increased quickly, and he wound his way to the peak of the northern peninsula. In the distance, where the shelf dropped off beneath the waters, he could now see the cabin lights of *Gretchen's Emerald* anchored in the bay a half mile from the beach.

The spot where he chose to park the Jeep was an isolated sliver of land protruding from the peninsula a quarter mile into the Aegean. A worn footpath took him to a point almost even with the yacht. From here, *Gretchen's Emerald* was only a quarter of a mile away tops. The sea was so calm, she appeared to be sitting on a black mirror.

Digging into his go-bag, he retrieved the case containing an ATN night-vision monocular. It was the first time he had used the latest Gen-3 gallium arsenide model, and after turning on the ATN and receiving the telltale green glow, he focused in on the yacht's hull.

He couldn't make out the numbers of the waterline markings, but he could tell she was running very low. That meant she was stocked, fueled, and the full complement of forty crew members, plus a few heavily armed security types, were already on board.

Shifting his view, he found the helicopter landing pad empty and the doors of the tender boat storage area closed. At the stern, the main cabin lights were off. Refocusing the ATN back to the villa across the cove, he noticed that Primo's bedroom lights were off and the tail of his helicopter protruded from behind a section of roof. That all made sense.

Liam focused the ATN on the yacht again. It was doubtful his father had managed to get past the guards at the villa, so the yacht was the most likely choice. His father was once a CIA contractor, a linguist, and a spy. Slipping aboard a yacht would be child's play.

But, if Primo had been telling him the truth, he wouldn't return from his trip until tomorrow. That meant Liam had some time to prepare. But so did his father.

After packing up the ATN and starting back along the winding roads toward Athens, Liam pressed the Speed Dial button on his phone. Primo's cheerful voice was in his ear almost immediately.

Liam switched to Greek. "I decided to take you up on your invitation and join you aboard the *Emerald*—brother."

"I would love nothing more than to see you again. But I have a trip planned with a friend. Perhaps you could join us. It will be like old times."

"I wouldn't want to intrude."

"Nonsense. I look forward to it. Call me when you arrive, and I will send the helicopter for you."

Liam said he would call, then clicked off and dropped the phone into the cup holder as the reality of what was about to happen hit him hard.

In twenty-four hours, years of searching for, and eliminating, the members of the NEST would finally come to an end. It was supposed to be the conclusion of a nightmare. Scratch that—*nightmares*. And with it, the beginning of a new life. *His* new life.

So why did it feel like he was about to commit psychological suicide?

CHAPTER 65

Moscow, Russia
Thursday, April 4, 1996
8:00 a.m.

Following Truscott's instructions, the team had dressed down and met Sanchez in his suite. Exactly five minutes later, Sanchez received a call, and the delegation left the room and took the stairs to the first-floor side entrance and ducked into the waiting Mercedes. Sanchez took the passenger seat, while Woody scrunched in the back between the two PAs. Pinard wedged himself by the door.

Woody tried to ignore her discomfort and thought perhaps they were going overboard with the cloak and dagger. But her mind changed when Truscott, now wearing a blonde disguise, explained the Mercedes belonged to a friend and was necessary for her to shake her usual FSB tail.

A few miles west of Moscow, the Mercedes turned down a newly paved street where mansions with grotesquely high walls popped up like bubbles in a bath. Truscott said, "I love the smell of rubles in the morning." Then, she pointed to a compound and announced, "That's Boris Yeltsin's private residence."

A mile later, the Mercedes turned down a side street, stopped at a T-intersection, then hooked a right following the Moskva River. As they drove, the road angled away, allowing room for more waterfront mansions. Woody imagined boat docks in the rear but at the same time hadn't noticed any pleasure craft on the river.

At the end of the road, Truscott pulled onto a paver driveway and stopped at the ten-foot wrought-iron gate. From a narrow man-gate, a serious-looking guard appeared with a submachine gun dangling beneath his armpit. Truscott lowered the window as the guard approached and examined the faces inside. He said something in Russian that Woody didn't understand but Truscott did. She said something back that didn't sound nice.

"Let me have your IDs," she said, reaching back over her shoulder. The one Pinard sent forward was fake and identified him as another member of the PA team.

After examining each one, and comparing the photos to the faces in the Mercedes, the guard returned them. A beat later, he disappeared and the gates parted.

The paver drive wound beneath tall Scotch pines until it ended in a circle around a statue of four angels spewing water from trumpets. On the portico between two of the six pillars stood a stout man in gray slacks and a blue shirt with the sleeves rolled up two laps. Behind him rose a magnificent brick-and-stone mansion. Woody recognized the man's face from intelligence briefs—and from *Forbes*.

Andrei Listin, oil, gas, and mining billionaire, greeted them with a smile.

"Welcome to my home," Listin's baritone thundered in jolly Russian-accented English. "Please, call me Andrei. And I ask that you leave the members of your security detail outside. My other guests have done the same." When he noticed Truscott searching the area, he added, "Of course, the others are waiting in the rear. We would not want any unfortunate mishaps due to unsupervised mingling, would we?"

Truscott, Pinard, and the two PAs climbed out first and stood at the rear of the Mercedes while Sanchez exited on the right. Listin extended a hand inside the rear door for Woody to accept. She did, and felt herself being yanked out.

"Thank you," Woody said, wondering when the feeling would return to her fingers.

"My pleasure. What a pleasant surprise, Madame Chief of Staff," Listin said, holding her gaze. "Are you surprised that I know you?"

Woody was surprised. But at the same time relieved that her attendance had only now been realized. "I'm flattered," she said. "And, it's ex–chief of staff."

Listin delivered a wink, then led Sanchez and Woody from the vestibule into a grand living area with twenty-foot-tall ceilings. Woody thought it might be called a *drawing room* in more affluent circles.

At the end of the room, to the left of the floor-to-ceiling stone fireplace, an ornate bar with a polished mahogany top jutted out from the corner, where three men occupied three stools. They all stood as the Americans entered the room, a drink already in their hands and scowls on two of their faces. Fear gripped the third.

The first man, an athletic blond with ocean-blue eyes, Woody didn't recognize but Sanchez seemed to. However, the other two, Woody knew instantly. And though they had never met in person, they appeared to recognize her too.

Woody and Sanchez stepped forward and introduced themselves. And in return, Jurg Ivanovich introduced his team.

The athletic blond turned out to be Felix Trubnikov. Ivanovich introduced him as his deputy. But when Sanchez shook his hand, he asked, "How are things at Directorate K?"

Trubnikov only smiled.

The last man was older, tall, lanky, skeletal, and tentative. Ivanovich introduced him as Franco Delgado.

Suppressing a smile, Woody stepped forward and shook Delgado's hand and said, "Mr. Delgado? Nice to meet you." The surprise on the man's long, hollow face spoke volumes.

After Listin mixed Woody and Sanchez drinks, he requested they all move to the sitting area. Woody pretended to power down her cell phone as she walked. In reality, she pressed a Speed Dial button and waited for the call timer to start before dropping the phone into her satchel. It was about to get very interesting.

Listin asked Sanchez's team to take the sofa to the right of the coffee table, while the Russians took the sofa on the left. Listin settled into the armchair at the end. Cordial chitchat lasted less than a minute before Ivanovich spread his arms across the back of the sofa and fired the first shot.

"Your assassin has failed," Ivanovich said.

"Let the games begin," Sanchez returned.

Ivanovich chuckled, almost playfully adding, "Your bomber, or—his parts—have been identified as Malik Anzorov, a Muslim Chechen separatist. The design of the bomb was the same as the one used in your Oklahoma City."

"It was also the same as one used in London two months ago," Sanchez added.

Ivanovich leaned forward and asked, "Why does your government wish to murder me, Mr. Sanchez? Perhaps to stop me from discovering the truth? Let me save you some time. I already know the truth."

A beat of silence fell on the room as Woody and Sanchez exchanged glances, putting the first step of their plan in motion.

Sanchez said, "First, let me express our condolences for the loss of innocent lives at the hands of a lunatic. Our embassy also lost two people in the explosion."

At first, there was surprise on Ivanovich's face as he glanced toward Trubnikov. Then he said, "Two spies."

"Really?" Woody added, "Two spies—who stopped the bomber from reaching his target?"

"Lies!" Ivanovich announced. "The two men were escorting the truck to its target when it exploded prematurely."

Sanchez's eyes went to slits. "Then why was Anzorov shooting at them? There must have been hundreds of witnesses, Jurg. Or did you bother to interview them?"

Ivanovich jabbed a thick finger toward the satchel at Trubnikov's feet. "We also have *proof* that a man named Jasper Pinard—a Canadian—delivered the bomb's timing device to Anzorov. Pinard is also a sniper who has been tracking my movements. We have photos and video of him in Ankara and at the Kempinski Hotel the same day as your spy, Bryant Curran. After that, he traveled to Langley, Virginia. A coincidence, Mr. Sanchez?"

Sanchez said, "We also have sources at the Kempinski. And we know Anzorov visited a guest named *Gustov Mikos*, who gave him a ton of cash before Anzorov delivered fifty thousand dollars of that cash to Pinard in exchange for the detonator. He then used the rest of the money to procure the truck and the bomb materials."

Across from her, Delgado uncrossed then recrossed his stilt-like legs.

Ivanovich opened his mouth to argue but then closed it as his head turned toward Delgado. His forehead wrinkled in a question mark. When he turned back, he said, "Then you admit your man supplied the detonator."

"You're half right," Sanchez said. "Pinard supplied the detonator, but he wasn't *our man*. Follow the money, Jurg." Sanchez pointed his finger at Delgado. "We know *he* was at the Kempinski. And you do too."

Woody said, "The CIA and the SVR both know that the real name of the man who paid Anzorov wasn't Gustov Mikos."

Delgado leaned forward and launched a skeletal finger across the table. "I do not deny I was at the Kempinski. I am there quite often. But I have never met this man, Anzorov."

"We believe you," Woody said. "Just like you never met Pinard face-to-face. You gave Anzorov instructions on where to pick up the money and how to pay Pinard for the detonator. They don't know you as Franco Delgado but as Gustov Mikos."

She expected someone on the Russian side of the coffee table to come unglued. But when Delgado smiled and leaned back instead, Woody and Sanchez quickly realized the Russians were not surprised to hear this story. And, maybe, as she suspected, Ivanovich didn't give a damn.

"We are aware that Mr. Delgado uses the name Gustov Mikos," Ivanovich said. "He had good reason to use this alias while staying in Moscow, as he once had a contract on his life."

"Which you put there," Sanchez said. "And have no doubt retracted in exchange for the so-called intelligence Mr. Delgado has been providing."

"That, of course, is true. But Mr. Delgado was not involved in the bombing," Trunikov added. "Anzorov had been using the farm of his deceased co-worker as a staging area for the bomb. After raiding the barn, we now know his plan was to kill Director Ivanovich. Mr. Delgado was in the limo *with* Director Ivanovich when the bomb exploded. Would Mr. Delgado plan to blow himself up? We think not."

"Nor do we. Anzorov's plan was certainly to kill Director Ivanovich. No doubt about it. But it wasn't *his* plan," Woody said, jabbing a finger at Delgado. "He had access to the detonator through his cell phone. His plan was to set off the device and kill hundreds of SVR agents at the headquarters while sparing Ivanovich to create an alibi for himself. And, to start a war." Woody then looked directly at Ivanovich. "And he hired Pinard to make it *appear* as though an assassination had also been hired. It was all for show."

"That is very imaginative," Delgado said.

Woody shook her head as she reached into her satchel for the file folder while, at the same time, she found her cell phone and pressed multiple random digits. Then, after disconnecting the call, she dropped the phone before sliding the folder across the coffee table.

Seconds later, Delgado visibly flinched.

Digging into his trouser pocket, Delgado produced a cell phone and stared down at the display. Turning to Ivanovich, he said, "I must take this call." Then, something remarkable happened.

Ivanovich leaned forward and nodded at Trubnikov, who stood

from the sofa and dialed his own cell phone as he stepped away. Then, from the rear of the mansion, a door opened and an armed man in a suit appeared. Woody assumed this man to be a member of Ivanovich's security team. The man motioned for Delgado to follow him outside while Trubnikov returned to the sofa.

Sanchez and Woody exchanged knowing glances. It was time to spring the trap.

Looking directly at Ivanovich, Sanchez said, "Earlier, you asked if we planned to kill you because of something you know. We assume that to be fabricated proof the United States was somehow involved in a plot to kill Leonid Brezhnev almost fourteen years ago—and that a CIA contractor named Karl Berger, also known as Bryant Curran, was directly involved. We freely admit the CIA put him inside the Kremlin as a spy. But not an assassin."

"Then why fake the deaths of his family?" Ivanovich asked.

Sanchez said, "Bryant Curran was being set up by members of the CIA to take the blame for opium trafficking coming out of Afghanistan."

Trubnikov said, "Are you suggesting his family's deaths were faked to *protect* them from the CIA?"

"That's exactly what we're saying," Sanchez replied. "Your source, Mr. Delgado, has been feeding you lies. Playing on what you *want* to be true."

Trubnikov pointed a finger at Sanchez. "And we know your source is Jaco Urmanov. A traitor. And he was the son of the traitor General Grigori Urmanov."

"It is a very creative tale," Ivanovich said. "You would say anything to deflect from your involvement in the death of Secretary General Brezhnev."

"If you enjoy *creative tales*, here's another one," Woody said. "The urgent call Mr. Delgado just received was from the so-called assassin Jasper Pinard. A man who should be dead. After Pinard had successfully made it appear an assassination was being planned, and he had delivered the device to Anzorov, he became a liability if he were ever caught. So, Delgado hired a man named Breckon to murder Pinard, to prevent you from ever finding him alive." When Ivanovich and Trubnikov exchanged glances, Woody added, "I assume you've sent your own people out to find Pinard?"

Ivanovich and Trubnikov turned stoically back her way.

Woody continued. "Pinard is still very much alive. It's Breckon who is dead. Only Delgado doesn't know this—yet. And my guess is that after he hangs up with Pinard, he's going to call Breckon to find out what went wrong."

Reaching into her purse, Woody retrieved the burner phone and held it up with two fingers.

"What is that?" Trubnikov asked.

"Breckon's phone," Sanchez returned. "And it's about to vibrate."

Woody tossed the phone to Ivanovich, who caught it solidly in his right hand. Then she said, "It will be very difficult for Breckon to answer the call, wouldn't you think?"

As if on cue, the phone in Ivanovich's hand vibrated, and he shot a glance toward Trubnikov before tossing him the device.

Trubnikov studied the display for a time, then, after it stopped vibrating, he pressed a few buttons before tucking it away in his trouser pocket.

Ivanovich asked, "How do we know this phone belonged to this man—Breckon?"

Sanchez said, "I have every faith that once your Directorate K dissects it, you'll be able to link it to both Delgado and Breckon. But to answer your question, we took it from Breckon."

"And you are giving us the phone?"

"If it will stop a war, absolutely. And there's one more thing," Woody said. "Given the way Delgado was escorted out by your own security team, you must be as suspicious of him as we are. Let me justify your paranoia by telling you that Delgado also uses the name *Gjon Rockman*, and he works for Primo Ruqur."

From the rear of the mansion a door opened, and moments later, Delgado and his escort returned. Trubnikov stood to let Delgado take his seat between him and Ivanovich, a sneer evident on his face.

"My apologies, everyone," Delgado offered. "Business never sleeps."

"I agree," Listin offered. "I hope it was nothing too troubling?"

"My apologies," Trubnikov said as he stood from the sofa and disappeared into the rear of the home.

Delgado returned to the sofa and said, "If it is not too much to ask, can someone please brief me on what was discussed while—" Delgado stopped in midsentence as he flinched again when his trouser pocket vibrated. "I am very sorry," he said as he retrieved the phone, eyed the display, swallowed hard, then continued to stare at the device.

"You should answer the call, Mr. Delgado," Ivanovich said.

"It can wait," Delgado replied as he returned the phone to his pocket. When his gaze finally lifted, and he realized all eyes were on him, his face faded to a ghostly white.

"Answer your phone!" Ivanovich demanded.

Delgado's shaking hand removed the phone from his pocket and pressed a button, then he swallowed hard and held the phone to his ear. "Yes," he said simply.

Then, from the back of the room, Trubnikov appeared—with Breckon's phone pressed to his ear.

Trubnikov said, "Good morning, Mr. Delgado. Or is it Rockman?"

CHAPTER 66

Delgado closed his phone and sent an angry look toward Woody. "What is this game you play?"

Trubnikov waved the cell phone in the air as he approached the sofa. "You called this phone—Mr. Delgado. But the display shows *GM*. Might that be—Gustov Mikos?" Trubnikov held out his hand, and Delgado surrendered his own cell phone.

Delgado thought for a quick moment, then said, "Perhaps. If the phone you have belongs to one of my associates." Then he spun on his heels and pointed at Woody and Sanchez on the sofa. "A phone the CIA obviously took from him."

"Who is Breckon?" Ivanovich asked.

Delgado ignored the question and asked, "What is it you believe you have proven, Ms. Woodburn? Because my Russian friends are well aware I use the alias *Gustov Mikos*."

"And Gjon Rockman," Ivanovich added.

Woody said nothing. Her gaze was locked on Trubnikov, who was cycling through the menu on Delgado's phone. When he finally looked up, it was in her direction—and his eyes squinted with doubt. Trubnikov then turned to Delgado and said, "The person who first called you—who was it?"

"Business," Delgado said.

At that moment, the sound of the front door opening and closing echoed from the foyer. A few beats later, three faces appeared in the vestibule and stood beneath the arched entrance to the drawing room. One was Listin's security guard. The second was Willow Truscott. And the third was Jasper Pinard, holding a cell phone in his hand.

Trubnikov's eyes went wide as he recognized Pinard's face. Looking down his nose, he said, "It is the assassin."

Truscott nodded at Pinard, and he dialed the cell phone.

The phone in Trubnikov's hand—the one he had taken from Delgado—vibrated.

After checking the number on the display, the questioning lines on his forehead deepened into rage. Then, reaching inside his shirt, his hand returned with a pistol. And he swung it toward Delgado.

Listin stood and demanded, "Not in my home!"

Ivanovich shook his head, and Trubnikov relaxed and tucked the pistol into his waistband. Delgado had moved to the fireplace, his hands slowly lowering.

Trubnikov took a step toward Delgado as he pointed an accusatory finger in his direction. "It was Pinard who called you earlier."

Delgado's skeletal frame stood poker straight as pride overtook good sense. He knew he had been cornered. There was no getting around it now. He'd be arrested and tried in a puppet court. Which was more than his father had received.

Pointing a bony finger at Ivanovich, Delgado stepped down from the hearth and said, "You murdered my father in Tirana! He was a priest, you bastard! And my mother—"

"A whore who took her own life!" Ivanovich interjected.

Trubnikov's gaze drifted from Ivanovich to Woody just as she saw Delgado make his move.

Using his long legs and even longer arms, he took a remarkably quick stride toward Trubnikov and, with an outstretched hand, ripped the pistol from Trubnikov's waistband before stumbling backward.

With the butt of the pistol resting in a palm, he swung the barrel from Sanchez, to Woody, to Listin, then stopped on Ivanovich. His finger wrapped the trigger and started to squeeze.

Then came the shot.

. . .

The Russian guard had fired from the adjacent room, splattering Delgado's brains across the fireplace before rushing in and positioning himself between Ivanovich and Delgado's still deflating corpse.

Listin, Woody, and Sanchez had all dropped to the floor, while Truscott, her own sidearm now drawn, duck-walked into the drawing room while pointing for Pinard to stay back.

Listin's guard followed close behind Truscott, his assault weapon readied.

Two more Russians poured into the room from the back while PJ's two PAs burst through the front door, taking up positions in the vestibule. Six barrels searched frantically for something to shoot.

Woody was on her knees preparing to duck behind the table as her eyes took in the scene that looked more like the OK Corral than a meeting in an oligarch's home. Delgado was certainly dead, but it seemed the danger had only now begun.

The PAs moved quickly to put themselves between Sanchez and the Russians. The SVR agents had positioned up near Ivanovich like twin sequoia trees. Trubnikov moved away from the scene as Sanchez, still on his knees, raised both hands in the air.

"Enough! It's over," Sanchez said.

His PAs remained steadfast, their weapons trained on the SVR agents.

"Stand down! Now!" Sanchez demanded.

Woody stood and inched toward the foyer while the SVR agents pressed Ivanovich down behind the Queen Anne chair. Sanchez motioned for Truscott to take Pinard and the PAs outside.

Ignoring the danger, Listin moved away from the group and stared down at Delgado's corpse, which was lying half on the fireplace hearth and half on the floor. "Who will clean up this mess?"

The words seemed to break the tension.

Ivanovich said something in Russian to one of his SVR agents, sending them across the room. One agent moved Listin back a step before grabbing Delgado's arms, and the other agent took his legs. It was a struggle, but they managed to carry him out the back door.

"It is time we return to our corners," Sanchez said.

Ivanovich eyed Sanchez. "Mr. Delgado is dead. And with him dies his plot. But he provided evidence that still holds true. Such as the email between two spies. One has been identified as Liam Curran." Then, he pointed at Woody. "The email claims you were asking about Karl Berger and Bryant Curran. We know of the relationship between Liam Curran, our dead Mr. Delgado, and Primo Ruqur."

"You'll never let this go, will you?" Sanchez said.

"Would you?" Ivanovich spat back.

"The email—is accurate," Woody said. "I did ask my team to look into those names. But only after your ambassador slipped them to Secretary of State Manchin at a private dinner. And if you know who gave those names to Ambassador Travkin—I'd love to know too."

"Who sent the email to Liam Curran?" Trubnikov asked.

"I'm not sure," Woody lied as Araseli's face appeared in her head, peering through the kitchen door at the Lake.

"I want to keep our channels open, Jurg," Sanchez said as he started toward the front door. Then, he turned to Listin and said, "On behalf of myself and my team, thank you for your hospitality."

Woody followed his lead, and they all stepped out into the midday sun, closing the front door behind them.

After stuffing themselves back inside the Mercedes and leaving the property, Truscott glanced in the mirror at Woody and asked, "Do you think we stopped a war?"

Leaning back in her seat, Woody thought about Liam and said, "Maybe this one. But not the one that's coming."

CHAPTER 67

Kalopigado, Greece
Thursday, April 4, 1996
9:45 a.m.

At the same time that Delgado's body was being removed from Listin's drawing room in Moscow, Primo Ruqur's jet landed in Athens in time to attend a meeting at the Hermes corporate headquarters with banking regulators (many of whom were on his payroll). Thirty minutes into the meeting, his assistant stuck her head in the door, nodded, then closed it again.

Primo grinned and checked his watch. Gabriela was waiting.

His plans had been for the two of them to take *Gretchen's Emerald* across the Aegean to Kusadasi, Turkey. Medicine to recover from his long trip and from the fake poisoning by his long-lost half-brother: a fact he had thankfully left out when inviting Gabriela because that same brother would now be accompanying them.

A Romanian beauty the world referred to as a super model, Gabriela was a woman accustomed to being wined and dined by the crème de la crème. After two days of sailing on the famous yacht, and three days at his home in Kusadasi, her mind would be blown, and the six-inch height advantage she had over Primo would be equalized.

Primo closed the meeting and saw the regulators to the door. Gabriela had been sitting in reception since the start of the meeting, and she glared at him over her magazine as he bid farewell to the men. He loved that a supermodel was waiting for *him*.

She stood in a huff but calmed when the beating of rotor blades from the Sikorsky S-76 helicopter grew from behind his office as it landed on the roof.

After landing at his villa to retrieve some last-minute items, his security detail, along with Gabriela, stayed on the running helicopter. As he pulled his favorite blazer from its hanger, his cell phone sounded against the low drone of the chopper's blades. Normally, he'd ignore the call and let it go to a generic voice mail. But the number on the display was not just any caller.

Flipping open the cell phone, he answered in Greek. "Liam? It is so very good to hear from you, brother."

Liam's voice was cold. "Have you seen the news from Moscow?"

Primo thought for beat. "The bombing? Of course."

"Have you spoken to Delgado?"

Primo didn't respond as dread took over.

Liam said, "I'm arriving tonight. I'll need a ride to the yacht."

"What is it Delgado has done?"

"We'll discuss that tonight."

Primo looked out past the lanai at the idling chopper, then across the bay at *Gretchen's Emerald*. Their departure was now postponed. Gabriela would have to understand. "Very well," Primo relented with a huff. "I'll have the helicopter—"

"No," Liam said. "Meet me at the pier. Ten o'clock. I'll take the landing craft back to the yacht after the entire crew gets off."

"The crew? I do not—"

"Every last one of them," Liam demanded. "When we have finished our business together, they can come back aboard. Tonight, it's just you and me."

"My head of security will never allow it. Especially after what happened in Brussels."

"He won't know I'm coming, and I'm in no mood for third-party intrusions. Afterward, you and Gabriela can be on your way."

"Fine. I will make the arrangements. The lander will—" He paused a beat, then asked, "How did you know about Gabriela?"

"Landing craft. Beach. Ten o'clock."

The phone went dead in his ear.

CHAPTER 68

Kalopigado, Greece
That Evening
9:15 p.m.

Liam guided the Jeep along the Aigaiou coast road until it peeled away from the shoreline, where he hung a right and followed a gravel path along the north peninsula until it ended at the cliffs overlooking the Aegean. The terrain was marked with scrub, shrubs, and small, bushy trees.

After parking behind a large bush, Liam slung the go-bag over his shoulder and walked to the edge of the cliff and started down the footpath cut by the local kids. It had been here as long as he could remember, and he felt a sickening sense of being home—but it quickly passed.

Once he was at the bottom and the lapping sea was but a few steps away, he placed the go-bag on a flat rock, unzipped it, removed the items he needed, then started his preparations.

He shed the jeans and sweatshirt he had put on over spandex thermal shorts and a T-shirt, then slipped into the wet suit. The temperature ranges of the Aegean Sea in early April were unpredictable, but thermals should be warm enough. After tugging and snapping the suit into place, he pulled on a set of dive boots. The next step was the CSAV.

The Combat Swimmers Assault Vest fit like a life preserver, snapping in the front. Unlike a preserver, it came with a bladder and rebreather, but he chose to leave it off, giving him more freedom to access pouches and Velcro straps to accommodate extra tactical toys.

Next, Liam checked the operation of his silenced Ruger .22 before slipping it and three extra clips inside the dry bag. He strapped the thigh holster to his right leg and the thigh sheath holding the black tactical knife to his left. After checking his gear once more, he stared up at the already disappearing moon. If the reports were accurate, he'd have ninety minutes of near total darkness. Checking the ATN for the last time, he could see the helicopter was still on the yacht.

And that meant at least one target was there too.

After slipping the ATN into the dry bag and stuffing his street clothes into the go-bag, Liam squatted on a flat rock in thought. He was under no illusion that Primo would follow his instructions to the letter, if at all. They might be half brothers, but Delgado, the Ruqur family enforcer, had been a staple for decades, and it was hard to believe Primo's only knowledge of the bombing in Moscow was from CNN.

Powerful people with world-order mindsets came with ulterior motives right out of their packaging.

As he stared at the lapping water, something his SEAL commander had always said popped into his head: *Every play in football worked perfectly until the ball was snapped.* Liam would treat this mission no different than any other. Primo was a devoted socialist, his sidekick was a perverted Albanian, and the third—was just an asshole.

Looking up at the darkening moon and the well-defined bite taken by the earth's shadow, Liam checked his watch once more, took two steps toward the rocky shoreline, donned his fins, lowered his mask and snorkel, then slipped easily into the crisp waters of the Aegean.

. . .

At precisely 9:45 p.m., the yacht's side hatch raised to reveal the tender boat storage area. Gears turned and lines tugged as the landing craft was coaxed to the hoist and then carefully lowered into the sea after which twenty-four souls followed the captain on board. The motor started and the captain guided the landing craft away toward the shore.

It took less than ten minutes to reach the shore, where the craft gently scraped the slope of the beach before the captain lowered the bow-ramp and counted each head as they stepped from the craft onto dry sand.

He was three heads short—as expected.

While the group milled aimlessly about the beach for several minutes before finally settling onto washed-up logs or the patio furniture of the local restaurant, the captain scanned the surrounding area for any signs of the man he was supposed to meet.

No one showed.

Then, as he turned back toward the yacht, his stomach churned and he swallowed hard when he realized the hatch to the tender storage had been closed.

CHAPTER 69

Gretchen's Emerald

Liam waited below the surface of the dark sea until the landing craft was a minute gone before paddling to the metal stairs and climbing into the tender storage area. There, just as he remembered, the buttons for the hatch were immediately inside the door, and he absently pressed the top one and watched as the stairs retracted and the hatch closed.

After removing the Ruger from the dry pouch, he dropped the clip and worked the smooth action a few times. Replacing the clip, he chambered a round, then checked the storage area for any brave stragglers who had not accepted the unwelcome invitation for a beachside lunar-eclipse-appreciation party.

When he was certain the area was clear, he slid the Ruger it into his thigh holster. Then he removed the mask, fins, and dry bag and stowed them in the dinghy closest to the hatch.

Let the end—begin, he thought.

Gretchen's Emerald had an eight-deck design, with A-deck being the highest, and the double-bottomed G-deck, the lowest. At 350 feet long, she could hold twenty-six guests in thirteen cabins, not to mention space for forty crew. The *Emerald* was one of the five largest private yachts on the water, basically a floating mansion.

Readying the pistol, Liam started toward the storage area, where twin Jet Skis hung from the ceiling. Across the way were the doors leading to the crew galley, cabins, and the stairs leading up to F-deck and down to the lower level of G-deck that housed the engine room, garbage, laundry, freezers, and potable water supply.

After a quick sweep of the tender storage area and the sleeping quarters of the crew, finding nothing, he moved to the stairwell, gripped the railing, and climbed to the F-deck, where the first signs of extravagance were revealed as he left the stairs and entered a mahogany-trimmed foyer at the center of the yacht.

Choosing to turn right, he moved quickly through the main dining room, saloon, spa, and sitting area. Finding them all empty, he moved to the other side of the foyer and the cabins. After quickly checking each one, he returned to the foyer and climbed the stairs to E-deck, where he checked even larger VIP cabins, the entertainment room, a hot-tub area, galley, and another dining room. He performed the same sweep of D-deck, and so far, the yacht was empty.

Maybe Primo had a change of heart.

Returning to the foyer, he ascended the stairs toward C-deck, or what was known as the owner's deck. And it was right before he reached the landing that he heard the first sounds of concern. Something squawked. Then, a whisper. Followed by a squawk.

A radio.

Pressing his back against the wall and using every angle for concealment, Liam moved right of the foyer toward the main cabin and the deck that opened up to the helipad. The helicopter was there, its blades secured to the hooks in the deck floor. Then, he moved to the opposite side of the foyer toward the private pool open to B-deck above.

Squawk. Whisper. Squawk.

Easing his way toward the pool's deck, he paused where he was still covered by the ceiling but could look up and see B-deck's railing on the opposite side. Nothing there but the returning moon through the retracted roof.

Moving to the right, sections of railing above revealed themselves. Then, as he took another step, he saw the faint outline of a person leaning over B-deck's railing, craning to see the pool. The figure bobbed ever so slightly from side to side.

So much for following instructions, he thought.

Resting the Ruger's silencer across the stone shoulders of a small statue and in the general direction of the figure above, he placed his finger on the trigger but stopped short of touching off a round. It was a long shot for a pistol. Accuracy would be minimal. Plus, there was another reason to pause. However likely it was that the figure was a straggling guard looking to protect his paycheck, there was another possibility.

It might be Stephanie Maguire.

Slipping back into the shadows, Liam crept to the foyer and eased up the stairs toward B-deck until the floor was at eye level. There, just ahead, standing by the railing and still searching the pool area below, was the figure. Too big to be a woman. In his left hand was a radio, and his right—a pistol. His back was turned.

After completing his ascent, Liam slowly eased toward the figure. The moon and her ending eclipse cast the man's faint shadow toward him.

When he was within reach, Liam lunged forward and body-pressed the man against the railing, nearly sending them both into the pool below. Liam took control of the man's pistol with his right hand while pressing the Ruger into the base of the man's skull with his left. The radio fell into the pool below as the man froze and Liam felt the burp of a fart vibrate through the man's jeans.

"Something you ate?" Liam whispered in Greek as he wrenched the pistol away. Taking a step back and spinning the man around, he recognized the face that belonged to the guard who had gut-punched him in Brussels.

"Please. Do not kill me," the man said.

"Where's Primo?"

The man pointed up toward A-deck. "He's with his woman."

"Gabriela?"

The guard nodded.

"What about Delgado?"

"He isn't here."

"Stephanie Maguire?"

A question wrinkled the man's forehead.

Jabbing the gun deep into the guard's neck, Liam led him outside to the deck looking out at the dark cove and the beach dotted with flashlights. No doubt the captain was there, staring at the yacht, wondering what happened to the other end of the radio.

Gripping the man by the belt, Liam sent him over the railing and into the sea. The man's scream came first, followed by a splash.

Unhooking a circular life preserver from the railing, he spun it blindly into the black sea, secured the pistol he had taken from the guard into an unused Velcro strap, then started back toward the stairs.

CHAPTER 70

Gretchen's Emerald

Primo stood on the sundeck marveling at the fading eclipse. He took a long, slow sip of whiskey from the highball and watched the flashlights from the crew still milling around the beach, wondering: *Why isn't the landing craft returning with my half brother?*

"How much longer?" Gabriela asked from behind him in her sweet, accented English .

"He'll come," Primo said as he turned and found the raven-haired beauty standing in the doorway holding a highball filled with wine.

The light from the bar burned through her sheer sundress. Her breast-length hair was down and blown forward, framing her high cheekbones.

"You should have gone with the others," Primo said. Given the vision standing before him, he found himself less than sincere.

"I want to meet your brother."

"Half brother," Primo corrected.

She stepped onto the sundeck and rested her arms on the railing. Siding up next to her, Primo joined in, gazing up at the moon and the retreating eclipse.

"How could you possibly think of experiencing this without me?" She let an arm drop to his waist. Then, the moment was broken, and they both lost their breath when her question was answered. But not by Primo.

"Because he's a self-serving prick, like his father was," the voice said. "And he's right. You should have gone to the beach."

Primo and Gabriela spun around in unison to find a tall figure blocking the patio door. The light was behind him, as it had been for Gabriela only moments before, but Primo didn't feel the same stirrings. The silhouette wasn't wearing a sexy dress. Instead, it was wearing the uniform of a cook.

"Why are you still here?" Gabriela protested before she realized the man had a pistol pointed at them. Then, she tried to melt against the railing while calculating the distance to the sea.

But Primo wasn't so easily fooled. The man might have been dressed like a cook, but his English smelled of an Irish brogue, and his athletic build wasn't by accident. And now that the moon had returned, Primo could make out the gray mixing with the jet-black waves of the man's hair.

"Who are you?" Primo asked, raising his hands in defense.

"First things first," the man replied. "Why did you send the entire crew to the beach?"

"You're just a cook!" Gabriela said. "And you're fired."

"Please," Primo said. "This man is not a member of my crew."

Her eyes squinted as her forehead wrinkled in thought. "Then who—"

"Does this bitch have an off switch?" the gunman asked.

Rearing back to deliver a punch, Gabriela then started to lunge forward, but her progress was stopped by Primo's hand finding her wrist. That's when the sound of a scream and a splash broke the tension, and they both turned to look over the railing.

Somewhere in the darkness below, flailing arms beat against the water. When they turned back to the gunman, they found him equally surprised, and he took a step backward, into the bar area.

"What was that?" the man asked as he raised the pistol and steadied it at Primo's head.

"Someone fell into the sea," Primo said.

"Primo, who is this person?" Gabriela demanded.

But Primo let her question go by.

The figure said, "Answer my question. Why did you order the crew off the boat?"

"Because I told him to," another voice said.

CHAPTER 71

Stepping toward the others, Liam leveled the Ruger in the general direction of the sundeck where Primo and Gabriela were pressed against the railing. Primo's hands were in the air and Gabriela's rested on her hips in defiance of Bryant holding them at gunpoint.

"Ginny was supposed to keep you away," Bryant said as he jabbed the pistol in Primo's direction. "This ends tonight. Eagle and the NEST are finished."

"Again, with this Eagle person!" Primo said. "We discussed this in Brussels, Liam."

Bryant ignored Primo and spoke directly to Liam. "You *discussed* this with him?"

"Let me get something straight in my mind first," Liam said. "I've been hunting Eagle for three years—a man you and Ginny tried desperately to convince me was a phantom. So, which is he? Guy or ghost?"

"I'm ridding the world of one more socialist."

"Answer my fucking question."

"Does it matter?"

"I see. So as long as I *believe* Eagle is dead, all is well? By killing five innocent people, you're *protecting* me?"

"Five?" Bryant asked. But when he saw the grin on Liam's face, he lowered his pistol.

"You killed Carmichael, George, and Stephanie in Athens," Liam said. "One guilty and two innocents. Now you're going to murder Primo, and—you couldn't possibly leave Gabriela alive.

I guess they were just collateral damage, huh?"

Lunging forward, Liam slapped the pistol from his father's grip, sending it across the floor. Surprised by the move, Bryant took a step away, but Liam had already closed the distance and planted a foot into his father's chest, sending him back against the bar. He collapsed to the floor.

Standing over him, Liam lowered the pistol at his father's head, his jaw clenched with rage. "I know Primo isn't Eagle—but you *are!*"

"You have lost your—"

Bryant's words ended with a grunt when Liam drove the toe of his diving boot into the side of his father's jaw, then waited for Bryant to recover and said, "It was Araseli who found the evidence: more than a hundred million dollars over three years transferred between Carmichael's phony corporations and HBC—the Hilliard Bearing Corporation. Money made by manipulating the markets using the phony nuke evidence the NEST and the CIA tricked *me* into planting on General Hussein Al-Jabori's computer. Then, when I started to eliminate the other members of the NEST, you and Carmichael divided up their shares as I took them out." Shaking his head in disgust, Liam chuckled and said, "You're fucking welcome!"

Bryant started to protest but then smiled a bloody grin. "It was never about *you.* It was about making the United States pay for betraying us in Moscow—after I gave them years of my life living as Karl Berger. For robbing me of a life with you—and your mother. For fucking nothing! Had it not been for General Urmanov and Ginny, those three graves in Moscow would be real."

"I used to believe that too!" Liam said, then pointed toward the sundeck, where Primo and Gabriela were still pinned to the railing. "Mom fell from that deck. Did you know that?"

Lifting his hand from the floor, Bryant pointed toward Primo. "Your mother's blood is on the hands of *his* father."

"And the blood of a four-year-old Kurdish girl is on yours!"

Liam said.

"We're back to that, are we?"

Liam pressed the pistol against his father's forehead as his hand trembled uncontrollably. One pull of the trigger. One microsecond between pin, primer, powder, and pow—and all his pain and nightmares would disappear.

Or would they?

"Brother, please," Primo said, easing up beside Liam. "This man is your father."

"This man is Eagle!" Liam said. "And he came here to kill you and Delgado!" Turning back to Bryant, he brought the butt of the Ruger down hard against his temple. "The CIA set you up in Moscow. Why would you help them set up your own son?"

"I didn't," Bryant said. "It was Cruxfield and Rehnquist. Cruxfield found out you were my son. They were the ones who sent you to Baghdad to plant the evidence and to get killed in the process. All I knew was that an operative code-named Lone Wolf was sent."

"Bullshit! Ginny knew. She had Araseli killed because she was getting close to the truth. And she sent you to kill Carmichael to keep me from finding out about you. She made me believe Primo was Eagle so that when one of us got to him, it would be over and the real identity of Eagle was protected."

"Ginny was trying to protect me."

"From whom?"

Bryant grinned. "The dipshit sitting on my chest."

Liam tucked the Ruger into its thigh holster and stared down at his father, the enemy he had been hunting for three years. Father, and betrayer of his mother. Patriot, and traitor. Bryant Curran, Karl Berger, Darren McFadden—and Eagle.

After drawing a breath and letting it out slowly, he said, "When you went after Carmichael, you didn't expect to find Stephanie, did you? That's why you killed her. Because she saw you. George did too."

Bryant closed his unswollen eye, squeezing out a tear.

Liam said, "They found George. Now, where's Stephanie's body?"

Bryant said nothing.

"You son of a bitch!" Liam drove a fist into his father's face, knocking him completely unconscious.

"Oh my God!" he heard Gabriela scream.

Using the barstool for support, Liam climbed to his feet and wiped his eyes clear of the hatred.

"You didn't come here for me, did you?" Primo said as he stepped closer. "You came for him."

"Mainly," Liam said. "Now, where's Delgado?"

"He never returned." Primo held out his hand, and Gabriela took it.

"You ruined our vacation!" she cried.

Liam locked gazes with her until she turned toward the sea.

"You're an animal!" Gabriela screamed.

"You're not wrong," Liam said. Then he turned to Primo. "Help me get this asshole down to G-deck so you and Miss Romania can finish your vacation."

CHAPTER 72

Off the Coast of Kalopigado, Greece
Friday, April 5, 1996
12:15 a.m.

After sending Primo away to deal with Gabriela, Liam secured Bryant's hands and feet with flex-cuffs. Then using an additional set, he tied his ankles to a link in the anchor's chain before dumping him onto the bow of the dinghy. Once he had lowered the dinghy into the water, he set the throttle on low and started toward the open sea until he had put *Gretchen's Emerald* between him and the beach. Then, he killed the engine and let the tide take them both to what had long been coming.

The eclipse had passed. With the moon bright, he had a clear view of the source of his life-long identity crisis and three years of nightmares lying motionless on the bow. He felt a spot of moisture on his cheek and flicked it away, adding his contribution to the Aegean.

Still, he had one more gift to give.

Beneath his arm, Liam balanced the dinghy's fifty-pound anchor on the gunwale. At the end of the anchor's first length of chain, a two-hundred-foot coil of rope lay in the floor with the other end secured to another short length of chain—and its last link, he had secured to Bryant's ankles with Flexicuffs.

Now, if only the man would come to, he could put this night behind them.

Liam shifted his gaze back to *Gretchen's Emerald* and her red and green lights rising and falling with the gentle waves. She had to be a half mile away by now. Flashlight beams from her multiple decks painted the surface of the sea, confirming the crew had returned and was searching for them.

In a flash, his mind took him back twenty years to the night his mother had gone overboard and how she might have seen the yacht while she drowned. Distant beams slicing the water. Angry waves churning her down until she lost the will to survive.

Glancing at the figure across on the bow, he shook his head at the irony of it all.

Or was *fortuitous* more fitting?

A rogue wave bucked the dinghy, nearly causing him to lose his grip on the anchor, and he hugged it briefly to prevent his retribution from ending prematurely. For three years, he had dreamed of this night and the many possible scenarios for putting an end to the life of Eagle. Remarkably, this particular option had never come up. Not that he was complaining. It offered two advantages hundreds of others hadn't: minimal cleanup and poetic justice.

But never in his wildest dreams had he imagined his own father on the receiving end of his vengeance.

Scooping water from the dinghy's floor, Liam sent a handful across the bow into Bryant's face.

Then again.

And again.

"Hey! Wake up!"

Finally, Bryant stirred, groaned, and opened his unswollen eye. A fat lip trembled, then the man spat bloody mucus onto the fiberglass bow.

Cough. "Where are we?"

"About a thousand feet above your grave. Give or take."

When Bryant's one good eye locked onto the anchor beneath Liam's arm, he laughed with a bloody cough.

"What's the joke?" Liam asked.

"You were always so melodramatic. And so fucking predictable."

"Well, then, this won't come as a surprise either." Liam lifted his arm and let the anchor fall into the sea.

At first, links of the steel chain tore against the dinghy's gunwale until the rope took over and hissed away what was left of Bryant's life. Like nylon sand in an hourglass, the coil on the floor started to disappear.

Bryant's eye grew wide in the moonlight, but then he rolled away, waiting for the inevitable.

"Where's Stephanie's body?" Liam asked as the rope buzzed against the gunwale.

Bryant rolled back toward Liam, his one open eye watching the rope disappear. "Even Ginny didn't know everything."

"Meaning what?" Liam asked.

"The NEST wasn't working *with* the CIA. We were *manipulating* them. They had long suspected Iraq was hiding nukes somewhere, and the NEST needed General Hussein Al-Rasheed dead. We put it in the CIA's head that the answer was on the general's computer. We even had a neat device to get it off the hard drive. But someone had to go inside and plant the device. Enter Lone Wolf."

"Me," Liam said.

Bryant swallowed hard. "Only, I had no idea Rehnquist would send you. Hell, you were living as Trevor Harmon in a cushy job at Grosvenor Square running the IRA desk, waiting to marry the ambassador's daughter. I didn't know Rehnquist had discovered who you were. Or that they had arranged for you get caught and die after the files were transferred."

"They gave me syringes to incapacitate the general and his staff. Someone switched the drugs."

"No one switched the drugs," Bryant said. "They were meant to be lethal. We needed the general dead, not sleepy. His wife and daughter were—"

"Collateral fucking damage. Right?" Liam spat back.

"Fog of war, boy."

The last foot of rope on the floorboard disappeared, and Bryant flinched as it went taut. But then he opened his eyes after realizing it had not yanked him overboard. Across the way, he found a section of the rope had been wrapped around a cleat.

Liam grinned at his father's terror. But the humor was soon smothered by his father's next words.

"Your lack of commitment is typical you."

Reaching across the bow, Liam gripped the taut side of the rope and pulled it away from the cleat. "Commitment is a moment away, old man."

Smiling and rolling away, Bryant faced the black horizon, an invisible line between the sky and the sea. He said, "When I found out the CIA had sent you, I shut down the NEST."

"But you didn't take out Rehnquist or Cruxfield."

"No. I knew you would do it."

"You didn't foresee that I would come after the NEST too?" Liam asked.

Bryant coughed a laugh. "Hell, boy! I was counting on it. I just never thought you would find *me*."

"I had a secret weapon. Araseli."

"Yours was better, I guess. I met Araseli once. Did you know that?" Liam shook his head.

"At the Lake. She was a feisty old broad."

"Yes, she *was*," Liam said. "Now, she's just more collateral damage, right?"

"That one's on you, boy! You got her involved. Turning her over to the CDG was Ginny's idea."

"And killing Stephanie was yours," Liam said.

"Araseli. The little girl. Stephanie. They're all the same, boy," Bryant said.

And Liam raged.

Drawing in a breath, Liam let go of the rope, and the tension on Bryant's ankles yanked him across the bow of the dinghy. But before going overboard, Bryant's fingers found a section of chrome railing, and he grunted in pain as the tension on the Flexicuffs cut into the flesh of his ankles.

Reaching out his hand, Liam said, "Tell me where to find Stephanie and I'll pull you in."

Bryant adjusted his grip on railing but said nothing.

"Those arthritic fingers must be hurting, old man." That's when his eyes zeroed in the back of Byrant's left hand and the healing gash there. "How'd you cut your hand?"

Bryant only fisted his eyes closed, his lips grimacing as he adjusted his grip once more. Then, an eerie calm washed over his face as he looked up, found Liam's eyes, and smiled. "I'm sorry..." he said.

Then let go of the railing.

. . .

"Nooooo!" Liam wailed as he watched his father's grin and fixed stare disappear into the black water.

Jumping onto the deck, he dove in headfirst, his arms reaching out into the vast nothingness, struggling to catch up with his father's vanishing face. His hands swept the blackness for an arm or leg or head or even a strand of hair—each hand battling the decision to cup and push against the sea or splay out to stop what his brain and lungs knew was inevitable.

Engulfed in frigid, liquid ebony, his lungs screaming for relief, Liam's brain had a different question: Which way was up?

Finally, his training kicked in, and he let out a little breath to catch a hint of rising bubbles to give him something to follow. As his head broke the surface of the water, he gasped and sucked for relief.

CHAPTER 73

BICA Headquarters
Washington, DC
Sunday, April 7, 1996
7:35 a.m.

Liam arrived early, dreading what was coming. In fact, the only reason he'd agreed to the meeting was the opportunity to get his fingers around the throat of Virginia Roosevelt-Woodburn.

Passing his ID through the car window to the guard at the gate, he watched the man in rain gear glance at it and check his face. "Good to see again, Mr. Curran," the guard said. "I'm afraid you'll need to have a new ID made. I can let you into the garage but not the building. Boss's orders."

Liam raised the window as the guard jogged back inside, and moments later, the steel door rolled up, and Liam eased the rental through. After reaching the seventh floor and parking, he strolled to the air lock door and tried his badge.

Nothing.

He tried his code.

Nothing.

Flipping open his cell phone, he punched in Curtis's number.

"We're coming," Curtis said, sounding out the syllables with unusual distinction.

Several minutes later, Liam detected movement through the smoky glass, and when the door opened, it wasn't Curtis's face he saw but Woody's.

"You're late," she said as she held the door, and Liam passed through without the machine turning on.

The first thing he noticed was her casual choice of office attire. Jeans, Tarheel sweatshirt, and plain white sneakers. She had pinned both sides of her short brown hair back over her ears. The second thing was the emptiness of the hallway. It was only the two of them, and building appeared post-holocaust empty.

"Where is everyone?" Liam asked, but Woody was already two steps ahead of him.

"We'll go over that," she said over her shoulder.

"Will it take long? I still need to find Delgado."

As soon as he said the words, Woody came to a dead stop, and he nearly ran into the back of her head. When she spun around, he saw that her brown eyes had become cold and black.

"No! You don't need to find Delgado!" she roared, poking him in the chest. And thanks to you and…" She stopped in midsentence. "It's been a very long weekend." Biting her lip, she turned and walked away.

Keeping his distance, Liam followed Woody to the office suite. It was empty except for Curtis, who rose from behind Amy's desk. On the other side of the suite, Ginny's office door was closed.

As if that would keep him from strangling her.

Curtis followed them into Woody's office, then shut the door. He joined them in the sitting area, where brand-new furniture had been positioned. The shelves along the walls were beginning to fill with books and knickknacks. Liam recognized a few titles. Specifically, *Charters of the Province of Pensilvania and the City of Philadelphia* by Benjamin Franklin.

The leather-bound hardcover had worn in spots to a pale yellow. Holding it up, he said to Woody, "Your mother has one of the originals from 1742." Then, when he opened the cover and read the publishing information, his jaw dropped. "She gave this to you?"

Woody nodded. "Next time, ask before handling my books. I'll give you gloves."

Liam replaced the book and sat at the end of the sofa. Today, there was no breakfast cart with bagels and coffee. Instead, Woody fixed three straight bourbons from a bottle of Woodford, which she placed at the center of the table before dealing out the glasses.

"Let's talk about Moscow," she said, then spent the next fifteen minutes bringing Liam and Curtis up to speed on her meeting with Ivanovich, Trubnikov, and Delgado. When she finished, her bourbon was gone. She refilled it from the bottle of Woodford.

Liam hadn't touched his. The moment he heard what had happened to Delgado, there was only one thought he was capable of processing: vengeance had been stolen—again. "What a fucking week. First Carmichael and then Delgado."

"Feeling cheated?" Woody asked. "Blame the Russians. With Delgado dead and Ivanovich knowing he's been played, he still isn't convinced we didn't kill Brezhnev. Thank God President Yeltsin isn't buying into his lunacy."

Liam said nothing.

"You lied to me," Woody said. Then, after wetting her lips with bourbon, she added, "You made me think you were going after Ginny. That explains a lot."

"Like what?"

Woody said, "BICA's board of directors held an emergency meeting Saturday morning. Ginny's been removed as the executive director. The vote was *almost* unanimous. Seems they take a dim view of their leaders orchestrating the deaths of BICA employees."

Finally, something that made sense, Liam thought. He turned to Curtis. "I never dreamed you'd turn on Ginny."

"I'm also an employee of BICA," Curtis replied.

Liam nodded.

Woody said, "Your father didn't show up to vote."

Liam said, "Well…he's gone dark, remember?"

Woody only shook her head, then sent a glance toward Curtis.

Curtis said, "His body was recovered yesterday off the coast of Makronisos."

"Whose body? Bryant Curran or Darren McFadden or Karl Berger or Ronald McDonald?"

Woody and Curtis exchanged glances. Woody said, "Want to give us your version of the story? Before you start lying, we know about HBC. And that Bryant was Eagle."

Liam finished his glass of Woodford in a single gulp. Curtis hadn't touched his, so Liam swapped glasses and finished it for him. Then, he told the story of the events in Kalopigado, the yacht and the dinghy.

"So—you were cheated out of killing Eagle too," Woody said, then instantly lowered her eyes.

"Fuck you!" Liam blurted.

"I'm very sorry for your loss?" Curtis said with a question.

"If you mean Stephanie—then thank you." Liam felt his jaw muscles grinding, so he took another sip of the Woodford. "I still have to find her body."

Woody shook her head. "Have you once stopped to ask yourself why Bryant would take his own life?"

"Don't care," Liam said. "All I know is that I still can't sleep."

"Lilliana still visiting, is she?" Woody asked. "Perhaps the medicine you chose was the wrong prescription."

"I think she's punishing *me* for Bryant's sins now."

Turning to Curtis, Woody said, "Can you get Liam his new ID?"

Curtis nodded, then left them alone in her office. Only then did Woody dare approach Liam.

"I want you to take some time off," Woody said.

"I quit, remember?"

"Whatever. Go back to Princeton, finish out the semester teaching—play your guitars. Maybe spend some time getting to know Sierra better." When Liam glared back at her, she said, "Or not. Do whatever. BICA has some healing to do, and the changes will take months to work themselves out."

"Rick Michaels told me coaxed him to join BICA."

"That's been a long time coming, and you know it," Woody said. After a pause, she added, "BICA elected me as executive director. That means I can't run ICEBRG."

"I'm not doing it," he said.

"No. You're not. PJ is resigning as director of the CIA."

Liam considered this for a time, then said, "Are you suggesting the head of the organization that once fucked over my entire family—and yours—could be my new boss?"

"It's under consideration." She watched Liam's gaze drift toward the window.

"Does he know I set off the bomb in Moscow?"

"No. And neither do you. We only assume you did."

"Do you people actually believe your own bullshit?" Liam said as he turned and started for the door.

"Brandon Maguire left the hospital yesterday," Woody called out. "He asked that I let you know he's hosting a private memorial for Bryant at his house, if you can make it."

"I'm busy," Liam said. But then, he stopped; his hand gripping the door handle. "Does he know about Stephanie?"

Woody seemed to consider it, then said, "I don't know. But you could both use a friend right now—I'm guessing. Take the BICA jet to the memorial if you want."

Liam turned to face her. "The only thing worse than spilling memories of Bryant at a memorial is collecting more of them dripped by others." He slammed the door as he left.

In the suite, Curtis was waiting and passed an envelope to him. Inside was his new magnetic pass.

After giving it his cursory attention, he thanked Curtis, then started to leave but was stopped when Curtis said, "I almost forgot. Your new pass code." Curtis pulled a folded sheet of paper from his front pocket and held it out.

"You wrote it down?" Liam said as he slipped the page into the envelope with the card. "Guess OPSEC has taken a back seat."

"It's eight digits. Didn't want you to forget."

"I can remember eight digits." He paused for a beat, then looked up at Curtis. "At National, after you gave Woody the envelope with Ginny's emails and texts, she told you it was the right thing to do."

"I remember."

"But then you looked at me and said, *We'll see, won't we?*"

Curtis said nothing.

"Where's Ginny now, Curtis?"

Curtis only grinned and said, "Have a good flight to Ireland."

"I'm driving back to Princeton, Curtis."

"Then have a good drive."

CHAPTER 74

Princeton, West Virginia
That Evening
6:18 p.m.

By the time Liam left BICA, the rain had stopped. Having leased a white convertible Mustang at National, and with the weather unseasonably warm that evening, Liam kept the top down the entire five hours to Princeton, West Virginia. If for no other reason than to air out the nasties gumming up his mind.

He tried to put the last week behind, but the one thought that refused to be boxed and taped was the question Woody had asked him: *Why would your father would take his own life?*

By the time he reached his exit, he had come up with several viable answers, ranging from the guilt of what he had done to his family to taking to the grave even more secrets the world should never know. In the end, the reason that seemed most plausible was that Bryant wanted to screw his son out of the satisfaction of winning.

But then, Liam wondered how to explain why he had tied the rope to the cleat before tossing in the anchor. Had it been simple trade craft to extract information from his detainee, or a crutch to help him through his own uncertainty? Then, after Bryant had let go and Liam had jumped in to pull him back out, had he done so to save his life? Or was it to reset the opportunity of throwing Bryant back in? Would that have stopped his nightmares of Lilliana?

Still, Owl and Eagle were gone. And the only *bird* left in the NEST was the crotchety Munir Kateb, the leader of the Popular Front for the Liberation of Palestine. Somehow, the thought of removing him now seemed unimportant.

Liam pulled into his garage right after six o'clock. The hours of wind and mountain air had calmed him. He spent some time resetting his go-bag and wiping away the dust of neglect. In the shower, he turned on the hot water and sat in the bottom and let the steam cook away the residue of the past weeks.

After toweling off and putting on a pair of sweats and a T-shirt, he sat at the kitchen table and rifled through the pile of mail, sorting the important from the letters that would line the bottom of the trash can. When the chime above the hall closet door sounded, he got up to look out the front window and found Bill Shipman opening the gate and driving through. Five minutes later, the skinny, leather-faced man was standing in his kitchen.

"Yo, brother. That your Mustang?"

"Yep."

"Selling the Beemer?"

"Nope. It's a lease."

Shipman opened the refrigerator and pulled out two beers. He handed one to Liam, then slid a chair from the table. They clinked the necks of their beers, and after they had both taken a second swig, Shipman answered Liam's unasked question.

"The two CDG pricks who hit Araseli are back in Matamoras. But you ain't goin' anywhere 'til you get some serious downtime."

Liam said nothing.

Shipman reached across and patted Liam's hands. "Want to talk about it?"

"You wouldn't believe it anyway."

Shipman chuckled. "I'm probably the one guy you'd never have to say that to." He paused a beat, then said, "I'll make us some eggs."

While Shipman scrambled and Liam sorted more mail, they talked about the farm, the planting, the coming spring, and how Sierra's tour was going. She had already called three times from Europe asking about him, but he let any waning interest pass.

After dropping the rest of the mail in the trash, Liam picked up the envelope Curtis had given him and opened it right as Shipman slid the plate of eggs in front of him. They ate to the tune of fork tines stabbing glass while Liam examined his new magnetic pass.

Shipman washed down a bite with a swig of beer and asked, "When are you leaving for Belfast?"

"Who said I was?" Liam replied absently as he unfolded the slip of paper to memorize his new pass code. But what he saw was more than eight digits. Much more. And he couldn't help but smile and think, *Curtis, you beautiful, beautiful man.*

"Hey, bro! Something the matter?"

Glancing toward Shipman, he said, "Guess I'm going to Belfast after all."

CHAPTER 75

Belfast, Northern Ireland
Tuesday, April 9, 1996
4:54 p.m.

Fasten your seat belt, Mr. Curran. We'll be landing soon. The weather is…"

Without complying, Liam held his gaze on the overhead speaker, where the pilot's voice was droning about the inconsequential while his mind struggled to recall the last time he had heard his real name used so loudly.

A chime dinged, and the attendant left her seat to start the cleanup process. During the seven-hour flight, when he wasn't sleeping, Liam had consumed a package of peanuts, a pre-wrapped sandwich, a Pepsi, and two miniature bottles of Macallan's. When she came down the aisle with the open plastic bag, he deposited his trash and offered a smile.

"Thanks, Trish," Liam said, hoping he had remembered the new attendant's name correctly. "If you're interested in *authentic* Celtic food tonight, I can steer you to the right places."

Trish was maybe five one and wore her brown hair cut short. Still, it shimmered in the cabin lighting, and her eyes turned upward into gleaming half moons when she smiled. It was his second flight where Trish had been the attendant but the first time he realized how attractive the young woman was—and how much she reminded him of his ex-fiancée, Tani Olsen.

"Thanks for the offer, but"—she leaned down to finish in a whisper—"I really don't like corned beef or cabbage."

Her perfume was haunting—something with *Liz* or *Gloria* in the name. And her Southern tones and whispered breath sent tingles from his cheek to his toes. He whispered back, "Good. Because corned beef and cabbage isn't actually an Irish dish. It's Jewish."

"Aren't you Mr. Alex Trebek tonight?" She smiled and started to walk away but stopped in the aisle and turned back. "By the way, I found the loveliest men's gold herringbone chain with a lobster-claw hasp."

Liam thought about it, touched his wrist, then swallowed hard. "Can I see it?"

"Sure thing." Trish disappeared up the aisle and returned with the chain. Squatting down, she opened the hasp and put it on his wrist. "It looks good on you. Is it yours?"

Liam nodded as a lump rose in his throat. His eyes closed, and a burning joy scorched his cheeks. "It was a gift from a very dear friend. Where did you find it?"

"In the cup holder where you're sitting now."

Liam thought back to when he was last on the BICA jet. Was it Brussels? No. It was Athens, the night Carmichael was murdered. Curtis had purchased a commercial ticket to get Liam from Brussels to Athens because the BICA jet wasn't available. Okay. So why wasn't it available to take him *to* Athens but was available to fly him home? It had also been the first time he'd noticed Trish, the new flight attendant. And it was her voice that brought him back.

She said, "You might want to have the hasp checked."

"I'll do that," Liam said. "Can I ask you a question, Trish?"

"Of course."

"When did you start with BICA?"

She gave it some thought, then said, "Last Saturday. My first leg was from Dulles to Athens when we picked you up. Why?"

"The BICA jet was in Dulles that night?"

"Yes. How else would I have gotten on it, silly?"

Liam let a wide grin spill across his face right as the plane touched down and sent Trish forward. Liam caught her free arm before she fell, and after righting herself, she leaned on the back of an adjacent seat, making no attempt to remove his hand.

"See you on the flight back," she said, then left to make her preparations.

After Trish was gone, he powered up his cell phone and typed a quick text message to Brandon.

MEET ME AT MOM'S

He hit Send, closed the phone, then picked up his duffle bag from the adjacent seat and started forward as the airstairs were going down.

As he passed Trish, he thanked her with a quick wink, then descended the airstairs to the tarmac, where he went through customs using his real passport. On the other side, he collected his rental car and made his way through farm country until he reached Enniskillen on the western coast.

CHAPTER 76

By the time he reached the cemetery, it was as going on seven p.m. When he finally arrived at the graves, the first drops of rain were beating holes in the fresh pile of dirt covering his father's new resting place. As he stood at the foot of the middle of the three graves, the dichotomy of lies and bitter truths stared back.

The headstone to his right read:

Liam Chase Curran
Born: March 17, 1960
Died: November 11, 1982

The name and birthdate were true enough. The hospital where he took his first breath still stood only two blocks away. The death date, however, was a total lie—and reflected the day of the fire in Moscow. And the grave held an empty coffin.

Before him was the grave of his beloved mother. Sadly, the information on the heart-shaped stone she shared with Liam's father was very real.

Wife Gretchen Suzannah Scott Curran
Born: March 7, 1940
Died: August 31, 1977

She was only thirty-seven when she was tossed from the yacht now bearing her name: a rumor he had hoped to turn into fact when he caught up with Delgado and beat the truth out of him. An opportunity he had been robbed of. And the fact that Liam was now only a year younger than his mother had been when she'd died hit him hard, and he knelt down at her foot marker.

Reaching out, he touched the well-settled earth holding her in and cursed the Ruqur family and Delgado.

He whispered, "I'm sorry I didn't kill him myself, Mother."

Over his shoulder, he heard a car pull up and park on the narrow gravel road. A car door slammed.

Without bothering to stand, he glanced at the fresh mound of dirt. Even through the settling soil, he could see his father's grin disappearing into the blackness of the sea. Glancing back at the heart-shaped headstone, he read the date that had long since been carved there.

Husband Bryant James Curran

Born, November 9, 1935

Died: November 11, 1982

The death date was the same as his own, as they had both supposedly died in the Moscow fire. But who had truly died on that date? Three cadavers doubling as the Bergers? Or had he and his father been the victims, only a decade or so late to the party? Did it even matter? The headstone should read, *April 6, 1996*, but what was one more lie between family—when one lie protects another?

Behind him, footsteps kicked gravel and a small stone rolled against his sneaker.

Liam plucked took the stone, rose to his feet, then tossed it onto the fresh mound of dirt as he felt the presence approach from behind. Closing his eyes, he drew in a deep breath and along with it the whisper of perfume as another raindrop spotted his nose. Reaching backward, he extended his fingers…and felt the warmth of a soft palm grip his own.

Liam asked, "Whose blood was on the wall?"

It was your father's blood. He cut his own hand and spattered the blood around the bullet hole."

Liam remembered the gash on the back of his father's hand that night in the dinghy. "How did he get you out?"

Stephanie said, "I put on one of Carmichael's overcoats and a cap, then left the building when the cops arrived. He was waiting for me two blocks away."

"And he put you on the BICA jet to Dulles."

"That's right. Sophya picked me up and took me to her house."

"In Columbus. Long drive. You should have contacted me then."

"Your father said it could get us both killed if anyone knew I was still alive." She squeezed his hand, forcing him to finally look at her. Smearing away pearls of tears, she glanced toward the graves. "I am so sorry, Liam."

He nodded as he turned back to his mother's grave. "Me too."

They both took in the moment for several beats as the rain intensified.

Stephanie asked, "Who were the men who kidnapped me? I got one of them with the tire iron."

"I know," Liam said, recalling the bandage on Breckon's shoulder. "You're a tough old broad. Still, you should have let me know you were okay."

"But I did," she said, then stroked the bracelet on his wrist with a finger. "I left it on the plane."

"I just got it today."

When Liam looked down at her, she said, "You left it on the nightstand." Wrapping her arms around his chest, she pulled him in until his arm fell over her shoulder. "Remember when I gave it to you?"

"Mm-hmm. My birthday. Three years ago."

They stood in silence for several beats, both of their eyes locked on the fresh grave.

She said, "The memorial was nice. Brandon had your father's casket placed in the living room. He stopped all the clocks and covered the mirrors for two days. Ginny flew in yesterday."

Liam only nodded as he thought about the note Curtis had slipped him.

"She's the executor of Bryan's will," Stephanie said. "In case you didn't know."

"Did Sophya come?" Liam asked.

"She didn't think it would be appropriate. Maybe because your father was being buried next to your mother."

"You mean—reburied," he quipped.

"I suppose. Someday you'll need to be a tellin' me that tale." When he didn't respond, she said, "It was only the six of us at the memorial. Brandon and Siobhan let the children come. Ginny told some stories about long ago—when you and Bryant and Gretchen first went to America."

Liam only watched the raindrops beat into the mound of dirt, marking the time of silence. Then, Stephanie broke it.

"Bryant left the home in Hilliard and the business to Sophya." Liam said nothing.

"He also left—"Then she stopped and stepped between him and the graves. "Sophya was very private while I was there. But I got the feeling that her marriage to your father was—an arrangement? I don't know." She squeezed his hand again. "Must have been very lonely."

Liam didn't respond. Mostly, because she was right—and for a moment, he felt on his hip the memory of the young girl he had once chased through the fields. Their first kiss was under the alder tree in his front yard.

Liam said, "When my mother died, she left me a trust I couldn't possibly spend and, honestly, I didn't earn. But *she* sure as hell did, married to that bastard Greek." He closed his eyes and said, "Bryant, on the other hand, stole his fortune. Whatever he didn't leave to Sophya, I don't want any of it."

"What *do* you want?" Stephanie asked.

"I want to come home," Liam said. "I just want—"

"What's stopping you?"

Taking his hand, Stephanie pulled him away from the graves and down the hill to the waiting Lexus, where Brandon was sitting behind the wheel.

"Good to see you up and about," Liam said as he reached through the open window and touched his old friend on the shoulder.

Brandon winced at Liam's touch, then passed him a small black sack closed by a drawstring. "Some items of Bryant's I thought you might like to have."

"Is this really the time?" Stephanie complained.

Brandon ignored his sister. "Did she tell you Brock Flannigan is home?"

"I heard," Liam said. "I'll go see him before I leave."

"I'll be a ridin' back to Belfast with Liam," Stephanie said. "We have somethin' we need to be a doin'."

Brandon gave Liam a knowing glance, then dropped the car into Drive. "We'll be expectin' you for a late supper. The kids will stay up to see you." He then raised the window and steered the Lexus along the gravel path and was soon gone.

Liam and Stephanie jogged through the rain to his rental.

. . .

After a fifteen-minute drive east along Feddan Road with Stephanie navigating, Liam turned up the familiar weed-cracked drive and stopped between the two crumbling stone pillars. The twin black wrought-iron gates were open, and one was off its hinges.

After a beat of hesitation, he continued over the rise until his dilapidated boyhood home rose up like a pimple on the earth. That's when he noticed the fresh ruts cut into the mud that led to a Lincoln Town Car parked in front of the graying farmhouse.

"Stop here," Stephanie said, then pushed the car door open and leapt out into the rain. "Take off your shoes," she said as she peeled off her sneakers, then waited for him.

Leaving his sneakers in the rental, he caught up to her. Stephanie took his hand and pulled him in a sprint up the drive until they were beneath the budding alder tree. "Remember when I would be sneakin' up on the porch roof to toss pebbles at your bedroom window?"

Liam glanced up at the shattered glass and dripping drapes. "I remember. And I used to sneak out and—"

"Broke your leg once, you did," she interrupted, then laughed.

"We got caught that night." He turned to face her and said, "We were so young."

"We still are," Stephanie scolded, then removed the chain with the claddagh ring from around her neck. "Your momma gave me this the night before you left for America. It's how I knew you'd be a comin' back. Your father knew it too."

"What do you mean?" Liam asked.

"He didn't leave everything to Sophya." She opened her arms and presented the home once again. "He left the Ó Corráin homestead to me. And a little money." She turned and looked up into his eyes, green fire begging to catch. "But I'm a believin' he left it for us."

If only she knew where the money came from, he thought. *What's one more secret?*

Liam dropped his gaze. "You know I'll always love you. But when it comes to making promises, I—"

She pressed a finger to his lips, then returned the chain with the claddagh ring to her neck. "This is all the promise I need. The rest is up to someone else. And I'm good with that. I'm just wantin' you to know that this will be here when you're ready to come home. I'll use some of the money to fix it up. Been thinkin' about movin' back anyway."

"Jesus! How much money did he leave you?"

She grinned, then kissed him hard.

Liam drew in a long breath and hugged her tight. "You can't trust the keeper of the stars to follow through with anything." Then, he felt her chuckle in his grasp, and he held her at arm's length. "What's the joke?"

"Oh nothin'," she said, nodding toward the Town Car and then to the house. "But I think the Keeper of the Stars would like a word with you."

Liam's jaw muscles knotted into stones as he jammed his hands into his coat pockets, feeling for the one item that had been in the sack Brandon had given him.

"I've been waiting to have some words with her myself," he said as he started toward the rickety stairs.

"Then you knew she would be here?"

"Yes—I knew."

CHAPTER 78

When he gripped the knob, it wobbled in his hand. When he opened the door, the guts of the home screamed as the wind swept up ghosts from his childhood and churned with the dust of neglect. Some caught in the corner cobwebs. He tried the light switch, but nothing happened.

"Power's off," the woman's voice said from the next room.

Liam took a step toward the arched opening and found the slender, stately woman standing on the far side near the fireplace; her back was to him. In the cast-iron grating, a single chunk of cold charcoal remained. She appeared to be fixated on it. Then, when she spun around, mascara striped both cheeks.

"I can't believe he's gone," Ginny sobbed openly.

Liam said nothing.

Taking a tissue from the pocket of her overcoat, she dabbed at her eyes and wiped her cheeks. She wanted to sit, but the dusty furniture coverings changed her mind, and she squatted on the raised hearth instead. "We were in love."

Her words weren't a total surprise. As even Stephanie had noticed, Bryant and Sophya's relationship had been more of a transaction and—well, people got lonely. He also noticed Bryant had started spending more and more time at BICA headquarters. Perhaps that was why Ginny put him on the board. It gave him an excuse to travel to DC.

Liam said, "Tell me *love* isn't why you had Araseli and Carmichael killed?"

"My only regret is that Araseli wasn't stopped in time," she said. Looking up at him, a Kleenex balled in a fragile fist, she added,

"Don't forget. I knew what you did to the other members of the NEST. I wasn't about to let that happen to Bryant."

Liam took a step toward her. "For years, you've been generating excuses to keep me from finding out my own father was Eagle. You sacrificed Araseli—and Carmichael. You even tried to convince me that Primo was Eagle. If I hadn't stopped him, Bryant was about to kill him. But I know you were hiding something much bigger than *love*, weren't you?" Then, he heard an odd sound. Something out of place in any setting.

Ginny had laughed.

She managed to stand without tripping on her overcoat and checked herself in the browning glass of the mirror over the mantel. When she turned to face him, he saw hints of the old Virginia Roosevelt-Woodburn: the once proud, Southern-belle matriarch of BICA.

Ginny said, "Was killing your father worth exorcising the ghost of one little girl?"

"Lilliana," Liam said.

"Yes. Lilliana," Ginny repeated. "A misfortunate casualty of war."

"Now you sound like Bryant. Don't bother trying to piss me off. One, I already know the truth about the drugs, and two, I'm already pissed." Liam took another step toward Ginny and said, "Araseli helped me find Carmichael and expose Eagle. And you killed her for it."

"To bury what *you* ripped open," Ginny barked.

Liam grinned as the truth he had been hiding begged to be let out. "Your bullshit is getting old. It didn't dawn on me until later, but Bryant had to have known all along how to find Carmichael. When you sent him the text to"—Liam raised twin air quotes—"*execute endangered species*, Carmichael was dead within twenty-four hours. But like I said, none of it was for love alone."

"Then what else?" Ginny asked.

"The two names Ambassador Travkin slipped to Secretary of

State Manchin. Travkin had to get those names from someone, and it wasn't the SVR planting them."

Ginny said nothing.

"There's only one person who had that kind of access to the Russian ambassador." Pulling the sheet from his pocket, he waved it in the air. "I have a copy of your text. You sent it immediately after you and Woody and Bryant met in your office."

"And whom did I text?" Ginny asked defiantly.

"Jaco Urmanov. Want me to read it to you?"

"Curtis," Ginny said under her breath. "How could I have been so—"

"Stupid? It was actually kind of brilliant. Karl Berger was a spy—fifteen years ago. The Russians were already digging up the Berger family, but they didn't know Karl Berger was Bryant Curran. That was Delgado's leverage, but you and Jaco took that away when he gave up the names to Travkin. The video of me and Bryant was all he had left to sell."

Ginny nodded ever so slightly. "I simply forced the issue to a head. After General Urmanov took his own life, I had to move fast."

"To use Jaco while he was still with the Russian embassy." Liam shook his head. "You know, if Araseli and I hadn't been using Webmail, they might have not picked up the leak."

"Sure, they would have. Araseli's little slip only sped things along," Ginny said.

"But then you had to kill her. To keep her—and me—from finding out the real truth."

Ginny reached out and let her hand slide across the mantel, then flicked dust from her fingers. "I've never been here before. You must have had a great childhood."

"I might have. If you and Bryant hadn't cut it short," Liam said, taking another step toward her.

"Suicide by drowning? I don't believe it."

"I tried to stop him."

"How hard did you try?"

"You're dodging again, Ginny. You and Bryant were hiding something bigger than him being Eagle."

Ginny said nothing as she stepped down from the hearth and started past him.

"I know the truth, Ginny," Liam said, gripping her arm as she passed. "It took me years to realize it, but now—I know."

"No, you don't!" she barked back. "Because I don't even know." Her lips pursed as her eyes squinted to slits. "And you'd better hope and pray that *you* don't know. Maybe that's why Bryant took his own life. To take the *truth* out of the equation."

"No. Someone else knows too."

Ginny reached out to touch his cheek, but Liam pulled back. After delivering a motherly smile, she turned to leave, and that was when Liam drew the gun that Brandon had put in the sack.

When he thumbed the hammer back, she stopped walking.

Liam cleared his throat. "In November of '82, Bryant asked me to come back to Moscow. I didn't know why until I got there, but it was so the three of us could die in that fire. But it wasn't to protect us from the CIA, was it? It was to protect us from what really happened in the Kremlin that night."

Ginny said nothing as she took a step forward.

"They did it, didn't they?"

Ginny stopped walking. "Did what, exactly?"

"They murdered Leonid Brezhnev."

"I wasn't there."

"Bullshit! That's why we're here. In my old house. No cameras or microphones. Only covered furniture and ripped drapes to bear witness. There's no way you were going to leave until you found out how much I know."

"You and I both need to forget what we *think* we know," Ginny said, turning to face him. "Unless you want to change your name again. Because Ivanovich will never give up."

"Sophya was there too, Ginny. She was Brezhnev's nurse, for Christ's sake. How long do you think it will take Ivanovich to send a Vympel hit squad after her?"

"He won't," Ginny said as she removed her hand from her coat.

"Why not? It's what I would do."

"Yeah. That sounds like you."

Liam noticed that Ginny was holding something in her right hand. "What's that?"

Ginny only shook her head as she placed the folded pages on a covered side table. Then, without another word, she left the room, opened the front door, then closed it.

Outside, the Town Car's engine came to life before gravel spun beneath its tires. Then, bare feet padded quickly up the creaking stairs. It was the first time Liam realized he was still shoeless. Decades of dust clung to his sweaty feet.

The front door opened again, and Stephanie asked, "You okay?"

Liam picked up the newspaper Ginny had left and passed it to Stephanie on his way out the door.

"What's this?" she asked.

Liam said nothing. He knew exactly what it was. The story it would tell.

Outside, the sun had dipped below the horizon. Sitting down on the top step, Liam took in the dusk as Stephanie sat beside him, straining to read the small print of the *Columbus Dispatch* as her mouth dropped open.

"Oh my Christ! Sophya took her own life!"

Liam said nothing.

"I can't believe it. I was just with her," Stephanie sobbed.

"Yeah. Tragic."

Reaching down, she took his hand. "Why would she do such a thing?"

"I need to go back," Liam said. "I'm the only one left to make the arrangements." It wasn't entirely true. Mika was Sophya's daughter, but God only knew where BICA had her on assignment.

"Will you at least stay with me tonight?" Stephanie asked.

Liam stood and pulled her up with him before kissing her nose. "We'll catch pneumonia if we stay here."

"I meant my place in Belfast," she said, squeezing his hand tight.

"I know what you meant."

"You're not very good at this, are you?" she said.

"So Woody tells me."

Liam started to say more, but Stephanie pinched his lips closed, then pressed her face into his chest. When he drew in a breath, she looked up into his eyes, pulled him down, and kissed him.

He had never enjoyed being told to shut up more.

AKNOWLEDGMENTS

As with every novel (especially mine) there is always much owed to many. Inspiration comes to mind first for without it, nothing flows from brain to heart to fingers to laptop. And from there, the real gifts arrive to prevent a fledgling story from failing in its early stages. Sometimes the gift is ballast, to keep me and my life stable and the story on life support.

First, I want to extend my deepest gratitude to you, my readers. Pouring one's soul onto a page is therapeutic but having it read is pure joy. And that exchange of happiness is why I write. If you keep reading, I'll keep up my therapy. Thank you all.

Inspiration flows from the depths and shallows of those in my life who have always been there and who, in many odd ways, I continuously try to impress. From a distant grandfather named Sir Thomas Wyatt of Henry the Eighth's court to my local newspaperman grandfather, James B. Davis, whom to this day I wish I had known; though he lives on through the stories from my mother, Emma. Thanks, will never be enough so I send my love.

My wife, Robin, and my daughter, Allyssa, are always at the front of my thoughts as I type away laying down (hopefully) entertaining fiction laced with some truth, though I refuse to disclose where those lines are drawn. Mostly to keep the readers guessing but also to shield me from unwarranted (and some deserved) judgement.

Much is also owed to those who stomached beta-reading the unedited sixth draft of Araseli's Web. Tapping through a PDF rather than leafing through pages is tedious and time-consuming and the brave folks called out here deserve more praise than one writer can give.

Among these beta-readers, I want to thank my best and life-long friend, Harry Bandy, whom I've known since first grade. And where most great friends would heave praises on their buddies, Harry has always dumped brutal honesty on me every step of the way. In life as well as my writing. After producing my first novel, it was Harry who read the massive draft and talked me into breaking it into several books. Thus, was born The Last Witness and Araseli's Web. Thanks for everything, Bear.

I also want to thank fellow author and extremely talented writer, Jim Roberts. His ability to lay down thoughtful, literary prose far exceeds my own. And his insights—and patience—with my story has been invaluable. Maybe one day you can help me write an effective short story. What a task that will be.

Also, a special note goes out to Phillip Smith. We've never actually met face-to-face but I'm looking forward to the day that I can shake your hand and slap your shoulder with a big thanks. I enjoyed your feedback on The Last Witness and Araseli's Web and I hope you will be available for the next ones.

On this novel, I went down a different path. And by different, I mean better. This leads me to owe much to my new-found editor, Michelle Hope. Talk about earning her keep. Her work on this novel was invaluable, detailed, insightful, and timely. I'd love to recommend her to every writer as long as I maintain the rights to her time first. And in her defense, she didn't get to edit the acknowledgement section. The mistakes here are all mine. Thanks Michelle.

Then, there's Paul Palmer-Edwards—the creative mastermind behind the novel's cover design, its interior and exterior layout, and the ever so important icing on the cake. Working with Paul has not only been a joy but also educational. It's refreshing to find a talent with real-world experience who is willing to share it with a fledgling author. I raise my symbolic goblet of wine in cheers and hopes that we continue working together.

Lastly, I want to thank those too numerous to mention individually but also too important to forget. Thanks to the fine people of Princeton, West Virginia for starting my roots and to the amazing community of Miami Township, Ohio who have given me my branches. It's great to have one hometown but to have two has been a blessing that still goes undeserved.

AUTHOR BIO

Michael Shayne grew up in southern West Virginia, served in the Air Force, graduated from West Virginia University (BSEE) and Wheeling University (MBA) before settling in Cincinnati, Ohio with his wife, daughter, and a dog. Goal Number One—check! What's missing from the tale perhaps begins with his 13th great-grandfather, Sir Thomas Wyatt, the official poet of Henry VIII. Or maybe his grandfather who was with the local newspaper. Or being named after Brett Halliday's sleuth. Either way, those Norman and Scotch-Irish genes have compelled him to spin yarns since he was old enough to hunt and peck on Smith Corona. A ravenous reader, he's usually engulfed in two novels, something non-fiction, iced with an audiobook at the same time he's writing. Outside of writing, he found himself working as an electrical engineer, project manager, product developer and business development executive in the electric utility and telecommunications industries.